The Courtesan's Wager

"Dain is a master of the Regency romp, and this one has witty repartee and an authentic setting." —*Romantic Times*

"Outrageous, offbeat, hilarious, and sinfully sensual, this romance employs lively, sassy dialogue, rare wit, and an effervescent sense of fun . . . Another winner."

—*Library Journal*

"Dain concocts another wonderfully witty story, complete with unforgettable characters, sparkling dialogue, a clever plot, and amusing situations." —*Booklist* (starred review)

Praise for
The Courtesan's Secret

"Clever, smart, fresh, and passionate, this lively romp is the latest addition to Dain's Courtesan series . . . Readers will find it as delightfully entertaining as the last."

—*Library Journal*

"The latest entertaining [novel] from Dain . . . Highly amusing repartee and some wickedly attractive open ends round things out." —*Publishers Weekly*

"Dain's clever tale of love and mayhem . . . Her talent for writing humor remains. That, plus her suggestive dialogue and a diverse set of characters, comes together in an enjoyable story." —*Romantic Times*

continued . . .

Berkley Sensation Titles by Claudia Dain

THE COURTESAN'S DAUGHTER
THE COURTESAN'S SECRET
THE COURTESAN'S WAGER
HOW TO DAZZLE A DUKE

The Courtesan's Wager

Claudia Dain

BERKLEY SENSATION, NEW YORK

THE BERKLEY PUBLISHING GROUP
Published by the Penguin Group
Penguin Group (USA) Inc.
375 Hudson Street, New York, New York 10014, USA
Penguin Group (Canada), 90 Eglinton Avenue East, Suite 700, Toronto, Ontario M4P 2Y3, Canada
(a division of Pearson Penguin Canada Inc.)
Penguin Books Ltd., 80 Strand, London WC2R 0RL, England
Penguin Group Ireland, 25 St. Stephen's Green, Dublin 2, Ireland (a division of Penguin Books Ltd.)
Penguin Group (Australia), 250 Camberwell Road, Camberwell, Victoria 3124, Australia
(a division of Pearson Australia Group Pty. Ltd.)
Penguin Books India Pvt. Ltd., 11 Community Centre, Panchsheel Park, New Delhi—110 017, India
Penguin Group (NZ), 67 Apollo Drive, Rosedale, North Shore 0632, New Zealand
(a division of Pearson New Zealand Ltd.)
Penguin Books (South Africa) (Pty.) Ltd., 24 Sturdee Avenue, Rosebank, Johannesburg 2196,
South Africa

Penguin Books Ltd., Registered Offices: 80 Strand, London WC2R 0RL, England

This is a work of fiction. Names, characters, places, and incidents either are the product of the author's imagination or are used fictitiously, and any resemblance to actual persons, living or dead, business establishments, events, or locales is entirely coincidental. The publisher does not have any control over and does not assume any responsibility for author or third-party websites or their content.

THE COURTESAN'S WAGER

A Berkley Sensation Book / published by arrangement with the author

PRINTING HISTORY
Berkley Sensation trade edition / February 2009
Berkley Sensation mass-market edition / April 2010

Copyright © 2009 by Claudia Welch.
Excerpt from *How to Dazzle a Duke* copyright © by Claudia Welch.
Cover design by George Long.
Cover art of couple by Richard Jones; cover background by Shutterstock.
Cover hand lettering by Ron Zinn.

ISBN: 978-0-425-23385-6

BERKLEY® SENSATION
Berkley Sensation Books are published by The Berkley Publishing Group,
a division of Penguin Group (USA) Inc.,
375 Hudson Street, New York, New York 10014.
BERKLEY® SENSATION and the "B" design are trademarks of Penguin Group (USA) Inc.

PRINTED IN THE UNITED STATES OF AMERICA

10 9 8 7 6 5 4 3 2 1

For my husband.
For everything.
Forever.

One

"IT defies all logic and every expectation," Lady Amelia Caversham, daughter and eldest child of the Duke of Aldreth, said to her cousin Eleanor. "I should have been able to find a duke by now."

"You've found enough of them," Lady Eleanor Kirkland said. "It's that they don't seem to want to marry you. Despite all logic," Eleanor added as a sop. It wasn't much of a sop.

If one wanted sympathy and tact, one did not go to Eleanor. Eleanor was uncomfortably forthright. One could only hope that she would grow out of it. Given that Eleanor was sixteen and fully matured in all other areas, it didn't seem likely. Still, for a woman who had decided to marry a duke before leaving the nursery, Amelia was not one to stare unpleasant facts in the face and wish for a prettier solution than the one which stared back at her.

She was the daughter of a duke.

Her brother, Aldreth's heir, was going to be a duke.

It had always seemed perfectly reasonable, indeed logical, for her to become the wife of a duke.

What was it about this current crop of dukes that made her plans seem so unreasonable? Surely the fault lay with them and not with her. She was extremely and eminently both appropriate and available, which she knew to be true because she had so assiduously worked at being appropriate her entire life. Why, any duke should be delighted to make her his duchess.

She'd made the acquaintance of nearly three dukes and not a one of them gave any appearance of being even slightly interested in her. It was beyond ridiculous, and she didn't have any idea what to do about it. Well, actually she had an idea, but it was a scandalous one.

Amelia wasn't at all certain that a woman on the hunt for a duke should engage in scandalous ideas. It didn't seem at all the thing.

"You know what I would do," Eleanor said, her dark blue eyes alight. "I would visit Lady Dalby and ask her for help. Just look what she managed for Louisa, and so quickly, too. Why, with Sophia's help, you could be married by Monday."

As it was Wednesday, it was highly unlikely . . . although where Lady Dalby was concerned, it just might be possible. Lady Dalby, Sophia to her many, *many* intimates, had been a courtesan in her past and had somehow managed to drag an earl to the altar twenty years previous. Scandalous, to be sure, and yet, if a courtesan could arrange an earl for herself, could she not more easily arrange a duke for a duke's daughter?

No, it was impossibly scandalous. Her father would scald her ears if he found out about it. Aldreth was very careful of his reputation and his reputation extended fully down to encompass his two children.

Although it wasn't as if Aldreth kept regular hours at home and would therefore know where and when she went. Eleanor, who knew Aldreth nearly as well as she did, then said, "It's not as if he'll find out about it."

"Of course he'll find out about it," Amelia answered, lying back on the striped, pale blue silk sofa and considering the shadows on the plaster ceiling. "He finds out about everything. Eventually."

Eleanor, whose own father was less than particular about how his daughters spent their days and could, therefore, not truly understand the force that was Aldreth, said, "Eventually. Are we supposed to care about *eventually* when you have a duke to catch?" *There was that.* "And don't you suppose that your own duke, once you've acquired him, can manage Aldreth?"

That was a bit more difficult to imagine, as Aldreth was quite the most forceful, autocratic, difficult man to manage. Was there a man who could manage him? Her thoughts drifted to the men of her acquaintance. Yes, there was one man who might be more than able to manage Aldreth. Yet more to the point, did she want to marry such a man? There were certain risks in acquiring a forceful man. Certainly her mother, what little she could remember of her, hadn't fared well against Aldreth, though Amelia certainly didn't fault her mother for that, because who *could* manage Aldreth?

Sophia?

Certainly Sophia did not give the appearance of being afraid of anyone, and she most definitely gave every appearance of being able to manage absolutely everything, particularly men. Most *very* particularly men. It was mortifying in the extreme that the same could not be said of Amelia. She seemed to have no talent whatsoever at managing men.

"You seem very certain that I shall marry a duke," Amelia said softly, still staring at the ceiling.

"Well, certainly," Eleanor said, shifting her weight on the oyster silk upholstered chair. "Aren't you?"

"I used to be very certain. Or perhaps I was only determined."

"There's hardly any difference, Amelia. Not a practical difference, anyway," Eleanor pronounced. For sixteen, Eleanor was very decided in all her opinions. It likely came from her reading so very many inappropriate books.

"Isn't there?" Amelia said extremely casually.

Really, with Louisa about to leave for her new husband's estate, there was only Eleanor left to talk to and Eleanor, unlike her sister Louisa, paid very much attention to everything that was said. It took rather a lot of concentration to converse with Eleanor because one had to be so very careful of what one revealed, particularly about men. In point of fact, it had occurred to Amelia that if things continued on as they had been for another year or two, she might find herself without any sort of husband at all.

And that naturally meant that she would live out the rest of her life with Aldreth, or the only part of her life that mattered, the youthful part. It was difficult to imagine a more unpleasant future. Just look what it had done to Aunt Mary; she was practically a five bottle a day drinker and she had not started out that way at all, no, not at all. Of course, Aunt Mary had also had to manage the Marquis of Melverley, Eleanor's father, and he was every bit as troublesome as Aldreth, although in a different fashion. But it did make the point most alarmingly that women without husbands and without a heavy purse did not fare well in the world at all.

Not at *all*.

"Now, Amelia," Eleanor said, sitting up quite straight and seeming determined to take charge of her wayward cousin, "you simply can't sit about any longer waiting for a duke to find you. You need help or you'll end up like . . . like Aunt Mary!"

It was truly most disconcerting that Eleanor was developing the tendency to read her every thought. It was quite a disturbing talent and if it continued, Amelia was going to be required to avoid Eleanor completely.

"What a perfectly dreadful thing to say, Eleanor," Amelia said.

"But the truth," Eleanor said, not at all contrite. "You need help, and the one person who you *know* can do the deed is Lady Dalby. What do you have to lose, Amelia? It certainly did Louisa no harm."

Yes, well, that depended entirely upon how one defined *harm*.

"You know as well as I do that Louisa had no intention of marrying Lord Henry. The only man she cared about was the Marquis of Dutton," Amelia pointed out. "It was after Louisa paid a visit to Lady Dalby that things got very muddled indeed and Louisa forgot about Lord Dutton entirely. Or at least she gave every appearance of forgetting him entirely."

Which was, of course, the entire dreary point. What if, after having sought Sophia's counsel and aid, Amelia forgot her goal of marrying the right man and found herself married to the wrong one? That would not do at all. If she did approach Sophia, she was going to be very firm; she was not going to find herself married to anyone other than her ideal choice, a man who she would not allow to even enter her mind at present because of Eleanor and her alarming ability to read Amelia's every thought. No, no matter what Sophia Dalby said or did, she was going to marry the right man.

Of course, without Sophia's aid, she might find herself married to no one at all.

"You have only to see Louisa and Blakes together to know that she's revoltingly content and Dutton completely forgotten, Amelia. It's almost impossible to be in the same room with them, to be honest. They're always sliding themselves off to a closet or a cupboard and coming out again all mussed and grinning. It's straight out of Fielding, I assure you."

"You really mustn't read such things, Eleanor. I'm quite certain it's not good for your character."

"Being in the same room with Blakes and Louisa is worse for my character. It's perfectly plain what they're about, after all."

They were rather obvious about it and it was entirely inappropriate, but it did look like such fun, in a perfectly astounding sort of way. In all her life, Amelia had never seen a married couple behave as Louisa and her Blakes did. Perhaps it would pass.

Yet perhaps it would not.

"They're leaving Town soon, are they not?" Amelia asked, flopping over onto her stomach and burying her face into a pillow. She felt unaccountably morose of a sudden.

Unaccountably? Of course it was accountable; she did not have a husband dragging her off into closets. That was the trouble with her, though the incessant rain didn't help. It had been cold and rainy for hour upon hour. The month of April did have that reputation and it should not have affected her mood. But it did.

"Tomorrow," Eleanor answered, "even if the rain doesn't stop. I think Blakes wants to get Louisa away from his many brothers."

And then she would be alone, left to find her duke without anyone to share the experience with her. Eleanor was too young and not fully *out*. Day after day spent trying to look appealing and sweet and lovely to a room full of people who all but ignored Amelia.

Well, the dukes ignored her and that was all that mattered, wasn't it?

Amelia and Eleanor said nothing after that, the mood of the day infecting them. The light in the room softened to pewter, the maid lit the candles, the fire blazed orange, and the two women sighed into the upholstery, pretending to doze.

That was when Hawksworth strolled in and of course that meant that Amelia had to put a better face on it, as one simply did not reveal any sort of weakness to one's younger brother.

"What are we doing?" Hawksworth asked, leaning against the doorframe of the library and studying them. Hawksworth did not stand on his own two feet if he could find anything at all to lean against.

Amelia and Eleanor sat up, Amelia ran a hand over her hair, Eleanor tugged at her sleeve, and Amelia said, "I suppose it should be obvious even to you, Hawks, that *we're* having a private conversation."

"I thought I heard snoring," he said, bowing a greeting

to Eleanor. Eleanor popped to her feet and curtseyed before promptly dropping back down to her chair. The four of them, Amelia and Hawks, Louisa and Eleanor, had always been far more like siblings than cousins, their family situations being what they were, which was that they were all without mothers and burdened with quite impossible fathers.

"I'm quite certain you did not," Amelia said.

"I might have been snoring," Eleanor said, again, as a sop. Again, it was not a very well-delivered one.

"No, it wasn't you, Eleanor," Hawks said, "I'm certain it was Amelia. I know the sound of her snores very well, and this snore had that particular rasping quality of Amelia's."

Need it be stated that Amelia and Hawksworth did not have the most cordial of relationships?

While Amelia was an entirely appropriate sort of girl in aspect and dress and deportment, and while Amelia had from an early age decided upon her life's course and pursued it with a singularity of purpose and passion that was truly remarkable, if she did say so herself, the Marquis of Hawksworth, her younger brother by three years, was and always had been bone lazy. He had no goals whatsoever. Getting him to get out of bed each morning was a truly Herculean task for his valet. He did not stand straight or walk straight or talk straight. Hawks simply ambled and sauntered and snoozed through his days and through his life. He was the most irritatingly aimless man she had ever known, and of course, he was the heir apparent to a dukedom.

Life was so ridiculously unfair.

"How do you know Amelia snores?" Eleanor said as Hawks ambled over to a chair by the fire and slouched into it.

"Coach to Scotland," he drawled. "She snored for six days straight. I'll never forget the sound of it, thought at first the wheel was working itself off the hub. But it was only Amelia."

"I was ill!" Amelia said, sitting up perfectly straight and all thoughts of dukes and marriage momentarily forgotten.

"And then there was the time—"

"Oh, shut it, Hawks!" Amelia burst out. Eleanor chuckled, her dark blue eyes shining in delight. Eleanor was such an *unusual* girl. When Amelia wasn't busy wondering exactly which duke would propose to her, she wondered how Eleanor would ever make a proper match at all. "I'm quite certain I sleep perfectly beautifully."

Which, she knew full well, was a completely ridiculous statement to make, but Hawks brought out the absolute worst in her. She was, truly, such a nice, normal, respectable sort of girl. It was perfectly obvious that she'd make such a lovely duchess.

"Actually, Hawks," Eleanor said, sitting up fully and leaning forward toward him. He did not return the gesture, as it would clearly require too much effort. "Perhaps you could give us your opinion on an important matter, something Amelia and I were just discussing."

"That would have to be which duke she hopes to marry?" he replied, checking his fingernails distractedly.

As Amelia was drawing breath to insult him, Eleanor answered, "Yes and no. I have been urging Amelia to seek out Lady Dalby for assistance. Certainly no other woman in Town would be . . . that is, could know . . ." Eleanor's voice trailed off, because how to say it? It was one thing to discuss these things as women, but with a man present, even such a man as Hawksworth happened to be, it was somewhat off-putting.

"How to snare a man into an inescapable net of matrimony?" Hawks offered cordially.

"Yes, something like that," Eleanor said. "What do you think, Hawks? Do you think the idea has merit?"

"What have you got to lose, Amelia?" he said.

"My dignity? My respectability?" Amelia shot back, bolting off the sofa and beginning to pace the room.

"If you want to ensnare a duke, you'll likely lose those anyway, Amy," he said, using the name he had called her when they had lived out their days in the nursery. It stopped Amelia cold. "You've been respectable and above reproach, why not try another tack to get what you want? Within reason, assuredly."

Perhaps there was some small morsel of truth in his observation. Forming an attachment should have been so simple, if one approached marriage logically and with clear goals. Which she did and she would. No mere man would be allowed to make a tangle of her plans.

"I had expected things to proceed along an entirely different course," she said calmly. "A course bound by amiable civility and a manner above reproach. Yet another course might be necessary. Certainly a different course does not necessarily mean anything dire."

"If you want things to be different, I'd trust the Countess of Dalby for that," Eleanor said. "She appears to excel at it, and things do seem ever to fall her way."

"That's true enough," Hawks said, shifting deeper into the upholstered chair, stretching his long legs toward the fire. "You have my approval, Amelia. You may speak to Lady Dalby."

"Blast it, Hawks! I wasn't asking your permission!" Amelia snapped.

Eleanor, that imp, giggled.

Two

BEING a woman of composure and fortitude, not to mention some urgency, Amelia left Aldreth House as soon as she had harangued Hawks on general principle for a good five minutes, sought out Aunt Mary without much enthusiasm, changed into a lovely afternoon dress of ivory muslin sprigged in green silk thread, swallowed her annoyance to ask Hawksworth to chaperone her to Lady Dalby's as Aunt Mary was not to be found, and then was made to wait while Hawks changed his linen before visiting as compelling a woman as Sophia Dalby.

It was late in the afternoon by the time they got to Dalby House. Amelia, showing the singleness of purpose and strength of character that she hoped she was known for, insisted that Hawksworth remain outside. She was *not* going to allow him to listen to what was certain to be a most uncomfortable and unusual conversation. She was also not going to allow the call to degenerate into a polite seduction of and by Sophia, which it was certain to do. It appeared to happen any time any man was within ten feet of Sophia.

Amelia, in most instances, found it fascinating. Today, however, it would have been singularly inconvenient.

Hawks, because he was too lazy to even fight with vigor, passed her over to the Dalby House butler, and then promised to walk up and down Upper Brook Street until she should come back out.

It was raining, but lightly now. Amelia didn't feel one bit sorry for him. Perhaps the rain would wake him up.

Amelia was shown into Sophia's famous white salon, famous because it was rumored to contain a piece of rare porcelain that had been a gift from either King George of England or King Louis of France, the rumors being rather more lurid than substantial. In fact, there *was* an exquisite vase of green Chinese porcelain prominently displayed in the white room, which added to the confusion more than cleared it as Amelia was almost completely certain that the porcelain was supposed to have been white, hence the name of the salon.

Where Sophia was concerned, rumor ruled the day more than Amelia found convenient. If she had not seen with her own eyes what Sophia had managed for Louisa in attaining a completely proper husband in a matter of days, she would discount everything, the vase included.

But there was the vase, and Louisa was most definitely married.

Amelia and Sophia made their curtseys to each other, took seats facing each other on matching sofas upholstered in milk blue damask, and Amelia was left with trying to determine how to communicate politely what she wanted of Sophia. It was not going to be simple.

"How lovely of you to come and see me today, Lady Amelia. You have brightened my day considerably. But, where is your chaperone, Lady Jordan?" Sophia said.

The first lapse in what she was certain was a perfect record of proper behavior. She was here, out, without her chaperone. Of all the places to be without a chaperone, Sophia's white salon was almost certainly the worst.

"I," she said slowly, "I am not quite certain, Lady Dalby.

She was out and I suppose, in my eagerness, I left before she returned."

"Eagerness? How flattering," Sophia said. "I was the source of your eagerness?"

"Lady Dalby," Amelia said, determined to say what she had come to say without dithering about, "please excuse me for being forward, but I . . . I was most impressed, that is to say, actually I found myself astonished by the chain of events surrounding Louisa's marriage to Lord Henry Blakesley. She is, even more astonishing, quite completely content in the marriage, and I . . . I, well, you may not know it, but we had our come out together and attended most functions together, with Lady Jordan, of course."

"Of course," Sophia said politely, her lips poised over her cup.

She was dithering. She could hear herself dithering and she couldn't determine how best to stop it while still appearing as innocent and virtuous as possible. Because she must appear so. She absolutely must. It was, she had determined, the best way of attaining Sophia's aid. If she were innocent, hopelessly so, Sophia might take some sort of interest in her situation and find it amusing to arrange a duke for her. Surely, Sophia Dalby was capable of procuring a duke. She had to be. It was almost certainly true that Amelia was not. After two years, certainly some duke or other should have stumbled into her arms by *now*.

"And now, now," Amelia continued, not at all reassured by the speculative gleam in Sophia's dark eyes, "I suppose that I don't know what's to become of me now. I am at a loss, Lady Dalby, and I could not but wonder if you would be so kind as to . . . help me."

There. She had said it. What more was there to say? Now, certainly, all that was left was for Sophia, if she agreed, to work her seductive will upon the currently available dukes of the ton and deliver a proper husband into Amelia's arms.

"Help you do what, Lady Amelia?" Sophia asked. "I am afraid I do not quite comprehend you."

Of course, Amelia did not believe that for a moment, but she had gone this far and there was little point in getting squeamish about it now. She was here for a purpose and she was determined to achieve her purpose. Surely, of all women, Sophia would appreciate that.

"Lady Dalby," Amelia said, feeling her cheeks flush with mortification at what she was about to say and ruthlessly ignoring it. "Lady Dalby," she repeated with slightly more force, "I would very much like to marry . . . to marry . . ."

Oh, this was most, *most* disagreeable. What a woman had to endure to snare a man. It was quite uncomfortable.

"Yes, darling, you would very much like to marry. Of course you would. Perfectly natural," Sophia said politely.

Amelia knew enough of the world to know very well that when a woman was *that* polite it was nothing but cruelty dressed in lace. She didn't care. There simply was no one else who could manage things of this nature as well as Sophia Dalby.

"I mean to say," Amelia continued, raising her voice slightly and stiffening her spine, "what I mean, Lady Dalby, is that I would very much like to marry a duke and I would very much like your help in acquiring one."

There. She had said it as plainly as it could be said. Let Sophia try and pretend ignorance *now*.

"Why, darling," Sophia said, leaning forward and taking Amelia by the hand, "that sounds positively riveting. I'm quite sure that, between the two of us, we can manage to snare one duke, don't you agree?"

"You truly think so?" Amelia said, her breath escaping her in a rush of pure relief, nay, exultation. Here was the answer to all her problems in attracting a duke. She should have come to Sophia two years ago.

"I have no doubt of it whatsoever," Sophia said, patting her hand and leaning back in her chair, her dark eyes considering Amelia with a scrutiny that was blatant and unsettling. "If I may speak plainly?"

"Of course," Amelia said, not at all certain that speaking plainly was ever desirable, but what choice did she have?

"You are, as I am quite certain you know, a very beautiful woman in the precise style of beauty that is so fashionable at the moment."

Amelia wasn't entirely certain that Sophia's observation ranked as a compliment, but not knowing what else to say, she said, "Thank you, Lady Dalby."

Lady Dalby smiled and said, "Lady Amelia, if you will allow?"

Amelia had no idea what Sophia was asking permission to do, but she nodded her assent. What could she do? Had she not just this moment asked for Sophia's help?

"You must never thank someone for complimenting you, particularly when the compliment is merely a statement of the obvious. And most particularly when dealing with dukes."

"I must not?"

"You absolutely must not," Sophia said. "You accept the compliment as your due and see where that leads. You must know your worth first before you can require anyone else to recommend you for it."

"Require?" Amelia said, well aware that she was repeating, but what was she to do? She found every word out of Sophia's mouth to be singularly strange and unique and, she hated to admit it, useless. Of what possible use could this odd advice on the receipt of the most ordinary of compliments be in the pursuit of a man?

"Yes, of course require," Sophia said on a sigh of frustration. "Naturally, I am aware that your mother died many years past, perhaps at the most crucial stage of your training, and you, through no fault of your own, have certain gaps in your knowledge of . . . things."

Things. That meant men. Ridiculous. She understood men very well.

"I am quite certain I understand *things* as well as any woman of my station," Amelia said a bit stiffly.

"I have no doubt that's true," Sophia said, smiling in what could only be termed a *calculated* fashion. "However, when a woman wants a duke for a husband, a bit more is required. You are quite certain you want a duke?"

"Completely certain," Amelia said.

"Naturally, your reasons are your own," Sophia said silkily, "and you are very fortunate that there are two dukes who are without wife this Season. You have met them, I suppose?"

"The Dukes Edenham and Calbourne?" Amelia said. "I have been introduced to the Duke of Calbourne only. I have not been formally introduced to the Duke of Edenham, though I know of him, naturally."

"You know the rumors of him, you mean to say," Sophia said, taking a sip from her cup. "Just because a man has had three wives die under him is no reason to think he is at fault. Some women are not entirely . . . sturdy," Sophia said thoughtfully.

Sturdy. Oh, dear. She did not see any need to discuss *that.*

"You do not mention the Duke of Hyde's heir apparent, the Marquis Iveston, Lady Dalby?"

"Oh, are you as broad-minded as to consider heir apparents? I do applaud you for your foresight. Hyde may well live for years, and naturally I do hope he does as I am quite fond of him, but he could die tomorrow of a fever and then there you are, a duchess overnight. Of course, that's assuming you've married Iveston."

Sophia smiled sweetly, as if she had not just said the most tawdry and obvious thing, even if Amelia and every other marriageable girl had been thinking it for years. One did not go about saying outright what one was ashamed to have thought. Unless one were keeping company with the Countess of Dalby. In her company, all rules of deportment had to be . . . readjusted.

"I do think he should be . . ." Amelia had no idea how to say it.

"On your list?" Sophia clearly knew exactly how to say it.

"Yes, if we're to call it that."

"Darling, what else *should* we call it?"

Amelia kept her tongue behind her teeth and waited for Sophia to speak. There was simply no point in engaging in a verbal battle with her only ally in this effort over a mere choice of words. Amelia had always had and would continue to have her goals clearly before her, and nothing and no one would distract her from achieving them.

"So," Sophia continued, "our list encompasses Iveston, Edenham, and Calbourne. They are, collectively, of a nice age, agreeable visage, and sufficiently wealthy. I have spent a delightful November at Edenham's Sutton Hall and you would find no fault with it, I assure you. As to Calbourne's estate, I shall have to ask Lord Ashdon; as they are quite close, he's sure to have seen it and will give an accurate report."

Amelia squirmed on her very pretty chair. She could not help it. It sounded entirely mercenary and unattractive to discuss her dukes this way, even if she had wondered about their estates and the state of their accounts. She certainly did not want to marry a man in need of a fortune, did she? Of course, she had her own fortune to contribute to their marriage, but would not find it at all attractive if her future husband were actually in dire need of it.

Very complicated business, this marrying for status and profit.

"That would be most kind of him," Amelia said, trying to keep her squirming to a minimum.

"Now, tell me," Sophia said, "do you have a preference or will one do as well as any other?"

There was simply no polite response to that. None.

"Come, come," Sophia said with a cool smile, "now is not the time for timidity. We must have it out clearly between us so that we may acquire the best man for you. That's what you desire, is it not? The best husband from the lot of them? I can assure you that I will think no less of you for being forthright; indeed, I will likely think the better of you. It is so delightful to meet a woman who knows exactly what she wants and pursues it with vigor. Yes, vigor is too often lacking in the young women of your generation."

In all her life, no one had ever accused Amelia of displaying vigor. She thought it was quite the nicest compliment she'd ever received, not that she'd ever received a surfeit of compliments.

"I must confess to you, Lady Dalby," Amelia said, leaning forward slightly, "that I do not know any of them well enough to have formed a preference."

"Nothing at all?"

"There was," Amelia said slowly, "the tiniest thought that it might be unwise to wed Lord Iveston. He is so very blond, you see, and I . . ." Amelia waved a hand in the direction of her own blond head.

"And you were nervous about the exact shading of your offspring," Sophia finished. "Entirely right of you, darling. While blond hair and a generally fair coloration is quite appealing in the right degree, it is positively revolting when taken to extremes."

"Exactly," Amelia said, relaxing her shoulders. Perhaps she had been more than wise in coming to Sophia. Sophia did seem to grasp every nuance with exact precision and a minimal amount of tedious explanation. "But I am also afraid, I do confess, of the possible consequences of a union with the Duke of Edenham. Given his history, I do have some slight fears for my future."

"But, darling, when one aims for a duke, there are always risks," Sophia said. "You simply cannot allow the fragility and plain bad luck of his previous wives to hinder you. Where is that stunning vigor I remarked upon? Surely not an illusion? And, having relegated Iveston to the third position, can you afford to remove Edenham? There are only so many dukes in any Season and that there are as many as three . . ." Sophia shrugged delicately. "I do think it is somewhat risky to put all your matrimonial eggs in Calbourne's basket. He's a charming man, as I'm certain you know, but he is possibly the least *tamed* of the three. Naturally, it is your decision entirely."

The least tamed. There was a phrase to send tremors down a virgin's spine. Calbourne was nearly a giant in size; though the fact that his clothes were perfectly tailored reduced the impact, nothing could hide the fact that he was always the tallest man in any room by a head, at the very least. Plain speaking was one thing, but she was not going to admit to Sophia that she was more than a little afraid that she couldn't *accommodate* Calbourne in the precise way that men so needed to be accommodated. It wouldn't do at all to have the marriage annulled for a failure of that sort.

"No, not at all," Amelia said. "I'm not so particular in my requirements. Merely a duke, that is all I require."

"Merely a duke," Sophia said, smiling. "If I may say so, your requirements in a husband have not gone unnoticed."

"I beg your pardon?" Amelia said, her voice barely above a mortified whisper.

Sophia put down her cup and leaned back slightly in her chair, considering Amelia more closely than was quite polite.

"Lady Amelia, you have hardly been discreet. Surely you were aware of that?" Sophia said.

"I'm quite certain I don't know—"

"Then allow me to make it clear to you," Sophia interrupted pleasantly. "You have been very singular in your interests and it has not gone unnoticed. Indeed, it has not gone unremarked upon, at least in certain circles."

Amelia put down her cup. It rattled against the wood, announcing her distress.

"Naturally, the men you have targeted are the most aware of your interest, as indeed they should be as they are the targets of every mama of every woman of the proper age and rank in Town. Men in that particular situation, which only a man would be so foolish as to find onerous, are very attuned to plans such as yours. How else to remain unmarried for more than a sennight? The fox does become wary whenever dogs are in the vicinity, does it not? Perfectly natural, though what a dog plans to enact upon a fox breaks the metaphor entirely."

Sophia was speaking in the most casual, most conversational tone possible. Amelia was quite sure of this even as her stomach was heaving up toward her mouth. She was going to be sick. There was nowhere to be sick in this room, if one discounted that very expensive-looking green porcelain vase. She thought she should discount it, at least for as long as she could.

"Lady Dalby," Amelia said, "I cannot think you are correct. Surely, you overstate it?"

"Darling, I never overstate anything. Are you feeling quite the thing? You look rather more pale than when you entered. Shall I ring for food?"

The thought of food at the moment did very unpleasant things to her stomach. She pushed the idea away with that mental vigor Sophia so prized.

"No. I'm fine," Amelia said, well aware that her upper lip was covered in sweat.

"I shall continue then, shall I?" Sophia said. "Of course, the thing to do, and you have begun it so well, is to continue on as you have done, only more so, naturally."

Amelia, of course, had her own plans in place for what this meeting with Sophia Dalby should have done, but this was rather more than she had intended. Quite a bit more, actually. She found that what she most wanted to do at present was to run from the room and demand that Hawksworth carry her home in his arms. Only he wouldn't because he was as lazy as a cat.

"I'm sorry," Amelia said softly. "I'm afraid I don't understand." In all truth, she was very much afraid that she understood all too well.

Sophia blinked and then smiled in exquisite patience. "The thing to do, Lady Amelia, is to *continue on*. You have a preference for dukes. It is not unknown. Let us only make it more known. Let us, indeed, require these three delicious men to interview for the post of husband. A most satisfactory solution and so very to the point, do you not agree? Lady Amelia, are you quite certain that you're feeling well?"

Amelia thought that, for the first time in her life, she might actually be on the verge of a faint. She did hope so.

Three

"WITH Blakes married now, perhaps Mother will let you slip a while longer," George Blakesley said in the least hopeful tone imaginable.

"Optimist," Iveston said from his slouch on the sofa in the second floor sitting room.

"Worse," Cranleigh said in a mumble of ill humor. "Liar."

It was the family sitting room, closed to all but those closest to the family, which meant a paltry fifty or so persons had ever seen it. In a house such as Hyde House, which took up a sizeable portion of Piccadilly Street and was therefore open to frequent large gatherings during the Season, the rooms in a house that were not under the public gaze were few indeed. The boys, that is to say, the sons of the fourth Duke of Hyde, spent considerable time in the family sitting room. In consequence, the room had a more than shabby appearance that their mother commented upon at every opportunity, yet she had relinquished the space to them fully, if not gracefully.

The room, large enough to be comfortable for the five

of them and yet small enough to encourage intimacy, had the benefit of a southern exposure and a fireplace that drew cleanly and evenly. In all, it was a comfortable place to complain about their lot in life, which meant that they were more often silently companionable than not. As the beloved sons of a very reasonable duke, they had very little to complain about. As the sons of a very pragmatic duchess, they knew it.

But, naturally and completely in line with the reasonable workings of the world, they could and did complain about women and marriage. They were, or had been until earlier in the week, contented bachelors, however much that discontented their mother. But Blakes, the fourth son, had precipitously married Lady Louisa and that singular occurrence, which should have settled the duchess into a pleasant state of satisfaction and complacency about marriage in general and her sons in particular, had almost certainly resulted in the opposite.

Molly, their Boston-bred mother, was more marriage-minded than ever.

It was a most singularly unexpected and horrifying development.

"You have to marry eventually," Josiah said, "why not get it over with and be done with it?" Josiah, the youngest son and aged twenty-three, was too young to marry and rested safely within that truth.

"Say the same when your manhood is on the matrimonial block," Iveston said.

The Marquis of Iveston, Hyde's eldest son and heir apparent, was on the hook and they all knew it, Cranleigh more than anyone.

"Amelia Caversham would do," Josiah said from his languid lounge upon the sofa farthest from the fire, which was only right as he was the youngest of the litter, "wouldn't she? She gives every appearance of being eager to marry a duke and as she is cousin to Louisa, well, it would make for cozy holidays in the country."

"Cozy for whom?" Cranleigh said abruptly, running his hands though his dark blond hair.

"Why, for Louisa, I should think," Josiah mused lazily.

"If you don't think Blakes will manage Louisa's coziness, you know nothing of either women or men, Jos," Cranleigh said a bit sharply, "which is hardly surprising, is it?"

Jos, as he was called among his familial intimates, took immediate offense, which was only proper and certainly the appropriate response.

"I am just back from Paris, Cranleigh!" Jos said.

"And hauled back like a squealing pig, as I understand it," Cranleigh rejoined, stretching his muscular legs out toward the fire. As the second born, he had a quite comfortable position by the fire. It was not a particularly chilly day, but one did not throw aside precedence merely on a technicality of that sort. "You weren't there long enough to lift a single skirt, I'd wager."

"I was there a full week!"

To which Cranleigh raised both brows fractionally and quirked his mouth almost invisibly. It was almost certain that Cranleigh's responses in general would be invisible to all but family. He was a most contained sort of man, much like the duke, actually.

"At least someone was made to squeal," George said, winking at Cranleigh.

"Get buggered," Jos said, scowling.

"Experience of that, have you?" George said, turning the knife.

Jos jumped to his feet and said, "You face down that Indian and see what you find yourself doing!"

"A valid point," Iveston said, putting an end to it. "How did they find you? I never did hear the details."

"I have no idea," Jos said, walking over to the window and staring sullenly out of it. "Having a good drunk, a giggling wench on my lap, and then we're surrounded by savages, wench gone, bottle gone, Paris," he sighed, "gone. I should never have gone with Dalby, it was because of him that they came."

"And you wouldn't have gone without him," Cranleigh said. "Hardly any fun in drinking and wenching alone."

Which would have sounded absurd to anyone outside of the room, certainly to anyone in London. They had discussed it once and reached the only possible conclusion they could: the duchess and her Boston upbringing had soiled them all. They could find fun only in small and carefully measured doses. It was most inconvenient as the ton did not practice frivolity in that particular fashion.

"Did you actually know about them, before you found yourself face-to-face with them?" George asked.

It was a likely question as none of them had heard even the slightest rumor that the Earl Dalby had blood relatives who were American Indians of the Iroquois variety.

"Not even a whisper," Jos said, which sounded almost as if he took it as a personal betrayal from his longtime friend, Dalby, which was a position of some merit as everyone in the ton knew everyone else's ancestry back to the Tudors, if not before.

"The duchess knew," Blakes said, entering the room with the same self-congratulatory expression he'd been wearing since his marriage to Louisa, which was most excessively annoying.

"Done rutting for the day?" Cranleigh murmured.

"I certainly hope not," Blakes replied pleasantly, which set the room to chuckling.

"But whatever do you mean?" Jos said. "Mother can't have known. She never said a word, in all these years."

"Not about that, no," Blakes said, "but she knew and has known. I know it for a fact."

"She told you that?" George said.

It was somewhat remarkable, what it did to five full-grown men to think that their mother had kept something from them with apparent ease for almost thirty years. It was quite inconceivable that a mother could possibly practice such discretion with, one might even say *against*, her own children.

"No, not precisely," Blakes said, "but Sophia said as much, without actually admitting a thing, naturally."

"Naturally," Cranleigh said wryly.

"That sounds precisely like her," Iveston said. "What little I know of her," he added. Iveston had, in fact, by way of his zealously guarded privacy, spent very little time with anyone, particularly women, and even more particularly if they were unmarried women.

"I have some trouble believing that the duchess has more than a passing acquaintance with Lady Dalby. It would be approaching scandalous and we all know how little the duchess cares for scandal," Cranleigh said.

"Where we're concerned, certainly," Blakes said, "she has as much toleration for scandal as any mother, which is to say, none at all, but this is about another woman and, as we all know, women have very different requirements where other women are concerned."

"Mother is a woman, that is true," George said somewhat reluctantly. It was most strange to think of one's mother as anything other than a mother. Most strange and not entirely pleasant.

They pondered that individually and silently, the room shifting as Blakes made a seat for himself next to Cranleigh on the sofa. There was hardly room, but Blakes didn't seem to care that Cranleigh had to put his feet on the floor and shift his arse over to accommodate him. Blakes, now that he had Louisa, seemed to think he could do anything.

"You still plan to leave?" Blakes asked him quietly.

"I do," Cranleigh mumbled, slouching down and extending his legs out.

"More now than ever, I should think," Blakes said.

"There is no *more now than ever* to it," Cranleigh snarled quietly, casting his brother a sideways glance. "I like the sea. I like Uncle Timothy, for all that he's an American. There is little for me to do here."

"You could marry," Blakes suggested.

Cranleigh snorted. "I have no need to marry."

"I believe that people marry not only for need, but for want."

"I want for nothing."

"And no one?" Blakes asked softly.

"And no one," Cranleigh answered stiffly, his gaze on his feet stretched out before him.

"Then I suppose it is wise of you not to marry," Blakes said evenly. "When will you go?"

"Next month, I should think. There should be an Elliot ship in port in the next few weeks. Timothy has offered me a place on any of his ships."

"Most kind of him."

"I've earned it," Cranleigh said, shifting his weight.

"No doubt of that," Blakes said. "I suppose the duchess will cry."

Cranleigh snorted again, this time in amusement. "I suppose she will not. She didn't cry the first time I took to sea. Why should she cry now?"

"Perhaps because it's the last time?" Blakes said softly, gazing at Cranleigh's profile. "You don't intend to return, do you?"

"Of course I do. What nonsense, Blakes."

"Is it?"

"Complete." But he did not look his brother in the eye as he said it. No, Blakes was far too discerning and saw too many things Cranleigh did not wish him to see.

"Well then, I'm glad to be wrong about it. I should miss you, I think."

"With that pretty bride waiting in your bed?" Cranleigh said with a half smile. "I think not."

"Oh, we do not restrict ourselves to beds, Cranleigh. Too pedestrian for my Louisa. She does like to get about, you know. Very ambitious, my girl. Quite like her cousin, Amelia, in that, though not in form, of course."

"Of course," Cranleigh said. "Not at all in form. Quite obviously."

"They're very close, those two, nearly like sisters. I

should think Lady Amelia will make herself quite at home here, or whenever Louisa is in residence at Hyde House."

"When are you leaving, by the way?" Cranleigh asked casually.

"As soon as the rains let up."

As it was April and had been raining for two days straight, Blakes might be in residence for another week or another month; it was impossible to predict. Cranleigh felt the urge to stand on a ship in the middle of the ocean rise up like a wave inside him.

"And until then?"

"Until then, we shall amuse ourselves as married folk do," Blakes said. "What will you do to amuse yourself, Cranleigh? Or should I ask, upon whom?"

"No, you should not ask," Cranleigh said, shoving his brother off the sofa until his arse hit the floor.

❧

"I must ask, Lady Dalby, if this is some rare jest?" Amelia said softly past her rolling nausea.

"About men? Never," Sophia said. "Certainly, they are quite amusing, but this business of marriage must be approached soberly and with great care. I am more than confident that you agree with me, Lady Amelia, or why else would you have shown such wisdom in seeking my counsel and advice? Most wise of you, most prudent. I only find myself wishing that you had come to me sooner. Yet, things are still quite manageable, and by *things* I mean men." At which point Sophia smiled slyly.

Amelia allowed that being sly was precisely the reason why Sophia could manage to get her married.

"I confess, Lady Dalby, that I don't quite comprehend what you mean by an interview process," Amelia said as calmly as could be expected.

"I mean, Lady Amelia," Sophia said, "that we shall advertise for a husband for you. Only dukes and heir apparents may apply, naturally. We shall make that very clear. It will come as a surprise to no one, which is precisely why we must boldly state both your intentions and your goals. It will have quite a good result, I should think. Men do so appreciate a forthright approach."

There was only one thing to be done in the circumstance. Amelia rose to her feet, her vision gone a bit gray about the edges. She slowly and very nearly gracefully slipped down to the floor in what appeared to be the most ineffectual faint any woman had ever endured.

"But, darling," Sophia said, staring down at her, "you've fainted? Are you given to faints? Not a bad thing, in certain circumstances. We might make some use of it."

It was then that Amelia knew she had made the worst possible choice in coming to Sophia Dalby for aid. The woman was as cold-blooded as an eel.

"Fredericks!" Sophia said, still staring down at her while she called for her butler. "Find Lord Hawksworth. I'm quite certain that he's wandering about down the street or some such. The women of his family do like to keep him cooling his heels. I think Lady Amelia needs her brother now. And he wouldn't want to miss this, would he?"

Amelia was sitting up when Hawksworth ambled into the room. One would think he might have hurried, but no. Sophia greeted him with a smile. He smiled in return. No one seemed particularly concerned that she was sitting on the floor. In fact, it might be said that no one even noticed, except for Fredericks, Sophia's American butler. Fredericks *winked* at her.

Oh, bother it all.

"Not feeling quite the thing, Amy?" Hawks said, when he could pull his attention away from Sophia for the barest minute. "Perhaps you should be bled."

Hawks leaned down and helped her to her feet. She rose with considerable charm, considering. Once she was in her chair again, her hands fussing with her mussed hair, she said stiffly, "I'm quite all right."

"No bleeding then?" Hawks said. "Pity."

Amelia cast him a look that was as sharp as glass and said, "I'm fine, Hawksworth. I simply had a start, that's all. A shock of sorts."

Upon which they both looked at Sophia, for who else could be responsible for shocks that resulted in faints if not Sophia Dalby?

"I'm afraid, Lord Hawksworth, that I am responsible for that," Sophia said without a shred of guilt or even shame.

"Is that so?" Hawksworth said pleasantly, stretching his long legs out before him. "I am quite certain you take too much on yourself, Lady Dalby. My sister has not been feeling well today. Why, not two hours ago she was sound asleep and snoring upon the sofa at Aldreth House."

"I was not sleeping, Hawks, and I was certainly not snoring," she snapped, her cheeks flushed. "I was *thinking*."

"And your thinking led you here, to me," Sophia said. "Perfectly understandable. Lord Hawksworth, Lady Amelia and I were discussing how she should best attain her marriage goals. You understand to what I am referring?"

"But of course," he said on a drawl, "it is to be a duke or no one for dear Amelia. That decision, to date, has resulted in no one, I fear."

"Hawksworth!" Amelia said, not at all amused.

"Yes?" he said, looking at her from beneath heavy lids and without a scrap of remorse. "One must face it squarely, Amy. What else is one to do in the circumstance?"

"One can retain some dignity, for one," she said. "I'm afraid I have wasted your time, Lady Dalby." Amelia rose to her feet and looked down at her brother. He sighed and rose slowly to his feet alongside her. *Dolt*.

Sophia rose to her feet as well, her smile looking almost genuine. It was quite remarkable. Amelia was in a very good position to know that good will was not in Lady Dalby's catalogue of skills. She was the most devious, the most ruthless woman that Amelia had ever had the opportunity to meet. Which of course was the reason she had sought her out in the first place.

"Lady Amelia," Sophia said, "are you quite certain?

As you are not feeling quite completely well, perhaps your decision is precipitous?"

"I am very much afraid, Lady Dalby," Amelia said, "that most of my decisions today have been precipitous."

"The desire to marry is certainly a most ordinary wish, Lady Amelia," Sophia said softly, her smile looking genuine for once, "and the desire to marry well is certainly always far beyond ordinary and always exemplary. You are only to be commended. And aided, if you will allow."

Sophia looked deeply and fully into her eyes, and for the first time Amelia was comforted by the dark sparkle in Sophia's gaze. Here was a woman in whom to put one's trust. She would not, unless provoked, betray either trust or confidence.

Amelia was entirely aware that she'd just made another precipitous decision, but perhaps this one would prove wise. It was not *entirely* impossible.

"Why would you help me, Lady Dalby?" Amelia asked in a voice just above a whisper.

"Because," Sophia answered swiftly, her smile growing, "should not every woman get exactly what she wants?"

Amelia felt her heart warm at the words. It was a startling philosophy. She thought it was completely brilliant. Sophia Dalby, when she had a moment or two, ought to write a small book on the subject.

"I should say that would depend entirely upon what it is a woman wants," Hawksworth said in an annoyed mumble.

Whereupon Sophia and Amelia exchanged a glance of ripe amusement and complete understanding. At Hawksworth's expense. Perfect.

Smiling at each other, Amelia and Sophia sat back down upon their matching milk blue sofas, Amelia taking her first full breath in perhaps two years. She was going to marry. Sophia would ensure it.

"Now," Sophia said, "we must make certain that we advertise in the precise manner to actually attract our quarry. I shall manage it, shall I? I have rather more experience in these sorts of things."

"Of course," Amelia said, leaning forward in her seat.

"Advertise?" Hawksworth said, leaning back on the sofa and gazing at Amelia with a look that was both bored and annoyed. "What are you advertising for? A husband?"

"Precisely," Sophia said. "How very astute you are, Lord Hawksworth. You do your father proud."

"Father," Amelia said, her confidence falling at the word. "How shall we ever manage to get this past Aldreth?"

Sophia smiled slightly and said, "I shall manage the duke, Lady Amelia. Never fear."

And for perhaps the first time in two years, Amelia didn't.

Four

THE Duke of Aldreth had a mistress. Having a mistress was not at all unusual and certainly no one would have thought to comment upon the fact, but Aldreth had enjoyed the same mistress, a failed French actress, for twenty years. That *did* excite some comment among those who knew, which was practically everyone. In fact, as Aldreth had been a widower for well over a decade, his mistress was blamed entirely for his negligence in not remarrying.

Zoe Auvray, his French mistress, deserved every bit of the blame, and because she was the sort of woman who would *be* a mistress, she did not even have the civility to feel at all guilty about depriving some English heiress of the chance of snaring Aldreth. Zoe quite liked keeping Aldreth all to herself and Aldreth quite liked being kept.

Which was the exact opposite of how these affairs were supposed to run, but she was French and he was a duke and there was no predicting events from that precise point of origin.

As Aldreth was a duke of rather formidable reputation and as he had a daughter of marriageable age and an heir of a somewhat peculiar degree of lethargy but, nevertheless, an heir apparent of sound mind and body, no one was in a particular hurry to beard Aldreth in his den concerning his mistress, his daughter, or his son, which was exactly as Aldreth liked it. Of course his mistress was not at all intimidated by his savage roars or savage silences or savage scowls, which was inconvenient in the extreme.

"One would think, Aldreth, that you have no wish for a husband for your daughter," Zoe said.

She was engaged in her toilette, an activity he found strangely and endlessly fascinating, and she was facing him in the mirror. She was not as young as she had been the night he had stumbled upon her in the theater at Drury Lane, but she was just as beautiful. He was quite certain he was unmistaken in that. She was, truly, just as beautiful, perhaps even more beautiful. Yes, she most assuredly was.

"Aldreth, you are wandering," Zoe said softly, studying him in the reflection. "We were speaking of your daughter, Amelia. She is quite ready for a husband."

"Yet no man has stepped forward for the role," he said. "What can be done? There must be something wrong with the girl." Though he could not see what. She was pretty and pleasant and endowed with a sufficient fortune to attract almost anyone, yet no one had stepped forward. It was very nearly remarkable.

"There is nothing wrong with Amelia, Aldreth," Zoe said. "She is perfectly lovely and has every advantage."

Which was exactly what he had been thinking for the past two years. Yet something had to be wrong with the girl. It was not at all difficult to find oneself married. People did it every day. Just look at Melverley's older girl, Louisa. She had found herself wed in a matter of days when no man had appeared willing to do the deed until it had actually happened.

Of course, Sophia Dalby had been involved in that somehow, he was almost entirely certain. Sophia Dalby, whom he had known even longer than he had known Zoe, though in a different capacity entirely, was in the habit of meddling in almost everything. Why, he was not completely certain even all these years later that she had not had something to do with his meeting Zoe. In twenty years he had not reasoned out *how* she could have done so, but the suspicion lingered.

"Yet no one appears to want her," Aldreth said. "What's to be done, Zoe? Certainly I can do nothing more."

"Ridiculous," Zoe said, turning upon her stool to frown at him. He found her frowns quite as charming as her smiles. "One can always do more, Aldreth. The poor child cannot be left as she is. Some man must be found for her. Someone worthy. Someone quite as wonderful as you are."

Aldreth smiled reluctantly. Zoe was always finding occasions to flatter him. He quite enjoyed it.

"Is anyone as wonderful as all that?" he said, rising to his feet and walking over to her.

"But of course!" Zoe said in a burst of unflattering enthusiasm. "There are so many lovely men about Town, truly and completely as delightful as you, dear Aldreth. You must not think so ill of men, Aldreth. Very many of them can be quite . . . satisfying."

Aldreth scowled instantly. Zoe was always finding occasions to tweak his tail. He had never quite got used to it.

"Hearsay, I presume?" he said sternly, glaring down at her.

"Aldreth, I am not a nun in a cloister," she said, grinning up at him. "I do manage, in my own little way, to find out the more interesting of the events that entertain the whole of Town. You cannot think that I spend my time doing needlework and waiting for you to arrive on my doorstep?"

"Actually, yes. I do think that is exactly what you should be doing."

"I suppose you'd like me to supply you with a portfolio of erotic needlework?"

"I'm not adverse to the idea."

He was grinning again. Zoe always managed to make him smile; he thought that it was likely why he found her so engaging and so endlessly fascinating after so many years.

She was no longer young, but she was still a coquette. And she was *his*, no matter what she said to torment him.

"I'm not particularly skilled with my hands," she said, running her hands up his thighs to his hips.

"I completely disagree," he said.

"How charming of you, Aldreth," she said, smiling up at him seductively. "Now, wouldn't it satisfy you deeply to have Amelia safely and blissfully wed to a man who finds her hands skillful and wants only to keep her for himself, as you so delightfully do me?"

Which, naturally, killed the moment completely as he did not care to think of his daughter in that way at *all*.

"Of course," he said, moving away from Zoe's hands, turning his back on her completely, actually. Zoe laughed, which was entirely in character for her. "But, I repeat, there is nothing I can do to change the situation as it now stands. If my daughter cannot attract a man of the appropriate degree of suitability . . ." He shrugged slightly.

"But Aldreth, she is a woman without a mother. Little Amelia needs help in achieving her man."

"She's hardly a child, Zoe."

"Of course she is not, but without a mother to guide her," Zoe said, shrugging her slender shoulders most expressively. "I, naturally, am in no position to aid her, though you know I would if it were at all possible, dear Aldreth."

"But you know someone who is in a position to aid her?" Aldreth asked suspiciously.

"But of course I do! Did you imagine that I would bring the subject up if I did not, even now, have the solution?"

"And the solution's name?" Aldreth asked, already knowing the answer.

"Sophia Dalby, as if you didn't know," she said, kissing him at the very base of his neck, which was quite as far as she could reach without standing on a chair.

"Sophia Dalby," he said sternly, staring down at her, holding her at arm's length. She didn't look the slightest bit alarmed by his severity, which was a continual problem in his dealings with her. "Why should Sophia help Amelia, and how could she possibly help her in any event?"

"Why? Because I have asked her to, darling Aldreth," Zoe said, smiling up at him. "As to how, I leave that entirely up to her, and so should you. She is, you know, responsible for me finding you that night in the theater."

"I don't see how," he said, allowing her to snuggle against his waistcoat.

"But of course you don't, Aldreth. It was never meant for you to see how, as indeed, no man ever sees how he ends up with a particular woman when there are so many other women available to him."

"I was under the firm impression that it was the man who did the choosing, Zoe."

"But of course you were, darling. Of course," she said, very nearly laughing. "And you shall be under that impression again, once Sophia arranges everything beautifully for Amelia. Then you may go back to thinking whatever suits you. And doing whatever suits you. What *does* suit you, my dear?"

Finally, a question he could answer without having to reason it out. Aldreth kissed her soundly, picked her up in his arms, and carried her to bed.

Five

"WE shall begin with Calbourne. He should do very nicely," Sophia said to Amelia and Hawksworth, who stared, slack-jawed, at her.

"But I thought you said that the Duke of Calbourne was more than, that is to say," Amelia said, casting an uncomfortable glance at her brother, "was a bit more than a girl of my years and experience could . . . manage."

"But, darling, he is not more than *I* can manage and I shall be with you every moment," Sophia said, smiling into her cup.

"I hope I shall be pardoned for sounding as green as grass," Hawksworth said with an idle air, "but how does one go about interviewing dukes, Lady Dalby? I'm quite certain I've never heard of it being done before."

"But of course it's been done, Lord Hawksworth," Sophia said. "The difference in this instance is that it will be done blatantly, which will make everything so much more interesting, not to mention more productive, don't you agree?"

Sophia clearly did not care if anyone agreed with her

or not. Amelia, who had spent her life to date making certain that everyone found her eminently agreeable, found Sophia's blunt approach remarkable. Sophia feared no one; on the contrary, most of the ton were careful not to annoy Sophia in the most minor fashion as it was well known that she made a spectacular enemy.

It was a skill, a trait, and a habit that Amelia believed had definite possibilities.

"We shall begin immediately, shall we?" Sophia continued, again, not waiting for anyone to agree with her. It truly was a useful skill. She simply must acquire it at the earliest opportunity. "I am scheduled to dine with the Duke of Calbourne tonight. I shall simply include you in our party, Lady Amelia. Of course, I do think things would go more efficiently if you were not present, Lord Hawksworth. You understand, I am quite certain."

The fact that Sophia spoke with a knowing smile did nothing to lessen the impact of her suggestion. In point of fact, it was rather more alarming than not.

"Unfortunately, I'm quite certain I do, Lady Dalby," Hawksworth said, showing just the slightest bit of warmth. It was entirely unlike him, and it was rather sweet. "I can't think that this could possibly be in Lady Amelia's best interests. Certainly reducing her to that sort of awkward situation would add another layer of tarnish to her reputation in Town, and she can scarcely afford another layer, can she?"

Dolt.

"I'm not tarnished in the least, Hawks," Amelia said stiffly. "My reputation is precisely as it should be—pristine. I am as pristine as it is possible for a woman of my years and station to be."

Which was nothing but the truth. She was twenty-one years old and quite as pristine as any normal twenty-one-year-old woman could be expected to be.

"And it is quite obvious to anyone with eyes to see that you are exactly so, Lady Amelia," Sophia said. "Pristine in the extreme."

It was most peculiar, but Sophia made being pristine sound like an insult when it was quite obviously nothing of the sort.

"As bad as that, then?" Hawksworth drawled, looking at Amelia in what could only be described as pity.

Before Amelia could draw breath to berate Hawks, almost completely past caring that Sophia Dalby would see her in a not entirely attractive light for doing so, and almost equally certain that Sophia might derive malicious amusement in revealing her lapse to her future husband, the duke, Sophia answered Hawks.

"Nothing, Lord Hawksworth, is as bad as all that," Sophia said, looking kindly at Amelia. "We shall act quickly, one might almost say with martial aggression, and the matter will be settled. Your sister, the lovely Lady Amelia, will find a most suitable match, and her reputation will only be enhanced by the endeavor. I trust that is satisfactory?"

It was with some horror that Amelia realized that she was being discussed in some mildly disparaging fashion for no cause whatsoever.

"There is nothing whatsoever wrong with my reputation!" Amelia said, not entirely certain what she was defending herself against, but somehow certain that she did require some sort of defense. Ridiculous, really, as she had lived her life beautifully and indeed, flawlessly. "I am exactly the sort of woman to make any man proud, and indeed I think I would make an ideal duchess. I am quite certain of it. *Quite* certain," she finished a bit heatedly.

Sophia smiled, her dark eyes flashing. "And it is just this level of conviction and fire which you must display before your suitors, Lady Amelia. A proper woman of proper fire is how they must see you. A natural fit for you, certainly. You shall not have a bit of trouble, I am quite certain. Why, I should not be at all surprised if the matter of your marriage is not settled within a week's time. The men of your list are all in Town at present, which is most convenient. A week's time, at the very latest," Sophia said musingly.

It was not at all reassuring. It should have been, but Sophia had the most unappealing gleam in her black eyes. It was nearly impossible not to shudder in anticipation.

"I do think that I should be present," Hawks said, sounding not at all glad about it. "I can't think that it would look quite the thing if I were not in attendance."

"Lord Hawksworth," Sophia said, leaning forward and giving Hawks a charming view of her décolleté, "surely you must realize that a man of your bearing and prominence in Society would hamper Amelia from making the necessary ... maneuvers a woman must deploy in snaring a duke of the realm. Surely you have ample experience at avoiding ladies with similar goals. You are, as you must be aware, a most compelling man with absolutely everything to recommend you. A woman would be a fool indeed if she did not do everything in her power to entertain your interest."

Hawks, the fool, was hanging on to Sophia's every word and looked as sophisticated as a four-week-old pup.

"True, true," he said in an outrageous display of false humility.

"Perhaps, to save your reputation and not make you the subject of speculation," Sophia said soothingly, "you would enjoy an invitation to Marshfield Park, the Dalby estate. My family is there now, doing all those things that men so love to do in the country. I'm certain they would welcome you into their midst with delight. Shall I make the arrangements?"

It was the most amazing thing, but Amelia could almost see Hawks imagining himself running amid the fields and streams of England in the midst of a pack of Indians, whooping like the worst savage. He was clearly enchanted by the vision. One only hoped he kept his shoes on. And his scalp.

"If it's no imposition," he said blandly, the worst bit of acting Amelia had seen in a year.

"Nothing of the sort," Sophia said, casting an amused gaze at Amelia, who found herself smiling in return.

Sophia Dalby could manage a man better than anyone Amelia had ever seen. It was positively inspiring.

And so it was that, except for the boring though necessary details, Hawksworth was disposed of.

∽

As far as boring details went, Amelia did think that it wouldn't be the worst idea she ever had to consult with Louisa about her decision to rely upon Sophia Dalby's plan. Or that would be the reason she gave Louisa for dropping in unexpectedly, if Louisa even asked. It was so very convenient to her plans that Louisa now resided at Hyde House as Hyde House was the London residence of the Marquis of Iveston, as well as all the other sons of Hyde. So very, very convenient. Louisa couldn't have married a better man for Amelia's schemes if she'd planned to do so for a decade, which she had most definitely not.

Amelia was admitted to Hyde House, a truly imposing structure, and escorted into the music room. It was a sumptuous room, newly papered, and littered with the necessary musical instruments to support its name. Neither the Marquis of Iveston nor any of his unmarried younger brothers were in view. It was most unfortunate that Iveston or even Cranleigh, the next oldest brother and an earl, was not littered about the music room with the harp and the pianoforte. Nearly before disappointment could find its way into Amelia's heart, Louisa entered with a saucy grin, her curling ginger hair looking slightly mussed. She wore a gown Amelia had seen her in often, a simple white muslin with clever pleating at the bodice and amber thread in a leaf design at the hem. Amelia was relieved that she did not look down-at-the-heel in her white muslin with the green-sprigged design. One did want to look one's best when calling at Hyde House, while at the same time not looking as if one had tried too vigorously to look just the thing.

"Lost your comb, Louisa?" Amelia said with a grin that she was certain Louisa would find cheeky.

"I find that there is no real point in taking supreme care

with my toilette, Amelia, as Blakes will make a mess of me within an hour," Louisa said. "He is most inconsiderate that way. It is quite annoying."

Naturally, Louisa did not look annoyed in the slightest. She looked completely delighted, which was perfectly understandable. Amelia could only hope that her future husband would delight her just as completely. In fact, she was determined that he do so.

"He sounds quite a handful," Amelia said, to which Louisa laughed and then blushed. *Oh, dear.* That could have multiple meanings, couldn't it? "You are most content, Louisa, are you not?

"I am. Truly," Louisa answered, the blush still pink on her cheeks and throat.

She appeared most sincere, which did give Amelia even more assurance that her minor conspiracy with Sophia would bear the appropriate fruit.

"But what of you, Amelia? Would you not seek your own contentment? You want a duke, and there are only two available, yet wouldn't either one of them do? Why, even Lord Iveston will be a duke one day. You might consider him."

Amusing, as usual. Did Louisa actually think that she needed to remind Amelia as to the number of dukes on the market? And as to Iveston, could Louisa possibly believe that Amelia had overlooked him? Regarding Iveston even more specifically, now that Louisa was part of the family, it did open up all sorts of opportunities for Amelia to have reasonable access to Hyde House. Had Louisa not realized that? Amelia certainly had.

Sometimes Amelia wondered if Louisa were as intelligent as she ought to have been.

"Louisa, I *have* considered him. The problem is that he has not considered me. Nor have Edenham or Calbourne. You see Iveston often now, as indeed you must see the entire family regularly; does he appear at all interested in marrying?"

"But of course he doesn't, Amelia. He's an eligible man

and they are the most unwilling sort of men, completely repulsed by women, by all appearances."

"How typical. And how unfortunate," Amelia said softly, casting her gaze to the design of the carpet beneath her feet. "It would be so much more convenient if he were at least mildly interested in me. You don't suppose I could entice him, do you? He is very much reserved; it is quite his most well-reputed trait. Perhaps I might be able to lure Iveston into some sort of observable interest?"

"Observable? Why on earth need it be observable, Amelia?" Louisa asked.

Amelia smoothed her muslin skirts and lifted her gaze to her cousin. "For the most simple of reasons, Louisa. If it is not observable, how am I to know if I have gained his interest? I can hardly read his thoughts."

"At certain times more than others it is quite possible to read a man's thoughts," Louisa said with another faint blush staining her throat.

Tea and cakes were brought in just then, which resulted in Louisa busying herself with serving and Amelia busying herself with smiling pleasantly as she accepted her cup and plate. Once the servants were out of the room, they resumed their conversation.

"Certainly there is more to it than that, Louisa. There must be. A man may think very much, yet do very little. Or may do the wrong thing altogether and then," Amelia said, shrugging, "nothing."

"Surely not *nothing*," Louisa said, leaning forward, her tea and cake entirely forgotten.

"Very nearly nothing. I could even find myself ruined."

"You don't sound very nervous about it, I must say," Louisa said.

"Don't I? But of course I am. I thought that was perfectly obvious."

"I still don't see how you can find yourself ruined by a man who does nothing. Are we talking about a specific man? What *have* you been hiding from me, Amelia? I've never seen you with any man, doing nothing or not. Or is it that some man has done the wrong thing? Have I got it all turned round?"

"But of course not. There is no man. There is no *nothing*. I was only speculating on how difficult it is to find the right man who will do the right thing. Before Lord Henry Blakesley dragged you off into that closet, you were quite of the same mind. I remember that most clearly."

Louisa eyed her curiously in response, to which Amelia smiled blandly and stirred her tea. It was quite a nuisance that Louisa had suddenly started to pay attention in a conversation that was not entirely about her. An air of innocence was what was required in circumstances such as these, and Amelia had quite a lot of practice at innocence. Or at least the appearance of it, which was more important than actually being innocent, wasn't it?

❧

THE Earl of Cranleigh came upon Lady Amelia Caversham in the foyer of Hyde House. She looked innocent, as was her habit. He knew she was not.

She looked fresh and flushed, bright and smooth, her hair glossy and shining with health and good soap, her cheeks soft as goose down. It was perfectly typical of her. She was wearing white with a green design and her eyes looked particularly blue at the moment.

He was not cheered to see her, which he hoped was obvious to her.

He was well aware that she was in Hyde House to see Iveston, the heir apparent and the unattainable prize of every woman of good family and good teeth for the past ten Seasons. Hard luck for Amelia that she had stumbled upon him instead of Iveston. He wasn't an heir apparent, was he? She would have hardly any use for him at all.

"Lady Amelia," he said, bowing to her.

"Lord Cranleigh," she said, making a very pretty and entirely proper curtsey. She had acquired the habit somewhere, likely in the same field where she had acquired perpetual innocence, of looking nearly perfect at any given moment. Naturally, as the daughter of a duke, this was to be expected. The thing was, she did it better than anyone else. It was most annoying. Calculated perfection was a thing not to be desired. If he were on easy terms with her, he would tell her just that. But he wasn't, and he wouldn't. What he would do was keep her away from Iveston. Iveston she could not have, no matter how she had perfected perfection.

Hell and blast. That sounded idiotic, but he knew it made sense. *Perfect* sense.

"What a surprise to see you, Lord Cranleigh," she said, her gaze raking him from his boots to his collar. If seeing him were a surprise, it did not look a pleasant one. Cranleigh slid his gaze to the butler and felt his pulse pound against his temples. "Are you all at home, then? Lord Iveston as well?" she asked sweetly, her blue eyes meeting his briefly.

"Lord Iveston is engaged at present, Lady Amelia. You shall be forced to make do with me, I'm afraid," he said, taking a step toward her. She took a step away from him, toward the front door, an awkward little dance between them. The butler looked on, stone-faced.

"Forced, Lord Cranleigh? That does sound a bit like you, I'm afraid," she said stiffly, straightening the seam on her left glove, avoiding his eyes. "You don't expect Lord Iveston to be available, then?"

"Not in the next few minutes, no," he gritted out between his teeth.

"How very disappointing," she said, lifting her chin and staring him fully in the face for the first time. Most irregular behavior for her and wandering very nearly into being not entirely proper. How peculiar. He could not think what had changed in the past day or so to make her behave so boldly.

Ah, but how stupid. Of course. Her cousin had married his brother. How difficult would it be for her to marry Iveston now?

More difficult than she dared to imagine.

"I'm certain it must be," he said coldly.

"Are you?" she said, her voice catching in her throat.

She coughed lightly and said, "Excuse me, I was merely going to ask if the rumor of your returning to sea is true?"

"It is quite true."

"How very intriguing," she said, her gaze wandering from his to survey the room behind him. Likely planning how she'd change the wallpaper once she was Duchess of Hyde, blasted snip of a girl. "I had no idea you were so taken with life aboard ship, Lord Cranleigh. What is it that draws you?"

"The complete absence of women?" he asked crisply. When her gaze returned to his, her blue eyes sharp with rebuke, he added, "A poor jest. Your pardon." Without waiting for her to grant him pardon or not, he continued. "Adventure awaits me there, Lady Amelia. I would grab hold of it. A man cannot drift upon the waves like so much flotsam, his plans shifting upon the tides."

"I understand completely, Lord Cranleigh," she said pleasantly, her eyes once again on his face, holding his gaze. His pulse hammered. He quickly shifted his gaze elsewhere, to the butler's feet, in fact. "It is, I fear to inform you, much the same for a woman. Drifting is not a desirable choice. Anything is preferable, wouldn't you say?"

"I would," he said.

"We have an accord. How pleasant. Shall I risk it by stating that a woman must grab hold as well?"

"Grab hold of what, Lady Amelia?" he asked.

"What would you suppose, Lord Cranleigh?" She looked at the room around him, at the high plastered ceiling and the richly colored walls and the fine furnishings. She took her time about it, too, cataloguing the place that she clearly wanted for her own. And then she looked straight into his eyes, her crystalline gaze quite clear, and said, "Why, grab hold of a husband, Lord Cranleigh. What else is there for a woman to grab? In fact, I have an appointment with the Duke of Calbourne in a few hours and I must make haste. Good day."

And with that she was out the door before he could think of a response, verbal or otherwise.

Six

THE Duke of Calbourne had lost a wager to Lady Dalby and because of that, he came very near to whistling whilst being dressed by his valet.

An intimate supper with Sophia Dalby had been the terms of the wager. Hardly a wager he was dejected about losing. He would dine, charm, and woo. He would, if things went well, find himself in her bed. Just one night, one tumble, was all he asked. That he had, at his advanced age of thirty, managed to miss seducing Sophia Dalby was not to be borne a moment longer. He was a duke. He did have his reputation to think of.

And because Calbourne, of all things, had a sense of humor, he laughed out loud at the direction of his thoughts. Life was very fine indeed if the seduction of the most beautiful and the most infamous of women counted as a task to be accomplished.

Calbourne arrived at Dalby House on time. A bit of reliable gossip was that Sophia did not hesitate to punish those who were not prompt. He was prompt. He was not going to start his seduction of her with a misstep of that paltry variety.

He was shown into the yellow salon, a large and beautifully proportioned room done up entirely in sunny yellow silk damask with costly deep blue porcelains of French origin dotted about, and made to wait. He had expected nothing less.

Calbourne was pretending to study one of the Sevres porcelains, a bit of truly remarkable artistry, but hardly something to hold his attention for more than a few seconds, when he heard Sophia enter the room. He did not turn immediately as he suspected she would expect that. He *was* a duke, after all, and some small measure of superiority and benign arrogance was due him.

When he did turn to face her, he turned slowly and with all the formidable grace his impressive size would allow. He was, rather famously, he thought, the tallest and, he was not too modest to admit, the most fit man in any gathering. He used his size to intimidate and to impress whenever possible. It was nearly always possible. He found that particular vanity about himself fully as amusing as almost everything else. Calbourne, blessed with everything the world could bestow, found life almost uniformly amusing and pleasant. Why should he not?

Sophia had indeed entered the room. She looked, as always, seductive and nearly attainable. He had given it quite a bit of thought and he had concluded that one of the reasons for Sophia's fame was her precise *degree* of attainability. She maintained a certain degree of elusiveness that men, at least defined by him, found mesmerizing. He strongly suspected she found that amusing. He was not at all inclined to fault her. Did he not walk through life finding it more amusing than not?

At Sophia's side was Lady Jordan, related through marriage to both the Marquis of Melverley and the Duke of Aldreth. Lady Jordan, as was perfectly usual, looked slightly foxed.

Here was an odd bit of business.

On the heels of Lady Jordan followed Lady Amelia Caversham, Aldreth's daughter and rather too obviously in the market for a husband. She looked completely lovely, as was her habit.

Odd again. He could find no explanation for this parade of women into what was supposed to have been an intimate dinner between sophisticated and healthy adults.

And the parade was still not at an end, for nearly on the skirts of Lady Amelia came Mrs. Anne Warren, a particular favorite of Sophia's and almost something of a project with her. Mrs. Warren, a woman of no particular credentials beyond her obvious beauty, was on the cusp of being married to Lord Staverton.

The women curtseyed. He bowed. They sat, clustered onto one side of the room, the candlelight playing delicately on their faces and across their coiffed hair, looking at him expectantly. Calbourne sat, slowly and without his usual grace.

Most odd.

"You look slightly bemused, your grace," Sophia said, "which is completely understandable. If I may explain?"

"Bemused?" he asked with a half smile. "To find myself in the cheerful company of four lovely women when only one was expected? I should not be much of a man to admit to being bemused. Say instead, Lady Dalby, that I am delighted. Explanations can proceed or not, at your discretion."

Sophia smiled and nodded her head once in acquiescence, or was it to hide a chuckle? One could never be completely certain of anything with Sophia Dalby.

"How very wise you are, your grace, to count on my discretion. I am, in all things, most discreet," Sophia said. Which truly was rare humor as Sophia was discreet in nothing, particularly where men were concerned. Unfortunately, he was a man. "We had an arrangement for dinner, which will be met, but before we go in I thought that, in the way of pleasant conversation, one which I hope will build the appetite, you could answer a few questions."

"Questions? Regarding what?"

"Why, regarding yourself," Sophia said pleasantly, but there was something twinkling in the depths of her dark eyes that was not at all pleasant. Calbourne crossed his legs and lowered his chin, a pose that had sent more than one person skittering from the room. In this instance, no one skittered. Most inconvenient. "As you may be aware," Sophia continued, "Lady Amelia Caversham is in the market for a husband." At this statement of fact, Lady Amelia blushed and blinked rapidly. It was not at all becoming on her.

"Is she? How very wise of her," Calbourne said, which was a most polite thing to say, after all. Far worse could have been said, but he was not in the habit of taunting young women, though he supposed he could develop the habit if it were necessary. Looking again at Amelia, blushing and blinking, he did not think he needed to develop the habit. At least, not at present.

"Isn't it?" Sophia agreed.

Calbourne studied the women arrayed before him. There were four, yet Sophia was the only one engaging him. What was the significance of that? He knew Sophia well enough to know that everything had significance, whether one saw it immediately or not.

"And in the spirit of that wisdom and indeed, Lady Amelia's unusual and exemplary boldness in pursuing her goals, matrimony in this instance, I have agreed to aid her in acquiring the proper husband."

A truly alarming statement in any situation. That Sophia Dalby had mouthed the words made it almost dangerous.

"The proper husband?" Calbourne repeated, for what could that phrase possibly mean? And how on earth did it apply to him?

"But of course, your grace," Sophia answered calmly. Calmly? When he could feel a bead of sweat moistening his left temple? "Proper. A woman would be a fool indeed not to seek a proper husband. Lady Amelia, like any well-brought-up woman, has her list of requirements and you, your grace, I am most pleased to tell you, fit them almost exactly. At least, what we know of you."

The single bead of sweat had turned into a cluster. He was not even remotely amused. Calbourne could not remember the last time he had not been amused. He was, he realized with a slight shock, in a distinctly uncomfortable situation.

"I beg your pardon, Lady Dalby," he said in growing annoyance, "*what you know of me*? What precisely is that supposed to mean?" And as Sophia was opening her mouth to answer him, he added in true irritation, "And what do you mean, *her list of requirements*? A list of requirements? As they pertain to me?"

"Why, naturally, Calbourne," Sophia said with a smile of pure malice. At least it looked like malice to him. In any other circumstance he might have thought her smile delightful and charming. But not now, and perhaps never again. "You must know that you are entirely eligible and that Lady Amelia, not to be distracted by a less than winning smile or a poorly cut coat as so many of today's young women are, has marked you as prime husband material. Surely, you should be as flattered as she is to be commended."

What the devil? Was his smile now being found fault with? He had a wonderful smile, truly one of his best features. His mother had remarked upon it often, or as often as she saw him. And there was nothing at all wrong with the cut of his coat. He engaged the finest tailor in Town. Still, he adjusted the sleeve with a rough tug. Perhaps the sleeve was a bit short. Damned tailor, was he turning him into a laughingstock? It was one thing to smile at other people's foibles, that was truly amusing, but to be found laughable was not at all tolerable. He was a duke, after all. No one should find it necessary, or indeed wise, to laugh at a duke.

"Indeed," he said stiffly, still fussing with his coat sleeve, "I am excessively flattered." He looked at Lady Amelia, who, shockingly, was studying him rather more directly than was entirely proper of her. "I am, however, not in the market for a wife."

"Are you not? Truly?" Sophia said, her smile almost

seductive. "Of course, you do have your heir in the darling Alston, but there are other reasons to marry, delightful reasons, your grace. Would you deny yourself?"

"As to marriage, yes, I would deny myself. I find this . . . situation most awkward, Lady Dalby. Perhaps we may arrange for dinner another evening, when it is more convenient."

"But this is entirely convenient, your grace, and there is the matter of the wager between us. This evening *is* the payment of that wager, as you must surely remember. I'm terribly afraid that there is no escape for you."

The look in Sophia's eyes was both amused and calculating. If he defaulted on their wager, she would make certain that everyone in Town knew of it before the week was out, as well as knowing all the particulars. That was not to be tolerated. The Duke of Calbourne was not going to be run out of a salon by four unmarried women. Calbourne took a deep breath, uncomfortably aware that his coat was tight across the chest. Blasted tailor.

"If there is no escape," he said, forcing himself to relax against the stares of the four women before him, "then I shall just have to relax and enjoy myself, a condition I have ample experience with, Lady Dalby. Continue on, Sophia, I will not make a break for the door, nor will I fight against the restraint of feminine bonds of curiosity. What more would you know of me, Lady Amelia? How shall I satisfy you?"

Lady Amelia, as was entirely proper, blushed brilliant pink. Well deserved, too. Blasted women, making a mess of what should have been a lovely and uncomplicated evening of seduction and mutual satisfaction.

"Is he not as I described him to you, Lady Amelia?" Sophia asked, eyeing him with blatant amusement and, dare he admit it, appreciation. He found he could almost smile in return. "A remarkably pleasant and delightful man, the Duke of Calbourne, and if any man deserves the ideal wife, it is surely he."

The ideal wife? An oxymoron of ridiculous proportions.

Calbourne had been married, after all, and had the son to prove it. He also had the most unpleasant and disagreeable memories. It had not been a pleasant experience, being married. He had done it only to please his father, marrying the woman his father had deemed ideal for him. His father had been deeply mistaken. When his wife had died, he had, almost disgracefully, breathed a sigh of relief. When his father had died, that had ended all thoughts forevermore of marriage. He had his heir, the Calbourne line was secure, and his duty was done. Life, from thence forward, was to be enjoyed. And he did; he enjoyed it devotedly.

But he was going to find a better tailor the first thing tomorrow.

"You jest, surely," Lady Jordan said.

Calbourne was more than a bit surprised. He had supposed that this was to be between he and Sophia, as it had been thus far; that Mary, Lady Jordan, had decided to speak was a bit of an unpleasant surprise.

"In what manner, Lady Jordan?" Sophia asked politely.

"In that a man, having found the ideal and, indeed, the proper wife, would hardly know it. Men," Lady Jordan said in an unattractive and entirely uncalled-for display of pique, "never appreciate a woman properly."

"Never?" Sophia said musingly, her dark gaze turning from Lady Jordan to Calbourne. "Surely that is not so. Certainly I have, upon more than one occasion, been very well appreciated."

Mrs. Warren made some noise. It might have been a giggle.

Lady Amelia blushed. Again. It was singularly tiresome. Could the girl not speak? Not that she would have anything remarkable to say. He had, by the merest accident, been forced to engage her in conversation only last week at Hyde House. He had been neither entertained nor impressed. Mrs. Warren, on the other hand, had been something of a surprise. She was, aside from being beautiful with ginger hair and greenish eyes, quite clever and completely charming. Small wonder that the Marquis of Dutton was making a complete cake of himself over her.

Of course, Calbourne had not and never would make a cake of himself over any woman, ever. The idea was ridiculous. He really didn't know what Dutton was thinking, to be such a complete and drooling pup over something as simple as a widow with red hair.

Lady Jordan, by way of response, merely grunted, her chin collapsing upon her chest. He had heard that, at some point in the far distant past, Lady Jordan had been quite a beauty. He could not see it.

"Should we not proceed, Lady Dalby?" Lady Amelia said.

It was the first word she had spoken and it did show the slightest bit of vigor on her part. Calbourne looked at Amelia Caversham a bit more closely. She was a good-looking girl, very fair, very blond, very fine boned. Her bosom was respectable, though not remarkable. She was the daughter of a duke, never a hindrance in arrangements of the marital sort, and she had, by every rumor, a hefty dowry.

All in all, she'd make someone a passable wife. But not him.

"Indeed we should," Sophia said, arranging her skirts in a very pretty display, her ankles showing briefly and, he was quite certain, not accidentally. "The duke will grow quite bored if we do not proceed with directness and decision, will you not, your grace? Is that not a true statement of your preferences?"

"I appreciate decisiveness, as does the majority of the population, I should expect," he said.

"Ah, we shall mark that down then," Sophia said. "Anne, if you would make that the first notation?"

It was then that things went from odd to bizarre as Mrs. Warren rose to her feet and went to a small table in the nearest corner of the room, sat down, and, taking quill to paper, wrote something down.

They were compiling a list?

Good God.

"You are making a list?" he said, still unable to quite believe it. "Concerning me?"

"We are," Sophia said. "Is it not completely flattering, your grace? I can assure you that not everyone in Town will receive such consideration. Lady Amelia is most particular, most exacting, as must be admitted are advantageous qualities to have in a wife. She will make some deserving man a truly spectacular wife. Of course," Sophia said with a smile, "he must be found deserving first. Hence . . ." She waved her hand gracefully in the air, encompassing the room, the people in it, and the entire exercise.

Calbourne rose to his feet in a fury. He would have none of it. Not a single moment longer of it. It was preposterous. It was degrading and insulting and not the least bit amusing. He was not sure what he found more offensive: the fact that he was being subjected to a test of his worth by a room full of, it must be admitted, women of a less exalted rank than his own, or the fact that he suspected that any amusement in this room was at his express expense.

"Your grace," Sophia said, not bothering to stand but considering him from a very relaxed posture on her very delicate chair, "you are not flattered? You should be."

"Hardly."

"How very strange," she said, eyeing him coolly. "I suppose there is nothing for it. You must be marked down as a man of less than amiable tendencies. Such a pity. I had always considered you to be the most amusing man of my acquaintance, and so very, very amiable. And then, of course, there is the wager. You are defaulting? Anne, write that down. The Duke of Calbourne is not a man of honor as he does not honor a wager freely made."

And, of course, there was nothing for it. He sat back down, his expression grim and his posture stiff. But he sat. If there was one thing he knew beyond any other and upon which every gossip in Town agreed, Sophia Dalby was a woman who did not threaten, she acted. What was more, she never forgot a broken vow or a slight and she always, *always* demanded and achieved restitution.

"Such an intelligent man," Sophia said, staring at him with blatant amusement. "Mark that down, Anne. The Duke of Calbourne is pleasantly intelligent. Such an important attribute and quite, quite impossible to put a price upon. But, of course," she said with a grin, "we shall."

He was annoyed and insulted and quite possibly more uncomfortable than he'd been in his entire life, but Calbourne, who did love a good jest above almost all else, found himself smiling with her. What did it matter? Let them make their little list. He was not going to marry, not Amelia, not anyone. What was perhaps of even more importance was that there was nothing Sophia could do to compel him to marry. Absolutely nothing.

At that thought, Calbourne leaned back in his chair, determined to relax and enjoy himself. Perhaps if he acquitted himself well, he might still find his way into Sophia's bed.

"And as you are marking things down, Mrs. Warren," he said, "please make sure my list includes that I am amiable in the extreme and I never default on a wager."

"Yes, your grace," Mrs. Warren said sweetly.

"So, my list includes amiability, intelligence, and a man of honor?" he asked.

"And decisive," Sophia said, "which has surely been proved. Not only do you value it in others, you display it within yourself. I just knew you were a stellar example of the dukes of England, your grace. Quite stellar."

"The dukes?" he said, leaning forward.

"But of course," Sophia said, leaning forward as well. It looked slightly challenging. He was entirely certain it was intentional. "You were not aware? Lady Amelia has, and very intelligently, too, made up her mind that only a duke will do for her. Aren't you so very pleased that you made the first qualification so easily? After all, all you had to do there was to be born of the right father, which, to be honest, is hardly to your credit, is it?"

And then she laughed, outright and with no restraint at all.

He decided then that he had no desire to find his way into Sophia's bed. He was more than certain that if he did, it was doubtful he would ever find his way out again alive.

Seven

AMELIA was completely aware that the Duke of Calbourne was being swept along by the force and allure of Sophia. That was to be expected. What she hadn't expected was to be almost completely ignored by the man.

She was not at all pleased. Not at *all*.

Of course, it was true that Sophia had got Calbourne into the room and got him to stay, all very well and perfectly lovely, but now that he was staying it was time for him to pay attention to *her*. She was an attractive woman with good hair and teeth. She had a dowry. She had an engaging manner. Did none of these lovely things matter anymore?

But what was she to do? Allow Sophia to walk off with Calbourne thrown over her shoulder? Amelia *needed* him.

"I do think," Amelia said, pleased that Calbourne was at least looking at her, "that . . . that it is quite fine to be the child of a duke. I know that I am very glad that I am a duke's daughter, and I am not," she said, wondering what to say now that she had Calbourne's full attention, "I am not at all certain that I should not be commended for finding myself in that position. Certainly, as the child of a duke, I do think I should be commended at every opportunity."

Calbourne looked at her in something approaching wonder, as if a dog had just burst forth with an opinion on estate law, which was the tiniest bit insulting, and then he looked at Sophia, his brows raised, and then he looked back at her. He was grinning. It was very difficult not to preen. She mastered the urge and sat with as much dignity and poise as a duke's daughter ought to display, which was considerable.

"I could not possibly agree with you more, Lady Amelia," Calbourne said. "I also believe that I am due commendation for nearly everything. I had no idea we had that trait in common. How very pleasant to find a kindred spirit in this room."

"Should I add that to the list?" Mrs. Warren said, looking at Sophia over her shoulder, her mouth twitching against a grin.

It might be possible that, at some future date, Amelia could actually develop a cordial relationship with Anne Warren. Certainly she did not mind in the least that Lord Dutton seemed so enamored of her.

When Sophia had arranged for this interview with the Duke of Calbourne, she had insisted, in direct opposition to the entire exercise, that propriety be maintained. Therefore, at least one chaperone must be present, which for Amelia meant her Aunt Mary as Hawksworth had been disposed of in the most innocent manner imaginable. As to Mrs. Warren's presence, Amelia had no explanation, but Sophia had insisted and that had been that. When one asked a favor from someone like Sophia, one did not look too closely into the horse's mouth. Not unless one wanted a finger chomped off at the knuckle.

"Oh, most assuredly," Sophia answered languidly. "Kindred spirits. Could anyone have anticipated it?"

Aunt Mary snorted and took a sip from her cup. She was drinking Madeira and she was drinking it very contentedly. Aldreth seldom supplied Madeira, likely because he knew it was one of Aunt Mary's favorite drinks. Of course, Aunt Mary had many favorite drinks; indeed, it was very difficult to think of a drink which she could not be tempted to enjoy.

"Do not pretend to modesty, Lady Dalby, for no one here shall believe it," Calbourne said.

"Very well," Sophia said, "*I* anticipated it. I should be very much surprised if you and Lady Amelia did not find yourselves to have much in common, your grace. She is, as you will discover, a remarkably pleasing sort of girl. As you are a man who likes to be pleased . . . though, actually," Sophia mused, "I cannot think of a single man who does not enjoy being pleased. Can you, your grace?"

"Not a one," he answered briskly.

Once more, Sophia had stolen the duke's attention from her. She refused to tolerate it, that was all. Simply refused.

"Actually," Amelia said firmly, leaning forward slightly, "I do not believe Aldreth to be the sort of man who enjoys being pleased."

"Is that possible?" Sophia said.

"It must be," Amelia answered stoutly, "for I have never seen him pleased. By anything. And I know him well enough, you must agree."

"Oh, yes, I must agree," Sophia said. It sounded suspiciously sarcastic, which was intolerable. Amelia did know Aldreth better than anyone in *this* room, certainly. He was her father, after all.

"It's quite true," Aunt Mary said, looking at Sophia. "Aldreth is . . . difficult."

"Perhaps all dukes are difficult," Sophia said, looking at Calbourne. "Perhaps they enjoy being difficult. Is that the source of your endless pleasure, your grace?"

"Ridiculous," Calbourne said. "It is a truer conclusion to state that all dukes enjoy making things difficult for others."

"Hardly complimentary," Mary said.

Oh, dear, Mary was always saying precisely the wrong thing to the exact wrong person.

"I think Aldreth is unique," Amelia said, "just as I believe the Duke of Calbourne is unique. Perhaps it is in being unique that the dukes of the realm make their mark upon the world."

It was a fine bit of calculated misdirection. She was quite proud of herself. She did, after all, have to manage both Sophia and Mary, who, she was certain, found their own perverse pleasure in being difficult. How else to explain their behavior? How to charm Calbourne with these mild insults flying about the room? No matter what anyone said about dukes, one thing was beyond dispute: they did not enjoy being insulted. In fact, they had no toleration for it at all.

"He is certainly unique in his height," Sophia said blandly. Calbourne came as close to preening as a man could while seated. "You did remark upon that, did you not, Lady Amelia? Having met the man, can you now over-look what you had deemed a hindrance?"

If there were any possible way to slap Sophia and get away with it, that is to say, continue to put forth the care-fully constructed aura of demure reticence and breed-ing that Amelia had spent a lifetime perfecting, she would have done so in that instant. Calbourne, as to be expected, looked completely annoyed and he was staring right at her with an affronted and, strangely enough, disbelieving look. Did he not know that he was excessively tall? Did he not once think that a woman, a carefully reared woman, might find his size not a little off-putting?

Oh, bother men and their vanity. It was such a cumber-some business to have to pet them at all times and about every single thing.

"The duke is a most . . . that is, he gives every appear-ance," Amelia stammered, "of being quite vigorous. Quite robust."

It wasn't entirely a compliment, but it could hardly be deemed an insult either. Amelia sat very still and waited for the duke's response.

"You have a gift for understatement, Lady Amelia,"

Sophia said before Calbourne could say anything at all. "The duke is quite vigorous and extremely robust. I have it on good authority."

Whereupon Calbourne looked quite close to blushing.

"But he is also, and this must not be overlooked, extremely tall and not at all slight of frame. Was not your pronouncement that he was *excessively* tall?" Sophia said with a smile.

"I am positive I did not say *that*," Amelia said briskly. "I am quite, quite positive that it is impossible to be excessively tall."

"Oh, come," Sophia said on a trill of laughter, "what of Lady Beauchamp's daughter? She is by every report extremely and most excessively tall."

"I am not interested in Lady Beauchamp's daughter," Amelia said through clenched teeth.

"Neither am I," Calbourne said. "If anyone's interested."

"But of course you should not be," Sophia said. "You would, between you, produce nothing short of giants. I can't think what it would cost you in tailoring, your grace."

Whereupon Calbourne frowned and tugged on his right coat sleeve. Odd.

"But we simply must keep on task, your grace, and that is why you must do all you can to assure Lady Amelia that your . . . size is not an issue."

Which of course put the most lurid emphasis on the issue. If Amelia were not so determined to interview a duke, she would leave this instant.

She stayed.

More important, Calbourne stayed.

In the end, that was all that mattered. She simply must find a way to make a good impression on Calbourne. Even with his disturbing size and his even more disturbing sense of humor, she could not openly discount him. There were only so many dukes to go around, after all. She could not afford to be *that* particular.

"I wonder if you would mind standing up, your grace,"

Sophia said. "I should like for Lady Amelia to stand beside you. A couple, even so exalted a couple as a duke and his duchess, must appear well together."

Mrs. Warren snorted in obvious amusement.

Aunt Mary snorted and shook her head a bit drunkenly, but she said nothing. Of all the times that Aunt Mary had spoken when it would have served Amelia better for her to be still, this was not one of them. Aunt Mary was, without qualification, the worst chaperone in the world. Fortunately for Amelia, she could usually make that work to her advantage. Now was not one of those times.

"I do not think that is at all necessary," Amelia said, feeling a blush color her cheeks. She only hoped it made her look virginal and appealing. She was perhaps beyond the point in this situation of appearing innocent. If Calbourne were not discreet, and why shouldn't he be, she would be the talk of Town by midday tomorrow. "A duke should never be required to endure such an examination."

"Why not?" Calbourne said, cocking his head. "Don't you think I can stand up to an examination? Are you implying that I shall be found wanting upon a closer look, Lady Amelia?"

Oh, dear. He was either honestly insulted or he was trying to be amusing. Neither option was very appealing. Calbourne might truly be more than she was ready to manage. Pity. It was rumored he had such a lovely estate.

"Don't pick on the girl, your grace. She's more than a little in awe of you," Sophia said. Calbourne grinned in male satisfaction. "Just stand, if you would, darling," Sophia directed from her seat. "How nicely you stand, your grace. You should do it more often. You have a definite skill for it."

"Do I, do you think?" Calbourne said, striking a pose, which was flatly ridiculous. Amelia couldn't help but smile. The Duke of Calbourne, quite unlike her father, did seem to get such a lot of fun out of being a duke, which was exactly what being a duke should be like. She couldn't think why her father had got it all turned round. Aldreth, to her knowledge, had never found joy in much of anything.

"I've been able to stand for most of my life, you understand," Calbourne said, eyeing Sophia in blatant humor. "I've got quite a bit of practice at it. I shouldn't be at all surprised to find I excel at it."

"Yes, you are truly remarkable," Sophia said, her eyes twinkling up at Calbourne.

It was just possible that, while Amelia might find herself married to Calbourne, Sophia might find herself in Calbourne's bed. Those sorts of alliances were not at all uncommon, but it did give one pause. She wasn't at all certain that she wanted to share her husband, at least not at the start. Perhaps she would be more than willing to parcel him out later, when she was quite bored with him. She studied Calbourne. Yes, that seemed entirely feasible.

This entire *duty to marry* business was so much easier to manage when one maintained a clear head.

"Now, Lady Amelia, if you would be so good as to stand at the duke's side? I should like to see how you two . . . fit," Sophia said.

Amelia would have blushed and refused, if Mrs. Warren had not at that moment said, "And what should I mark down, Lady Dalby? Perhaps an illustration?"

It was perfectly plain that she was laughing under her breath, and not at all discreetly either.

At that prompt, and knowing full well that Calbourne expected her to refuse, Amelia got to her feet and walked very gracefully to where he stood. She smiled into his somewhat startled face and took her place at his side. And then she faced Mrs. Warren and smiled. Mrs. Warren, far from being shocked, smiled back at her and then took up her pen and began what appeared to be a sketch.

It was a victory, but of what type Amelia was not certain. Still, a victory. Any sort would do after two full years on the marriage mart.

Calbourne did, truly and completely, tower over her.

Why, her head did not even reach the top of his shoulder. They looked dreadful together, she was certain of it. But then, how often did a duke and duchess appear in public together? Not more than once a year, surely.

"How well you look together," Sophia said, confounding Amelia's most logical conclusion, "your coloring so complimentary. Calbourne, I do think that you and Lady Amelia would produce quite the loveliest children in Town."

"Do you think so?" Calbourne said, preening. "Of course, I do have a son, Lord Alston, and he is quite a handsome lad."

"And should you not like another, your grace? What sort of man is content with only one child? Surely you have it in you to father scores of them," Sophia said.

Amelia took a deep breath. *Scores?* Sophia had the most wicked sense of humor.

"I am content with Alston," Calbourne said, smiling at Sophia like a fellow conspirator.

Which made all very clear to Amelia. She felt herself awash in rigid anger. It was all just a jest, the entire evening. Calbourne and Sophia were flirting with each other and she was the prop to the event, though she could not imagine why two such dissolute people, two people given to such flagrant and frequent affairs of the heart should require a prop to their mutual seduction of each other.

All this humiliation, at her expense, mind you, was at an end. She was going to end it and she didn't care what anyone said about it. Fortunately, Aunt Mary appeared to be snoring.

"Oh, how unfortunate," Amelia said stiffly, "I am not at all interested in having scores of children with such an . . . excessively *large* man," she said, for spite. It felt wonderful. "It has been a delightful evening, your grace, Lady Dalby, but I must excuse myself for the rest of it. If you will allow?"

Calbourne, to her intense joy, looked positively startled. And insulted. Perfect.

Sophia rose to her feet gracefully, and said, "I'm so

sorry, your grace, but that appears to be that. You have been removed from consideration. Of all things, Lady Amelia is most decisive, but do not despair. I'm certain that there must be another woman who will not find you so . . . excessively unsatisfactory. Shall we go in to dine?"

Calbourne did not choose to dine. Calbourne chose to leave immediately. He had the most perplexed expression on his face. Amelia, however, felt perfectly fine.

Eight

It was at two o'clock the next day, a perfectly dreadful time of day when one was still half foxed from the night before, that Calbourne found himself sitting in White's coffee room and scowling into a glass of whiskey.

"Bad whiskey?" the Marquis of Ruan asked.

Calbourne glanced up and nodded to Ruan, which Ruan took to be an invitation to sit. He sat.

"Bad night," Calbourne answered. "I dined with Lady Dalby. Or was supposed to."

Ruan raised his brows in surprise. "I didn't think it possible to have a bad night with Sophia Dalby."

Calbourne grunted and scowled into his drink. He hadn't thought so either. He also was not in the habit of discussing his affairs with anyone, but he was in such a state of mental disturbance and the Marquis of Ruan was known to be such a discreet fellow, as well as being a man who knew his way around the knottier tangles of life, that Calbourne, still slightly, just slightly, foxed, found himself confiding in the man. He was certain he would come to regret it. He was equally certain that he didn't care. The worst had happened. What more could be done to him?

"She was not alone," Calbourne said, to which Ruan raised his dark brows and smirked. "Yes, well, it wasn't like that," Calbourne continued. "She is conducting . . . interviews." At this Ruan's brows raised themselves even higher. "For a husband." Ruan's eyebrows plummeted to their proper position in an obvious state of unpleasant shock. "For Lady Amelia Caversham."

Ruan's breath appeared to have caught in his throat. He coughed, nearly choked, before regaining his composure. Which had been precisely Calbourne's response, until he had done what any reasonable man would do under the circumstances; he had got himself good and drunk.

"And you do not want to marry Lady Amelia?" Ruan asked mildly.

"Of course not," Calbourne grumbled, taking another drink.

"Then why did you accept her invitation?"

"Blast it, man," Calbourne snapped, "I didn't know that was what she had in mind. We had a private wager between us and dinner was the outcome. Naturally, as it was a wager, I could not leave and retain my honor."

"But you did leave?"

"Blast my honor," Calbourne said sullenly. "I was rejected. A man does not linger when he has been rejected."

"Perfectly logical," Ruan said. Calbourne, who did not know Ruan well at all, had always had the sense that Ruan was a very calm and reasonable sort, the sort of man who did not require tedious explanations. He was glad to have been proved correct. Certainly he was overjoyed to find he had been correct about something; the situation with Sophia and that slip of a girl could not have been more bungled. "Yet your honor?"

"I cannot think that Sophia would not agree it has been satisfied. After all, I did stay for the interview, did I not?"

"Did you?" Ruan asked with the barest smirk.

"Why not? It was a flimsy bit of fun, but I could see the humor in it. I'm not going to marry, after all. Let these women have their jest."

"These women?"

"Sophia, Amelia, her chaperone, and Mrs. Warren, who took notes."

"I beg your pardon?"

"She took notes," Calbourne repeated, not at all happy to be required to do so. "How else to keep an account of all the interviews?"

"I'm so sorry," Ruan said. "You seem to have lost me. There are others?"

"Don't be dense, Ruan," he said. "Do you think I am the only man without a wife? Of course there are others. Although," he added with some pride, "I was the first. Top of the list, I should think."

Ruan was silent at that, his green eyes thoughtful, and his gaze on his shoes. Quite nice shoes; Ruan did know how to dress to the demands of fashion. He was rumored to be fabulously wealthy, something to do with land in Canada. Or perhaps it was in Barbados. Somewhere foreign, of that Calbourne was certain, or nearly so.

"It's quite a nice bit of work, isn't it?" Ruan said eventually, jerking Calbourne out of a doze. "I do wonder why Lady Dalby should be so interested in the marital prospects of Lady Amelia. Is she friends with Aldreth?"

"I have no idea. I shouldn't think so," Calbourne said, his thoughts swirling in a sea of whiskey. "Though, I do seem to remember that Sophia is or once was closely acquainted with Zoe Auvray, Aldreth's mistress."

"Is that so?" Ruan mused with a half smirk. "That might explain it."

"Explain it? There is no explaining it," Calbourne said.

"I wonder who else shall be summoned?" Ruan said.

"Who else? Why, it's perfectly obvious who else. Certainly the Duke of Edenham. He's available, though I can't think how he'll pass." Calbourne smirked and crossed his *excessively* long legs. Excessively, indeed. Blasted women and their ridiculous notions. He was an exceptional-looking man. Exceptional in the extreme. "And then there's Iveston. He'll be a duke one day. I don't see that they'll overlook him."

"Dukes? Dukes are all that interest her?" Ruan said, sitting up in his chair, looking very nearly alarmed. Well, why should *he* be alarmed? He wasn't a duke. He was free and clear of the whole business.

"Isn't it perfectly obvious? Lady Amelia is only interested in becoming a duchess. I thought I'd explained that."

"Oh, right," Ruan said, leaning back against the cushion. "Lady Amelia. Yes, well, it's very forthright of her, isn't it? Not many girls have that sort of singleness of purpose, and it's not an unworthy goal, is it?"

"Not unless you're a duke, then it's a blasted nuisance," Calbourne said. It was insulting as well. Especially as he'd been rejected.

Blasted women and their foolish ideas. There was nothing wrong with his height, or with his coat either.

Calbourne reached out to put his glass on the small table in front of him and felt the stitches rip at his shoulder.

Blasted tailor.

⤳

BY six o'clock that afternoon White's was buzzing with the news of Lady Amelia's *interview*. After the initial astonishment, things proceeded as they always did at White's. Wagers were placed as to who would be called, who would attend if called, who would be found acceptable by Lady Amelia, and how Aldreth would react when he heard the news.

It was a very busy afternoon at White's and the betting book was a mass of wagers and counter wagers.

One wager stood out in that sea of impossible wagers and that was if Calbourne had been rejected by the mild Lady Amelia, who had before this day been considered so demure and so proper as to be nearly invisible in any gathering of more than four people, or if Calbourne had done the rejecting. Odds were on Calbourne.

That Lady Amelia intended to interview Iveston was a foregone conclusion, the proof being that there were no wagers placed on that. Not even one.

The Earl of Cranleigh was not in the least bit amused. He was quite determined to force Lady Amelia Caversham into dropping the entire idea of marriage as it pertained to Iveston. Quite determined. He was simply not going to allow her to marry his brother. She could have anyone else she could get her grasping little hooks into, but not Iveston. He would have thought that should have been perfectly obvious to her.

As to the interview, as to that blasted interview of Calbourne, that he laid firmly at Sophia Dalby's feet. Oh, Amelia Caversham was no innocent lamb led into ridicule by the merest of enticements. No, she knew what she wanted and she was pursuing it without shame or the slightest care for protocol. To be honest, he had not thought she had it in her and he could not quite puzzle out why she had stooped to such tactics now.

Yet she had. And he would respond as he must. She would not get Iveston.

He had every expectation that things would be permanently settled regarding Iveston by tomorrow dawn as tonight there was a ball at the Prestwicks' to which nearly everyone had been invited. The elder Prestwick, newly made a viscount by the normal route in that it had been tidily bought and paid for, was quite eager to make his new and exalted mark in Society. Cranleigh wished the entire family well with the endeavor as he did not know the Prestwicks even slightly. He had not intended to attend, but as Amelia was now flagrantly in the market for a duke, she would certainly attend and there would hardly be a better, that is to say, more convenient time to make his position known regarding Iveston.

She was not going to marry Iveston.

Put thus, Cranleigh hardly expected any sort of trouble at all from her. She would marry where she willed, but not into the Hyde family. Let her have Edenham or Calbourne, though his gut clenched at the thought. Grasping, ambitious, calculating female. He would force her out, back, and away from his brother. The question, really, was how he would accomplish it. He would prefer to keep any fuss to a minimum, but if that were not possible, if she made it impossible, well then, he was prepared to do what he must to drive her off. He was entirely confident that whatever action was required would come to him at the proper time.

That resolved, at least in his own mind, Cranleigh settled into a game of whist. He had hours yet before the ball was to begin. Hours in which he intended to enjoy himself before seeing to Lady Amelia Caversham.

∽

"BUT of course Lady Amelia will find herself enjoyably wed," Sophia said from the depths of the most comfortable chair in the white salon. "You can't think I would do her a disservice of that sort. She is simply in the market for a husband, a very particular sort of husband, and you know there is nothing simple at all in acquiring the right sort of husband. Husbands, as a rule, are exceptionally easy to acquire, but she wants a duke, clever girl, and dukes are not at all that straightforward. I'm just trying to help, Zoe. Certainly you cannot think otherwise."

"I can't think what will happen if Aldreth hears of it, Sophia. I've done what I can to keep him occupied," Zoe said.

"I'm certain you have. You look quite lovely as a result, darling. Keeping Aldreth occupied agrees with you completely."

As Zoe had been Aldreth's mistress for almost two decades, she was quite in the habit of looking lovely, and of being told so.

"Yes, but even I must tire, Sophia," Zoe said, leaning forward, a single chestnut curl falling forward over her bosom. "I am not, I blush to confess, as rigorous as I once was."

"Liar," Sophia said, grinning.

"Flatterer," Zoe rejoined, smiling.

As they had both been young courtesans making their way into the deepest pockets in London at approximately the same time, and as they were both deeply pragmatic and exquisitely beautiful women they had, naturally, formed an alliance that had quickly become a friendship. Sophia had married her earl and Zoe had made a life with her duke, and they were still friends. Which must be conceded was a very unusual thing to have happened between two women who had been in London for as long as they had.

"If we are to trade compliments," Sophia said, "then I shall win all, darling, for you have kept Aldreth so fully entertained that while all of London is buzzing about his daughter's interview of the Duke of Calbourne, Aldreth gives every appearance of being blissfully ignorant of the entire evening."

"So far," Zoe said. "Are you certain that this will end well for the girl, Sophia? I do like to think of her as being satisfied with her life, finding resounding joy with the man who is her heart's desire."

"Still so French, my darling Zoe," Sophia said gently. "Amelia will find her man and then she will either find joy or not. As to her heart's desire, some might argue that she is too inexperienced to know what, or who, that is."

"Certainly she must want love!" Zoe said in a huff of outrage. After twenty years sharing Aldreth's bed, she felt more than a little protective of Aldreth's children by his wife. As they had no mother to look out for them, she had taken on the duty, albeit from an extreme distance.

"Certainly?" Sophia said softly. "Of course she wants love. But can she clasp love by the hand and tuck it beneath her bodice ties? That is not as certain."

"How very tragic," Zoe said, leaning back in her seat and taking a sip of chocolate. "How will you proceed?"

Sophia smiled, her dark eyes glittering, "I will simply

make certain that love not only shakes her by the hand, but throws her over his shoulder and carries her off."

"That sounds completely alarming," Zoe said sternly. Then she smiled and said, "And perfectly romantic. Of course," she added, once again serious, "none of this throwing can be done with Aldreth in Town. I shall insist he escort me to Paris. He will do as I ask and he will be completely captivated by me and shall give no thought to his children for at least two weeks. Can you manage it all in two weeks' time?"

Sophia smiled and said calmly, "I can safely promise that Amelia Caversham will be carried away completely within two weeks. Have no doubts at all, darling. No doubts at all," she repeated, her gaze quite contemplative.

Nine

Of course, while nearly everyone of any note had been invited to attend the Prestwick ball, very few persons of any note had any intention of attending. Until the *interview*.

The Earl of Dalby, the dowager countess Lady Dalby, her daughter and new son-in-law, Lord and Lady Ashdon, had been invited, as had Lady Dalby's special friend, Mrs. Warren. As Lady Dalby was the only member of her family in Town and as she was known to have developed the habit years ago of making the acquaintance of everyone in Town who could possibly be thought interesting in any way imaginable, it was widely known that she would accept, Mrs. Warren tangling in her train.

If Lady Dalby was present at the Prestwick ball, and there was not a wager on any book that she would not be present, then it was almost certain that the interviewing of dukes would continue. On that nearly everyone agreed. Sophia Dalby would not let a minor thing like the giving of a ball in someone else's home stop her from doing whatever she wanted, particularly as Lady Dalby had made it perfectly plain to all of her afternoon callers that Lady

Amelia Caversham would also be in attendance at the Prestwicks'.

That settled everything.

The Prestwick ball, for entirely unexpected reasons, was likely to become the event of the Season.

Miss Penelope Prestwick was not at all pleased.

Of course, as the only daughter of a viscount newly made, she had hoped to be the center of all speculation and observation during the course of the ball. Her father had spent quite a bit of money in putting on the ball, which had not been his idea at all but hers, for how else was she supposed to meet the very people she planned to spend the best days of her life with, and now that the money had been spent and her dress crafted and her brother, George, made to promise to behave as the son of a newly made viscount ought to behave, now, at the hour of her premiere upon Society, she was to be upstaged by a very disreputable countess and her strange manner with men, dukes, to be precise.

It was quite intolerable, but she would tolerate it because Penelope had no choice at all about the matter. She was more than a little aware of what she could and could not do. She could not make a fuss. She could only put as placid a face on it as possible, and much was possible as Penelope had early on learned to tolerate quite a lot, and appear unconcerned and only mildly interested in what was certain to be a lurid scene. Perhaps even a series of lurid scenes.

Of course, as was to be expected, she had heard of the scandalous events involving Lady Louisa Kirkland and Lord Henry Blakesley at Hyde House. Of course she had wondered along with the rest of Society why Lady Dalby clearly found it an irresistible impulse to aid in the ruination of any girl who circled too closely to her orbit, for while it was publicly announced that Lady Dalby had had not the slightest involvement in not one but two separate ruinations, one of them her own daughter, privately everyone knew she had done something to arrange each seduction down to the last undone button. No one knew how she had done it, or why, but she had.

Naturally, this had made inviting Lady Dalby to the Prestwick ball something of a necessity, for who would not want the most talked of woman of the Season, perhaps of the decade, at her ball? Penelope was quite well informed and much better educated than girls who had been born into the higher reaches of the ton, and therefore had nothing to prove and less to gain by appearing intelligent. But she was. Very.

"Have you decided how you'll manage it?" George asked.

George, her older brother by two years, was as darkly handsome as she was darkly beautiful; as she was an intelligent and forthright girl, she did not see any point in denying the facts to herself. Modesty was perfectly well and good as an outward manifestation of good breeding, but one should be honest with oneself. And she was. Very.

"Of course," she said, and then mentally winced. She had picked up the habit somewhere of saying *of course* rather more often than was attractive. She was determined to lose the habit as soon as possible. "I shall be demure and modest, displaying as often as possible complete ignorance as to any event that involves Lady Dalby. I shall be deemed an idiot for being unaware of what everyone in Town knows, but I do think that men prefer idiocy in a wife. I have seen little to disprove the theory."

"Idiots don't have theories, Pen," George said placidly. "You're doomed. You'll be forced to marry a man who does not require an idiot for a wife. I predict a long Season for you. You might want to learn to embroider."

"I know how to embroider. It's only that I hate to embroider. Silly thing. All girls are taught to embroider," she said, checking her hair in the mirror of the second floor hall. It was quite a nice mirror and her hair looked perfect.

"Pity you couldn't be taught how to like it."

"George, you know perfectly well that liking anything isn't the point of anyone's education. It's only that you must be proficient. A fondness for *anything* can be manufactured."

"Or *anyone*," he said, checking his own hair in the mirror, imitating her. She hit him on the shoulder.

"Stop teasing me. This is the most important night of my life to date and I won't tolerate being distracted. You will behave, won't you?" Before he had a chance to answer, because she did assume he would agree with her and therefore obey, she said, "And watch Father, won't you? You must make certain he does not talk business. And keeps his voice lowered. And doesn't pull at his waistcoat."

"Perhaps we should put him on a lead?" George said. "He found his way into a viscountcy but shan't survive one evening as a host?"

Penelope, who loved a jest and a laugh as well as anyone, but not on the most important night of her life, gifted George with a cold look. "You know perfectly well I'm right. How will I ever become a duchess with a father who shouts his opinions?"

Because of course, that was the entire crux of this evening's problem. Penelope had decided to marry a duke. Lady Amelia Caversham had made the same decision. The trouble was that Amelia had help in the form of Sophia Dalby and they would likely proceed with their pursuit tonight at *her* ball. And where did that leave her?

Without a duke, of course.

Penelope winced. Breaking habits was easier said than done. Marrying a duke would likely prove the same.

THE Prestwick town house, which everyone knew they were leasing as it had been in the Hyde family for a full twenty years, looked quite as respectable as it had when the Elliots were in residence. This spoke well of the Prestwicks, as everyone, at least those who had chosen to attend the Prestwick ball and so could discreetly observe the condition of the plasterwork and the skirting boards, had wondered how a viscount who had more money than pedigree would do in a first-rate house in Town. Viscount Prestwick appeared to be doing very well.

It was a bit of a denouement and the ball had not even properly begun.

It was in situations such as these that the ton of London looked to its reliable notables for entertainment. They were not to be disappointed.

Amelia had never felt so on display in her life. After two years of being virtually ignored during the Season, a situation she had loathed, she found she did not at all prefer being the center of attention. She was being stared at. She was being whispered about. She was being speculated upon.

She knew this as firmly as she knew her own name. She had done it herself, to others, and it had been wildly entertaining. It was no longer entertaining.

"Why, there is the Duke of Calbourne," Sophia whispered from behind her fan. "It does show such fortitude that he should come, does it not, Lady Amelia?"

Amelia was jerked out of her contemplation instantly and, without intending to do so, found her gaze going to the Duke of Calbourne. He was, as always, difficult to miss as he was and ever would be the tallest man in any gathering. He did, however, look quite handsome in an excessively tall sort of fashion. He did not look pleased to be at the Prestwick ball, but that could have been because everyone was staring at him.

And then, as she was coming to expect, they stared at her.

It was most uncomfortable.

"I assume he was invited," Amelia said to Sophia, a bit curtly. She wanted to turn her back on Calbourne, but it was possible he might see it as a slight. Of course, since she had done far worse than slight him at Dalby House, she didn't suppose that anything else she did would matter now.

"But of course he was invited," Sophia said. "I should be very surprised if everyone in Town was not invited here tonight. The Prestwicks do have so much to prove, do they not?"

Of course they did, but it was so common to remark upon it. Perhaps she should not have allied herself with a woman who had been a common courtesan. Then again, things could hardly have reached a worse state. If this interviewing of dukes did not turn the tide, she did not know what would.

"But now that it is known that you rejected him," Sophia continued, waving her fan gently, the wispy curls at her temples lifting in concert with the motion, "I should think that everyone in Town, who would not have crossed the Prestwick threshold last week, will push through the door to see whom you will discard next. Pity that you found Calbourne not to your liking. I've always seen certain advantages to large men. Perhaps, once you are married and more experienced, you will come to agree with me."

If that wasn't the most . . . the most lurid and vile comment to make to a virginal and innocent lady, then Amelia . . . then Amelia . . . Yes, well, having interviewed a duke for the position of husband might have severely damaged her reputation as an innocent, though being a known innocent had hardly helped her, had it?

"I don't think that is likely, Lady Dalby," Amelia answered with cool civility.

Mrs. Warren chuckled. Mrs. Warren was something of a permanent fixture when dealing with Sophia. Amelia, while she had not actively disliked Anne Warren before, liked her less the more time she spent with her, likely because she was suspicious that Mrs. Warren was laughing at her.

"You are amused, Mrs. Warren?" Amelia said with noticeably less civility.

"Lady Amelia, I am often amused by the things Lady Dalby chooses to say. She has a distinct ability to make truth sound scandalous."

But perhaps only when the truth *was* scandalous. Naturally, Amelia kept that thought to herself.

"Oh, look who has come to entertain us," Sophia said, changing the direction of the conversation. One hoped. "It is Lord Iveston and his brothers, minus the lovely Lord Henry, of course. Did he and your cousin not leave Town?"

"Yes, I believe so," Amelia said absently, her thoughts momentarily overtaken by the arrival of the four unmarried Blakesleys, who were, taken as a whole, unfortunately spectacular.

All blond. That was the first firm impression. The eye was positively arrested by the sight of all those gleaming gold heads.

Then tall, so very pleasingly tall. Not at all like the nearly gigantic proportions of Calbourne, but merely so very nicely tall.

And handsome. So startlingly handsome, though not mirror images of each other, they all had blond hair and blue eyes and remarkably fit physiques. Of course, she had met each of them at one time or another, but she'd never actually seen them clustered together in a knot of such raw masculinity before now.

"What a close family they appear to be, to come as a throng to the Prestwick ball," she said. Cranleigh stood shoulder to shoulder with Iveston, which was not unexpected given what she knew of Cranleigh.

Sophia eyed her with an amused smile before turning her gaze back to the sons of the Duke of Hyde. "They are a very close family, yes, I do believe so, but as to why they are in attendance at the Prestwick ball, surely you know the reason for that."

"Do I?" Amelia countered.

"They are here, darling Amelia," Sophia said, closing her fan, "for you."

"I beg your pardon?" Amelia asked, snapping her own fan closed. She was not entirely certain, but she did think that Anne Warren was smiling in sympathy at her.

"They are here," Sophia said softly, "to protect their darling Iveston from a woman such as you, Lady Amelia. Was ever a woman more complimented than that? Three men to defend against a single, fragile woman. It's perfectly delicious. You are to be congratulated."

"Lady Dalby," Amelia said firmly, "I hardly think, that is to say, I am sure you must be mistaken. I have done nothing to Lord Iveston and wouldn't *think* of—"

"Think of, Lady Amelia?" Sophia interrupted. "But how absurd. You must do all; indeed, hold nothing back. Lord Iveston must be snared, at least as far as an initial estimation of his compatibility with you. Would you marry him without even a conversation to mark the moment? No, no, I know you are eager, but I must insist that you at least talk to the man you intend to marry."

"That is not *at all* what I meant, Lady Dalby!" Amelia's voice, raised to an unusual level, caused more than one person to turn and stare at her.

"But then what did you mean, darling?" Sophia said politely. "Certainly you have not marked Lord Iveston off your list? We have just got rid of the delightfully entertaining Calbourne. I do think we should proceed to Lord Iveston, don't you? Or would you prefer to meet with the Duke of Edenham first? Oh, and there he is! This is turning into a quite grand affair. The Prestwicks shall be so pleased. Miss Prestwick must also be in the market for a husband, don't you agree? Are you two not of the same approximate age? And still unmarried? Well, some girls do like to take their time about such things. I, however, knew what I wanted and proceeded to acquire it. I should say the same is true of Anne. Mrs. Warren, how old were you when you married your lovely first husband?"

"Eighteen, just," Mrs. Warren said.

As if what Anne Warren did at eighteen was of any interest to her. Yet, the point had been made, as if she needed it to be underlined. She knew why she was here and she knew what she wanted. Why else go to Sophia in the first place? But she had made *her* point, should anyone look into it. Had she not appeared most uncomfortable and very nearly reluctant to talk to Iveston and his many brothers?

She had.

"I should like to meet Lord Iveston first, if that is quite agreeable to you, Lady Dalby," she said firmly, her bosom held regally high and her chin quite firm and unyielding. "If the situation requires it, then I shall require an introduction to the Duke of Edenham. He is last on my list, after all, and I don't see any need to rearrange the order now."

The fact that Edenham was in all likelihood the most handsome man she had ever set eyes upon was not going to move him up the ladder. She knew what she wanted. She was as much a woman of the world as . . . well, not as much as Sophia, but enough. Enough of a woman to get what she wanted from a man.

She was going to get it before Penelope Prestwick, too.

"Would you be so kind as to lead the way, Lady Dalby?" Amelia said regally. "I would be so pleased to be formally reacquainted with Louisa's husband's brothers."

"Ah, yes, family," Sophia said with a very wicked smile. Amelia wasn't entirely certain if Sophia knew how to do *anything* that wasn't wicked. "You are related by marriage now, aren't you? How very, *very* convenient. That will make as nice a start as any, though I do think you underestimate the comprehensiveness of London gossip, darling."

Amelia was not going to think about that, not now, not ever, if given the choice. She was quite certain that, once married, this entire escapade would, if not disappear, become an entertaining and highly amusing story. One day. Eventually. Certainly her husband should be able to arrange it tidily.

"I do think now is the time, Lady Dalby," Anne Warren said, redirecting the conversation slightly. "Are they not looking this way?"

They were, all four of them. They did not look pleasant at all. They looked, oddly enough, almost hostile.

How very typical.

"Don't they look charming?" Sophia said, her dark eyes glittering. "They appear very eager to speak with us, which is quite a lovely compliment. Let's allow them the pleasure, shall we? I do think that now is the time, Lady Amelia, for you to unleash all your considerable experience at sparkling conversation."

Amelia was quite certain that she had no experience whatsoever at sparkling conversation. She was not going to let that small detail interfere with her sparkling all over Iveston. "I am quite prepared, Lady Dalby," Amelia said. "If you will lead the way?"

"Lead the way? Oh, darling girl, no, no. That is not at all how it's done. They must come to us, you see. I thought that was perfectly obvious. We may beckon them. We may ignore them. We may charm them. But we must never approach them. Men do love to run after things, pursuit being their preferred leisure activity. No one of any intelligence understands why this is so, but the matter, understandable or not, is not up for debate. A man pursues. A woman eludes. It is the way of things."

Amelia was very much afraid her mouth was hanging agape and presenting a most unattractive view of herself. She snapped her mouth shut.

"But Lady Dalby, by your very words I am becoming famous for interviewing the Duke of Calbourne! Is that not pursuit? Is that not precisely why I am here tonight and why I should speak to Lord Iveston?"

"Darling," Sophia soothed, "you are confusing the issue completely, mixing together two separate acts that do not require mixing. You will have your interview, indeed, I should be much surprised if Iveston, and even Edenham did not insist upon it."

"*They* will insist upon it?" Amelia said. She was developing a headache behind her right ear. It took all her composure not to rub the spot. "Whyever for?"

"Pursuit, darling Amelia," Sophia said softly. "They *must* now pursue. They are men, poor dears, they are very nearly compelled to do so."

"Lady Dalby—" Amelia said, very much afraid she was sputtering, which would have been entirely unattractive and, as fully one quarter of the room was now staring in her direction and at least ten people actively listening to their . . . well, what else to call it, their argument over how men behaved with women, which really was absurd as no one in the world understood how men behaved with women more than Sophia Dalby, which was the very reason Amelia had gone to her in the first place . . . Amelia's head pounded, the spot behind her ear spreading upward in an arch of distraction.

"Lady Amelia," Sophia interrupted, "you must know that men absolutely detest being left out of any competition. You have provided them with a very unusual competition. How can they resist? Surely you can see that."

Sophia was looking at her as if she were the worst sort of fool, the sort of fool who did not understand men.

Amelia, knowing by now that nothing she said would reflect well on her, said nothing. Perhaps that was the best course when dealing with Sophia. Certainly speaking with her did no good at all.

"Of course," she said, capitulating completely. Things were slightly, just slightly, out of her hands and out of her control. All she could do was hope that her husband would understand one day all she had endured to find him. "What should I do now?"

Sophia smiled at her encouragingly, which was obviously insulting. "Do? Why there is nothing *to* do. Iveston and his lovely brothers are on their way to you now. Did you expect otherwise?"

There was only one answer to that.

"Of course not," Amelia said.

Ten

THE Earl of Cranleigh, the Marquis of Iveston's more direct and, some would attest, ruthless brother, watched Amelia Caversham in hushed council with Sophia Dalby, openly consorting with a woman of highly questionable reputation, though there really was no question about it at all, was there? Sophia Dalby was the worst sort of woman and Amelia had taken up with her, openly. Lady Amelia Caversham had made a bad secret of the fact that she was in hot pursuit of a duke for a husband. It was one thing for a woman to want to marry; that was a normal, if annoying pursuit, but to make a list and conduct interviews, that was quite beyond decent and clearly ruinous. How had such a sheltered girl wandered onto such dangerous ground?

Lady Dalby had led her there, naturally.

No matter. A woman, even such a well-bred and, admittedly, beautiful woman as Lady Amelia was not going to be permitted to run through the Prestwick ball and snatch Iveston up like a trinket at the fair. No.

Of course she was beautiful.

There was something about the planes of her face, some

deeply etched tracery of feminine nobility, that was compelling in a way that mere prettiness was not. Her eyes were blue, her hair was blond, yet she was not pretty. She was beautiful.

Not that it mattered in the least. Pretty or beautiful, she was not going to trap Iveston into an unwanted alliance, no matter that Iveston himself suddenly seemed less than outraged by the prospect. Cranleigh laid that at Sophia's doorstep as well. Iveston only recently had come under Sophia's rather famous spell and, because Amelia was allied with Sophia, Iveston was prepared to make allowances. Cranleigh was not. More to the point, the very fact that Amelia Caversham had chosen to ally herself with the infamous Lady Dalby spoke volumes about her intentions and not a single one was flattering.

It spoke of desperation, surely, and a lack of discretion, even a certain coarseness that was flatly reprehensible. Surely Lady Amelia understood that, which brought the circle back round to desperation.

He was only thinking of Iveston, who, mesmerized by Sophia Dalby, could not readily fend for himself. He would take care of everything. Amelia Caversham, under the questionable tutelage of Sophia, would not find Iveston easy pickings.

The Viscount Prestwick had rented, for himself and his family, a house on Upper Brook Street, just down from Lady Dalby's residence. It was a very nice address and the house was well appointed. As it was on the end of the street, it had the advantage of a small conservatory off the drawing room, the scent of green mixing pleasurably with the scent of beeswax candles. Quite a nice house. It was rumored that Prestwick could afford almost anything he wanted. What he wanted, presumably, was a husband for his daughter.

Another girl looking for a husband. This business with Amelia Caversham blatantly pursuing Iveston, Edenham, and perhaps even Calbourne had put a crease in Cranleigh's firm plans to return to sea and he intended to be done with the entire mess by the end of this ball. Let Amelia, and even Miss Prestwick, if she was observant and had her wits about her, find that Iveston at least was not on the menu for hungry young ladies of a matrimonial bent.

"Lady Dalby, how delightful to see you again," Iveston said with a curt and perfectly executed bow. Would that his manner was curt; Iveston, now that he had actually met her, seemed to genuinely like the woman. Blame Blakes for that. He had an unnatural fascination and respect for a woman who had made her way through London on her back. Her husband, the late earl, had likely died of exhaustion. "Lady Amelia, Mrs. Warren," he said, bowing in turn.

"Lord Iveston," Sophia said when she had risen from her curtsey, "how charming of you. Of course, we expected *you*, but to bring your delicious brothers with you, and all unmarried, that was generous. One might say to a fault?"

"Is there fault to be found in attending a ball, Lady Dalby?" Cranleigh said coldly before Iveston could answer her. "Or is there only fault in being unmarried?"

Sophia smiled at him and said, "But I am unmarried, Lord Cranleigh, thus I would never find being unmarried to be a fault. As you are unmarried as well, would you not agree?"

"I find myself being forced to agree with you, Lady Dalby," Cranleigh said. "It is a firm expectation of yours, I suspect."

It was hardly polite, but then neither was interviewing dukes for husbands. She had pushed beyond the boundaries, let her live with the broken fences in her wake.

"Suspect no longer, my lord," Sophia said, not a hint of shame marking her elegant features. "I do love it when men agree with me, forced or not. In fact, sometimes force adds a certain extra pleasure to the experience. Will you agree with me again, my lord?"

"Don't punish him, Lady Dalby," Iveston said softly. "Cranleigh is not possessed of a soft and yielding temperament. He cannot bend against your jests but must stand and crack beneath them. As he is here for love of me, I must protect him, even from so delightful a woman as you."

Cranleigh turned to stare at his older brother. Truly, he had rarely heard Iveston say so many words in one breath outside the family hearth. It was then, oddly and for the first time, that he wondered if Sophia Dalby might, in some strange way, be good for Iveston.

Most peculiar.

"Perhaps," Lady Amelia said softly, "if Lord Cranleigh is punished, he might soften and learn the pleasure of yielding." She was blushing by the end of it.

Well should she blush; it was a most indelicate comment. Cranleigh stared into her eyes. She stared back, her blush fading into white composure.

Sophia smiled. "He might at that. Do you think it possible, Lord Cranleigh?"

"There is no pleasure in yielding," Cranleigh said, staring hard at Amelia. "A woman of virtue would know that, wouldn't she?"

He did not name her, but he looked directly at Lady Amelia. His point was obvious.

She blushed again, vigorously. He was not a bit repentant. A girl, no matter who her father was, should not be so coarse in her language or her manner.

"A woman of virtue knows many things, Lord Cranleigh," Mrs. Warren said, joining in the debate, her fair features showing no sign of a blush, "and the first of which is what pleasure is available to her and what pleasure denied. Certainly yielding to the wisdom and wit of an earl must rank as being pleasurable, or else how is a lady to survive in Society?"

Iveston laughed. The Earl of Cranleigh could not see what was so vastly amusing about being verbally bludgeoned by a trio of women.

"You're overmatched, Cranleigh," his brother George said, his gaze focused on Mrs. Warren. She was a pretty thing, all white skin and glowing hazel eyes, her ginger hair gleaming in the candlelight.

"Hardly," Cranleigh said tightly.

"I must agree with Lord Cranleigh," Sophia said. "It is not possible, at this early stage, for the earl to be in any danger at all from the three of us. Why, are we not mere women?"

Precisely.

"At this early stage?" Iveston said, dipping his head. "That sounds ominous, Lady Dalby. What do you intend?"

"Only what you yourself will agree to, Lord Iveston," Sophia said. "Is that not why you are here tonight? Or had it been your intention to attend the Prestwick ball when the invitations were issued weeks ago?"

She was playing the pure coquette. Cranleigh was not amused by it. Glancing at Amelia Caversham, he was of the impression that she was equally unamused.

"I should think that over half of those in attendance tonight had declined," George said, "until the details of your interview became widely known."

And here all eyes turned to study Amelia, as was only to be expected. To his surprise, she did not blush and avert her gaze. Instead, she lifted her chin and her bust and stared thoughtfully at Iveston. As if she were considering him! As if she had the right to just snatch him up.

"Odd, isn't it?" Sophia said, gazing at each of the brothers in turn, even though Josiah had yet to say a word. Smart lad.

"What's odd?" Cranleigh said. "That a woman would debase herself and her family name by exhibiting such poor judgment?"

Amelia swallowed heavily, but she did not lower her gaze. He was reluctantly impressed. He pushed all thoughts of admiration from him instantly. *Nearly* instantly.

"Lord Cranleigh," Sophia scolded with a seductive lifting of her sable brows, "you surprise me. I had it from the duchess that you were widely traveled. Do you mean to say that you learned nothing of the various cultures of the world in all those miles put beneath your feet? Certainly a woman should always be commended for doing her utmost to make a good marriage. Do you not agree?"

"Of course I agree," he said. "But this is hardly—"

"Hardly ordinary," Sophia interrupted. "I so agree with you. But then, Amelia Caversham is hardly ordinary, which I think must be obvious, especially to you."

His gaze went to Lady Amelia. He had neither the time nor the inclination for these feminine games of man-baiting.

"Especially to the Duke of Calbourne, I should think," Iveston said, surprising him again. When had Iveston become so talkative, and with a woman, too? "You caught him wrong-footed, it's being said. 'Tis quite a rare thing, that."

"Darling Lord Iveston," Sophia said, "if it's being said, it's being said by the duke himself. Certainly he was as charming and as entertaining as he ever is and certainly Lady Amelia found him quite—"

"The word was *tall*, Lady Dalby," Amelia said with some force. "The Duke of Calbourne is quite, quite tall. Wouldn't you agree, Lord Iveston?"

Amelia Caversham turned her striking blue eyes upon Iveston and very nearly tried to burn him with an intense gaze ripe with meaning and invitation. Even Cranleigh could feel it. By George's slight cough, George felt it, too. Josiah remained silent, which was something of a miracle.

❧

IT was a miracle of sorts. Amelia had spoken, interrupting Sophia and her unfailing ability to make herself the center of male attention, and by speaking, she had garnered attention unto herself. The very avid attention of each Blakesley male. It was quite lovely.

Of course, it had required her to be very rude and very obvious, and yet she had their full attention, which certainly must be all that should matter. All she cared about for the present was that Lord Iveston, who truly was a quite respectable-looking man, was staring deeply into her eyes.

His brother, the irritable Lord Cranleigh, who spoke far too much and not at all pleasantly, was staring at her bosom.

She could feel it, and she thought it perfectly dreadful of him. Of course, her bosom was perfectly lovely, but did he have to make such a point of it? He clearly, if she had to judge only by this most recent conversation, had no restraint and very nearly no civility at all. She forced her gaze back from Cranleigh to Iveston.

Lord Iveston, who would one day be the Duke of Hyde, was tall and of a somewhat narrow frame, an altogether elegant-looking man with light blond hair and vivid blue eyes. Iveston's brother Cranleigh, not nearly as blond and with eyes the color of an arctic wolf, looked very much like a common sailor. He was wearing a well-tailored suit, but that did not disguise the fact that he was powerfully built and rather thick about the neck. Common. He clearly took after his mother, the American-born Molly, not that she would ever allow such a thought to even enter her head once Molly was her children's grandmother.

Now that she had seen Iveston with his brothers, and now that she had spent an hour with Calbourne, she was more certain than ever that she wanted Iveston. Edenham, with his trail of broken wives and nursery full of children, was off the list. Well, not completely off, but barely on. She was not so foolish as to mark off Edenham before Iveston had been fully secured.

He was very nearly secured now. He was staring at her, after all, and he did not look too displeased, and she was a more than merely attractive girl, and her father was a duke.

That should settle things nicely, shouldn't it? Sophia was completely unnecessary from this point on. Now that Iveston had noticed her and actually approached her, she could manage on her own.

The first order of business, besides inducing Iveston to beg for her hand in marriage, was to make it clear to Cranleigh that he was unwelcome. The other two could stay or go, she did not much care which. But Cranleigh, the sailor, had to go. He was rude and arrogant and he was not at all shy about giving every appearance of entertaining an actual dislike of her. Certainly, if he found reason, however paltry, for disliking her, he should keep it to himself. Besides, there was no reason at all for anyone to dislike her, especially a man who looked like a sailor.

"Calbourne is quite tall," Iveston said mildly, answering her. "I believe it suits him, though, don't you, Lady Amelia?"

"I believe it does," Amelia answered with a soft smile. "It does not suit me, however. Is excess in any form ever truly desireable?"

Iveston smiled blandly. The sailor scowled. And then Sophia said, "Lady Amelia is a woman with very set standards, which is surely commendable, even admirable. Too many of our young girls today marry simply anyone who shows the slightest interest. Lady Amelia has far more confidence in herself than to treat herself so lightly."

"I think we all understand what Lady Amelia's standards are," Cranleigh said, nearly snarling.

Bother it. Couldn't he find a puppy to kick? Was he going to stay by Iveston's side all night? That might become nearly unpleasant.

"But of course, Lord Cranleigh," Sophia said sweetly, "that is the entire point. What is the use of having standards if no one knows what they are? Stop me if I have this wrong, Lord Iveston, but, knowing of Lady Amelia's standards and her rigorous pursuit in maintaining them, are you not intrigued by her?"

"I find everything about this exercise intriguing, Lady Dalby. Were you going to interview me, Lady Amelia? I did make the list, did I not?" Iveston said.

He was almost smiling. It was a quite a coup as everyone knew that not only did Iveston rarely leave his house, but when he was caught out, he even more rarely smiled. He certainly never spoke. It was one of the reasons that Society had deemed him a bit peculiar. Though, speaking to him now, he seemed more retiring than peculiar. She could manage a retiring husband, it might even be very convenient to have one. Certainly no sane woman would enjoy having a husband of Cranleigh's type, who scowled and bullied out of pure habit.

Cranleigh did make a most powerful impression. A most unpleasantly powerful impression.

"You've heard about that, Lord Iveston?" Amelia said, before Sophia could speak first.

"Everyone's heard about it," Lord Cranleigh snarled, not at all discreetly.

Sophia smiled and tilted her head. Amelia spoke quickly, having observed that Sophia tended to tilt her head coquettishly before speaking to men.

"And you are not offended?"

"To have made your famous list? Not at all," Iveston said, looking at her shyly. It was quite charming. "I feared only to have not made the list at all."

"It is not an actual list, Lord Iveston. I am not so crass as all that," Amelia said, planning her wedding breakfast as she spoke. Iveston seemed nearly desperate to sign the marriage contracts, which was so delightfully pleasant of him. Things were going to work themselves out beautifully.

"And particularly as there are only a very few men who meet Lady Amelia's standards, certainly they need not be written down," Sophia said in an excessively sweet tone.

Bother it, she had to pay strict attention or Sophia would run away with the entire evening. She'd have time to plan her wedding breakfast later.

"Yet crass enough to demand a duke for a husband," Cranleigh said softly, staring at her with his pale blue eyes.

She felt a shiver slide down her spine. Small wonder *the sailor* was rarely out in Society. He could not even be civil when the occasion demanded it.

"Demand?" Sophia said. "I was not aware that any demands had been made, Lord Cranleigh. Must I remind you that Lady Amelia speaks only of standards? Certainly you cannot object to that."

It was perfectly obvious that he would indeed object to that. And Sophia had spoken *again*, drawing all eyes to her. It was simply not to be borne.

"As your brother finds no objections to my very reasonable standards, Lord Cranleigh, I do wonder why you should," Amelia said, and very curtly, too. Cranleigh was not the only one who could be less than civil.

"You may not have noticed it, Lady Amelia," George Blakesley said, his features of a most arrogant slant, "but Iveston is not of a temperament to readily take offense. And Cranleigh is."

"How unpleasant for Lord Cranleigh," Amelia said, turning her own blue eyes upon Cranleigh. "And to everyone who knows him, I daresay."

Oh, yes, it was rude, excessively so, and bold, and perhaps even crass, but there was something so very, *very* pleasant about annoying Lord Cranleigh. Why, just look at how his silvery eyes burned in outrage.

Why, he was almost as much fun to torment as Hawks. If he did not stop hampering her attempts to wrangle Iveston into a proposal, it might be very necessary to torment Cranleigh nearly endlessly.

Amelia smiled just thinking of it.

"My, my," said Sophia, speaking *again*, "you have made a strong impression, Lord Cranleigh. Is that common?"

"I should say most things about Lord Cranleigh are common," Amelia said.

At that point, Mrs. Warren gasped.

Lord Iveston blushed and ducked his head.

Amelia hardly noticed. Her attention was completely held by the look of pure, icy determination upon Cranleigh's rugged features. He looked quite completely enraged. She couldn't possibly have been more pleased. Why, it was almost impossible not to laugh in his face. He didn't have much to say now, did he?

"As to common, Lady Amelia," Cranleigh said, "I believe you have outstripped me. I can't say where Iveston falls on your infamous list, but I can say with complete certainty that you have fallen off his. Good evening." He bowed, stiffly and very reluctantly, and turned to leave. He clearly expected his brothers to follow him. And they might have, if Sophia had not then spoken.

"But, no, truly?" Sophia said. "I had not thought the Blakesleys to be so skittish in the face of friendly fire."

"Friendly fire?" Cranleigh said, looking over his shoulder at, not Sophia, but Amelia. Amelia's breath caught in her throat. He looked completely lethal.

"But what else?" Sophia asked with a smile. For once, Amelia was happy to allow Sophia to take the lead in the conversation as she couldn't have formed a syllable if given half an hour. Cranleigh's look had impaled her. She hated him for it, even more than she already hated him. "Is this not all part of the marriage dance, which is danced, badly, at every ball during the Season? Lady Amelia is more forthright than any woman you've yet to encounter, but is that just cause for retreat? Lord Iveston, are *you* frightened of this pale and slender girl?"

The Marquis of Iveston considered Amelia slowly and with complete detachment. She wasn't sure if that was a good thing or not. When he had finished his perusal of her face, he said, "I find no need to fear Lady Amelia. She is a woman looking to wed, which is hardly cause for alarm as women possessed of the same goal populate every salon in Town."

"How wise of you, Lord Iveston," Sophia said, her dark eyes sparkling merrily at him. "I'm quite certain your brothers will follow your lead, trusting in your discretion."

At which point, Cranleigh swallowed heavily, scowled at Amelia pointedly, and stayed exactly where he was.

Amelia was not at all sure if she should be relieved or upset. As Iveston had decided to stay, she decided to be relieved. She would indulge in an upset about Cranleigh later, when she had the privacy to be upset properly and without restraint. She predicted it would take approximately an hour, give or take.

Eleven

As she was the hostess, Miss Penelope Prestwick could not indulge in a proper upset, but she wanted to. She was an observant girl, and it was her house, after all, so she had noticed to the second when Lord Iveston had entered and made a direct path to Amelia Caversham. He had been ensnared in conversation with her for a full fifteen minutes and showed no signs of leaving her to circulate among the other guests.

"Stop staring at them," her brother George said under his breath. "We'll be finished here soon and then you can run him to ground like a stag."

"Lovely. I suppose that makes me the sweaty horse," she whispered, before arranging a pleasant expression on her face to greet the next guest.

"Not at all, Miss Prestwick," the Marquis of Ruan said with what might have been a smile. "You don't resemble a horse, sweating or otherwise, in the least."

Penelope was quite certain she had never blushed in her life, and she did not do so now. But she wanted to.

"Lord Ruan, good evening," she said, refusing to comment upon his observation. What could she have said that would have saved the situation? Best just to ignore it and soldier on.

"A mesmerizing gathering, Miss Prestwick," Ruan said, his brilliant green eyes studying the room, halting on the Marquis of Iveston, though why he should care about Lord Iveston was a mystery. "Mr. Prestwick, a pleasure."

"A pleasure indeed," the Marquis of Dutton echoed.

Penelope greeted Dutton with a pretty curtsey, eyeing him discreetly. He looked foxed. The gossip was that ever since Sophia's daughter had married Lord Ashdon, Dutton had been more foxed than not. It appeared to be nothing but the truth. Did Dutton harbor a *tendre* for Caroline? It was possible. Caroline was a dark-haired beauty, a diamond of the first water. Penelope delicately tossed her own black hair, but Dutton's slightly reddened eyes only looked at her briefly before fixing on the knot of people that was dominated by Sophia Dalby and Lord Iveston.

Blast it all, she couldn't even capture the attention of a man who was cup-shot. A massive fortune clearly wasn't as enticing as it once was.

"Yes, I had hoped that my little ball would attract," Viscount Prestwick said with very ill-disguised pomposity, "that is, would be found favorable among Society's elite. I am delighted that it was found to be so. I begin to wonder if my house can hold them all."

Penelope groaned inwardly, particularly as sardonic amusement was writ large all over Lord Ruan's rather rugged features.

"I should think it obvious, Papa, that we shall be forced to dance in the streets," Penelope said bluntly. "We were expecting fully half to decline our invitation, the Season being what it is."

"Busy?" Lord Ruan said with wry humor, his green eyes sparkling.

"Yes, Lord Ruan, busy," Penelope said genially.

But, naturally, they both lied. Such pretty lies ought to be fully embraced as the truth would never serve so well.

The truth was that Lady Amelia's interview of the Duke of Calbourne was what had brought them here tonight, the anticipation that she might interview another prospect within their hearing too delicious a chance to miss. That the circulation of guests was becoming knotted at the precise spot where Amelia was talking to Lord Iveston, and that the knot was growing larger by the minute, only proved how fully their hopes had been achieved. Everyone's hopes except hers, naturally. Poor Papa had no idea about Amelia Caversham or the interview or the true reason for everyone on their invitation list actually choosing to attend their ball. Papa was of the misguided notion that Society was welcoming him fully into its ranks.

Papa was an idealist. It made dealing with him somewhat exhausting. He did think so well of himself and he fully expected everyone he met to adopt his position on the matter. She and George knew better as they were not crippled by rosy idealism and a well-fed sense of superiority, as Papa was. No, they understood very well that they were newly hatched, as it were, and that what they had in their favor was, not to be ridiculous about it, a dose of healthy good looks and a vast fortune, the fortune being the most critical item on the list.

With both her fortune and her looks, she fully expected to get what she wanted, namely, a duke. What else was required? Certainly a sterling pedigree was never amiss, but lacking that, a fortune would more than make up for it. Certainly Society was awash in those who had only pedigree and attractiveness, and look how they struggled. No, a fortune was the essential ingredient. She had one. She did not see any difficulty in attaining a duke.

Except for the fact that Amelia Caversham most obviously had the same goal. That was a problem. That Lady Amelia was beautiful, possessed of a fortune, and had a pedigree few could match made it a problem of epic proportion. The solution was obvious. Amelia had to leave the marriage mart immediately, preferably without a duke in her pocket.

"You are to be commended, Prestwick," Dutton said, holding himself very erect. He was a very handsome man, tall and lithe, with chiseled features and deep blue eyes. He was rumored to be a rakehell, a scapegrace, and a scoundrel. Penelope would have overlooked all of that, but what she could not overlook was that Dutton was a marquis and not a duke. Some things simply put a man beyond the pale. "This evening may well go down as the event of the Season. I, for one, had no intention of missing it."

"I am most pleased to hear it, Lord Dutton," Papa replied, puffing out his chest. As his coat was perfectly tailored, puffing did not mar the line. "Please, enjoy yourselves. Lord Ruan?" Papa bowed elegantly, Penelope dipped her head, and the two gentlemen moved on. Penelope watched them wind their way into the crowd and was not at all surprised that they moved relentlessly toward the knot that was Amelia Caversham and Lord Iveston.

Blast and bother, this simply could not continue or her ball, by which she meant the reason she had given it in the first place, would be ruined. She had to do something about it. If only she could think what.

∽

"IF the girl wants to marry a duke, I don't see what I can do about it," Dutton said. "Or that I should care one way or the other," he added in a somewhat sullen tone.

Dutton had been sullen ever since Ruan had met him at White's. Ruan attributed it not to himself, but to the fact that Dutton had cast up his accounts twice in the past three hours. Even a three-bottle man could not become a six-bottle man in a single week, though Sophia Dalby could drive a man to try.

"As I said earlier," Ruan answered, "you should care because Sophia Dalby is quite obviously punishing you for something. Do you mean to stand about and let her have at you?" Ruan paused. Dutton grunted and averted his gaze. Ruan continued, "As to what you can do about Lady Amelia, nothing. She will marry whom she will marry, but as

Sophia is the obvious source of this particular manhunt,
I would think that would be motivation enough for you.
Am I wrong? Are you beaten yet again by that particularly
adept woman?"

Naturally, it was enough to arouse even the most blatant
coxcomb to stand and deliver. As Dutton was not a coxcomb in any measure, the challenge was caught up without
any hesitation.

"Don't be absurd," Dutton said, brushing past a group
of three women who giggled the moment he glanced in
their direction. Which only proved how easy it would be to
distract Sophia and hobble Amelia.

"Very well," Ruan said, glancing at the three women
himself. They did not giggle at his look. No, they hushed,
their eyes going very wide, their cheeks going pink. There
was a difference in degree when dealing with rakes, let
there be no doubt about that.

&

SOPHIA watched Ruan and Dutton approach and did nothing at all to hobble her smile. Ruan and Dutton. How amusing. They had formed an alliance of sorts, though how she
could not imagine. The why of it was far easier. Dutton was
desperate. Ruan was . . . dangerous. Yes, slightly dangerous. He was unlike any man she had met since coming
to London more than twenty years ago. She did not enjoy
enigmas of the male variety, though she did not fear them
either. Ruan was a man, and as a man, he was predictable.
And malleable.

"Ah, you've found us," she said before even the bows
had been made. "How mighty the hunter who finds his
quarry on the first . . . thrust," she said, staring pointedly
at Ruan.

Ruan's mouth was shaped in such a way, the corners tip-
ping up slightly, that he looked amused even at his most
relaxed. It was a convenient arrangement of features as she
was certain he went through life being endlessly amused

by nearly everything. It was a pleasant trait for a man to possess and certainly spoke in his favor with her.

"Lady Dalby," Ruan said softly, his low voice even and calm, another trait she enjoyed. Ruan was not the hysterical type, and so many men, in the guise of manly outrage, became hysterical over the smallest of things. "I had not thought it in you to describe yourself as any man's quarry. I confess I don't know what to make of it. Except to thrust." His green eyes smiled at her unrepentantly. She liked that, too.

"A bold hunter," she said, the noise of the gathering fading as they faced each other, all ears pricked to hear the next ribald reply. She hadn't had this much fun in years. "The first thrust is, of course, the most vital. Miss, and your quarry escapes. Having learned your scent, you will never draw so near to her again."

"Scent can be masked," he said.

"Not enough to delude an elusive quarry. Every hunter knows that."

"Only hunters who miss on the first thrust," Ruan answered with a slight smile.

"Oh, for heaven's sake," Mary, Lady Jordan, snapped. "Can you not conduct your seductions in private? This is a ball, not a bawdy house."

"I'm afraid, Lady Jordan," Sophia said into the shocked silence, "that Lord Ruan, knowing he would not find me in a bawdy house, must make do with ballrooms. Is that not so, Lord Ruan?"

"Lady Dalby, I would seek . . . and find you, anywhere," he said, bowing, his eyes never leaving her face.

"Is that the orchestra?" Amelia said, robustly inserting herself into the midst of what was a most blatant seduction.

"I believe it is," Iveston said, smiling first at Amelia and then at Sophia. Iveston was such a lovely man, so affable and reasonable. What a delicious husband he'd make for some deserving girl. "Shall we proceed in? Or shall the interview take precedence?"

Amelia flushed, which gave her such a sweet and delicate air, and she knew how to use that air to her advantage, clever girl.

"I think, Lord Iveston, that you may have quite befuddled Lady Amelia," Sophia said, turning away from Ruan and ignoring him completely, though not so completely that she didn't know to the precise degree his eyes stopped sparkling and his mouth etched downward in a subtle frown at being so ruthlessly ignored. "Do you mean to say that you *want* to be interviewed for the post of Lady Amelia's husband? I must confess that I suspected you would be eager, but I do not think Lady Amelia shared my prediction. Would you mind terribly explaining to her, and to her dear aunt, precisely why you are so eager?"

Iveston, a truly elegant man in all respects, directed his answer to Amelia, who looked up at him in all her virginal, blond splendor. "Why Lady Amelia, surely it must be plain to you that, having conducted an interview upon the Duke of Calbourne, I should find myself slighted egregiously to be found lacking of even the opportunity to present myself for your consideration. I am not a duke now, but I have every hope of becoming one. Can your list stretch to include me?"

Sophia turned her gaze upon Amelia, who blinked once and then said with delicious sincerity, "How charmingly put, Lord Iveston. Put thus, how could I refuse to add you to my list?

"Hell and blast," Cranleigh spit out, not at all discreetly, which of course, was equally charming, but in an entirely different way.

Men. They were so very entertaining.

With the tuning of the orchestra, the mob, keeping a careful eye on which direction Sophia and her troop were heading, moved ponderously in the direction of the music. The Prestwick town house—on let from Molly, the Duchess of Hyde's sister, Mrs. Sally Elliot, a fine coincidence—was on the end of Upper Brook Street with a fine view of Grosvenor Square. The light was excellent and so a study on the front of the house had been converted a few years back into a petite conservatory that was just now filled to bursting with roses in the first flush of full bloom. Delightful.

The house was not exceptionally large, but it was supremely well appointed with fine boiserie in lustrous walnut lining the walls of the dining room, which tonight had been transformed into use as a ballroom. The dining room was not open to the conservatory, although they shared a wall, but had only one opening into it, that from the hall. Once in the dining room-cum-ballroom, it would be very difficult to get out again. Intriguing possibilities there.

The hall, beautifully done up in Flemish tapestries of exotic locales, also led into the drawing room, where the guests were gathered in advance of the dancing. The drawing room, quite a sumptuous room, was done up in scarlet silk damask, the walls fetchingly sprinkled with family portraits and the odd landscape or two.

That the crystal chandeliers were sparkling, the woodwork gleaming, the floors waxed all spoke to the care the Prestwicks were devoting to keeping the house in top form. That they had let the house from a close relative of the Duke of Hyde was hardly something that had come about by chance. Little Miss Prestwick, quite a stunning girl of black eyes and black shining hair, was shopping for a husband. Sophia didn't suppose that the girl would mind it at all if she found one among the sons of Hyde. The man did have five sons; Miss Prestwick couldn't possibly have anticipated that Lord Henry, his fourth son, would be snatched up quite so quickly by Louisa Kirkland, but that still left four.

Sophia's gaze drifted away from Miss Prestwick and on to Lady Amelia. She was managing Lord Iveston quite well, Cranleigh growling, the two younger sons of Hyde listening, watching, smiling.

"You had hardly a word for Lord Dutton, Lady Dalby," Ruan said at her side. "Has he displeased you in some way?"

"Darling Lord Ruan," she answered, "are you fishing? You make the most abysmal fisherman."

"But a fine hunter?"

"That remains to be seen, doesn't it?"

He looked down at her, a smile playing around his mouth, and she felt a flutter under her heart. The last time she had fluttered was with Dalby. How peculiar and so unexpected. She hadn't thought to flutter again and she wasn't sure what to make of it. It wasn't unwelcome, but it was . . . uncomfortable.

"Is that a promise, Lady Dalby?" he said softly.

"I rather thought you were the one making promises, Lord Ruan. A mighty thrust and all that," she said, considering him. The tiniest flutter, again. Yes, definitely uncomfortable and very distracting. "But as to Lord Dutton," she said, changing the subject completely, and permanently, "I find him as entertaining as I normally do." Ruan lowered his black brows and studied her, encouraging her to continue by his very silence. "He is a handsome man, which never hurts, and he knows how to talk to a woman."

"He flatters her?" Ruan said, his mouth quirking into a smile.

"Profusely. And then he sobs into his whiskey. It's irresistible," she answered, smiling.

"He can't have done this with you. No man would find cause to sob with you."

"Why, Lord Ruan," Sophia said, almost forgetting that she had determined to put Ruan out of her thoughts not a moment ago. The man was nearly mesmerizing. "Are you aping Dutton's technique? Flattery and then . . . oh, but you can't sob now. I haven't given you cause. Yet."

"And you can't convince me that you gave Dutton cause," Ruan said. "But Mrs. Warren, he might well throw himself off of Westminster Bridge for her."

"Can he swim?" Sophia asked brightly.

Ruan chuckled. "If I knew, should I tell you? You might push him off yourself."

"Might I?" she said, laughing up at him. He was quite

tall and she always had preferred tall men. "Why should I do that?"

"I wish I knew," he said.

His voice was serious, but not alarmed. He thought he knew something and wished to know more. But could that not be said of everyone? What they thought they knew and what they wished to know, such a chasm, nearly uncrossable.

"Darling Lord Ruan, you assign much to me. I bear Lord Dutton no ill will. He is perfectly safe from me."

"But is he safe from Mrs. Warren?"

"I'm afraid only she can answer that, Lord Ruan."

Twelve

THE Marquis of Dutton, unpleasantly sober, wanted nothing so much as to grab Anne Warren by the back of the neck, drag her into a dark corner, and kiss her until she melted in his arms. Unfortunately, not only did Society frown on behavior of that sort, it was not at all the plan that he and Lord Ruan had devised. Actually, Lord Ruan had done the devising. Dutton had done the scowling and the arguing. In the end, Ruan had won his point and convinced Dutton to proceed accordingly. Dutton might have agreed, but he was still scowling.

"Mrs. Warren," he said, drawing near to her as the crowd continued to shift as they made their way into the ballroom. "You're looking well."

She was looking bloody marvelous, but he wasn't going to confess any such nonsense as that. Women positively fed off that sort of thing and, where Anne Warren was concerned, he meant to starve her into compliance. He'd landed wrong-footed with her, though he still could not see quite how it had happened.

He had noticed her.

He had approached her.

He had kissed her.

She had promptly got herself engaged to Lord Staverton, a viscount fully three times her age. Well, perhaps only twice her age, but he had not aged well and he had an eye that wandered erratically. Literally. Still, for the daughter of a failed courtesan, Anne Warren had done well for herself. That she had done it to spite him he knew without a doubt. Unfortunately, that knowledge had no value whatsoever. Anne Warren, perhaps because of his bold kiss or perhaps because he had only become interested in her when he discovered her mother had been a doxy, was ignoring him. He suspected that she was doing it to drive him mad; the problem was that it was, literally, driving him mad.

"And you, Lord Dutton, are looking sober," Anne said sweetly, her hazel green eyes as sharp as knives. "Can't find the whiskey?"

"And you, Mrs. Warren, used to be sweeter. You give every evidence that the prospect of marriage to Lord Staverton does not agree with you," he said, which was not at all the conversation he was supposed to have had with her, but dammit, she was being unreasonable. All he wanted was a tumble. Certainly she could give him that. It wasn't as if she were a virgin and it wasn't as if she didn't understand what a man wanted from a woman.

"Naturally," Mrs. Warren said with sweet acidity, "you have got it all twisted, Lord Dutton. It is you who does not agree with me. I find myself ever out of sorts in your company. If you will excuse me?"

"I will not," he said sharply. He moved to lay hold of her upper arm, but she gave him such a look that his hand dropped to his side. Someone gasped on his right. He didn't bother to see who. It was the worst folly, to engage her this way. It was not at all to plan.

Blast Ruan and his damnable plan.

"I beg your pardon," he said, swallowing his annoyance. "I am not myself. I had only wished to bid you good evening and to, if you will allow, ask a favor of you."

"No, I will not kiss you, Lord Dutton. Nor will I lift my skirts for you. If you have any pearl necklaces hidden upon you, I do not want them," Anne whispered harshly, her eyes flaring bright. She had the most remarkable eyes, a greenish hazel that could look pewter soft in candlelight. She was in candlelight now, but they did not look soft. She looked as wild as a cat, her red hair gleaming like sunset.

"My pearl necklace days are over, Mrs. Warren. After Lady Caroline's rather scandalous acquisition of one, mine have been locked away in safety, a gift for my future wife."

She drew as still as a doe at the words and he thought for the first time that Ruan might have a plan at that.

"In fact," he continued, "I had wondered if you could help me with that."

"With what?" she said crisply, her cheeks growing slightly flushed.

"It is being rumored," he said softly, watching hungrily as she leaned closer to hear his words, "that Lady Amelia is on a quest for the ideal husband and that she is, oddly enough, conducting interviews."

"Yes?"

"It is also rumored that you are aiding her as a clerk of sorts, a most trusted position, to be sure," he said, lowering his voice even more. She leaned closer, so close that he could catch her scent and see how the light glimmered off her porcelain skin. Dutton blinked a few times and grabbed hard for his purpose. He must not lose his way now, not even if she did smell of roses. "I wondered if you could help me there."

Anne looked up at him, her eyes wide and clear, her breath catching in her throat. He almost had her. In a second, he could be kissing her, would be, if they weren't in the middle of a noisy throng in a well-lit room.

She must have read the thought in his eyes, for she pulled away and swallowed audibly.

"Help you? I can't see how, Lord Dutton. And, I must say, these matters can't concern you."

"But they might concern me, Mrs. Warren, if you would but help," he said, turning slightly so that his arm brushed against her. She trembled slightly. He was relieved he was sober enough to notice. "If you could just arrange for me to be on that list, Lady Amelia's marriage list, I should be so grateful. I do think she'd make a wonderful wife and, as you have pointed out, I do need a woman to settle me. I fear, Mrs. Warren, that I have fallen into debauchery. Who better than a wife to pull a man back onto the straight and narrow?"

She looked, if he could be immodest, and he could, like she wanted to faint.

Damned if Ruan wasn't a genius.

❧

LORD Iveston was behaving beautifully, walking quietly at Amelia's side as they entered the ballroom, listening to her exclaim over the beauty of the boiserie, the gilded plasterwork on the ceiling, the sweetness of the violins, all the things a woman said to a man when she could think of nothing to say. Amelia was entirely certain that the reason she could think of nothing to say to the elegant Lord Iveston was that Lord Cranleigh was hovering at Iveston's side and staring at her with his icy blue eyes. The man could freeze a volcano.

It was perfectly obvious that Cranleigh was making the point that the only way to avoid *him* was to avoid Iveston, which flatly was not going to happen. She wasn't about to be manhandled into giving up Iveston now.

"I had no idea," Cranleigh said, practically cutting off her latest comment regarding the cellist, "that a discussion on the merits of string instruments was part of your interviewing process, Lady Amelia. One can but wonder how it pertains to the issue of marriage."

"I'm sorry," she said, staring around Iveston's well-tailored shoulder at his thuggish brother, "I should have guessed that a discussion about the merits of music would effectively remove you from the conversation, Lord Cranleigh. Perhaps you might find other conversation elsewhere that interests you. Perhaps with the . . ." She was so very tempted to say *with the footmen*, but as she did not want to appear unnecessarily ungenerous and surly in front of Lord Iveston, she said, "hostess, Miss Prestwick. A charming woman, by all accounts."

"Yes, she appears to be," Cranleigh shot back. "So demure. So reticent. The very blush of feminine perfection."

"By all appearances," Amelia concluded snidely.

Stupid man, to be so impressed by appearances. They could all, with very little effort, put on the appropriate appearance. Of course, she found it very difficult to do so with him, but that was surely his fault and not hers. If Cranleigh would only behave appropriately, then she would as well. His having the manner and look of a deckhand was singularly off-putting.

"But Cranleigh makes a point, Lady Amelia," Iveston said, and because he spoke, she gave him every attention. Cranleigh muttered something under his breath. "What did you speak of with the Duke of Calbourne? I would not have short shrift."

Sophia was so right; men did find themselves nearly compelled to compete with one another. How odd, yet so convenient if one was aware of it. Small wonder that Sophia Dalby had such a reputation for success with men when she understood them so well. Knowing them did lend a rather obvious air of manipulation to the whole thing. Not that she minded. Far from it. After two years on the marriage mart, she finally felt she had been given a leg up. If only Aunt Mary had bothered to explain things to her before her come out, although it was highly likely that Aunt Mary didn't understand a thing. There *were* reasons why Sophia was . . . Sophia.

"Why, Lord Iveston," Amelia said as the ballroom filled, "we simply talked, of nothing in particular. To be frank, he was not so eager to talk as you are."

"Truly? I've always heard that Calbourne is quite adept at conversation," Iveston said.

"But not, perhaps, adept at being interviewed," Cranleigh said. "As to that, I should think you'd need your clerk, your chaperone, and your mentor to witness this interview. Will it be valid without them? Will you know what to ask and how to interpret my brother's responses?"

"I am perfectly capable of speaking to a man without aid," Amelia snapped.

"I'm sure," Cranleigh said dismissively. "Practice, have you? Solitary conversation with a man something you do regularly?"

"That is not what I meant!"

"If you can't be clear about what you mean, I fail to see how you can conduct a revealing interview," Cranleigh said.

"I can be perfectly clear, Lord Cranleigh," she said, stepping in front of Iveston to face his brother. "I should think that you, of all people, can have no doubt as to that."

"He does grate on one, doesn't he?" Iveston inserted mildly.

At which point Amelia took a shaky breath and remembered her purpose, a purpose that had nothing to do with the Earl of Cranleigh. He was leaving Town on the first Elliot ship, wasn't he? Had admitted as much to her himself earlier. He had his plans and she had hers, and there was clearly no reason for their plans to tangle. None. Nothing could be more clear to her than that.

"No, not at all, Lord Iveston," she said sweetly, refusing to look at Cranleigh. Cranleigh, as he was solidly built, was impossible to ignore completely. "He is merely acting like a brother, a very protective one, though why he should feel you need protection from *me* . . ." She let her voice trail off and smiled sympathetically.

Cranleigh opened his mouth to speak. Iveston made some movement of his arm, Cranleigh grunted, and kept his mouth closed. Had Lord Iveston actually elbowed his brother in the ribs? How spectacular. What an efficient way to get him to mind his own business. She would have to remember that particular move with Hawksworth the next time he said something that annoyed her. Of course, it would be difficult to do as Hawksworth was so rarely standing up.

"He is very protective of me," Iveston said. "Always has been. I thought at one time that it was because I am the heir, but now I believe it is simply his nature to . . ." Iveston's voice trailed off and he looked at her to fill the gap.

"Bully?" she said brightly, looking first at Iveston and then at Cranleigh as she said it. Iveston smiled. Cranleigh scowled. She didn't care. No, that was untrue. She was delighted.

"Oh, yes," Iveston said, "I suppose that's possible, but I was going to say intervene. He does have a habit of intervening."

"Does he?" Amelia said, so enjoying the fact that they had fallen into discussing Cranleigh as if he were not present, and yet he was. So very, completely, and eternally present. Why, she could feel raw energy coming off of him like waves. "He certainly did not intervene in any way that I could see when my cousin Louisa was ruined by your brother Henry in the closet at Hyde House. Perhaps he wanted to see her ruined? Is that possible?"

Of course, it was Iveston's brother Henry, as well, who had ruined her cousin. Not a very politic reminder, but she did so want to bludgeon Cranleigh with something and Louisa's ruination and, to be fair, marriage into their family was such a handy bludgeon.

"No man of sense wants to see a girl ruined," Cranleigh said. His voice was soft, low, but not gentle. He sounded more menacing than soothing and she was quite certain it was intentional.

"A man of sense?" she said, unable to stop herself. She should be ignoring Cranleigh and focusing all her attention on Lord Iveston. She should and she would, once she'd got this conversation behind her. There was something about him, such arrogance and surly disdain of her, which was ridiculous as she was the most likeable girl in Society. Everyone, absolutely *everyone* liked her. She had made it a point to be as likeable as humanly possible, which was saying quite a lot. "Not a man of decency? Not a man of honor?"

"Sense," he growled at her. "For if she's ruined, then he is required to marry her. No man of sense wants a ruined girl when he can have one who's above reproach and gossip and suspicion."

If that wasn't the most unkind, unprovoked attack! How completely like him. How perfectly and supremely like the horrid Lord Cranleigh to throw that comment in her face.

"My cousin," she snapped before he had fully finished speaking, "was and is the most proper, the most lovely girl until *your* brother arranged to meet her in a darkened room and . . . and . . . did something to her! And then he ruined her! It's common knowledge!"

"It certainly is," Cranleigh said flatly, which made the whole thing somehow Louisa's fault, when it wasn't, or it shouldn't have been.

"He ruined her!" she said, challenging him to deny it.

"According to her, she ruined him," Cranleigh said. "What's more, she's proud of it."

Of course, it was at this moment that Amelia realized that Iveston hadn't said anything in rather a long time, and that she wasn't engaged in even a spirited conversation but a heated debate, and that the entire room, which was quite full now, was staring at her. At them. At her fighting with Lord Cranleigh, the Duke of Hyde's son.

Of course it was completely Cranleigh's fault. Obviously. She couldn't, not after all these years of appearing perfect, have fallen into public disgrace in a single hour.

Oh, very well, a half hour.

"As they are contentedly married," Iveston said mildly, "the point seems moot. But certainly no one, for any reason, would want to see a girl ruined."

Is that what they had been arguing about? How stupid. Of course no one wanted to see a girl ruined. Even the gleam in Cranleigh's cold blue eyes affirmed it, which was hardly surprising.

It was so difficult to credit that he was the son of a duke. He bore himself like a street tough. A sailor. As to that . . . Molly may have jumped the fence and . . . no, no it was ridiculous. And even if it were not, she was not going to think of her future mother-in-law in such a light. It would make dealing with her at family gatherings so awkward.

"If you believe that, Iveston, then you shouldn't get yourself involved with Lady Amelia and her infamous interview. You'll ruin either yourself, or her, or both," Cranleigh said.

Infamous? Was she infamous? She felt a tiny thrill, uncertain if it were a bad thing to be even slightly infamous after two years out. It might not be so bad. In fact, it might be worse to be invisible, which she certainly had been until tonight. Never before had any gentleman during the Season been more than passingly polite to her and now, now she had two men at her elbows. Of course, one was the thuggish Lord Cranleigh and he was an absolute horror, but the other was the future Duke of Hyde and he was quite nice, entirely pleasant.

How pleasant and serene life could be as his wife. Why, she might go days without knowing if he were in the house or not, he was so very quiet and polite. Certainly, a woman could hardly do better than that, as husbands went.

How lovely. Only a few days after consulting with Sophia Dalby and she had her man. Oh, well, not precisely *had* him, but it was a near thing. All that was left to do was to arrange for him to ask her, ask her father, ask his father, get the license, arrange the day, agree upon the terms of the contracts, sign the contracts . . .

Oh, very well, there were still a few details to be worked out, but she had decided to put all her efforts upon Lord Iveston. As he was sticking to her side so very agreeably, he clearly had made the same decision. The real problem facing her was how to get rid of the ever scowling Lord Cranleigh. He did put such a damper on courtship. It was very nearly amusing. Yes, she most definitely did feel like laughing.

"Lord Cranleigh," she said politely, or as politely as was possible when talking to Cranleigh, "as an interview, such a formal word for what is, in truth, simply a discussion, and as a discussion is simply a conversation, and as yet, no man or woman has been ruined by a conversation, I fail to see the source of your concern. I will not harm your brother. I can say with complete confidence that he will not harm me. You are free to seek your entertainment elsewhere."

She barely refrained from giving him a shooing motion with her fingers. Barely. She only refrained because she thought he was entirely capable of reaching out and breaking them off at the knuckle.

"She has a point, Cranleigh," Iveston said.

Amelia smiled a bit savagely.

Lady Dalby was watching her from a few feet distant and nodded her approval, or what Amelia assumed was her approval. Certainly Lady Dalby had done her part in keeping Aunt Mary out of the middle of things. How she had done so, Amelia couldn't imagine for, even deeply in her cups, Aunt Mary could be so intrusive. Amelia was completely certain that if Aunt Mary had been conscious and not snoring on the sofa, Louisa would never have found herself married to Lord Henry, Iveston's younger brother. Of course, Louisa hadn't wanted Lord Henry at all, but rather Lord Dutton, yet she had been distracted somehow by something that had happened in that closet and Dutton had been forgotten from that point onward.

Amelia was not going to allow herself to be dragged into any closets. There were many things that a man might do in a closet to confuse a girl.

"I am quite certain Lord Iveston will not ruin me," she said, hoping Cranleigh would pester someone else. Her gaze scanned the room and settled on Penelope Prestwick, looking very fetching in white muslin with cream and black embroidery at the hem and her ever-present diamonds at her ears and in her hair. They looked quite spectacular against her black hair, which was obviously why she'd chosen diamonds as her jewel. That, and the Prestwicks were rumored to be fabulously wealthy. "Miss Prestwick is quite lovely, Lord Cranleigh. Perhaps she would be interested in your thoughts about conversation. Unless you fear she might ruin you somehow."

She oughtn't to have said that last bit, but she couldn't seem to stop herself where Cranleigh was concerned.

"She is a beautiful woman," Cranleigh said, staring across the room at their hostess. Amelia felt a small stab of annoyance to hear him say it. "I should very much enjoy getting to know Miss Prestwick better, but," he said, turning back to face her, his cold blue gaze piercing her, "I dare not leave Iveston unchaperoned. You could well ruin him. It might be a family trait, mightn't it?"

At which point, her annoyance became a gleaming sword of immense weight.

"I would like him to stay, if you don't mind," Iveston inserted pleasantly, his brows lifted in question. "I do think that having a witness of sorts can only be to the good. To preserve your reputation, I would not break with tradition."

Which meant she had no choice at all and had to agree to let Cranleigh hover at Iveston's elbow. There were worse things; it could have been Aunt Mary. But at least Mary drank.

"Before the music fully starts," Iveston said, "would you not like to ask me something? I should so hate to come up short when Calbourne insists we compare our interviews."

"I beg your pardon?" she said.

"Somewhere in your nursery rhymes," Cranleigh said, intruding yet *again*, "you must have learned that men *do* talk. They compare. They judge. They even, Lady Amelia, are known to make coarse jests."

"Darling Cranleigh," Sophia said from behind her. "How generous of you to instruct Lady Amelia, who is surely the most innocent woman of my acquaintance, in the habits of the man about Town. Certainly, if a woman is to find her way to the altar, with the *appropriate* man at her side, she does need keen instruction. Naturally, her brother, the Marquis of Hawksworth, is not the man for the job, as no brother ever is for a sister. But you, you have risen up to help Lady Amelia. I don't know the last time I've seen such gallantry in action."

Lord Cranleigh was struck dumb. They all were. It was something of a relief.

"Were you next going to explain to her that men also offer marriage? In the best circumstances they offer a lovely cash settlement or a first-rate house in Town. Sometimes, they offer both," Sophia said with a seductive smile. "Yet sometimes, Lord Cranleigh, a woman would rather have cash than a husband." When Cranleigh turned white about the mouth, a truly lovely sight, Sophia added, "But obviously, that would depend entirely on the man offering himself up for consideration, and certainly neither you nor your brother would be refused consideration. Isn't that so, Lady Amelia?"

"I . . . ah . . . that is," Amelia stammered. What to say? There was nothing to be said that would not be crass and obvious and crude, but then, in for a penny, in for a pound. "I should consider any offer most carefully, as I believe any woman would." That sounded fairly mild, considering. "Of course, some decisions can be made very quickly," she added, staring at Cranleigh, the oaf.

"Then Lady Amelia is not looking for a husband?" Cranleigh asked of Sophia while staring at her. He was such an unpleasantly brutal man, quite the sailor of reputation.

"Only the right sort of husband, Lord Cranleigh," Sophia answered smoothly. "As you, one day, will seek out the right sort of wife. If there is scandal in that, London truly has gone dull. I may be required to do something about that."

"Move?" Cranleigh said brusquely.

Sophia laughed and, tapping his arm with her fan, said, "Leave London? No, darling Cranleigh, I would simply and completely have to stir things up a bit. Whatever occurs,

London must not be allowed to fall into solemnity and respectability. How hopelessly dull that would be."

Amelia had never before heard respectability referenced as dull, and it did explain much about Sophia Dalby and the course her life had taken. It also, like a worm burrowing into the side of a well-built ship of the line, caused the tiniest hole of speculation as to what her life would be like without the armor of respectability. Certainly she had gone about her hunt for a husband with both respectability and solemnity as armor about her. And what had it got her? Respectability and solemnity. Not a duke. Not anyone.

"But as to what questions were asked of the Duke of Calbourne," Sophia continued on, the men held silent by her combined allure and authority, a truly remarkable and useful combination of assets, "surely that would be indiscreet to divulge. You can't want your own interview to be bandied about, Lord Iveston. I did think you a modest, private man."

Sophia did not give him a chance to either confirm or deny the observation. Could he have done either and retained a speck of dignity? Continuing on was actually something of a mercy. Yes, it could be thought so.

"As to what you would like Lady Amelia to ask of you," Sophia said casually, "perhaps you have taken the concept of an interview too literally."

The occupants of the room pressed in on them without any trace of shame. Certainly at least twelve people could hear every word spoken between them and one of them was the Marquis of Ruan. How perfectly odd. What interest could he have in any of this? Amelia had only met him last week at Hyde's, during that scandalous dinner where Louisa had got herself ruined and engaged.

There was that pairing again, scandal and marriage. Were they ever to be tied irrevocably together? Perhaps only when Sophia Dalby was involved. Well, she was involved very deeply with Amelia, but Amelia was both certain and determined that she would not be ruined, not now. No ruination for her. Though, looking at Iveston, he did not appear to be the sort to ruin a girl, not by accident and certainly never intentionally.

Her gaze strayed to Lord Cranleigh. *He*, on the other hand, looked exactly the sort to ruin a girl by simply being introduced to her. *Sailor.*

"Have I?" Iveston said, giving his full attention to Sophia—again. Really, this was not to be borne. Every time Amelia paused to think and ponder and consider what best to do next, Sophia swooped in and monopolized every man within sound of her.

"Or perhaps he has not," Amelia said boldly. It was a very scandalous thing to suggest, and she had no idea what to say next, but all eyes were once again on her and she intended to keep it that way for as long as she could. "I don't think it amiss for a woman to ask a simple question of a man, particularly as he appears so very eager."

"A simple question?" Sophia said, smiling. "Of course, he should be more than willing to answer a simple question. Was your question of Lord Iveston to be simple, Lady Amelia?"

Blast and bother, now that put an even more scandalous turn to the situation. It was almost as if Sophia were challenging her, but that was ridiculous. What purpose could Sophia have to do that? There was something odd about Sophia's brand of help.

"I shall leave Lord Iveston to determine whether my question is simple or not," Amelia said diplomatically. "Lord Iveston, I should very much like to ask you why you appear not to find my interviewing, to use your word, of potential husbands to be *scandalous*?"

"Perhaps *insulting* would be a better word," Cranleigh said stiffly. Amelia ignored him.

"Lady Amelia," Iveston said, after looking censoriously at his annoying brother, good man, "no matter what word is used, I do believe it shows a levelheaded and logical approach to marriage, which I must confess is not often on display in the women I've met to date. Scandalous or not, it is very practical and I do find myself ever an admirer of practicality."

Well. That was surprising.

"Chamber pots are practical as well and one doesn't drag them into the center of the dining table."

No need to speculate as to who had said *that*.

"Are you comparing me to a chamber pot?" she asked, turning the full force of her gaze, indeed her full attention, upon Cranleigh.

"I wouldn't think of it," Cranleigh said in a stiff undertone. "*I* still maintain the boundaries of decorum."

"I think you are mistaken, Lord Cranleigh," she replied swiftly, before Sophia could reinsert herself into the conversation. "I do believe that, in trying to manage your older brother's life, you step beyond many boundaries."

Cranleigh leaned close to her, his icy blue eyes as hard as shining blades. She held her breath, but did not take a step away from him, though she wanted to. Certainly she wanted to. Most definitely.

"And if I do, Lady Amelia," he breathed in cold disdain, "who is to push me back within the bounds? You?"

There was only one answer to that. She didn't think. She didn't debate. She didn't ponder.

Amelia set her palm against Lord Cranleigh's massive chest . . . and pushed.

Thirteen

Miss Penelope Prestwick almost laughed out loud.

Amelia Caversham had her hand squarely in the middle of Lord Cranleigh's chest and appeared to be trying to push him, right in front of Lord Iveston, too. It was the strangest way to acquire a duke that she'd ever seen and it was sure to fail, if one could judge by the expression on Iveston's face, though, he did not look offended so much as amused. That *was* odd. In fact, Iveston looked, why, he almost looked as though he might actually laugh.

That was not good.

The fact that pushing Cranleigh, who was built like a monument, was sure to prove impossible had very little to do with anything, except to prove, if proof were needed, and she hoped it were, that Amelia Caversham had no idea how to comport herself around men of title and fortune. A rare fact as Amelia was the daughter of a duke of healthy fortune. Certainly, for a girl who had every advantage, Lady Amelia had no idea how to take advantage of her assets.

Penelope was sure to do better.

"Whatever can she be doing?" George asked her.

"Making a fool of herself?" Penelope replied to her brother.

"What lovely entertainment you've provided," the Marquis of Penrith said at her elbow. "And I'd only expected a small orchestra. You have gone quite above the mark, Mr. Prestwick, Miss Prestwick. My compliments."

Oh, dear. *He* had come? Penrith had been invited, of course, as everyone had been invited, but she hadn't thought he'd come. In fact, she'd almost hoped he wouldn't come.

The Marquis of Penrith had the most dangerous of reputations in regard to young, unmarried women. It was rumored, and of course Penelope paid as much attention to the Penrith rumors as she did to every other, which is to say she considered them carefully and then swallowed them whole, that Penrith could and did with astounding regularity seduce innocent girls into doing all sorts of scandalous things merely by suggesting that they do scandalous things. It was his voice, you see, a husky, velvety murmur of masculine amusement and vague arousal that was his weapon. Even girls who knew nothing of arousal, vague or not, understood it at once, once Penrith had got them alone.

Penelope, perhaps not as innocent as some—as she had exchanged a few *mostly* innocent caresses with a very attractive groom at her father's estate the day she had turned twenty, because the day had seemed to call for something in terms of a rite of passage, and she had no regrets as she still was not married and a girl did like to have some small experience of men before she found herself married to one for life—knew enough about Penrith's reputation that she took a step away from him to be nearer to her brother.

And then she looked into Penrith's cat green eyes, let her eye travel over his tousled dark blond hair, and discreetly cast a glance up and down and up again his lithe form . . . and took a step nearer to Penrith. Her brother was at her side. What could happen?

"I'm afraid, Lord Penrith," Penelope said a bit stiffly, which was mortifying as the worst a woman could do was appear nervous when talking to a man, "that I must redirect your compliment to Lady Amelia and Lord Cranleigh, who are acting independently and outside the bounds of propriety."

Once the words were out of her mouth, she wanted to gobble them back in. She sounded like the worst sort of prig. Penrith would hate her instantly.

Penrith, tall and lean, looked down at her with an amused expression. Perhaps he did not hate her?

"Miss Prestwick," he said, and a shiver worked its way over her skin, "you notice that Lady Dalby is standing not a foot away from Lady Amelia?" Without waiting for her reply, he said, "I can promise you that Lady Amelia is not acting independently. Nor is Lord Cranleigh, though he may not be aware of it."

Illogical nonsense. Is this how Penrith and his mesmerizing voice had gained infamy? By spouting gibberish? Of course, his gibberish had sounded lovely enough until one bothered to try and make sense of his words. How did Lady Dalby figure into the events of the evening? She was infamous, true enough, but not for persuading young women to manhandle titled gentlemen.

Or was she? Penelope had heard some rather lurid rumors about Sophia's own daughter, pearl necklaces, and a closet in Hyde House, not to mention a rigorous jaunt down Park Lane; actually, some of the rumors had been that she'd run down Park Lane, her new husband chasing after her. Penelope enjoyed a luscious rumor as much as the next person, but when they became out-and-out ridiculous fabrications, then rumors were in danger of losing all their entertainment value as a window into the private lives of the titled class. An abuse of their function, surely, and such a waste. If one couldn't rely on the stoutness of rumor, well then, what was left?

"I should think that would annoy Lord Cranleigh," George said mildly. George was often mild; it was what made his company so pleasant, and so rare in a brother. Most of them were simply horrid by her observation. Why,

Amelia's brother was a perfect example: Lord Hawksworth rarely went out, and when he did, he hardly spoke a word, unless it was to annoy Amelia. "Do you think he knows?"

"Knows that he's annoyed?" Penelope said a bit too sharply, considering that Penrith was smirking down at her, his smirk more alluring than many a man's cordial smile. The man could simply get away with nearly anything. "I should think he would."

"I think," Penrith said softly, his voice causing another shiver to pass over her skin, this time deeper and . . . lower, "that it is a rare event indeed when a man knows he is being managed by Sophia Dalby, and if he does know—"

"He doesn't mind," George finished, smiling conspiratorially at Penrith.

Good heavens. This sort of conversation served no purpose whatsoever. What could George be thinking?

"I find that," Penelope said, trying very hard not to sound priggish, "puzzling."

"If you're puzzled, Pen," George said, "just think how Cranleigh must be feeling. Look at him. He looks—"

"Deadly," Penrith finished.

Penelope looked. He did. Cranleigh looked truly deadly and he was looking fully at Amelia Caversham. For a moment, Penelope felt almost sorry for Amelia.

But then it passed.

❧

WHATEVER Amelia had been expecting when she laid her hand against Cranleigh's chest, it was not that he would be hot beneath her glove, or that a jolt of fire would pass through his skin to hers, or that the look in his pale blue eyes would be so blatantly intense. So dangerous. The word clanged through her thoughts, screaming into her blood.

Dangerous.

"Are you pushing me?" Cranleigh asked, his voice nearly a hiss of derision. "I can't feel anything."

It was a lie. She knew it instantly for a lie. The look in his eyes, the ragged intake of his breath, which surely matched her own hoarse gasp for air, the pulsing heat of his massive chest all declared it a lie. He could feel it, feel her, and it enraged him.

And she was glad.

She forgot about Iveston, about Sophia, about Ruan, and all the rest. She only saw Cranleigh. She only wanted to beat him. To push him off. To push him and push him until he moved.

Until she could move him so far and so deeply that he would not be able to deny it. He would be moved. And he would know that she was the woman who had moved him.

She pushed.

He did not move. His eyes widened slightly, frozen and hard, immovable.

She pushed again slightly and raised her other hand to add in, to pile on, to defeat him by a single push.

His brows lowered, scowling. He was always scowling. She didn't care if he scowled. She only wanted him to move. It was the most important thing, instantly and illogically, the most important thing. There was nothing else. Just this man and his adamant refusal to be moved by her.

She pushed again, harder, putting her back into it, very nearly a shove.

He grabbed her wrists and pulled them down and away, a strong, effortless move that infuriated her as nothing in her life had done. His chest was scant inches away from hers, his face hovering above hers, his eyes like shards of ice, his mouth a line of anger, his body nearly twitching in repressed violence.

No, not repressed, delayed. He would, he wanted, to get violent. He wanted to yell at her and pummel something and have his way in this, in everything.

And he didn't. And he wouldn't. It was nearly enough to make her laugh.

Except, except the feel of his hands on her wrists made her want to do anything but laugh. No, she wanted to move him still. In any way. She wanted to best him and frustrate him and make him suffer.

"Did you feel that, Lord Cranleigh?" she whispered, her breath washing over his face. He was so close. He had a scowl line right down the center of his forehead, between his eyes, honestly earned, obviously. He made a business of scowling—it was only right that his body be marked for it.

"No," he growled, scowling hard. Naturally.

"But you feel this," she whispered even more softly, twisting her wrists in his hands, feeling his grip loosen. "You feel *me*."

He released her at the words, clearly stricken. He stepped back, one step, and then two.

"*Pushed*," she chided softly, smiling, unable to look away from his eyes, so blue and so hard.

"I'd say," Iveston said mildly into the fury of their silence, "that she's done it, Cranleigh. Well done, too, a most unusual approach."

"But so very effective," Sophia said.

Amelia and Cranleigh continued to stare at each other in something very nearly horror. But not quite horror. Not quite.

❧

Miss Penelope Prestwick stared at Lady Amelia Caversham and the Earl of Cranleigh in ill-disguised horror. Actually, her feelings were likely not at all disguised, in any degree.

It was a debacle.

Her ball would not be remembered for having the finest orchestra, and she had imported them from Naples, or for having the earliest blooming and most spectacular roses in her conservatory, for which she had paid a fortune as neither she nor George had any skill with horticulture at all, which required her to buy the roses and let the assumption stand that she had grown them, or for her having the finest muslin gown with the most delicate and exotic black silk embroidery at the hem, a fashion statement her modiste had assured her was about to become the latest thing.

No, her ball would be remembered because Amelia

Caversham had shoved Lord Cranleigh until he positively, and understandably, recoiled in revulsion.

"She's done it again," Penrith said, his green eyes sparking in what was clear to see was not horror. Most odd. "Would you care to wager on when the wedding is to take place?"

George smirked and said, "I shouldn't admit it, but I have no knack for these seduction wagers. I lost ten pounds on Louisa Kirkland, thought for sure she'd hold out for Dutton."

Penelope gaped at her brother until he said, "So sorry, Pen, I shouldn't be discussing this in front of you. Lapse of judgment, but as this latest has happened in our very own home . . ." He shrugged. "Just think what this will do for our reputation."

Ruin it, obviously. Men. They were such infants when it came to rumor and reputation.

"Quite right," Penrith agreed, nodding his head. "It will be talked of for months, perhaps years. Good bit of luck there," he added, studying the grouping that was made up of Sophia, Ruan, Iveston, Cranleigh, and Amelia . . . where was the girl's chaperone? Penelope scanned the room and finally spotted Lady Jordan in heated conversation with the Duke of Calbourne. Calbourne? When had he arrived? She had not greeted him. "Though," Penrith said, "as Sophia Dalby has made something of a project of finding Lady Amelia a duke for a husband, I can't think it's good luck for Sophia. She does like her plans to stay firmly fixed. I wonder if she wagered on it?"

"There's nothing on the book at White's," George offered, as if they were not discussing the most absurd and horrendous things, and discussing them casually.

And she had always considered George such a pleasant, almost harmless man. Certainly he had seemed so to her. Perhaps she didn't know her brother as well as she'd thought. She eyed him now, very nearly scrutinized him. Penrith, of course, was known to be a rake and so she didn't put anything past him, but George was her brother!

It didn't seem at all right that he'd put forth one face to her and another one to the bucks at White's. Not a bit fair.

"She wouldn't be down under her own name," Penrith said, looking down at Penelope pleasantly, including her without shame in their speculative conversation. *Confirmed rake.* "She always gets some member to bet for her. Makes it tricky because she very nearly always wins. If she had a steady, confirmed alias it would throw off the odds considerably."

"She can't have wagered on *this*," George said, staring across the room at Amelia and Cranleigh.

Penrith looked instead at Sophia before answering. Penelope found herself staring at Sophia as well. If she had placed a wager and lost it, though what the wager could have been and how she could have either won or lost it was a mystery to Penelope, she looked remarkably calm about it. In fact, Sophia looked almost pleased. By what, for heaven's sake? Penelope's ball had just been *ruined*.

"I don't know," Penrith said. "I wouldn't have thought so, but . . . she hardly looks upset, does she?"

And of course, Sophia didn't. But why should she? It was Penelope who was upset and for very good cause, though George and Penrith seemed to have not considered that at all. Penrith was clearly the most horrid influence on everyone he met, including dear George. Penelope was determined to rescue him from Penrith's influence immediately, or at least once the ball was over, which would have to be soon enough.

❦

"I can't think why you're bothering me about this, Calbourne," Mary, Lady Jordan, snapped. "It was hardly my idea and I scarcely endorse it. I should think you'd be glad to be free of it."

Mary had been dealing with the Duke of Aldreth, Amelia's father, for more than twenty years. She was not in awe of dukes, no matter how tall or how demanding they happened to be. Certainly, Aldreth was far more demanding and awe-inspiring than Calbourne could hope to be, at least as far as she was concerned. At the moment, Calbourne was acting like a child who had been deprived of his pony for a week. In an hour, he'd likely forget he'd ever had a pony, distracted by a new indulgence. Dukes were like that.

"How can I be free of it when I was dismissed like a boy at school?" Calbourne asked.

They were thinking along the same lines, obviously, at least in thinking that he was behaving like a spoilt child.

"I suppose you wanted to be considered, evaluated, judged, and then married in July?" Mary countered, because that was the only option, at least as far as Sophia was concerned.

Mary had, reluctantly, allowed Sophia to have her way with things as they pertained to Amelia, but only because of how well things had turned out with Louisa. In truth, neither Louisa nor Amelia had done well on the marriage mart, for entirely different reasons, but results hardly cared about reasons. Mary had done quite well in her Season, as had her sisters, one of whom had married Melverley and produced Louisa; the other had married Aldreth and produced Amelia. Good Seasons, good husbands, at least from the look of it, miserable marriages.

Sophia had, with her brother John's reluctant help, convinced Mary that what had been done for Louisa could also be accomplished for Amelia. Mary, who was profoundly reluctant as well, had gone along with it. She did want better for her nieces than what she and her sisters had wrought, namely, perfectly miserable marriages. Of course, Martha, her sister and the Duchess of Aldreth, had claimed with her very last breath to have been content in her marriage, but Mary didn't believe a word of it. Any man who maintained a French mistress from almost the outset of his marriage to this very day was not a man to make a wife happy. That much was perfectly obvious. Martha had put a good face on it, as anyone would, and gone into her grave with a smile for Aldreth.

Mary wanted better for Amelia, Martha's daughter.

Sophia implied, for she never promised anything, that, with her aid, Amelia's husband would be assured.

As Amelia wanted a duke for a husband, Mary had, somewhat ungraciously, allowed the interviewing process to proceed unhindered, or at least unstopped, by her. Calbourne had got out with his skin intact, if not his pride. If he had any sense, he'd know he was well out of it. But he was a man. And a duke. He had no sense.

Unless he was infatuated with Amelia and devastated that he'd lost his chance with her?

Mary snorted in amusement. He was a man. And a duke. He had more pride than sense.

"I might have," Calbourne said, lifting his chin and looking the picture of a proud duke. What else? "I do think I didn't get a fair run at the thing."

"By *the thing* I suppose you mean Amelia?"

Calbourne colored slightly. "I suppose that is not precisely what I meant, but surely I deserve another chance to make a favorable impression."

Mary shrugged, and not at all discreetly. She was far past the age, and too often pleasantly foxed, to care what dukes or earls thought of her. She knew what she thought of them and that was enough for her.

"Why should you care, Calbourne?" Mary asked. She was older than Calbourne by a good ten years. She could call him what she liked.

Calbourne, who truly was an attractive man, even though he *was* very tall, looked around the room a bit in apparent discomfort. He looked clear over her head without any trouble whatsoever. Mary was very petite, a fact she more than liked about herself.

"It's on the book at White's," he said in an undertone, still surveying the crowd. "That I was discarded. That I was rejected. For my *excessive* height."

"Only Amelia thought it was excessive," Mary felt duty bound to say.

Calbourne was not a *bad* man, for a duke. As far as dukes went, he was very pleasant. As far as dukes went.

Yes, she was repeating herself. It bore repeating. Dukes, as everyone knew, were not known for being particularly pleasant. As to that, neither were duchesses, although her sister Martha had been a positive joy, if a bit complacent, and she was certain that Amelia would make a stellar duchess.

"But it's on the book!" Calbourne said, rather urgently, too.

Men and their betting. It had ruined her husband and, consequently, it had ruined her. He had died inconveniently and left her without a farthing. After he had been dead for a sennight, it had become abundantly clear that what had been inconvenient was his debt, not his death. Was there any other reason why she was locked into place as the perennial chaperone for Amelia and Louisa? Now that Louisa was safely married, she had only Amelia left to see to. Of course, Eleanor would have her come out, but then, perhaps Louisa could see to her. An older married sister ought to be able to adequately see to her younger sister, see her settled properly.

Though Louisa did not put much store in what was proper. Just look at the bungle she had made of her own come out. If Mary could only get Amelia married to a lovely duke, then she could see to Eleanor.

As lovely dukes went, Calbourne wasn't bad. Certainly he was better than Edenham, who might well kill Amelia. Having had Martha effectively killed by Aldreth, through childbirth, she did not relish the same fate for Martha's daughter. Besides, Edenham had already put three wives into the ground; he'd had his share and more besides.

Mary looked Calbourne up and down somewhat sloppily. She was more than half cup-shot, a circumstance that didn't alarm her in the least. In fact, she preferred it. Amelia could do worse. And he seemed very eager, which was preferable to being forced. Usually.

"I don't see why you shouldn't," Mary said, "have another go." That sounded rather too blunt, even for her. "What I mean to say is that, you were rather rushed out of the running, I do agree with you there, and so, I should think that you ought, in fairness, be allowed to continue a conversation with Lady Amelia."

There. That sounded better. Very nearly respectable.

"You think so?" Calbourne said, looking very eager, very boyish. It was slightly charming. Even Mary was not so jaded that she was blind to it. "You will allow it?"

"But of course," she said with dignity. "Fair play and all that. Have to."

Which, again, sounded a bit less dignified and proper than what an elderly female relation ought to say to a virile man about Town, but, again, Amelia did deserve her duke and this one was as good as any other.

"Have to," she said again, nodding, very pleased with herself. Very.

Fourteen

ANNE Warren and Lord Dutton, along with everyone else in the room, had been caught up in watching the spectacle that was Lady Amelia attempting to shove Lord Cranleigh from her path. Most peculiar behavior from a girl who had hardly had the spine to even dare being noticed before now. Of course, she was taking counsel and guidance from Sophia Dalby now, and that explained absolutely everything about the situation. Although, perhaps, it did not explain why a woman who wanted to marry a duke, and Iveston would be a duke one day, if he lived long enough, would push that man's brother about like a lackey. Strange methods, but then again, Iveston didn't look particularly alarmed. No, in fact, he looked almost amused.

Well, that was something. Iveston, when he did venture out, which was a rare occurrence, looked more often uncomfortable than amused, so perhaps it was not a bad strategy after all.

"It seems that Lady Amelia has been introduced to Lord Cranleigh," Dutton said to Anne as casually as he possibly could. It was a bit of a stretch.

Anne looked particularly fetching tonight in unadorned white muslin with a few pearl pins scattered in her brilliant red hair. She looked like a goddess, though not quite as pure as goddesses were supposed to be. So much the better. He would lure Anne Warren into his bed, married or not. Staverton would never know, if Anne married him at all. It was not impossible that she might be induced to change her mind.

Dutton was very well aware that Lord Ruan was not ignorant of the fact that he was slightly obsessed with Anne Warren. Ruan, discreet to a fault, had not made an issue of his knowledge, which Dutton appreciated as it was embarrassing in the extreme. For a marquis of England to have anything more than a casual interest in an insignificant widow of reduced circumstances was in the worst taste, and he was not in the habit of displaying bad taste. He couldn't help but think that Ruan's plan would rid him of his obsession with Anne by delivering Anne into his bed, where all obsessions sputtered to a damp and predictable death.

So it would be with Anne. If he could only get her to bed and so begin the end.

"He does seem to have . . . alarmed her somehow," Anne said mildly. "I can't think what he might have done to earn such a response."

"Can't you, Mrs. Warren?" Dutton said suggestively. When was she to wed Staverton, a week from now? Two? Why couldn't she simply make matters simple for him and tumble into his bed? "Perhaps I could help you solve that particular mystery."

Anne, far from looking alarmed, which he had half intended, looked nearly amused. And superior. Superior-looking women did not often tumble into beds, at least with the men they were acting superior toward. What the devil had gotten into Anne? Why, before she had got herself engaged to Staverton, he could raise a blush in her cheeks by simply looking at her directly for more than a few seconds.

To be blunt, she had stopped her blushing habit the moment he had kissed her in Sophia's white salon, but he didn't like to dwell upon that. Coincidence, most likely. Make that definitely. Definitely coincidence. Anything else was unthinkable.

"Lord Dutton," Anne said sweetly—too sweetly. "You are at your most amusing when you try so very hard to act debauched, a seducer of girls in shadowed corners. I am no girl, my lord. Had you failed to notice that?"

"And I am very hard, Mrs. Warren. Had you failed to notice that?" he countered, a bit rashly. Oh, dash it, very rashly. This was not the sort of conversation to woo a woman into bed. It was too hasty, too rough. Though . . . it might work, with a certain type of woman. Was Anne that type?

Anne allowed her gaze to travel down the length of him, at his straining breeches, at the precise place where he was hard.

"Lord Dutton, there is nothing about you that I have failed to notice, including your belief that I must fall into your arms simply because you think I should. It is a very boyish quality, this blind belief that your every whim must be met, but I have outgrown my fascination for boys and prefer a man. Lord Staverton, to be precise. Now, if you will excuse me," she said, her sweet tone belying the sharpness of her gaze. When he opened his mouth to, it must be admitted, stop her, she said, "And even if you will not—"

"What of my desire to be introduced to Lady Amelia?" he interrupted.

"But you have met Lady Amelia, have you not? Were you not intimately involved in her cousin's engagement to Lord Henry Blakesley? If you wish to speak to her, go to. There is no one here to stop you. But I should warn you, Lord Dutton, that you do not meet her qualifications in the slightest. Nor, I fear to tell you, do you meet mine. Good evening."

And with that, she pushed her way through the crowd. Yes, *pushed*. He was, he was ashamed to admit, left standing with his mouth open and his plans thwarted. Again.

❦

THE musicians did try. They were tuned. They were ready. It was only that no one was lining up for the dance. How could they? They were all too busy staring at and speculating upon Lady Amelia and Lord Cranleigh.

"The entertainment appears to be stalled," Sophia commented. "I wonder, is there anything to be done about it?" As she was looking inquisitively at Cranleigh as she said it, he was well aware what she wanted. In point of fact, he was of the same mind.

"I shall remove the hindrance, shall I?" Cranleigh said, and without waiting for approval or disapproval, took Amelia Caversham by the arm and led her from the ballroom.

She did not go willingly. No, he could feel her stiffness, her reluctance, but she daren't do anything so bold as to defy him.

"I don't care to leave!" she said, locking her knees, defying his expectations. Again. Horrible habit of hers. She really ought to be rid of it.

"But when others care for you to leave, you really should do the polite thing and leave," he said grimly. Grimly, yes, because being forced to touch her was not at all to his liking.

She was forward and presumptuous and unruly. Traits he abhorred in anyone, man, beast, or woman, and in that order, and he could not abide them in her, this woman who sought to drag his mild and mannered brother to the altar simply because of an accident of birth. Let him be the firstborn, the heir to Hyde, and she'd face a different quarry, one not so pleasant and certainly never docile. Would she want the future Duke of Hyde if that man were he?

He knew the answer to that.

He dragged her, as politely as possible, through the throng, who did part to let them pass as curiosity aroused them as very little else did; out of the ballroom; through the drawing room, which still held far too many people for his purposes; and into the conservatory.

She did not stop protesting the entire way, which only proved how stubborn she was. When there was no stopping something, the thing to do was to go along with it as gracefully as possible. But perhaps this was as graceful as she could get. Though, he had thought of her as being more graceful than this. The night of Blake's ruination of Louisa, the night that it was decided, almost by vote, that they would marry, Amelia had sat upon a settee, looking very innocent and unblemished and screamingly virginal, at least when she suspected Iveston was looking at her. When Iveston was not looking at her, the majority of the time, and she'd been studying Iveston, an entirely different look had crossed her features. One of determination. For his title. That was all. That was eminently plain.

Little Amelia, blond and bored, wanted to be a duchess.

Little Amelia could go rot. She was not going to use his brother for his title. Iveston deserved better.

The conservatory was not exceptionally large, particularly crowded as it was with large pots of roses. Roses in every shade of pink to purest red, a wide range of rosy color, a delicate and aromatic backdrop for Amelia in her white muslin gown, her golden hair gleaming beneath the three crystal chandeliers suspended above them.

It was a very pretty picture, a setting for seduction, which was flatly ironic.

She looked a spitting fury as he released her, taking in instantly that he was blocking the only door back into the main portion of the house.

"If you think to ruin me, Lord Cranleigh, I shan't allow it!" she snapped.

Ruin her? Is that what she thought he'd dragged her in here to do?

He *could* ruin her. It would be simple enough. It would take little effort on his part, and certainly his brother had ruined her cousin in a similar manner just days ago, a fact that must be as fully in her thoughts as it was in his.

It was a simple thing to ruin a girl.

Ruin her? He wouldn't ruin her because then he'd be forced to marry her. And he didn't want her. Not one bit of her. Not her crystalline blue eyes, nor her golden hair, braided and twisted into something vaguely Grecian, not her mouth, which was a bit on the thin side, wasn't it? Just a tiny mouth with lips not at all lushly drawn, but rather, perhaps, if one took the time to study them, just a bit more elegant than lush, but so easy to devour. So effortlessly simple to taste her.

"You shan't?" he asked, taking a step closer to her, his coat brushing against a rose shrub, pink petals scattering onto the brick floor. "How shall you stop me? Will you push me?"

He took another step.

She took another step. Backward. Her eyes were quite large, quite her nicest feature.

"I'll do more than that, Lord Cranleigh," she said. "Very much more."

She let the warning fade, hoping to intimidate him, no doubt.

Couldn't she see that he couldn't be intimidated? It wasn't in his nature. And certainly never by a mere bit of a girl, blond braids gleaming, a single braid looped into a loose coil, nearly begging to be pulled out and set free.

"What will you do, Lady Amelia?" he asked softly, taking another step. Another rose shuddered and fell to the floor in a pink cascade of petals. There was something symbolic about that, but he couldn't, or wouldn't, think what. "Have you learned how to fight for your honor? Have you learned how to defeat the advances of very proper young gentlemen who pursue you rather too vigorously?" None of that, he knew. Not a bit of that. "Or have you learned," he continued, "that if you want Iveston for a husband, you'll have to go through me to get him? You think I'd just let you snatch him up?"

She stopped backing up, which was a pity. He had almost come to enjoy chasing her slowly into the roses.

"Why not?" she snapped. "He must marry and I must marry."

"He must marry. But he must not marry *you*."

"Why not me?" she said, her eyes large and demanding, her voice sharp. "I am available, aren't I? I'm so very available, Lord Cranleigh."

"Why?" he asked.

"Why to what?" she asked, surrounded by roses, buried in blooms. The candlelight twinkled through the prisms of the chandelier, like starlight through midnight leaves. Midnight leaves? He was being ridiculous.

"Why Iveston? Because you want to be a duchess, Amelia, that is all. Iveston is nothing to you beyond a title. And I have made up my mind that he shall not be cast at your hem for you to pick up like a broken flower."

He said it hotly, angrily, when he had meant to be cold and distant, to hold her beauty away from him, to keep her off, to keep her out.

She studied him, unmoving, perhaps unmoved by his declaration.

"Why not, if he wants to be plucked?" she asked. "I shall make him a fine wife."

"A fine duchess?"

"Again, why not?" she said coldly.

"But being a wife is not the same as being a duchess," he said, taking another step nearer to her. "Can you simply pick a man's name from Debrett's, spreading your life and your legs out for him? Can you do that, Amelia?"

He was being crass, to shock her, to scare her. She did not so much as flinch.

"It is done every day, Cranleigh. Every single day. Why should it be any different for me?"

She backed up, just a sliding step, almost casually, but another step removed from him. Or so she hoped. How far would she retreat to avoid him? How far would he push her into the conservatory? Until her back was pressed against the cold glass? Until her hair was caught and snagged by rose branches? Until the word *duchess* was driven from her?

There was no place that far. No place on earth that far.

"Why, Cranleigh?" she said, her blue eyes wide and imploring. "Why are you fighting this so? I must marry. Why not Iveston?"

"Never Iveston," he said. "You think he cannot see what you are?"

"What I am?" she countered, her eyes clear of tears, which he had not expected.

"Taken," he snarled, taking another step nearer, pushing her back into the roses, the petals encompassing her, the thorns grabbing at her gown. And still she stepped away from him. Still she would not relent in her pursuit of Iveston. He could read it in her eyes.

"Taken? *Taken*, Cranleigh?" she said, lifting her chin. "I am the furthest thing from taken."

"No, Amy," he said, his voice hoarse in own ears. "Not the furthest thing."

"Nearly, my lord," she said. "Who has taken me? Who has ruined me? No one. And no one shall. Now let me pass."

"No."

"Let me pass, Cranleigh," she said again, more firmly.

She was trapped within roses, could she not see that? She couldn't get away now, not even if he allowed it. Even so, he could not resist. He never could. He never had.

He raised his arms out toward her, and with his fingertips, he pushed against her shoulders. She stumbled back slightly, more fully wedged in rose petals, the thorns grabbing at the muslin, holding her fast, holding her deep within their embrace.

Embrace, yes, that was the word.

He moved forward, lifted her chin with a fingertip, gazed once more into her luminous eyes, and for what had to be the last time, what *must* be the last time, kissed her on the mouth. She opened beneath his lips like, yes, like a flower. Warm and moist and ready. And the kiss deepened and lengthened far beyond what he had intended, though he had intended none of this, and he fought the urge to pull her against him, but he kissed her still.

Kissed her amidst the roses.

Kissed her in the dark quiet of the conservatory.

Kissed her, knowing that he would never be the man she wanted.

And when the kiss ended, when *he* ended it, let it be remembered, he pulled away from her slowly, studying the passion-glazed look in her lustrous blue eyes, ran a hand over her hair, knocking the braid loose so that it fell in a line across her shoulder, and stepped away from her.

She was breathing heavily, as was he. Just like before, that long-ago kiss in that long-ago time, before she had entered Society and before he had learned that she planned to be a duchess and nothing less.

"Pass, Amy," he said, his voice still hoarse. "Pass and be gone. You will never marry Iveston. I shan't allow it."

And then he turned and left her there, stranded amidst the roses and caught up in thorns, the sound of her harsh breathing echoing against the glass.

Fifteen

It was something of a mystery as to where Cranleigh had dragged Lady Amelia, but after Cranleigh reappeared at Iveston's side only ten minutes after leaving the ballroom, it was supposed that Lady Amelia, who had only barely escaped ruination, which was a delight to her chaperone and a disappointment to all else present, had left the Prestwick ball.

It was not until fully fifteen minutes had passed that Lady Amelia had appeared, the first set well under way, her fine muslin dress torn irreparably and, it looked, repeatedly.

Naturally, all eyes had gone immediately to Lord Cranleigh.

Cranleigh, as he was a stalwart fellow, had ignored them all nearly blissfully.

Amelia, it was duly noted, gave a fine performance of ignoring Cranleigh.

Well, what to think but that Cranleigh had dragged the girl off to some dark corner and practically ripped the clothes from her very shapely body?

The most peculiar, that is to say, interesting facet of the entire thing was that Lord Iveston did not seem to be bothered by any of it in the least. Nor, it should be mentioned, was the Duke of Calbourne, who made his way to Lady Amelia's side almost immediately and began talking her up.

Well. If that didn't put a fine spin on things. The room nearly exploded with speculation, not the least of which came from the younger Blakesley boys.

"Do you think *he's* responsible for that?" Josiah asked his brother George, obviously referring to Cranleigh, who, if it were not already too late, would be referred to as *he* by the entire company for the rest of the evening. And perhaps into next week.

"I can't think why he should be," George Blakesley answered, looking slightly less sure of himself than usual, "but I can't think that he didn't."

"Because of Iveston," Josiah said solemnly, studying Cranleigh as he stood next to Iveston, his expression a stony mask of social boredom.

As they were all standing within six feet of each other, it should not be supposed that Cranleigh did not hear every word spoken by them. If he had a comment to make regarding his guilt or innocence, he refused to make it. Both George and Josiah—particularly Josiah, who was the youngest and did have a need for more experience where women were concerned, a fact he was grossly aware of—logically felt that, by discussing the situation in Cranleigh's hearing, he would, by necessity, have to defend himself, his actions, and his honor. Cranleigh rarely, if ever, felt required to do anything of the sort. They ignored that fact. What else could they do?

"But what did it accomplish? Except to ruin a very nice dress," Josiah said. Unlike his four older brothers, he did not have blue but pale aqua green eyes. Other than that, he looked much like the other Blakesleys in that he was well formed and blond-haired. He could not, by all appearances, take his pale aqua green eyes off of Amelia Caversham and her torn gown. "I should think she'd go home, wouldn't you?"

"Which is what it was supposed to accomplish," Cranleigh said, not turning his ice blue eyes anywhere near the vicinity of Amelia Caversham. Which did strike one as being excessively deliberate. "Her dress, though not the lady herself, is ruined. One would suppose that she'd hie off home, glad to have escaped with only a ruined dress."

"One would think so," Iveston said mildly, looking at Amelia. "I find myself surprised by how well it looks on her, torn as it is. I hadn't thought myself the sort of man to enjoy seeing a woman so disheveled and, frankly, tossed about, but . . . she is lovely, isn't she? There's something so pleasant about her. Even torn."

Cranleigh swore mildly and then held his tongue. Most inconvenient. How was anyone to find out what had happened in the conservatory if he wouldn't speak of it? Cranleigh had always been a stubborn lad, fully the most stubborn of them all.

Into Cranleigh's stubbornness strode Sophia Dalby, looking quite relaxed and full of cheer, even though her current pet project stood across the room in an alarming state of dishabille.

"A woman of such beauty and poise looks lovely no matter her state of dress," Sophia said, "or undress. As to that, I've asked Miss Prestwick to allow Lady Amelia to borrow some sort of covering as Lady Amelia seems determined not to leave the ball. Stalwart girl, isn't she? Such a pleasure to see girls with a bit of spine to them. Ah, and there's Miss Prestwick now, and isn't that a very pretty shawl she's handing her? Such a generous gesture."

The fact that Sophia had needed to prod Miss Prestwick to make the gesture was not deemed worthy of comment.

"As Lady Amelia is staying," Sophia continued, "and as there is some speculation as to the manner in which her dress sustained injury, well, to be perfectly frank, it is nearly destroyed, isn't it?" She looked at Cranleigh as she said it. Cranleigh returned her look and said nothing.

Damned Cranleigh, never letting loose of his tongue. It made learning anything at all nearly impossible. "The only way to silence the most aggressive of rumors is for you, Lord Cranleigh, to ask her to dance."

"I beg your pardon?" Cranleigh said stiffly.

"Oh, I shall speak so you cannot fail to understand me," Sophia said with deceptive civility. Deceptive surely, for the air fairly sizzled between them. Of all the Blakesley brothers, Cranleigh was the only one who had never had a pleasant word to say about Sophia Dalby. The others may not have had *any* word to say, not knowing her, but Cranleigh was one of the few men about Town who didn't seem to care for her in the least. Which made everyone very curious indeed. "The music is rather loud. I shall repeat then, shall I? You must dance with Lady Amelia, Lord Cranleigh. There is simply no other way to salvage her reputation and you surely must want that. I can't think why a gentleman of your reputation would want it bandied about that he'd ruined a girl merely to keep her from his brother."

The silence that comment engendered could have been cut with a sword. And Cranleigh looked like he wanted to do just that.

"I would be delighted to dance with Lady Amelia," the Marquis of Ruan said.

Sophia did not so much as turn to look at him. "How amiable of you," Sophia said dismissively. "But as this does not concern you, Lord Ruan, and as you clearly don't understand the intricacy of the situation, you should, by all means, find your entertainment elsewhere."

"I can't imagine being more entertained than I am at this moment," Ruan said with a pleasant smile. His intent was not at all pleasant and that was obvious to all of them. Ruan, fulfilling his reputation to perfection, did not seem to care a whit whether anyone but himself was pleased or not.

"Such a limited imagination," Sophia said. "I would hardly have thought it. You did imply otherwise."

She gave Ruan a look of amused annoyance, much the

look one would give to an irritating but beloved pet. Ruan bowed crisply and said, "Whatever you imagine, Lady Dalby, shall be fulfilled. That I promise you." And then he wandered across the room in the general direction of Lord Penrith. Sophia watched him for a moment, watched as Ruan turned when he was perhaps fifteen feet from her, winked at her in bold flirtation, and continued on.

Sophia very nearly chuckled. She swallowed the sound whole.

"As I was saying," she said when Ruan was gone, "it must be Lord Cranleigh, mustn't it?" The Blakesleys stared at her, not quite able to make the shift in conversation as quickly as she could. "As his name is linked to hers, poor dear"—and it was not clear exactly who was the poor dear, Cranleigh or Amelia—"and as her dress is evidence of something, it must be Lord Cranleigh who silences every possibility of scandal by dancing with the girl."

"I fail to see what that will accomplish," Cranleigh said.

"You are not so untutored, Lord Cranleigh, that you cannot anticipate precisely what it will accomplish," Sophia countered. "If you had ruined the poor dear"—ah, so Amelia was the poor dear—"then you would naturally avoid her now. If nothing unfortunate happened in the conservatory, then you would be as guileless as a lamb in approaching her now."

As no one in the northern hemisphere would ever accuse Cranleigh of being guileless, no matter what the cause or what the evidence, that was pushing the point a bit too far. But no one argued the point. To what purpose? No one wanted to see Lady Amelia ruined.

Not even Cranleigh.

"I would have thought that, by approaching her," Cranleigh said, "I would be confirming whatever suspicions might be entertained. Surely, giving the lady a refined distance is all that is required."

"My lord Cranleigh," Sophia said softly, "a gentlemen

must do more than is required, must he not, particularly where a lady is concerned? Oh, but perhaps another solution is presenting itself even now. The Duke of Calbourne is at her side, which surely must please them both. They certainly look well pleased, and as this set is ending, it does appear that they will dance the next set. How perfectly lovely," Sophia said cheerfully. "It looks as if you are not needed after all, Lord Cranleigh. I should think that the duke will handle things admirably, as dukes so often do."

What to say to that?

"I would not put my duty to Aldreth's daughter upon some other man's shoulders," Cranleigh said abruptly, leaving their party to make his way across the crowded floor, everyone in the room watching his progress. Everyone, that is, with the exception of Lady Amelia, who kept her back aimed precisely at the spot where Lord Cranleigh had been. Miss Prestwick, still somewhat bound by hospitality and feminine concern over something so horrendous as a torn gown, and nearly rooted to the spot by the fact that the Duke of Calbourne had joined their small party, was at Amelia's side when Cranleigh reached them.

"I do think you should prepare yourself, Lady Amelia," Penelope said, staring at Cranleigh in something very nearly a trance.

Amelia knew precisely what could induce a fine, healthy girl to get that approximate look: Cranleigh. He was good at freezing innocent girls with a mere gaze. She did not find it a relaxing experience in her own case and found it even less enjoyable when watching it happen to another female.

"Prepare myself for what?" Amelia said in abundant unconcern. "I have been through the worst, Miss Prestwick, a torn gown at the most fashionable ball of the Season. I shall fear no mere man."

"Even if he steps upon your toes, Lady Amelia?" Calbourne asked with a smile.

"Even then," she said. "I can and will defend myself. You have been forewarned," she said with a teasing smile as Cranleigh joined their circle. The smile was directed at Calbourne, but it was meant for Cranleigh.

"'Tis a woman's right," Calbourne said.

"'Tis a woman's duty," Cranleigh interjected, refusing to look at her, directing his gaze to Miss Prestwick instead. "Is it not so, Miss Prestwick? A woman's first concern is to protect her honor?"

"I believe the word you mean is *chastity*, Lord Cranleigh, which seems to become a man's first concern upon leaving the nursery," Amelia said as Penelope was forming her answer. "He seems equally determined to either want to rob her of it or cast her high upon some distant shelf where she will die of dusty chastity." Calbourne's mouth hung agape. Miss Prestwick seemed to have forgotten how to breathe. Cranleigh bore his usual expression of grim annoyance. "I see I haven't shocked you, Lord Cranleigh, which certainly proves my point. But excuse me, Miss Prestwick, I spoke hurriedly, yet would you not agree?"

Miss Prestwick, to her credit, rallied quickly. "I suppose it must depend upon the man," Miss Prestwick said. "Certainly a brother is a man and yet he does not seek to steal his sister's . . . honor, does he? A certain logic must be applied, don't you agree?"

"A logical woman," Calbourne said wearily, a fact he didn't bother to hide. "I suppose you have been educated, Miss Prestwick?"

"I know my alphabet, your grace," Penelope answered, looking extremely uncomfortable.

"And your numbers, too, I should hope," Amelia said. "It is to a man's advantage to keep a woman uninformed, uneducated, and untutored. How else to keep her from besting him?"

"She could always fight him in a duel," Cranleigh said sarcastically.

"Pistols or swords, Lord Cranleigh?" Amelia swiftly replied, staring at him sharply.

"Are you adept at either, Lady Amelia, or would you cajole a man into taking action on your behalf?" Cranleigh snapped. "I do think that is the way a woman gets what she wants."

"As long as she gets what she wants, Lord Cranleigh, and the man gets a good fight in the bargain, then both shall find themselves well content. It is no secret that men of a certain vigorous disposition do enjoy a small battle or two; even you should be aware of that, by hearsay at least. Though I don't recall asking you what you think about the matter, Lord Cranleigh," Amelia said. "But I do care what you think, Calbourne," she said, turning her gaze from Cranleigh and his icy rage to Calbourne's startled expression. "Do you think a woman should be kept ignorant?"

"Of certain things, yes," Calbourne said.

"Of maps and mathematics, of art and philosophy?" Amelia said earnestly.

"Of pistols and swords?" Cranleigh sniped.

"Or merely of men who use pistols and swords?" Penelope said, falling into the rhythm if not the tone of the game.

Into the stilted silence that followed, Amelia found it almost impossible not to glare at Cranleigh, and really, why shouldn't she? He had tried by the most unchivalrous and calculated way possible to drive her from the ball. What a horrid shock it clearly was for him that she refused to be driven. She was not to be distracted by something as ordinary as a tear in her gown, though it was rather more than a single tear and there had been something more to distract her than ripped fabric.

He had kissed her. Again. She had not wanted it, she had not sought it, and she had not run from it. But that was only because she was trapped within roses and couldn't move. That was the sole reason she had stood stock-still and allowed him to kiss her.

She had reasoned this out while trying to disentangle herself from the roses, and she was fairly well pleased by her summation of events.

As to why she had kissed him back, she hadn't worked that out yet to her satisfaction. But she would. All she knew at the moment was that her heart had hammered and her skin had flushed and her breasts had . . . Well, he couldn't possibly know what her breasts had done as a result of his touch so there was little point in counting that. In this secret war they had been conducting between them for two years, only obvious defeats and victories counted. Or that's what she had decided. She didn't know or care what Cranleigh thought of any of it. He probably didn't think at all, he just scowled and snarled and reacted in any fashion he thought right to him.

Sailor.

What he did not yet realize was that she had taken their war public.

She never should have let him kiss her that first time. It had been unwise in the extreme, and just look at how it complicated everything. Of course, he had taken the kiss rather than asked for it, and no matter how she went over it in her mind, and she went over it far more than was necessary or helpful, she couldn't see how she could have prevented it. It was going to be a tad difficult to be married to Iveston with Cranleigh kissing her at almost every opportunity; a fact which ought to be perfectly obvious to him.

Could he stop? It hardly appeared so.

Could she stop? Most assuredly not. He had started it, after all, yet it was perfectly obvious that she would have to finish it. If that wasn't just like a man.

Certainly Cranleigh had muddled things up nicely. It was all his fault, every bit of it. She hadn't been the one to kiss a man at the innocent age of eighteen, especially as that man wasn't likely to become a duke. She did have her priorities in order, and had done since the age of six, at the very latest. By ten, her resolve had only firmed up into something akin to mortar. By sixteen, seeing that her teeth were straight and white, her bosoms firm and round, her skin clear of pox, she had known it for a fact; she would wed a duke. She had everything needed to acquire one.

At the age of eighteen, the year of her come out, she

had met Lord Cranleigh, and that had changed everything, instantly. Not that he seemed aware of it.

Cranleigh, older and wiser and certainly more experienced, had used his wiles and his magnetism and pure brute force to take her in his muscular arms, press her against his hot chest, and kiss her boldly. It had taken him the better part of a day to get round to it, too, which really had been most annoying of him. She had thought he was never going to make his move, then he had, and then he had done nothing about it. Nothing at all. Not a marriage proposal in two long years. Nothing but torrid kisses and a few mostly innocent caresses, and no proposal. He was clearly the most obstinate, stupid man in England.

If she didn't know better, she might begin to think he didn't *want* to marry her!

The only thing that had kept her at all sane during the two years from that first kiss to this moment was that no one, *no one*, knew what had happened between them. She was quite pleased about that, nearly proud. Certainly Louisa would be shocked, as Louisa believed she knew every thought in Amelia's head. She very nearly did. Some thoughts, however, were not meant to be shared and what she thought of Cranleigh fit firmly in that category.

They did meet each other less than she would have liked as he was not the most sociable man she had ever met, not that it diminished his appeal. No, far from it. In fact, the danger inherent in their encounters added quite a nice dollop of excitement to what, it must be admitted, were rather boring social affairs of the most repetitive type. Cranleigh dragging her off into an alcove to kiss her at the odd recital made the pianoforte nearly bearable.

And when he could not drag her off, it was miserable.

There had been one near moment on the night Louisa had been ruined by Lord Henry Blakesley, Cranleigh's brother. They had been in the same room, not alone naturally, for nearly an hour. That had been a challenge. They had ignored each other as best they may, not an easy task as

Cranleigh was flatly impossible to ignore. He had scowled at her a few times and she had turned her back on him a few more, and they had got through it.

She did try to be a proper duke's daughter, but Cranleigh made it so difficult.

Then there had been that unfortunate weekend spent at a house party at the Earl of Quinton's estate. Quinton's heir, the handsome Lord Raithby, had very nearly stumbled upon Cranleigh kissing her in the maze. She had not *wanted* to be in the maze, mind you, but as it was the afternoon's entertainment, she had been obligated, as a good guest only. That Cranleigh had found her there had been purely by chance, she was nearly certain. Upon reflection, and she had reflected upon it often since then, it had seemed to her that Cranleigh had hunted her down. How else to explain his luck at finding her in a maze? In that particular instance he had come toward her at a trot, grabbed her round the waist before she had the wit to protest, bent her backward and begun kissing her on the swells of her breasts, securely and demurely tucked away beneath scads of sturdy fabric, and proceeded upward until he had her mouth firmly beneath his. As she had been bent backward, what was she to have done? She'd held on to his waist and tried to keep as quiet as possible. It was a house party, after all, and they were out in the open. Anyone could have come upon them, and nearly did in the form of Lord Raithby.

There had been other instances over the years, all of them similar in basic substance, all of them amorous assaults on her person that should have resulted in a speedy proposal. No proposal had been forthcoming, yet he could not stop kissing her. Ridiculous, really, as she was not the sort of girl to go about letting a man have his way with her without benefit of marrige. Or she hadn't been that sort of girl until meeting Cranleigh.

She really considered it a service to the Hyde name that she hadn't made public what an absolute barbarian Cranleigh was. He truly fit the description of a sailor on shore leave, and looked like one as well. If they only knew how it had begun, how innocent of all guile and false purpose she had been and would still be if not for falling in love with the most inconvenient, impossible man. And now she was reduced to using guile to attain him, for what else was the dukes list but a bit of guile? Just look how he had changed her! At eighteen, what had she known of guile?

Oh, very well, some little bit even at eighteen, but Cranleigh had started it. Cranleigh always started it.

She remembered that first kiss vividly, as was surely to be expected.

It was late winter, the eighteenth of March, to be exact, and Aldreth was at home on one of his rare visits to Sandworth, the ancestral estate. As he was at home and as it was winter and as he was bored, he allowed that a small and intimate party of not more than forty guests were to be invited to entertain him, and each other, if it so happened. Oh, and his children, who were rarely offered any sort of entertainment whatsoever.

Naturally, Aldreth being what he was, a duke, a widower, and a father, in that order, did not make mention of any of those particulars, but Amelia and Hawksworth, not being completely dull, understood that that is what had occurred.

The guests who arrived were the Duke and Duchess of Hyde, along with most of their sons, Lord Iveston markedly absent, the dowager Countess of Dalby and the Earl of Dalby, Lady Caroline, at fourteen, being forced to keep to her lessons, the Duke and Duchess of Edenham, his third wife who was in the very first flush of pregnancy, and various others who were too unimportant to bother about. Naturally, she had been very excited about meeting the Marquis of Iveston. It would not have been at all amiss and she certainly would not have minded in the least to have snared Iveston before even her come out. It would have saved so much bother and, indeed, been something of a coup to formally enter Society as the wife of the heir apparent to the Duke of Hyde.

But Iveston, ever reclusive, had not come to Sandworth. The Earl of Cranleigh had.

He had not, and indeed still did not, look like anyone she had ever met before. He was muscular in the extreme, nearly like a laborer and, worse, it did not put her off in the least. His manner was rigorously contained and he appeared nearly inarticulate, which naturally made her want to break into his iron self-control and entice him to pour out his silent heart to her. But it was his eyes which captured her beyond rescuing, as blue as arctic ice, as cold and sharp as snow, and as full of unspoken shadows as to lure the most innocent of girls, which is precisely who she had been until meeting him.

He had cornered her in the picture gallery when everyone else, or most everyone else, had been in the saloon playing at cards. As she didn't care for cards, she had wandered in nearly complete innocence a full two rooms and one hall away from the saloon to the picture gallery, and Cranleigh had followed her. She was quite certain he followed her, for how else to explain how he had found his way into the picture gallery? Naturally, she had done everything she could possibly think of to lure him to follow her, and it showed such promise for a lifetime of pleasure that he had followed her unspoken instructions so well.

The room faced east, the light was quite soft in the room, lighting the portraits of her ancestors delicately. She had looked, she suspected, quite lovely in that gentle light, for Lord Cranleigh, who never had before that instant had much to say, started talking to her.

Staring at the portraits, he compared her eyes to an aunt three generations removed.

She thought the comparison thin.

He compared her hair to a great-grandmother on her father's side.

Perhaps there was a slight similarity.

He thought that her nose was quite that of her father's.

Completely absurd and she told him so. As Cranleigh

was standing quite close and as he had been running a fingertip down the length of her nose as he spoke, turning to argue with him had been . . . well, she had been innocent until that moment. Though not quite so innocent as to not understand that turning to face a man who stood not six inches off was a very good way to get kissed.

He had, without any hesitation she could discern, kissed her lightly on the mouth.

She supposed it might have been possible that the moment he lifted his mouth from hers that he would have stepped away and apologized. As she had placed her hands on his chest and looked up at him in rapture, lifting her mouth for another kiss, he had never quite had the chance to apologize, if he had been intending to at all. It was definitely not a sure thing.

He had pulled her to him, both hands around her waist, and kissed her again. She had kissed him back. Fully. Without restraint. With a great deal of ardor, truth be told.

They had kissed until the sun set, leaving the picture gallery in purple shadow. She remembered that especially, how his eyes had looked in shadow, still so icily blue that they shone almost like a wolf's.

The sounds from the saloon had drifted to them, a changed sound, coming closer, breaking apart. They might be discovered any instant.

He'd kissed her again, almost ruthlessly. It had been . . . scandalous and wonderful. Not that she would ever admit as much to him. But she had thought, and it was perfectly logical to think so, that their arrangement was all but secured.

It was not, and she still could not reason out the why of it. Clearly, he was deeply in love with her. Oh, of course, there were men who were not at all honorable about things of that nature, she was not a dolt, after all, but Cranleigh, for every impossible trait he possessed, and there were more than a few, was honorable. He was most assuredly honorable.

He hadn't offered to marry her, you see; after two years and this the start of her third Season out, he had yet to offer and, worse, was about to go back to sea.

What was she to do? Force him? Take her slender fist to his icy blue eyes and beat him into doing right by her?

No, instead she had sought out Sophia Dalby as an ally, and that was bearing most interesting fruit. She would somehow force Cranleigh into offering for her, or she would entertain an offer from one of the men on her list. If it came to that. Surely Cranleigh would not allow it to get to that point. Didn't he, after all, have some fighting blood in him? Could he not be made to claim her? To date, his prowess seemed exclusively in bullying her about, kissing her, and not offering for her. Cranleigh really ought to have learned by now that she would not be bullied by him. But he hadn't and so he still tried.

It was exhausting, but what could she do about it? She couldn't stop him and he clearly wouldn't ruin her outright; he could have done that long ago and if he had, they'd be married by now. Why, just look at how quickly Blakes had ruined Louisa. A single evening's work and he had snared the woman of his heart. Cranleigh certainly was not cut from quite the same bolt as his brother, which was most odd.

Her thoughts must have shown on her face, giving her a most distracted air, she was sure, for into the stilted silence, the Duke of Calbourne spoke.

"Would you care to dance, Lady Amelia?"

"I'd be delighted," she answered and, taking his arm, she allowed Calbourne to lead her onto the floor for the next set.

She could feel Cranleigh glowering behind her. That delighted her almost nearly as much as dancing with Calbourne. Perhaps more.

Sixteen

OF course, what else was Penelope to feel but that she'd stumbled and fallen badly in the conversation with the Duke of Calbourne? What was to have been a display of her wit and vivacity had turned somehow into a display of her education and logic. Men hated that sort of thing, positively loathed it. She'd have to do better if she wanted to be a duchess, that was all. Simply have to do better. She was quite confident that looking a bit stupid and gullible was not at all difficult. Logic simply screamed that it should be nearly effortless. All she had to do was keep her mouth closed and her opinions to herself. Time enough after she was a duchess to speak her mind.

The question, and she had not worked this bit out, was how to attract a duke when speaking was not actually encouraged?

She'd love to ask Lord Cranleigh, as he seemed a forward sort who might actually be willing to give her a straight answer on the subject, but as he was busy staring firebolts at Amelia Caversham and the Duke of Calbourne he did not look readily available. Though, by the look of things, it did seem that somehow it should be possible to use the clear animosity between Amelia and Cranleigh to ruin things between Amelia and Calbourne. Penelope did not see at all *how* this could be done, but she did feel that it ought, and indeed, *should* be done.

"If you hadn't given her that shawl, she might have left by now," Cranleigh muttered. As she was the only one standing near him and as she had been the one to loan a shawl, Penelope presumed he was speaking to her.

"I only loaned her a shawl, Lord Cranleigh," she said as politely as possible because, after all, Cranleigh had a brother who was going to be a duke and he simply must, for that reason alone, be mollified. How stupid of Amelia Caversham to be so irritating and combative with Cranleigh. No wonder the girl had not managed to marry in two full years, coming up on three. Of course, Penelope hadn't married either, but she didn't have a duke for a father. With that sort of advantage, there truly could be no excuse. It really was imperative to get Amelia married off, clearing the field, as it were. "I felt I had little choice, the condition of her gown being what it is."

"Ruined," he whispered, staring at the dancers distractedly. At Lady Amelia? Possibly. In hatred? Distrust? Annoyance?

Penelope was far from an expert on men, but it did seem, almost, that Cranleigh watched Lady Amelia with . . . longing.

Longing?

Oh, dear, that could be made use of, though how she could not quite imagine. Certainly there must be some way to *push* Cranleigh in Amelia's direction. Oughtn't things somehow fall into place from there?

"Yes, it is quite fully ruined," Penelope said, staring at Cranleigh's profile. He was quite a hard-looking man, not at all the look one associated with nobility, even if he were an earl. Ah, well, men rarely looked as they ought and a woman made do with what was offered. "Did you happen to see how it occurred?"

Cranleigh turned his head slowly to look at her. It was a bit chilling. His eyes were a remarkable shade of blue, very pale, his gaze very steady.

"I believe she got herself tangled up in the roses. In the conservatory. Are they yours?"

Are they yours? Oh, the roses. Cranleigh's eyes, his icy stare, were enough to freeze the air in her lungs. If Amelia had been studied by those eyes, small wonder she had dashed into a bed of thorns to escape them, or rather him.

"Yes, Lord Cranleigh," she said, and they were. She had paid for them, hadn't she?

"You have a knack for flowers." It was not a question, which was such a relief as she might have been required to lie.

She smiled a reply. Let him draw whatever conclusion seemed logical to him.

"You were in the conservatory?" she asked.

Cranleigh almost smiled. "Briefly. It was quite impressive. Tell me, what is the name of the rose with the deep pink center?"

Oh, dear.

"You are familiar with horticulture, Lord Cranleigh?" she asked with a charming and innocent lilt.

"No, not particularly. It merely caught my eye."

Penelope let out a discreet sigh of relief.

"Rosa perpendicillum," she said. That sounded vaguely Latin and should do the job.

"Rosa perpendicillum?" Cranleigh said, a disturbing twinkle in his eyes. "Interesting."

"Yes, a very interesting, very rare variety," she said, "but I shan't bore you with the particulars."

"I assure you I am not bored, Miss Prestwick," he said. No, he did not look bored, but he did look amused. That would not serve her interests at all.

"No, you certainly don't give anyone the impression of being bored, Lord Cranleigh, but perhaps a bit perplexed? However Lady Amelia tore her dress, you clearly did not expect her to stay."

Cranleigh's amused look vanished like mist at the dawn, for which she was entirely relieved.

"I should think I am not alone in that, Miss Prestwick. How often does a woman stay at a ball with a torn gown?"

"How often at a ball does a woman's gown become torn?" Penelope answered.

"I should think, darling, that would depend wholly upon her partner," Sophia Dalby said, having come up behind Lord Cranleigh.

Penelope was relieved. Having to manage Lord Cranleigh on her own, particularly where her roses were concerned, was a bit of a stretch. He was a man who required so much *work*, which was the absolute worst that could be said of a man.

"And if it's the proper partner," Sophia continued, smiling at the sight of Amelia dancing with Calbourne, "then she doesn't mind at all. Don't you find that so, Lord Cranleigh?"

"Why ask me, Lady Dalby? I am not a woman with a dress to tear," he said in a most surly fashion. Penelope found it difficult not to take a step away from him, he was so off-putting. Sophia Dalby apparently experienced an entirely different reaction.

"Hardly," she said with a delicate smile, "but I do think you must admit to having some experience with tears and fine muslin gowns, musn't you? I shan't be so bold as to say you have some experience with Lady Amelia, for that would be too forward by half, wouldn't it?"

"It most certainly would," Cranleigh snapped. "And you would be entirely off the mark. I am acquainted with Lady Amelia only. As you may have observed, we are not on entirely cordial terms."

"Not *entirely* cordial," Sophia repeated softly, staring up into his formidable face. "Yes, I'm sure that's true, isn't it? How very awkward that will be if she chooses to marry Iveston."

"Iveston? She's dancing now with Calbourne," Cranleigh said, staring at Amelia and Calbourne as they did their turns like he wanted to throttle one or the other of them, perhaps both.

"Well," Sophia trilled, "what is that? A woman may dance with one man and marry another. She may even enjoy a quiet respite in a conservatory with yet another. Why not? She is a beautiful woman and beautiful women have a remarkable freedom, do they not? At least I have found it to be so."

"Are you implying that something untoward happened in the conservatory?" Cranleigh said, his gaze averted nearly reluctantly from Amelia and Calbourne to glower down at Sophia Dalby.

Penelope was delighted in equal parts that Cranleigh was not glowering at her and that Sophia was making all kinds of malicious digs at Amelia's reputation. What could be lovelier?

"Besides a ruined dress?" Sophia said silkily. "No, not at all. And it's quite clear that neither Calbourne nor Iveston believe anything at all happened, beyond an unfortunate accident, which must surely leave Lady Amelia innocent of both suspicion and rumor," and here Sophia glanced at Penelope, and Penelope, to her horror, felt her cheeks flush. "Calbourne has no hesitation in taking Amelia up and neither, darling Cranleigh, will your brother. Look now. The set has ended and she is being nearly swept away by Iveston's attention. He will claim the honor of partnering her for the next set. And isn't it lovely of him to do so? There is nothing quite so delicious as a gentleman devoted. Or don't you agree?"

It was quite obvious by the look on his face that he did not. But Cranleigh said nothing. Penelope said nothing. Sophia, who had said quite enough, said nothing more, at least for the present. What they all did was watch Amelia dance with Iveston.

❧

"CRANLEIGH is watching you, isn't he?" Iveston asked Amelia as she passed him in the dance. To her left was

Anne Warren, dancing with the Duke of Calbourne, which didn't bother her in the least as Anne Warren was to marry Lord Staverton. Calbourne, as much as he clearly liked to flirt with Anne, was safe. To her right was one of the Earl of Helston's daughters, which one Amelia wasn't certain as there were four of them and they each were green-eyed brunettes. And beautiful. And unmarried.

Everyone had come to this ball; it might as well have been held in a public room.

As she, whichever one she was, was dancing prettily with the Marquis of Penrith, Amelia decided that she could and would ignore it. As long as the girl kept her eyes and her intentions off all the dukes in the room, including the Marquis of Iveston, Amelia would continue to smile charmingly and with more delight than she had ever shown at any of these affairs since her come out.

She was going to convince Cranleigh that she was determined to marry a duke. She was quite certain that she was being very convincing. All that was left was for her to make her choice. Iveston was being attentive and Calbourne had been nearly devastating in his charm, and in his insistence that he deserved another interview.

Amelia, to her horror, actually felt slightly sick to her stomach, not at all the reaction she was supposed to be enjoying at this moment of her brilliant success on the marriage mart.

"It is amusing," Iveston said genially. "I can't remember when a woman was as sought after as you are, Lady Amelia. It is a situation that should be enjoyed to the fullest."

"You are very gracious, Lord Iveston," she said when they passed near each other again. He was so elegantly tall and such a graceful dancer, not at all like Cranleigh, who danced passably but was not nearly as elegant.

"And very, perhaps excessively, polite," one of the daughters of Helston said. She was very beautiful. She was also very rude.

"An odd sort of compliment," Anne Warren said as she passed near, Calbourne at her side.

Amelia tugged as delicately as possible at her borrowed shawl. It was a poor substitute for a flawless line of muslin, but it was allowing her to remain at the ball and for that she thought it the most beautiful shawl ever devised, even if it was a rather unattractive shade of red. She did not look her best in red, which was likely why Miss Prestwick had decided this was the perfect shawl to lend her. Oh, there was no doubt as to that. It was precisely what she would have done in similar circumstances.

"Can a compliment be odd?" Penrith said as they all passed near each other again.

"Obviously it can," Amelia said.

She was not going to share this moment with that woman, whatever her name was. She had been married, Amelia was nearly certain of that, but she had lost her husband somehow. Any woman who was careless enough to lose a husband once acquired should not go about making uncalled-for remarks to a woman who gave every appearance of soon becoming a duchess.

"As to being polite, I don't think anyone has ever accused Cranleigh of it," Iveston said. "Would you, Lady Amelia?"

Bother it, she didn't want to talk about Cranleigh now, or in fact, ever. Just hearing his name did horrible things to her composure. She had ten score of images of Cranleigh, memories that had no place and yet she couldn't expunge them. Not that she'd tried overly hard. She saw him rarely during the Season, perhaps ten or twenty times in all, and that wasn't very much, was it? Not when he was the only one who even looked at her as if he could actually see her. As if she was a desirable woman. A woman worth wanting. A woman worth taking. Her stomach rolled against her ribs. She ignored it.

"I certainly wouldn't, but perhaps I would if I knew him better," Amelia said, trying to appear pleasant.

What if Cranleigh didn't offer for her? The list was known, both Calbourne and Iveston appeared interested, indeed were insistent upon being interviewed, yet

Cranleigh still did nothing. If one discounted pushing her into a bed of thorns, which she did.

She had considered that something like this might happen. She was a logical, forward-thinking girl, after all, a girl who made plans and then threw them away when the first man who looked twice at her kissed her on the mouth. Still, a logical, rational sort of girl and she had considered that Cranleigh might not be brought round to doing the right thing, that is, marrying her, and that she would be required to follow through on the promise of the duke list.

She might actually have to marry a duke. She would marry *someone*. She was more than a little tired of sitting on the shelf, and if Cranleigh couldn't do right by her, then she'd do right by herself.

She was going to marry. Perhaps even Iveston. He certainly appeared amiable to the idea.

Marry Iveston.

Amelia looked him over as they parted again in the dance. He was not a bad-looking sort, certainly elegant of form and with quite refined features. It might be nice to be married to someone who didn't look like a street tough, someone who didn't grab her whenever there were no witnesses about. Someone who didn't kiss her and set her blood on fire.

Her stomach rolled again. She missed a step in the dance. She smiled at Iveston and pushed Cranleigh out of her thoughts. He stayed out for a full two seconds.

It was going to be so difficult as Iveston's wife. Perhaps Cranleigh would settle in America. Her stomach twisted and she quelled it sternly.

"Don't people become less polite as you know them better?" Helston's daughter said. As if she didn't have enough trouble tonight with both a torn gown and Cranleigh alternating between glowering at her and talking in an entirely too friendly manner to Penelope Prestwick, now she had this woman, a widow of some ill repute, if she wasn't mistaken, pestering her as well.

Life was going to be so much more pleasant as a

duchess. She was quite certain people would be so much better behaved. Just look how she and Hawksworth were so very careful around Aldreth, and he was their father. An acquaintance ought to be very easy to manage.

"Lady Paignton," Lord Penrith said to his partner, which was such a help as now she remembered the story completely, "you are not concentrating on the steps."

"Lord Penrith," Lady Paignton replied when they passed near to each other again, "I know all the steps. I thought you understood that."

Whereupon Mrs. Warren smiled and shook her head at Calbourne, who smirked and very nearly shrugged. At Mrs. Warren! It was not to be borne. She had not quite, *quite* decided upon Lord Iveston, and she did not at all appreciate the Duke of Calbourne being literally snatched up before her very gaze, nearly from beneath her very hand.

At least no one was paying any particular attention to Lady Paignton, which was perfectly understandable as she had been properly married to a complete rogue who had got himself killed in a duel defending her honor, which had required considerable defending, the rumor went. Looking at her now, Amelia believed it completely. Lady Paignton was the most overtly seductive woman she had ever encountered, not including Sophia Dalby naturally. Lady Paignton was so much more common about it. *Very* much more common. By every rumor, Lord and Lady Paignton had been well matched, except that now he was dead, of course.

Amelia had been out long enough to be aware of which women she had to be wary of: women who wanted dukes, women who wanted husbands, women who were beautiful, women who were clever, women who were seductive, women who had fortunes. The list was long and comprehensive, the result being that it was the rare woman indeed who was not a threat to her search for a husband. In fact, looking about the room now, there were only two women she even remotely trusted not to steal a man right out from under her, no pun intended—Aunt Mary and Sophia Dalby.

It did strike her as odd that Sophia Dalby, a perfectly deadly sort of woman where men were concerned, was on her very short list of trusted females, but she was and Amelia, perhaps because the list was so very short, was disinclined to remove her from it. In fact, with the way the evening was becoming more complicated with each step of the dance, Amelia more than ever wanted Sophia's aid.

In keeping Anne Warren away from Calbourne and Cranleigh.

In keeping Lady Paignton away from Iveston and Cranleigh.

In keeping Miss Prestwick away from Calbourne, Iveston, and Cranleigh.

In fact, the only man that Amelia was perfectly willing to throw into the arms of any available female was Lord Dutton. Lord Penrith was far too pleasant a man to throw about that way, but Dutton, he should be punished for making Louisa's life such a misery until Louisa had discovered that she loved Blakes and not Dutton.

It also occurred to her, as she was making her final move in the dance, that she was developing the loathsome habit of making lists.

It also was perfectly obvious that Cranleigh was on every list she mentally complied. Of course, the tears in her dress would explain that; he was in her thoughts, how could he not be? He'd very literally attacked her, as he was in the habit of doing, as long as she was making lists of habits, which she was *not* going to do.

Cranleigh was so ill-mannered, so effortlessly and eternally ill-mannered. Why, he never should have kissed her that first time. What could he have been thinking? Certainly not that she was irresistible. Two full years out had proved how very resistible she was, especially to him.

He had not offered for her.

She wasn't particularly beautiful, not nearly beautiful enough. She was attractive enough in a very predictable sort of way, but she certainly wasn't as ethereally lovely as Anne Warren nor as seductively tempting as Lady

Paignton, both forced into her speculations as they each stood not two feet away from her. And then there was the classically beautiful Penelope Prestwick, who was still chatting up Cranleigh, who looked not at all disposed to move away from her.

For the most obvious reason her gaze stayed on Cranleigh and Penelope Prestwick. What a perfectly devious woman she was, to try to make inroads with Iveston through his brother. For that was what it was, clearly. She couldn't, wouldn't have any interest in Cranleigh and he none in her. Why, he had a well-established habit, one might even call it a compulsion, to attack Amelia with kisses every time he saw her.

Amelia smiled, forgetting all about Iveston and Calbourne and certainly about Penrith, but not forgetting a single thing about Cranleigh.

He did like to kiss her.

"A lively dance," Mrs. Warren said to the Duke of Calbourne, her eyes shining.

"A lively partner," Calbourne answered. "I thank you, Mrs. Warren. You never disappoint."

Yes, there was that. Mrs. Warren had something of a history of being lively with Calbourne. She had done it at Hyde House not a week past and here she was doing it again. Amelia had no personal animosity toward Anne Warren, none at all, but she did think that for a woman about to be married, Mrs. Warren was out in Society rather a lot. And without her future husband, too.

"I should think Lord Staverton must be most disappointed that he so rarely sees you, Mrs. Warren," Amelia said. "Or I presume so as I never see you with him."

Anne turned her very pretty face from Calbourne's to Amelia; her eyes looked silvery in the candlelight, her skin like pearl. It was most inconvenient.

"Lord Staverton is visiting his various properties in advance of our marriage. He wants all to be in order before we leave on our wedding trip," Anne answered without a hint of irritation. She was clearly a superb actress.

"And when is the wedding to take place?" Lord Dutton asked, having elbowed his way into their small circle of conversation. It was a pity that he hadn't managed to elbow Lady Paignton out of it. Amelia was forming a fast dislike of Lady Paignton as it was becoming obvious that she was nearly brazen.

"Within the month, Lord Dutton," Mrs. Warren answered firmly. "Hardly any time at all to make my preparations."

"You must have them well in hand to be out as often as you are," Amelia said.

Mrs. Warren smiled and answered, "Lord Staverton insisted, as does Lady Dalby. I believe it is so that I will find my feet in Society before becoming Lady Staverton. I should so dislike being a disappointment to my husband."

"An impossibility," Calbourne said. "Wouldn't you agree, Dutton?"

Lord Dutton stared at Mrs. Warren with an intensity that was not at all called for. "I would."

"If you will excuse me?" Iveston said, already drifting away. "I did enjoy our dance, Lady Amelia."

Amelia could feel panic rising in her throat. Penrith and Lady Paignton had already left the room, Mrs. Warren was smiling beguilingly at Calbourne, who was smiling back at her. And Dutton, dear dreary Dutton, was looking at Mrs. Warren with all the subtlety of a tiger.

"As did I, Lord Iveston," Amelia said, attempting an even tone. As it was hardly possible, she supposed she could be excused for the tremor in her voice. "It was a lovely prelude to our interview. Where shall we conduct it? Someplace more private than this, surely."

Everyone stopped, turned, and stared at her. She couldn't have been happier. She was so very tired of everyone ignoring her at the first opportunity. Everyone except Cranleigh. If being slightly scandalous and forward was what was required to keep a man's interest, well then, that's what it required. There was little point in bemoaning the fact. She had suspected long ago, long before Cranleigh's first kiss, that men were little better than ravaging beasts. After Cranleigh's first kiss, and indeed upon all his subsequent kisses, she had known it for a fact.

Iveston looked down at her from his very compelling height, his brow furrowed in surprise. He glanced around the room almost negligently, smiled slightly at her, and said softly, "Perhaps the conservatory?"

Amelia swallowed firmly and answered, "Why not?"

Seventeen

THE entire room watched Lord Iveston escort Lady Amelia Caversham from the ballroom, through the drawing room, which was scarcely empty, and into the conservatory, which was. It was just as it had been, the roses scenting the air, the chandeliers overhead casting a twinkling light against the dark glass, the sound of the music coming from the other side of the wall.

Iveston did not close the door, but he didn't need to. His two younger brothers, by some silently communicated command, stood guard at the portal. Guarding her against ruination, was all she could conclude. She and Iveston were not alone, not actually, not with both George and Josiah Blakesley within sight if not earshot.

Iveston's hair was very blond, quite unlike Cranleigh's shade, which was very dark. She couldn't help but notice the difference as she had *just* been in the same room with Cranleigh. It would have been rather silly of her not to make a comparison, wouldn't it? Very logical. Some might even argue that she was *forced* to make a comparison. She certainly would.

Where was Cranleigh?

It was logical to wonder. He had watched her leaving the ballroom with Iveston, watched her like a wolf watches a rabbit, and she did not care for the comparison to a rabbit at all. She was not a rabbit.

Where *was* Cranleigh? He was not guarding the door, which she couldn't imagine him doing anyway.

"You had a question for me, Lady Amelia?" Iveston asked politely.

He was such a nice, calm man, so pleasant and mild, even if a bit quiet and withdrawn. That could be so restful. Surely she should enjoy being married to a restful man.

"Thank you, Lord Iveston," she said, wrapping the shawl tightly around her and keeping well clear of the roses. "I did. I first must say again how thoughtful it is of you to indulge me this way. It is an indulgence, I know, and it is only your superb manners and remarkable disposition that are responsible for this rare opportunity."

"Lady Amelia," he said, ducking his chin to his chest and smiling almost shyly, "it can hardly be deemed a rare opportunity when Calbourne has already . . . indulged."

Was that a jest? A play on words? Could it be that Iveston was attempting to be witty? "As to my remarkable disposition, do you know me well enough to claim such intimate knowledge?"

She had offended him. It was a perfectly dreadful beginning. This is what came of trying to charm a man. Best to just speak plainly and hope for the best. It had worked well enough with Calbourne, obviously, as he was still in the game.

In the game? She was becoming as common as any actress.

"No, Lord Iveston," she said, looking at him directly, "but I would. Hence, the interview."

"Proceed, Lady Amelia." Iveston leaned his shoulders back against the only solid wall in the room, the shared wall with the ballroom. He looked the picture of negligent elegance.

He looked almost nothing like Cranleigh. He behaved almost nothing like Cranleigh either. Cranleigh, after as many minutes as this, would have had her back against the wall and would have been kissing her breathless.

Amelia sighed and remembered her resolve.

"Do you enjoy horticulture, Lord Iveston?" she asked.

"I enjoy the results of horticulture, Lady Amelia."

"Do you like roses?"

"I like them well enough when they don't tear pretty dresses."

"Do you enjoy being in Town for the Season?"

"I enjoy Hyde House, Lady Amelia, and being among friends, in Town or not."

Amelia sighed again, heavily. It was not going well. It was going exactly like an . . . interview. Not at all what she had in mind. It was so much easier to talk to a man when Sophia was doing most of the talking. Yes, well, she wasn't inviting Sophia into the conservatory. She would manage on her own.

Bracing her spine, Amelia said, "Do you find me attractive, Lord Iveston?"

Iveston came up off the wall. It was an improvement.

"I find you very attractive, Lady Amelia, as I'm certain everyone does."

Oh, bother, that was hardly the right answer. It was so very *mild*. Perhaps being mild was not such a good thing after all.

"At the moment, Lord Iveston, I care only what you think."

"You are a beautiful woman, Lady Amelia," he said softly, his blue eyes shining at her. "Surely you have been told that before now?"

If one counted Cranleigh, then yes, she had. But she was not counting Cranleigh.

"At the moment, I care only what you think," she repeated, smiling.

"But, Lady Amelia, you must care what I think for

always and must care only what I think. Isn't that the point of this exercise? You want a husband."

Amelia's smile faltered and died, her cheeks flushed in embarrassment. It was to be hoped that it was too dark for Iveston to observe that.

"I do want a husband," she said. "Do you not want a wife?"

There. She'd said it plainly.

Iveston left the wall entirely and walked toward her. She did not move, feeling no need to back away from him, to put distance between them. How different he was from Cranleigh. How different this all was from Cranleigh dragging her into the conservatory.

This was better, obviously, but it *was* different.

"I think the question, Lady Amelia, is whether I am the husband you want," he said, standing very close to her. She felt . . . nothing. "Whether you are the wife I want," he finished in a hushed undertone.

"And you do not," she said, feeling . . . nothing.

"Answer first for yourself, Amelia," he whispered, taking her hand in his and lifting her fingertips to his mouth for a brief brush of his lips. "Do you want *me*?"

No.

But she wouldn't say it, couldn't say it. She didn't want anything or anyone but Cranleigh when he held her, kissed her, touched her. When Cranleigh was in the room, she felt *something*. Not the nothing she was feeling now.

"I don't know you well enough to know that, Lord Iveston," she said instead.

What else could she say? She wanted to marry. Cranleigh, after two years, had not offered for her. If not Cranleigh, then *someone*. She *would* marry and she would marry well, and Cranleigh would suffer to see her so well married. She would be happy and Cranleigh would suffer. That's all she wanted.

"Then know me better," he said, dipping his head down and kissing her softly on the mouth.

Too softly, too gently, too mild a kiss from too mild a man. It was a disaster from start to finish, which was mercifully swift. He lifted his head and smiled down at her. She smiled back. And then she laughed. And he laughed.

And then Cranleigh entered, shoving past his brothers, and no one laughed.

❦

"LORD Cranleigh doesn't look at all pleased, does he?" Sophia said.

"And why should he look pleased?" Lady Jordan snapped, "Cranleigh can't want Iveston to be forced into marriage. It only just happened with Henry!"

Sophia cast her gaze down to Mary, who was very petite. "I suppose it would be awful for you, to have two nieces in as many weeks find themselves ruined and married into Hyde's family. I shouldn't think Melverley would let you anywhere near Lady Eleanor if that happened. Once can happen to even the most diligent of chaperones, but twice . . ."

Mary's brow furrowed in frantic thought. As she was not entirely sober, thinking took a bit more effort than usual.

"I suppose that would look queer," Lady Jordan said.

"Naturally, it's perfectly obvious to all present that you had nothing to do with it, but as Aldreth and Melverley are never at these things . . ." Sophia shrugged.

"I never should have agreed to this, Sophia," Mary grumbled. "It was only because of your brother that I did, and now he's gone off again."

It was a little known fact, but of course Sophia knew it and all the details that accompanied it, that her brother John and Lady Jordan had been quite intimate at one time and that they each remembered their affair fondly. Perhaps it was truer to say that Lady Jordan, whose life had not been the most pleasant, remembered John with longing while John remembered Mary with tenderness. She was speculating, certainly, but it was solid speculation and she didn't doubt the basic truth of it for a moment.

"He wanted to get the boys out of Town for a bit. You can certainly imagine how being in a city hampers their activities." Ah, yes, their *activities*. "He'll return."

"Yes, but when?" Mary snapped.

It was a peculiar truth that Mary, Lady Jordan, had very little tolerance for Sophia, based upon some ancient misunderstanding of events, she was positive, while enjoying a deep fascination, even an infatuation with John. Life was full of these little oddities of circumstance. John found it entirely pleasant, as well he should.

"It shouldn't be long now," Sophia answered truthfully. "But about Lady Amelia, you will continue on with it, won't you? It won't do her a bit of harm and will result in a perfectly lovely marriage. I am quite certain of that."

"You're always certain of things, Sophia. It's not entirely proper and it's never comfortable."

"Odd, I find it extremely comfortable," Sophia answered brightly. "I'm certain Lady Amelia would agree. She is doing so well now, the men simply lining up. I do think that it's good for her and does Aldreth credit."

"Aldreth credit? You don't know him at all if you can say that."

"Possibly," Sophia said mildly. "Another week then?"

"Do you think John will return in another week?"

It was a bargain, pure and simple, and they both understood it as such.

"Possibly," Sophia repeated.

Mary nodded, and that was that.

❧

"You've just arranged something, Lady Dalby. I wonder what it is," Ruan said.

Mary had wandered off in the direction of the necessary and Ruan had wandered over to her. Although it was perfectly obvious that Ruan didn't wander anywhere. He always made it a point to be precisely where he wanted to be. That he wanted to be with her was hardly surprising.

"An assignation?" she suggested.

"Impossible. I've yet to be told the time and place. Hardly an effective assignation without those necessary details," he said.

"Lord Ruan, you are not the only man in the room."

"Lady Dalby, I am the only man that matters."

"Doesn't that depend upon what a woman needs from a man?"

"A woman only needs one thing from a man and we both know what that is," he said with the barest hint of a smile.

"A cash settlement?" she asked.

"No, Lady Dalby," he whispered, leaning down so that his mouth was a scant few inches from her cheek, "a good inducement to scream."

Sophia smiled and moved her head away from his mouth. "Lord Ruan, I scream most regularly, but thank you for the offer. It shows such pluck."

"Pluck?" he said, his mouth twisting into a wry smile. "Perhaps I should compose a rhyme, an invigorating poem of perfect couplets?"

"Lord Ruan, you astound me. Is there anything you won't attempt?"

"No, Lady Dalby, there isn't," he said, and he wandered off into the crowd in the drawing room.

But, of course, he didn't wander at all.

❧

CRANLEIGH hadn't wandered into the conservatory, far from it. Unfortunately, he wasn't the only man who was attempting to enter. The Duke of Calbourne was there, demanding in a rather loud voice to George Blakesley that as there was a perfectly accessible conservatory in the house he be allowed to access it.

Not only Calbourne, but the Marquis of Dutton was skulking about, clearly trying to browbeat Josiah into letting him enter the conservatory, though why Dutton should have any reason to see a conservatory was beyond comprehension. Dutton, it was widely known, had no interest in flowers or Amelia and those were the only attractions in the conservatory. Unless he wanted to see Iveston? No, but that was ridiculous.

About as ridiculous as this entire evening.

As Cranleigh was pushing his way through the ever-deepening throng to the glass doors separating the conservatory from the drawing room, the Duke of Edenham bumped into him.

Hell and blast, another duke.

"Excuse me," Edenham said. "It's turned into quite a crush. I had no idea."

"Who did?" Cranleigh mumbled.

"Who did?" Edenham repeated comically. "Why, Sophia certainly. She's the one who's arranged all this."

"All *this*?" Cranleigh said, knowing he sounded like an idiot and unable to stop himself.

"Of course," Edenham said pleasantly, as if this were the most ordinary conversation in the most ordinary of circumstances when it was nothing of the kind. "It's quite entertaining, isn't it? And quite impossible to avoid falling into. The sort of thing that one must be a part of or be forever found lacking."

"I beg your pardon? I'm not following," Cranleigh said, elbowing a gentleman who had pushed into his kidneys, jarring him unpleasantly. Everything about this evening was unpleasantly jarring.

"Aren't you? But how is that possible? You are one of the main players, Lord Cranleigh," Edenham said almost jovially. "I wasn't witness to your performance of dragging Lady Amelia into the conservatory, but everyone is talking of it. That, and her ruined dress. Naturally, no one is holding you accountable for that, but it certainly made for high entertainment. As these balls are notoriously dull, I can only thank you. What did you discuss in there? And do you think your brother is having a similar discussion with her now?"

"Bloody hell," he muttered, an image of Amelia caught among the roses searing him, her mouth swollen by kisses.

After that, Cranleigh had no trouble at all pushing his way to the front of the crowd. One look at his face and both Josiah and George gave way and allowed him entrance, which did set up a fuss with the other twenty or thirty men pushing for their chance at Amelia in the conservatory.

God above, what had he started? He never should have dragged her in there. He never should have torn her dress. He never should have kissed her again. Again and again.

But after that first time, how could he not have kissed her again?

He never should have kissed her the first time, that was the truest answer.

Truest? No, not that. He had to kiss her. It had been impossible to not kiss her. That he had kept it to kissing for two long years was the true test of his resistance. Small wonder he was in a foul mood most of the time.

Into the lightly scented conservatory he strode for a second time that night. But this time, instead of blazing up like a volcano in his arms, Amelia stood with her hand against Iveston's chest, laughing up into his smiling face. No, more than that, they were *both* laughing. And Amelia had just been kissed. He knew what she looked like having just been kissed, none knew that particular look better than he.

He was going to have to kill his brother. Damned inconvenient bit of work.

Seeing him, Amelia stepped away from Iveston. Good move, but late.

"Oh, hello, Cranleigh," Iveston said pleasantly, not even bothering to put on an appearance of shame or regret or anything remotely appropriate to the situation. "We were just finishing up. I think Lady Amelia knows everything she needs to know about me now."

Hell and blast!

"Does she? And what does she know, besides how you taste?" Cranleigh said, striding into the room, his coat catching on a few rose branches, nearly toppling the pots that held them.

"Lord Cranleigh!" Amelia said sharply, the color rising in her cheeks. Whether from shame or from the kiss it was impossible to tell. "This can't possibly concern you."

"It most certainly does concern me," Cranleigh said. "He's my brother. I can't allow him to get tangled up in soiled skirts, if you take my meaning, *Lady* Amelia."

"Soiled skirts?" she blazed. "You are presumptuous, sir. If you will excuse me, Lord Iveston," she said, her voice a hiss of anger, "I shall return to the ballroom. Thank you for speaking to me privately."

"Privately?" Cranleigh said, catching her by the arm and turning her so that she faced the doorway to the conservatory, where she could plainly see the thirty or so men pressed there, kept out only by George and Josiah, and what looked to be the addition of five or six footmen. "You have been far from discreet, Amy. The whole world wants just the sort of interview you gave to Iveston. You look a ripe girl. I'm certain you can manage them."

"Really, Cranleigh, it's not at all what—" Iveston said, looking seriously alarmed. He should look alarmed. He'd kissed Amelia and there was no going back from that.

How was he going to explain to Hyde that he'd killed his heir? It was going to be awkward, to say the least.

"Iveston," Cranleigh interrupted, "I've always entertained a healthy fondness for you, but I am very close to killing you. Try to make it hard for me, will you? Don't say another word. It would help very much if you'd leave. Now."

Iveston, because he was a reasonable sort on most occasions, closed his mouth, bowed crisply to Amelia, and left the conservatory. The crowd parted beautifully and then closed ranks again, but not before the Duke of Calbourne had shoved his way in, the Duke of Edenham following on his heels.

It was almost like a bearbaiting. And Cranleigh was the bear.

"You've had your chance, Cal," Edenham was saying as they entered. "It's been decided against you. Step aside, man, and let another attempt it."

Amelia turned a stunning shade of white, her lips looking particularly rosy by comparison. Or perhaps that was only because she was surrounded by pink roses. He didn't suppose it mattered either way, unless it was because she'd just been kissed, then he'd have to revisit the idea of killing Iveston. He'd never known Iveston to be so much trouble. Amelia, on the other hand, was nothing but trouble.

How all Society could think her sweet, docile, and nearly invisible was a mystery to him. She was anything but invisible; it would have been a help if she had been. Sweet and docile? Even further folly. She was fire and flame, exploding all over him whenever he was near her, for instance, when they were both in London at the same time. That was more than close enough to do him damage.

"See what you've done?" he snarled at her.

"*I've* done! I'm not the one who stormed in here and made a fuss over a simple, private conversation!"

"We both know what happens when you try to have private conversations with men, Amy," he whispered, pushing her behind him, into the rosebushes, again. Not that he cared. "You find yourself kissing them in no time."

"I do not!"

He gifted her with a look that was only fitting to her denial.

She gifted him with a shove, and a hard one, against his shoulder. It was a solid shove and did her credit.

"Lady Amelia," Edenham said, looking eminently dignified, which was an accomplishment, considering the situation, "I've been made aware that you are conducting interviews for a post and are considering only a very select few for the position."

The Duke of Edenham was a very handsome man, even Cranleigh could see it. He was tall and elegantly constructed, his hair brown, his eyes brown, and features quite remarkably arranged. He was, it was to be supposed, every young girl's dream. As to that, he was likely every old girl's dream. His title was one of the oldest. His estate was one of the loveliest. His fortune was deep and his children were small. There was the small matter of his having buried three wives, but for the honor of being a duchess, it was to be assumed that a woman could overlook that tiny incumbrance.

"I can't think how you could have heard that," Amelia said softly, trying to push past Cranleigh. Cranleigh reached behind him and shoved her back into the shrubbery. He heard snagging fabric. Perfect.

"It hardly matters, does it?" Edenham said. "These things do get round. I only wondered, and in fact hoped, that I had made your very select list. Have I?"

He said it like a love-struck suitor when he was no such thing. He damned well had better be no such thing.

"You very much have, Duke," she said, laying the flat of her hand on Cranleigh's back and trying to push him out of the way. He wasn't in any frame of mind to be pushed. "In fact, I should greatly enjoy getting to know you better."

"She certainly would," Cranleigh said, "unfortunately, she is unable to do so."

"I certainly am able," Amelia said, pushing to get around him. As she was wedged rather neatly between no less than five rose shrubs, all of them nicely thorny, he had the satisfaction of knowing she was well and truly trapped.

"Are you?" Cranleigh said, and turning to face her, he very simply and without any trouble at all, ripped a long and gaping gash in her fine muslin gown. With his bare hands.

It was most satisfying.

She stood there, her dress a ruin, the red shawl a ruin, her chemise and stays intact, but that could hardly matter.

There was the sound of rending fabric, to be sure, and then there was silence. Even the throng in the drawing room fell silent. Edenham and Calbourne were most definitely silent.

Amelia was not, at least not for long.

Ignoring Cranleigh completely, something she had long practice at, Amelia gathered her dress and shawl around her and, upon some final ripping from the thorns grabbing at her muslin, she walked like a queen, or a duchess, around Cranleigh to face Edenham and Calbourne as they both stood there in mild shock.

"I shall be At Home on Saturday. I look forward to our conversation," she said sweetly, as if Cranleigh were not there. As if he hadn't just ripped the clothes from off her body. Something he'd dreamed of doing more than once, now that he thought about it.

"Lady Amelia," Calbourne said, elbowing just a bit past Edenham, "allow me to assist you."

"Thank you," she said, taking Calbourne's coat round her white shoulders, still so icily calm that Cranleigh wanted to kiss her out of it. And he could, too. Years of practice and all. "Please, come round on Saturday also, if you wish. It wouldn't hurt to rethink some of my previous decisions."

"I would be honored, Lady Amelia," Calbourne said, looking at Edenham like he'd won at the Newmarket races.

And here she looked over her shoulder at Cranleigh, her look not frozen, but blazing. Just for him. Just for him she blazed. He got rare pleasure out of that.

"You, Lord Cranleigh, are a thug," she said.

Cranleigh bowed and said, "No need to rethink that, is there, Amelia?"

She didn't answer him. He hadn't expected that she would.

Eighteen

"I'LL never be able to wear that shawl again," Penelope
Prestwick said, idly shuffling cards by the fire.

"You never liked that shawl much," her brother George
answered her. He was lying on his back on the sofa in the
family drawing room, studying the shadows on the ceiling.

"She's got them all now," Penelope mused. "All of them.
Being interviewed."

"If you're clever, you'll auction that shawl off. You could
make a fortune," George said, caught in his own musings.

"You wouldn't think a duke would tolerate being treated
that way. I certainly wouldn't, were I duchess."

"I wonder if you should auction it whole?" George ran
his hands down his waistcoat. "Perhaps in pieces is the way
to go. Two-inch strips?"

"By the time she makes her choice, whoever's left
will probably leave Town in disgrace at being so publicly
rejected."

"How many strips do you think, at two inches wide?"

"She's bound to choose one. Why not? I would. I wonder which one? Iveston's the youngest and he's never been

married. That counts quite a lot. No woman would actually choose to be second, would she? And Edenham and Calbourne already have heirs. No, she'll choose Iveston."

"Given how the shawl got itself torn, the thing to do might be to offer it to Lady Amelia, whole, or as whole as it is. She might be willing to pay dearly for the evidence. Especially as she'll be a duchess soon. She can't want something like that in someone's library, framed, on show. You should make the offer, anyway. Let her choose."

"What?" Penelope said, dropping the cards on the table. "Of course she'll choose. Isn't that what I've been saying?"

"What?" George said, lifting his head from off the sofa cushion. "I'm just agreeing with you, Pen. She'll choose. Why not?"

"Of course why not? She has every man in Town worth having simply lining up. It's disgraceful."

George looked at his sister and then dropped his head back down on the cushions.

"It may be disgraceful, but it's effective."

Yes, there was that.

❧

SOPHIA studied the print fresh out of Hannah Humphrey's shop on St. James's Street. "It's very effective, isn't it?"

"Effective as what?" Anne asked.

"Why, as a prompt, naturally," Sophia said.

"Sophia," Anne said with a sigh, "I can't understand any of this. How is this going to help Lady Amelia get a husband? No husband can want this sort of thing going around about his future wife."

"No, I shouldn't think he would," Sophia said with a laugh that was not entirely polite.

"You haven't got some secret revenge going against Lady Amelia, have you? She seems a sweet girl, innocent of even good sense."

"Yes, she does have that air about her," Sophia said pleasantly, holding the print in better light, studying it with a grin of almost animal satisfaction.

"Sophia?" Anne prompted. "This isn't about revenge, is it?"

"Against that darling girl? Don't be absurd, Anne. You're seeing . . . why," Sophia smiled, "you're seeing an Indian behind every tree."

It was not at all confidence inspiring as a reply.

❧

AMELIA stared out the first-floor window and felt whatever confidence remaining within her tear into pieces, much like Penelope Prestwick's red shawl. They were lined up. Literally. She was formally At Home and they were lined up, nearly into the center of Berkeley Square, blocking traffic, both foot and horse.

Aldreth House was large, indeed grand, but the butler, Yates, hadn't been prepared for such a large crowd and so had begun to refuse admittance, which resulted in the crowd growing. Apparently, when a man could not get what or where he wanted, getting it or there, or her, became *all* he wanted. She hadn't understood that about men at all. But she would have wagered her dress, the Prestwick shawl, and her reputation that Sophia Dalby did. And, in fact, she had wagered just that.

"Yates?"

"Yes, my lady," Yates said. He looked overwhelmed, very nearly sweaty.

"Send someone round to Dalby House. Have the messenger request Lady Dalby's presence here, as soon as is convenient for her."

"Yes, my lady," Yates said. He sounded relieved. Clever man.

❧

"BUT, darling, how glorious," Sophia said when she was admitted, to the protest of the men standing at the door. "You have them precisely where a woman wants a man, standing at the ready, eager to provide her with every pleasure. Isn't this fun?"

It was not fun.

Sophia had come alone, for which Amelia was grateful. She couldn't have borne dealing with Anne Warren just now. Or with Aunt Mary. Mary, ever since the night of the Prestwick ball, had not been readily available. She would have suspected that Aunt Mary was busy with Mr. John Grey, Sophia's brother, since it had recently and most shockingly been revealed to her by Mary herself, rather more deeply in her cups than was usual even for her, that she had at some younger point in her life engaged in some sort of relationship with Mr. Grey.

Amelia was positive that it was the most innocent and tenuous of relationships. Or nearly positive. Still, that Aunt Mary had at one time been on more than speaking terms with an Indian, and worse yet, clearly would like to be on more than speaking terms with him again, well, the only reason that Amelia did not suspect that Aunt Mary was abandoning her function as her chaperone was because Mr. Grey was at the Dalby estate of Marshfield Park. Which left her with only one conclusion available, that Aunt Mary had abandoned her because of the scandalous events on the night of the Prestwick ball.

Just when a girl needed a chaperone most, she was left with Sophia Dalby. That was an odd form of justice, to be sure.

Yates had shown Sophia into the library at the front of the house and they were looking out the large window together, Sophia in delight and Amelia in horror.

"This isn't at all what I expected, Lady Dalby," Amelia said.

"No?" Sophia asked brightly. "You didn't expect to be pursued by every available man in Town?"

"Of course not!" Amelia said sharply, keeping her gaze out to the street below. "And *he's* not even available," she said, pointing. "I met him at a musicale a year ago and he's married! Lord Stilby or Stillbough or some such."

"Are you certain?" Sophia said, her brow furrowed in disappointment. "Perhaps she's died."

"Then he should be in mourning!"

"A man can only mourn for so long and then he becomes tired of it," Sophia said. "Men are so easily bored, particularly when it comes to remembering women."

"That is not the point, Lady Dalby," Amelia said. "I only wanted, that is, I only agreed to consider dukes. These men, this crowd, is not a crowd of dukes!"

"Well, of course, darling," Sophia soothed. "There are only so many dukes to go around. But you can't have expected all the other men in Town to be discarded without the opportunity of presenting themselves for your scrutiny."

"I certainly did expect that! I expected precisely that, and why should I not? Dukes, Lady Dalby, dukes are—"

"But darling," Sophia interrupted, "men can't be sorted quite as easily as all that. Of course, a woman *will* sort them, naturally, but they never tolerate being obviously sorted. I thought you understood that. Men are quite unyielding in that regard. They simply must be seen to measure up, to compete and to best all other men. Of course, they can't, but they must feel they've had their day, you see. I thought I had explained all this to you. The need to compete? The drive to win?"

Yes, that did sound unhappily familiar.

"Then this throng has nothing to do with the events at the Prestwick ball?"

"Don't be absurd, darling," Sophia said. "Of course it does. Didn't you expect some sort of a response to having the dress nearly torn off your very lovely body?"

Amelia had no answer to that. She was too appalled to even blush.

"Oh, look, there's Cranleigh now," Sophia said with a smile. "Fighting his way in, I see. He is rather a brawler, isn't he? I begin to wonder how you escaped the conservatory with your chemise intact. You *were* wearing a chemise?"

"Of course!"

"Just wondering," Sophia said casually, keeping her

gaze on the street below, where Cranleigh truly was . . . brawling, just like a common sailor.

"He appears to be trying to get them to disperse," Sophia said. "Small chance of that. He's quite outnumbered."

He was that. Cranleigh, built not unlike a young ox, was pushing and shoving and punching all the men who stood between him and the door to Aldreth House. There had to have been thirty men, conservatively. He didn't seem to care.

Amelia felt her heart hammer to bursting in her chest just watching him.

Fighting his way to her? That was precisely to the point.

"Will your butler allow him entry, should he make it to the door?" Sophia asked. "Oh, that was a cunning blow," she said, sounding almost wistful. "I must say, Cranleigh can hold his own. I do find that an attractive quality, don't you?"

She most certainly did.

"Why, look at that," Sophia said, smiling at the scene below them. "I do think Cranleigh has just hit Calbourne on the mouth. Calbourne doesn't look at all pleased, but then, who would?"

Amelia shamed herself completely by standing riveted at the window, watching Cranleigh hit everyone within reach just to get to her door. He *was* a complete brawler. It was slightly adorable of him.

"Was that Dutton who just took a fist to the belly?" Sophia said. "Yes, it was, wasn't it?" Shaking her head in obvious amusement, she added, "That does seem to happen to him quite frequently, by all reports. I've heard a rumor, unsubstantiated, naturally, that he might not be allowed back into White's. He appears to instigate all sorts of violence in the other members. He always seemed so pleasant to me." Sophia shrugged and smiled. "But then, I do find most men to be pleasant, don't you?"

Amelia dragged her gaze away from Cranleigh, who was now arguing with Calbourne and pointing at Edenham.

Edenham was here as well? Amelia had just enough time to scowl in annoyance at Sophia before Penrith leaned down to help Dutton to his feet, and was shoved by Dutton into Edenham for his efforts. Edenham did not look pleased.

Neither did Dutton.

Neither did Penrith.

"Penrith, too?" Sophia said. "You *are* doing well, Lady Amelia. I thought he had the beginnings of an *affaire* started with Lady Paignton. You seem to have quite eclipsed her."

Amelia couldn't help herself. She preened. Just a bit. If Lady Paignton were standing here, she'd snap her fingers in her face.

"I want to say again that I did nothing to encourage any of these gentlemen. I can't think what's got into everyone," Amelia said. "All I did was talk to Calbourne. That's all."

Sophia's dark brows rose in mock astonishment. Amelia was quite certain it was mock.

"That's *all*? Darling, don't think you can dissemble with me. I was there. Of course you only talked to him, no one thinks otherwise, but it is what you said to him that began all this. Once you had spoken honestly and clearly to one duke, did you not think that all the others wouldn't demand the same? They are men, darling. They are not going to step aside and let another man take the field, as it were. Fighting is in their nature. Just look at Cranleigh if you require even more proof."

She did look at Cranleigh. His coat was torn at the collar and his pantaloons filthy. He had a bruise coming up on his left eye and a bloody lip. He didn't look at all alarmed by any of it. No, in fact, he looked energized. Empowered. Alive. Male.

"He is quite a dashing-looking man, if you like the sort," Sophia said, staring down at Cranleigh. "If I weren't so close to his mother, I do wonder . . ."

"Wonder what?" Amelia snapped.

Sophia smiled fractionally and, her gaze trained on Cranleigh, which was most annoying, said, "It's difficult to explain to a virginal girl."

"Try," Amelia said, crossing her arms over her chest.

"I am good friends, old friends, with Molly," Sophia said, watching Cranleigh with an ardent gleam in her eyes, "but even so, I can't help but wonder how he'd be."

"How he'd be what?"

Sophia laughed lightly, the sound clawing at Amelia's nerves.

"In bed, darling. How he'd be in bed. Like a tiger, I should think. Ravenous. Powerful. Perhaps even a bit ruthless. Which, as I hope one day you will find out, is quite a delicious experience."

The only reason, the *only* reason why Amelia did not physically assault Sophia in the next instant was because Yates entered the library at that precise moment.

"My lady? Are you at home for the Earl of Cranleigh?"

"I most certainly am," she said, glaring at Sophia.

Sophia merely smiled and sat herself down in languid ease on the sofa.

"I'll stay as chaperone, shall I?" Sophia said. It was not actually a question. Amelia could plainly see that Sophia was in the library to stay, perhaps for all time.

Cranleigh entered the library like a, well, like a tiger. Surely the only reason Amelia would think such a thing was because Sophia's bewitching words were still ringing in her head. A tiger. Yes, perhaps Cranleigh was a bit like a tiger. *Ruthless in bed.* There was an image to make a virgin blush.

Amelia was not blushing. All those kisses had clearly rubbed the fear off of her, at least where Cranleigh was concerned.

Cranleigh was covered in dust, his blue eyes blazing white, and something was crushed in his hand.

"Have you seen this?" he said, looking at Amelia, ignoring Sophia completely, which was quite nice of him.

"Good day, Lord Cranleigh," Amelia said stiffly, forcing

him to keep to protocol, or at least trying to force him. Tigers did not readily submit to force.

Cranleigh swallowed heavily, bowed, and said, "Good day. Lady Amelia. Lady Dalby."

"Lord Cranleigh," Sophia said silkily, her dark eyes shining, "how fit you look, quite robust. The manly arts clearly agree with you."

"You saw?" he said, looking at Amelia. "You see what's happening?"

"Well, I only arrived just before you did, Lord Cranleigh," Sophia said, answering when Cranleigh had obviously not been speaking to her at all. Really. The woman was so forward. "But I certainly saw enough to be both impressed and entertained. Well played, my lord. Of course, Lady Amelia deserves every bit of the credit for managing things so well."

"Managing things?" Cranleigh snapped. "Things are not managed, Lady Dalby, not in this fashion. She is made a laughingstock and a scandal, her name all but ruined."

"All *but* ruined?" Sophia said casually, checking the seam on her glove. "Well then, that's nothing to be upset about, is it?"

"No man will marry her now," Cranleigh said, staring at Amelia. Amelia could only stare back at him. He did look rather lovely, all dusty and bruised.

A tiger in bed. What would that entail, exactly?

"No man?" Sophia chuckled. "Impossible. I can think of three who'd take her today."

Three?

"Lady Amelia," Sophia said, "I do hate to be a bother, but could you ring for refreshment? It's been an invigorating day. Perhaps something to settle the blood, cool the ardor?"

"I'm so sorry. Of course," Amelia said, hurrying to the door to call for Yates. "Tea?"

"Madeira," Sophia said.

"Yates. Madeira," Amelia said briskly and then turned back to Sophia and Cranleigh.

Three?

"Impossible you say?" Cranleigh said. "You have yet to see this?" And he uncrumpled what he'd had clenched in his fist, shoving it at Sophia.

Sophia barely glanced at it before saying, "But of course I've seen it, Lord Cranleigh. It's a perfectly delicious print, isn't it? The rendering is quite well executed, I must say, and so quickly done. I got mine the moment the shop opened and there was quite a run on them, according to Freddy. I'm surprised there are any left."

"There weren't," Cranleigh said. "I got this one off Dutton."

Ah, the hit to the belly was now fully explained.

"A print?" Amelia said, feeling herself go light-headed. "A satire?"

"Yes, darling," Sophia said in clear delight. "Gillray did one up and it appeared in Humphrey's shop this morning. Quite a coup for you, naturally, as Humphrey only carries the best and Gillray only does the most compelling *on dits*. Why, I can't think of a girl who's had a satire done of her at your stage of life. You truly are the talk of the Town."

Amelia's knees—far from collapsing, which she did wish they'd do, to be followed by a healthy faint, which would take her out of this situation—locked in place and her breathing stilled in her lungs.

A satire. Of course there were duchesses who'd had satires made of them, the Duchess of Devonshire first and foremost among them, but they did not have satires made of them *before* they became duchesses. That was an important distinction.

Aldreth would send her to a nunnery in Castille. Did they still have nunneries?

"And when Aldreth hears of it?" Cranleigh asked Sophia, not at all politely.

"Isn't he out of Town?" Sophia asked in return, as if that solved anything. Yes, he was out of Town, but no one stayed out of Town forever.

Yates knocked at that moment and brought in the Madeira on a tray with many more than three glasses. When Amelia looked at him, the question in her eyes, Yates responded, "In the event that any of the other callers are admitted, my lady."

Yates, very forward thinking, but not altogether practical in this instance.

"How very clever you are, Yates, quite up to form," Sophia said. "I should think that Lady Amelia will begin admitting one or two at a time very soon now."

Yates? Did Sophia know Aldreth's butler? *How* did she know Aldreth's butler?

"She'll be admitting no one," Cranleigh said, beginning to pace the library as if on a very short leash.

She did wish he'd stop doing things that reinforced Sophia's tiger reference. She had enough problems already without imagining him prowling into her bedchamber, kissing her raw.

Amelia shuddered at the thought, and not in distaste, which was most inconvenient at the moment.

"Whyever not?" Sophia said, looking at Amelia. "They're here, practically storming the gates. They've seen the print, *everyone* has seen the print, and they are not alarmed by it as Lord Cranleigh so clearly is. Why is that, Lord Cranleigh? Don't you enjoy prints?"

"I am not going to do battle with you over this, Lady Dalby," Cranleigh said tightly, the veins in his neck showing most clearly.

"Aren't you?" Sophia said, leaning her dark head against the pale blue damask sofa cushion. "That sounds rather pointedly like you, Lord Cranleigh."

Cranleigh stared at Sophia, his jaw muscle working, his eyes like January frost.

"I haven't seen the print," Amelia said into the tension. "I should like to. Actually, I shouldn't like to at all, but I think I must."

Cranleigh tore his gaze away from Sophia and walked

over to where Amelia stood by the Madeira. Without a word, with only the look in his eyes to prepare her, Amelia took the crumpled print from his hands and spread it out on the secretary.

It was typical Gillray, which made it very bad indeed.

How often had she laughed at the satires done of others in her class? *Constantly* would be an accurate summation. Having a satire done of oneself was not at all laughable.

It was a rendering of the Prestwick conservatory. Amelia, looking more voluptuous than she was in fact, was shown surrounded by pots of roses, their blooms reduced and their thorns increased. Her dress was torn, her body exposed, her expression delighted. She had been made to look debauched and thrilled by the fact.

Cranleigh had been made to look worse, which should hardly have been possible. Cranleigh was a rose. He had a rose for a head, from which his face peered out from the shadows of the petals, and his hands were thorns. With his thorny hands, he was ripping her dress. Hence her delighted expression.

Oh, and another part of Cranleigh's anatomy had been made into a gigantic thorn. It protruded out of his breeches and curved wickedly in her direction.

The caption read *Lady A gets pricked.*

"Isn't it marvelous, Lady Amelia?" Sophia said. "It's quite a distinction. The Duchess of Devonshire, who has had quite a few satires done up of her, never achieved one *before* becoming a duchess. But you have. Only think what you will manage once you are a duchess in fact."

Amelia sat down slowly on the chair by the secretary, the sounds of the brawl in the street coming clearly through the library windows. "I shall never be a duchess," she whispered, still staring at the satire.

Why had Gillray drawn her as being so delighted to be mauled by Lord Cranleigh? Why should he think that a girl of good family would be delighted by such a thing, by such an act, by such a man?

By such a man.

Her gaze drifted up to Cranleigh's, who was looking at her in such stern protectiveness that it caused her breath to catch in her throat.

"Never be a duchess?" Sophia exclaimed. "Don't be absurd, darling. You are eminently more appealing now than you were a month ago. Just look out the window if you doubt me."

Cranleigh, his eyes never leaving her face, slowly dropped to one knee at her side.

"Is it still all of dukes, Amy?"

All of dukes? Did he think that was what she was, what she wanted? Hadn't he understood what kissing him meant? That all other men were dust; all other men and all other dreams were dead because Cranleigh breathed himself into her heart?

And then, because he was Cranleigh and because the library was quiet, and because he had that look and when he looked at her that way there was only and always one result, he kissed her.

Sophia was forgotten.

The satire was forgotten.

The brawl on Berkeley Square was forgotten.

It was all of Cranleigh and his mouth and his heat and his touch. He swept her up, swept her out of herself and her fears until there was only Cranleigh and only Amelia and nothing else. And nothing else was wanted. Because all that there would ever need be was right here, right now, in Cranleigh.

His mouth on hers, open and hot and seeking.

Her mouth opening in welcome, their tongues meeting like old lovers, starved for contact.

She put her hands on his chest, near his throat, and felt his heat and his strength.

His mouth moved down to her throat and she leaned her head back, letting him kiss her neck, his breath covering her, his scent enfolding her.

And then the door to the library from the vestibule opened, letting in an unwelcome rush of chill air and harsh reality.

"Amelia!" her father's voice rang out. "Remember yourself!"

Amelia jerked and pushed against Cranleigh's massive chest. Cranleigh did not jerk. Cranleigh, his expression as hard and resolved as she had ever seen it, rose to his feet, turned to face Aldreth and said, "I have just asked Lady Amelia to marry me. She has accepted. Will you give your consent?"

"I will," Aldreth said stiffly. "Is a special license necessary?"

By which he meant, was she possibly pregnant? She wanted to crawl under a rug.

"No, but I would prefer one, if you can arrange it," Cranleigh said.

How was it that Cranleigh was not quaking when confronted by Aldreth? Everyone quaked when facing Aldreth. Although, Sophia likely did not.

Whatever had happened to Sophia?

Sophia was seductively sprawled on the sofa, her head nestled against the cushions, her neck arched back and exposed. Her eyes were closed and her breathing heavy. Asleep?

"I can," Aldreth said, scanning the room. "Where is Lady Jordan? And why is Lady Dalby here?"

"Oh," Sophia said, seeming to come awake on hearing her name spoken. "I should never drink Madeira. I have no head for it. Your grace," she said, rising to her feet, looking not at all embarrassed, but then, she never did, "back from France so soon? You didn't find Paris to your liking?"

Aldreth's pale blue eyes narrowed at Sophia. Sophia smiled indulgently at him in response. Amelia would love to know how she did that, how she had acquired that fear-no-man attitude to the most intimidating of men.

"Lady Dalby," Aldreth said, his eyes glinting suspiciously, "how is it that you are in the position of chaperoning my daughter? Inadequately, I might add."

"Inadequately?" Sophia said, rising to her feet to approach Aldreth. To actually approach him! Who drew nearer to Aldreth when his eyes had that particular glint? "Have you not seen your front door, your grace? Your daughter can choose from any man among them. Is that not the point of having a Season in Town? As this is her third Season out, I should think that you would have got round to the idea of her actually marrying."

"She is to marry me. The issue is settled," Cranleigh said, in a most unhappy tone of voice.

Amelia felt the very tiniest prickling of annoyance.

"Is she?" Sophia said. "I must have missed that. Did Lord Cranleigh actually propose, Lady Amelia?"

Sophia was staring at her. Cranleigh was staring at her. Aldreth was staring at her. Both Cranleigh and Aldreth looked impatient and slightly hostile. Sophia did not. Sophia smiled at her pleasantly and tilted her dark head in inquiry.

"No," Amelia found herself saying, "not *actually*."

Cranleigh jerked slightly and scowled. Aldreth scowled. Amelia found she was not intimidated in the least. It was quite refreshing.

"Well then, shall we fling wide the doors to Aldreth House and let the gentlemen enter?" Sophia said, lifting her hands to check the condition of her hair.

"We shall not fling wide anything, Lady Dalby, as I'm sure you must know," Aldreth said.

"Whyever not, your grace? Surely you must want your daughter to marry."

"She will marry," Aldreth said. "She will marry the man who ruined her."

"Ruined her? How completely absurd. I've been in the room the entire time and Lord Cranleigh did not ruin Lady Amelia in the least."

"Not in the least? He was kissing her as I entered!" Aldreth said, raising his voice.

"A girl is not ruined by a single kiss, your grace. Certainly it requires more than that to force a girl into a premature marriage," Sophia said, apparently unmoved by Aldreth's temper. "Wouldn't you say so?"

For some reason, that remark resulted in Aldreth closing his mouth and turning to the window, to look down on the scores of men jostling in the street in front of his house.

"What of her dress? What of Gillray's satire?" Cranleigh said, his voice just as sharp as Aldreth's.

"You, of all people, Lord Cranleigh, know the truth of that," Sophia said. "Lady Amelia's dress was torn on rose thorns."

"But the satire," Cranleigh said.

"Certainly Mr. Gillray must make his way in the world like everyone else," Sophia answered, walking over to the window that faced the street. "If he should take the fact of Lady Amelia's torn dress, a dress innocently torn on an innocent rose shrub, and make a few pounds off his artistic and highly fictionalized account of how her dress became torn, should Lady Amelia be held to account? Indeed, should she be forced into marriage because of a satire?"

Put that way, it did sound absurd. Why should Amelia allow Mr. Gillray to choose her husband for her? Ridiculous. She was a duke's daughter, wasn't she? Who was Mr. Gillray to manhandle her?

"You're twisting things," Cranleigh snarled, pacing the room. "You're always twisting things to get what you want."

"I?" Sophia asked innocently, dark eyes twinkling in anything but innocence. "I have no wants here. But you, Lord Cranleigh, you have wants. I should say, based on your abrupt behavior of just minutes ago, and your being the one to have . . . invited Lady Amelia into the conservatory in the first place, that . . . well, *someone* had to give Gillray the idea for his satire."

Aldreth turned from the window at that remark and considered Cranleigh coldly. "That's very true," he said.

"It may very well be true," Cranleigh answered, just as coldly, "but I am not the man responsible."

Aldreth nodded and said, "Certainly it can't be proved."

When Cranleigh narrowed his eyes at that, looking exactly like a man who was about to call another man out onto the dueling field, Sophia spoke.

"Oh, proof," Sophia said with a negligent wave of her hand. "There has never been any proof required by anyone regarding satires. Proof resides in a court of law only, and barely there."

"What did you mean, Lady Dalby, when you said Cranleigh invited Amelia into the conservatory?" Aldreth asked. "How did she and Cranleigh find themselves there, together, alone?"

"You could ask me," Amelia said, feeling very much annoyed that no one apparently thought it important to speak to her about any of this and very much tired of being overlooked by absolutely everyone, Cranleigh most especially. "I was there, after all. I should know how I got into the conservatory."

Aldreth looked at her as he usually did, with arrogance dipped in civility. "And how did you?"

"I walked in, obviously," Amelia said. "I walked in and . . . and the flowers were lovely."

"She walked in because I forced her to," Cranleigh said, standing next to her. It was quite nice, very nearly chivalrous.

"You did not force me to anything," Amelia said over her father's stern gaze at Cranleigh. "I cannot be forced." Because it was the sort of thing that required a dueling field and she didn't want to see anyone hurt, not even Aldreth.

When both Cranleigh and Aldreth looked at her in blended pity and disbelief, Sophia said, "How true that is. You must know, as you are here in London again, Aldreth, that Lady Amelia and I have formed an alliance, the purpose of which was and is to find her a most specific sort of husband. Your daughter, much like her father, is quite, quite specific and, dare I say it, relentless in her standards. She knows what she wants and she cannot be turned from it."

Amelia forced herself to stand in dignified silence while her father and Cranleigh stared at her in something akin to alarm.

"Why, she has already declined the Duke of Calbourne and he, as you must be aware as you know his character, is most put out. He simply cannot believe he has been passed over. But there you are. Lady Amelia has found him lacking. She will not change her thoughts about him simply because Calbourne wishes it to be so. No, nor even though he even now is pressed against the doors of Aldreth House like a hound seeking shelter from the rain."

"You rejected Calbourne?" Aldreth said, looking at her most strangely. In fact, it was a rather strange occurrence for Aldreth to look at her at all. He did not seem to enjoy spending time with his children, which was not at all remarkable in a duke, but was not at all pleasant either.

"I did," Amelia said, looking at Cranleigh. Cranleigh did not look back at her, the oaf. He truly was excessively dull not to understand all she had done.

"Of course she did," Sophia said. "It must be perfectly obvious to everyone that Lady Amelia is not the sort of woman to be picked up and carted off by the first interested party. She has standards and she holds to them. You must be so proud, Aldreth."

"Of course," Aldreth answered a bit awkwardly. "Yet there is this situation and it cannot be talked around. There is the conservatory and there is the satire. And there is Lord Cranleigh." He did not look at all pleased by the recitation, but then, Aldreth rarely looked pleased about anything.

"There certainly is," Cranleigh said. "I am not to be talked around either."

"But, darling, no one is trying to do that," Sophia said, turning her back to the window fully. "It is only that you have made your somewhat tepid offer of marriage under a false presumption, that being that Lady Amelia has been ruined, however accidentally, by you. As we have determined, she has not been ruined. No satire can ruin her. No dress torn on a careless thorn can ruin her. Certainly the men below do not see her as ruined."

Cranleigh looked like he wanted to strike something. Sophia, most likely. Sophia, as Amelia was coming to expect, did not look alarmed in the least by Cranleigh's hot expression of impotent rage. *Impotent*, not a word she had ever before conjoined with Cranleigh.

"They see her as *something*," Cranleigh said on an explosion of air.

"Available?" Sophia offered.

"*Extremely* available," Cranleigh said.

"How absurd," Amelia snapped. "Has it just not been demonstrated that I am not extremely available? I am certainly not available to the Duke of Calbourne, much to his surprise, I should say. I, also, Lord Cranleigh, am not available to you, extremely or otherwise."

Aldreth looked at her in almost complete shock. Cranleigh did not. Cranleigh looked at her in annoyance, which he did often enough, whenever he wasn't kissing her. He was a terribly contrary sort of man. She couldn't think why she'd tolerated his kisses for all these years.

Oh, very well. She could, and much more than tolerate, too. *Crave* was a word that came to mind.

Why couldn't he have asked her to marry him two years ago? If only he had done, this all could have been avoided. But he hadn't and, worse, he was leaving England on the first ship he could find, and so she had been required to do *something*.

She hadn't anticipated precisely this, of course.

"Well then," Aldreth said slowly.

"Well then," Sophia continued, "I do think that, the excitement of the satire behind us, the gentlemen be allowed entry. Perhaps by fours? That should whittle them down to a manageable number before we must dress for dinner."

"Lady Dalby," Aldreth began.

"Lady Dalby," Cranleigh said, cutting off the duke in his

very own house, "I know this is rare fun for you, but there shall be no whittling, no interviewing, no dining room escapades such as befell Amelia's cousin Louisa. There shall be nothing of the sort. Lady Amelia is not under your care."

"And I am not under yours, Cranleigh!" Amelia said sharply. "I am not yours to order or coddle or protect. The event of the conservatory was . . . a mistake, a mischance, a . . ."

"Mésalliance?" Cranleigh asked softly, his blue eyes smoldering. She was not going to let smoldering eyes hinder her.

"Yes, that," she said, walking up to him, staring up into his eyes, showing him that she could resist him and that she was not going to tumble into his arms every time he touched her. Why had he waited two years? Mustn't he answer for that? "All of that. Completely that. I have formed an alliance with Sophia Dalby and I *will* see it bear fruit. I will. Do not mistake me in this, Cranleigh. Believe me," she said, aware that she was whispering by the end of her declaration.

"Amy," he whispered, "do not mistake *me*. No mercy. No quarter."

"No quarter?" Sophia said briskly. "Is that what I understood you to say, Lord Cranleigh? How very martial."

"For once, we are in agreement, Lady Dalby," Cranleigh said, and with a glance at Amelia, he made his bow and left.

The room felt empty without him. It always did.

"What brought you home, Aldreth?" Sophia asked, pointedly changing the subject. "I'll never believe you found Paris lacking."

Aldreth turned his very cynical gaze upon Sophia. Sophia soaked it up like a sponge. "I was warned to return to London, Lady Dalby."

"It sounds thrilling. No one ever warns me about anything," Sophia said with a tilted smile. "You clearly took the warning seriously."

"Clearly," Aldreth said, his voice a dangerous rumble. "I was warned to make haste to Aldreth House or see my daughter ruined completely."

"And how reassuring to see that she is not ruined completely at all," Sophia said. "But who warned you, Aldreth? Someone who clearly did not have your best interests at heart, to ruin your trip abroad so callously."

Aldreth almost smiled. It was a rueful movement of his mouth, a twinkling in his light blue eyes that he quickly damped down into sodden arrogance again.

" 'Twas the Earl of Westlin, Sophia," he finally answered. "Which I do not believe surprises you one whit."

"Not even two whits," Sophia said. "He does love to spoil anyone's good time. He's most reliable that way. I'm somewhat surprised that he was able to . . . manage you so well, your grace."

"Yes, I do feel managed," Aldreth said, this time almost actually smiling in fact.

It was quite rare to see Aldreth smile. Amelia was not certain she had seen it even ten times in her entire life. And how did Sophia manage Aldreth so well? No one managed Aldreth. Well, perhaps with the exception of his mistress. By every rumor, she managed Aldreth like a trained bear.

The analogy was entirely intentional.

The door to the library opened abruptly yet again, causing Amelia to jump. At least this time she wasn't kissing Cranleigh, or rather being kissed by him. That was truly the more accurate summation. Stupid of her not to remember it properly. The events of the day had clearly unsettled her.

It was Hawksworth, looking dirty and tired and rumpled. And not the least bit pleased. The shock of seeing Hawks dirty was quite enough of a jolt. One did not often get dirty from continual napping.

"Amy! What's—oh, good afternoon, Father," Hawks said, nearly skidding to a stop on the polished wood floors upon seeing Aldreth in his own home. Aldreth had never developed the habit of being home much. "I thought you were on the Continent. Lady Dalby! I did think to see you here."

"Did you? What a cordial remark, Lord Hawksworth. You have managed to produce the most cordial, accommodating, and pleasant of children, Aldreth," Sophia said, smiling winsomely at Hawksworth. What Sophia did not say and what was hanging silently in the air above them all was the question: *How could Aldreth have done it?* Aldreth was not cordial in the least.

"But what are you doing here, Hawks?" Amelia said. "I thought you were for the country, a bit of hunting, wasn't it?" For how else could she communicate in front of Aldreth her absolute horror at seeing her brother present at the most important moment of her life? That of snaring a husband by the most unorthodox means possible. And by that she meant Sophia Dalby.

"Yes, well," Hawks stammered, glancing at Aldreth, who looked entirely too interested in both Hawksworth's departure from Town and his unexpected arrival. "I, that is . . ."

"Don't tell me you weren't welcomed warmly at Marshfield Park, Lord Hawksworth," Sophia said. "I shan't believe that my son closed the door upon you."

"He did not," Hawksworth said, for he was not such a fool as to insult Sophia's family in such a way. "Nor did Mr. Grey, who was most hospitable, it was only that he, we, it was thought, that is, it was decided that being in Town might be preferable. At present. And it does seem so, doesn't it?"

As Hawks was clearly speaking to Amelia, she had to form some sort of answer that would be acceptable to her father. She couldn't think how it could be done. Aldreth found very little acceptable in the best of circumstances. This was hardly the best of circumstances.

She was saved from having to answer Hawks by the entry into the library of the Earl of Dalby, his uncle Mr. John Grey, and his three sons, the various Mr. Greys of the

Iroquois nation. He had dragged them home, here, now? Hawks was entirely worthless.

The introductions were made in a perfunctory fashion and then Hawksworth said, "You're to marry Lord Cranleigh, then? I had not thought, that is, I had not considered him to be someone of interest to you, Amelia."

"I beg your pardon?" Amelia said stiffly. "I am not going to marry Lord Cranleigh. Not at all. Whyever did you think so?"

"Because he is declaring it himself, to everyone gathered in front of the house."

"What? You mean, now?"

"I mean precisely now. This instant. You didn't know?"

Of course she didn't know, but she should have. Cranleigh could be so forceful at the most inconvenient times. She rushed to the window, everyone else in the room following her, and it was a crowd, and looked down upon Berkeley Square. The outdoor crowd had diminished by about half, but those who remained were engaged in a very loud and very agitated argument with Cranleigh, who looked quite ready, even eager, to duel the lot of them at the first opportunity. As dueling was illegal, first opportunities were not easy to arrange.

"My, he is determined," Sophia said on a wistful note. One might even say she sounded appreciative. Amelia looked at her askance for a moment, not at all in a friendly manner. Sophia Dalby was entirely too aware of Lord Cranleigh and everyone knew that when Sophia became acutely aware of a man, he wound up in her bed. "Such an endearing quality, is it not?"

"It is not," Amelia said. "Not when it is presumptuous and uncalled-for."

"Uncalled-for?" Sophia said and then added in a whisper that could be heard by everyone, likely even Yates out in the vestibule, "Darling, he did kiss you, most ardently in fact. I think he feels he must do something about it. Something primitive."

Amelia could only stare at Sophia in shock, her mouth unattractively agape. What could she say to that in front of her father?

"Amy? You kissed him?" Hawks asked, driving home the point, the fool.

"He kissed *me*. Briefly," she answered, not certain that was a response that put her in the best light, but unable to think of an alternative.

"Small wonder he thinks he is to marry you," Hawks said.

"Small wonder, indeed," Mr. John Grey, Sophia's brother echoed, his expression looking entirely off-putting. Why, was she to defend her behavior with Cranleigh to an American Indian? She would not.

She *could* not. But that was neither here nor there.

"Amelia declined something that was not quite an offer, not five minutes ago in this very room," Aldreth said, studying Sophia.

"But of course she did," Sophia said, staring back at Aldreth. "No one can expect Lady Amelia to accept any sort of offer of marriage that is less than the kind of offer she fully expects, kiss or not. Satire or not. Rumor or not. She simply has far more fortitude than Cranleigh has credited her with. And far higher standards than he relied upon."

What was that supposed to mean? That Cranleigh had arranged for her to be very nearly forced into a situation that would very nearly require her to marry him? There was nothing further from the truth. And she ought to know. She'd been kissing him for more than two years and he had yet to do a single thing to damage her reputation or her chances for a good marriage.

That didn't sound quite right, but it was correct in theory. And practice.

"She kissed him? Right here in this room?" Sophia's fully grown, and what was to have been assumed, sophisticated son asked. He sounded like a simpleton. Where did it matter where Cranleigh had kissed her? Why, as to that, he had once kissed her on the seventh step of the Duke of York's staircase for upwards of half an hour.

"Markham," Sophia said, sounding almost weary, "please do try not to be tiresome. Certainly a man may kiss a woman and not have the world come to halt. I'm entirely certain that both Lord Cranleigh and Lady Amelia are both sophisticated enough to know that a simple kiss . . . or two, between friends, can't possibly do either of them any harm. Unless, of course, one of them wants to do harm. Then it is another proposition entirely."

"I don't know as to harm," Hawks said, actually beginning to pace the room. Hawks, as a very firm policy, never engaged in anything as energetic as pacing, particularly not when there were six perfectly good sofas available, and ten chairs. It was a well-equipped library, after all. It even had a pleasingly arranged assortment of books. "I do know that he's convincing nearly everyone out there," and here he pointed vaguely at the window that overlooked the street, taking in three or four Indians with the gesture, "that he's going to marry you. He's *very* convincing."

"Of course he's convincing," Sophia said. "I'm quite certain that he's simply trying to clear the area in front of Aldreth House for Lady Amelia's sake, her reputation being of his utmost concern. Wouldn't you agree, Lady Amelia?"

"I most certainly would," she said stiffly, not daring to look at Aldreth. He *had* seen her kissing Cranleigh, after all. In certain lights, it might appear that Cranleigh had other things on his mind than her reputation. "I was most definitive in my refusal of his offer of marriage. I even have witnesses."

"You certainly do," Sophia said. "And I'm quite certain that, if required, Aldreth and I will give accurate and detailed accounts of what occurred in the library concerning Lady Amelia and Lord Cranleigh. But only if required." Sophia smiled at her as she said the last. It was not a pleasant sort of smile. Why, it looked very nearly malicious.

"As she is soon to marry," Aldreth said, studying Amelia

with more care than she found comfortable, "I shan't think it will be required. Her husband will dispel any lingering rumors, as is his right, as well as his duty."

"And his pleasure," Sophia's brother said, his black eyes mere slits of speculation as he looked her over, "if he's the right kind of man. This one," and he made a gesture with his head that clearly indicated he meant for her to look out the window, which she did not as it would have been seen as entirely too forward by the mob below, "seems the right kind. What's wrong with him?"

"Nothing!" Amelia said sharply, feeling very safe about being sharp with an Indian as she was in the very heart of Aldreth's house. On the open street would have been another matter entirely. In the park, she would have said nothing at all, no matter the provocation. And she had been provoked. Dreadfully. And all because she had kissed Cranleigh . . . blast, he had kissed *her* . . . she really had to get that bit straight, and because Cranleigh was out on the street trying to salvage her ravaged reputation.

Which wouldn't have been ravaged if he hadn't practically torn her dress off of her very unwilling body in the Prestwick conservatory. Well, very nearly unwilling. Some small part of her had felt the slightest thrill when he had laid his hands on her, his icy eyes burning with . . . passion? Anger? Frustration? Something very like all three. There was very little to it, after all, a simple misstep, a torn dress. It happened almost every day, didn't it? Something to be quickly forgotten.

Or it should have been if not for that scandalous satire.

Oh, very well, she might have been slightly responsible and things might have got just a bit out of hand because she had been found in Iveston's very brotherly arms. Certainly brotherly. Why, she felt as much passion in Iveston's arms as she did in Hawksworth's, which is to say, none whatsoever.

Couldn't Cranleigh see that for himself? How could he be blind to something so very obvious?

•

"John," Sophia said, "things are not as simple as that, particularly in this country. Why, a man and woman must have all sorts of ties and alliances to bind them. Mere physical attraction and a good character are not enough."

True, completely and utterly true, and yet so unpleasant when put forth so blatantly.

"Good family is essential," Aldreth said, sitting down on the sofa closest to the window and crossing his legs.

"There is nothing wrong with the Blakesleys," Amelia said.

"No, perhaps not," Aldreth said. "Still, Hyde, as a general of some repute, didn't perform up to expectations when the colonies revolted." Aldreth shrugged slightly, his most damning gesture.

"Truly?" Sophia asked. "I can find no fault with his performance. We have differing standards, apparently."

"Apparently," Aldreth echoed, not at all perturbed. Why, he looked very nearly relaxed and the whole world knew that Aldreth never relaxed.

"What's to be done about Cranleigh?" Hawksworth asked. "If he's not to marry Amelia and as he's even now putting it out that he is . . ." He let the idea trail off, as it would have been too much effort to complete a sentence.

"As Lady Amelia's brother," the Earl of Dalby said reasonably, "I should think the duty should fall to you, Lord Hawksworth."

Two or three of the Indians, most attractive men in a primitive sort of way, particularly the elder brother, a Mr. George Grey, who had the most alarmingly attractive dimple in his left cheek when he smiled, which he was doing right now, grunted in what she assumed was agreement to Lord Dalby's suggestion.

Spending a few days with Lady Dalby's exotic relatives had apparently done nothing to firm Hawks up. "I could attempt it, I suppose," Hawks said with absolutely no enthusiasm.

"If I go out it will look entirely too official," Aldreth

said, "as if there is actually something to his assertions. I don't think that would serve Amelia's best interests."

"No, it certainly wouldn't," Sophia said thoughtfully. "Perhaps you should do it, Lady Amelia. It would certainly quell every hint of speculation if you were to be seen publicly denouncing Cranleigh's claims. I should think it would be obvious to those who remain, those who see the two of you together, that Cranleigh is wildly off the mark in claiming an alliance, indeed, an arrangement between you. Don't you agree?"

She most certainly did not. However, as the entire room was arrayed against her, she didn't see that she had much choice. As to that, she had always found Cranleigh to be almost usually reasonable as long as they weren't alone; she didn't anticipate any problem in dealing with him on a public street.

It was truly remarkable how wrong she could be in her expectations, starting with her alliance with Sophia, which was not proceeding as smoothly as she had wished, and ending, she hoped, for she was truly quite exhausted by the events of the past week and still without a proper proposal, with Cranleigh.

Cranleigh, his coat off, his shirt nearly undone, was very close to brawling in the street, her street, to be exact. *Again.* It was entirely scandalous. That Cranleigh was brawling with . . . oh dear . . . with *Iveston.* Why on earth was Lord Iveston here? Hadn't they mutually decided that a marriage between them was not a thing to be desired? As he was not a man to be desired, at least by her.

Amelia moved cautiously down the steps, just one or two; she couldn't see any requirement that she actually go down amongst the men. Two footmen stood at the entrance of Aldreth House, watching the fight with overt delight, which was not at all helpful.

The Lords Dutton and Penrith were in the crowd, near the front; at Penrith's side was Lord Raithby, the Earl of Quinton's son, which was most peculiar as she had only met Raithby a half dozen times at best and Hawksworth didn't have a fondess for him at all, which might explain the peculiar look of delight on Raithby's rather handsome face.

The younger brothers of Cranleigh were quite visible, and doing nothing to stop their brothers' fighting, which was so very like a brother. The Dukes of Calbourne and Edenham were far to the back, but for all that, they had an unobstructed view of the fight and, in fact, seemed to be wagering on the outcome. As to that, Calbourne looked a bit rumpled about the cravat; perhaps Cranleigh had knocked him another glancing blow? She did hope so. For all that Calbourne was a duke in the very prime of life, she did find him a bit of a nuisance. He had been discarded. Could he not accept the fact and forget her?

Apparently not. It was to be expected that dukes in the prime of life had little experience at being rejected for any reason.

"Cranleigh!" she said, holding her shawl tightly around her. It was not a red shawl, as depicted in that horrid print, but it was a shawl nonetheless and she realized in the next instant when every man gathered in front of Aldreth House, and there were more than a few, stopped watching the fight for the barest instant to look at her, that she should not have worn a shawl of any color. By the very speculative gleam in all their very debauched male eyes, she should *not* have worn a shawl.

She also should not have called out to Cranleigh. No, not Cranleigh. His name on her lips was perhaps, just perhaps, too intimate an act for public consumption.

Cranleigh, to his credit or against it, she could not decide which, did not look at her upon hearing his name. He did take advantage of Iveston's momentary loss of concentration to hit him firmly in the vicinity of the third button of his waistcoat. Iveston turned a bit red in the face, and then white about the mouth, and then Cranleigh turned to give her the most unpleasant glare.

Well, *really*. What had *she* done? She was not going to feel guilty about merely saying his name, though by the look on his face, actually by the looks on all their faces, she should be simply drenched in guilt. And shame.

Blast. Men were such prudes.

"Would you all please leave?" she said, rather shrilly she was afraid. "The duke is in residence and he does not care for such displays on or near his property."

There. Throwing Aldreth's name about ought to run them off. It was not terribly enjoyable to have a stern father, but it was somewhat convenient to have a stern duke about when things got out of hand. Things were rather completely out of hand at present.

"Amelia, go back inside," Cranleigh barked at her, as if he had the right. Prudes and *bullies*.

"I would love to, Lord Cranleigh," she said, watching as Iveston rubbed his belly and Dutton chuckled not at all discreetly. She had never liked Lord Dutton much; she liked him less nearly by the hour. "It is only that, as you are instigating a brawl in front of Aldreth House, and the duke has indicated that I should put a stop to it, I find myself in the position of being out in the street and trying to do just that!"

She was shouting by the end of it. She couldn't seem to help herself. Cranleigh, as was so very typical of him, did whatever he pleased and expected her to comply. Had he not kissed her at every opportunity for the past two years, making opportunities arise when none presented themselves quickly enough for him? Had he not pushed her into thorns? Had he not ripped her dress for no other reason than he thought to drive her from the Prestwick ball?

The man was the worst sort of bully, the sort who targeted his urges upon innocent, unmarried women of good family. If she had any sort of useful brother at all, Hawks would call Cranleigh out and shoot him through the heart.

Looking at Cranleigh glowering at her, his eyes frosty, the muscles in his neck bulging, she thought that, perhaps, Cranleigh might only require being shot through the foot.

He couldn't dance well anyway, so it would be a small loss to the community.

"Lady Amelia, do not go back inside, not unless you will allow me to escort you in," Calbourne said, coming forward from the edges of the crowd, Edenham walking at his side, smiling. At what she couldn't imagine.

Amelia sighed heavily, clutching her very pretty and very ill-conceived blue shawl about her shoulders. It was starting to rain.

"She will allow no such thing," Cranleigh said. "I believe I must have made clear to you by now that Lady Amelia is to be my wife. This absurd jest, this," he said stiffly, "uncivilized contest for Lady Amelia is *over*. Done. I must insist that you leave, that you *all* leave."

"Does he speak the truth, Lady Amelia?" Iveston asked, still trying to catch his breath and truly looking the worse for having tangled physically with Cranleigh, but still so civil, still so pleasantly polite. Why couldn't Cranleigh have half of his brother's mildness of temperament? "Have you agreed to his suit?"

"His suit?" she said, a bit sharply, true, but she was being so horribly pressed from all sides, particularly the side Cranleigh was on. Her left side, actually. She was always acutely aware of Cranleigh's presence, and it was supremely annoying to be so aware, but she had given up trying to ignore him years ago. "*His suit?* Lord Cranleigh has made no suit. Lord Cranleigh has made declarations of intent. Lord Cranleigh has made proclamations. Lord Cranleigh has made an ass of himself!"

She was shouting again. It was beyond inexcusable. She simply had to get control of herself, but being anywhere near Cranleigh always made that so difficult.

"He has, hasn't he?" Penrith said, coming nearer to the steps, Dutton and Raithby at his side.

Dutton was a rake, confirmed, and a sensual assault upon the senses of ignorant girls. As Cranleigh attacking her with kisses upon every opportunity had left her less ignorant than most, Dutton had never made a favorable impression upon her. Raithby was not quite a rake. Raithby was soft seduction in a well-tailored coat of blue superfine. His hair was brown, his eyes were blue, and his expression was invariably sultry. He was reputed to be a horseman of superb ability, which was likely why Hawksworth disliked him so. Hawksworth was best known for riding a sofa.

"I do wonder," Penrith said with that famous voice of his, "if he has not had some motive in his behavior that is not entirely . . ." He clearly wanted to say *honorable*, but no man, no man of any sense, would dare to insult Cranleigh in that fashion, not unless he was eager to face Cranleigh on the dueling field.

"Entirely . . . ?" Cranleigh prompted, his jaw muscle working.

"Clear," Penrith said.

"What is unclear to you, Lord Penrith?" Cranleigh asked. "Lady Amelia seeks a husband. She has found one. I am that man."

As Amelia was opening her mouth to tell Cranleigh he was being overbearing in his manner with her, *again*, Dutton said, "Yet there is the matter of the wager."

Wager?

"I can't think what you mean," Cranleigh said.

"Can't you?" Dutton asked. "Is it possible that you are not aware of the wager on White's book that Lady Amelia would—"

Amelia was most assuredly interested in what the wager had her doing, but just at that moment Cranleigh struck Dutton a hard blow to the face. Dutton went down, crumpled actually, into the dirt and stayed there. Neither Penrith nor Raithby helped him to stand. He probably couldn't have stood anyway.

"So you have heard of the wager?" Penrith asked mildly, one brow cocking in sardonic amusement.

"There are many wagers on White's book," Cranleigh said. "Certainly it is not a topic for Lady Amelia's ears."

Cranleigh, aside from kissing her all over Town, was never one to want her to have any amusement at all.

"Yes," Penrith said, "I suppose that, now that she is to marry, it should be her husband's decision as to what to tell her. Or not to tell her, as he determines."

How perfectly dreadful. She was certainly not going to endure a husband like *that*.

"I am not going to," she said, "that is, I have not agreed to marry Lord Cranleigh. Indeed, I have not agreed to marry anyone. As yet."

"As yet?" Edenham said, walking most elegantly toward the Aldreth House stairs. "That does sound encouraging. May we not come in out of the rain, Lady Amelia? As Aldreth is At Home, it would be convenient to call upon him. And his daughter."

Oh, dear.

Amelia had never stood quite so close to the Duke of Edenham before now. In fact, most women kept a healthy distance from him, the rumors of his lethal quality being what they were. Amelia now perhaps wondered if Edenham was lethal in an entirely different manner.

He was devastatingly handsome. Truly and remarkably handsome. Tall and lithe, dark brown hair and eyes, a brow worthy of a sonnet, and the most elegant nose she'd ever seen. Lethal, yes, most assuredly.

"You're not going to let them in," Cranleigh snarled softly in her direction. "Not when I've thrashed half of London to keep them out."

"It is my father's house, Lord Cranleigh," she said, sounding more brittle than was attractive. Edenham smiled fractionally. Amelia felt something skitter along the backs of her knees. She might have giggled; she did hope not. "I wouldn't think of turning away Aldreth's guests."

"Hell and blast, Amy!" he said in a rumble of annoyance. "You're doing this to torment me."

"Am I?" she said sweetly. "How convenient." Cranleigh looked at her in such a fashion then that she turned quickly away from him. When he got that look in his eyes, well, dragging her off into a closet to kiss her senseless was his usual next move. She did hope he could find a closet quickly. "Gentlemen? I do believe the Duke of Aldreth is At Home."

And, before Cranleigh could reach her, Amelia scooted past the footmen and into the house.

Nineteen

"It looks like she's admitting them," Sophia said from her post at the front window. "How clever of her."

Aldreth, who was standing at Sophia's side, looked askance at her.

"You intend her no harm, Sophia?" he asked softly, his blue eyes both cynical and vulnerable.

"Is that what Westlin told you? That I wanted to hurt you by hurting your daughter?" Sophia asked.

The rest of the men in the room, Sophia's family and Aldreth's, kept themselves apart, talking quietly amongst themselves in the far corner of the room. Hawksworth was even on his feet, a rare sight.

Aldreth nodded fractionally, his gaze not leaving Sophia's face. He had aged well in the twenty years they had known each other, but then, so had she.

"Aldreth, I forgave you long ago," Sophia answered, looking at his profile, seeing the muted trace of the angled jaw of his youth. "That night at the theater, that night when you rescued Zoe from the streets, was enough to settle any differences between us."

"Rescued her by making her my whore?" Aldreth said softly.

Sophia smiled. "Don't think you can lie to me, darling Aldreth. The uninformed rabble may think she is your whore, but you and I both know she is your salvation. And you love her for it."

Aldreth grunted in answer, his eyes smiling, though his mouth did not. "Westlin was very certain that you wanted me away on the Continent so that you could work some mischief against me, my house, my heir."

"Westlin is very certain of very many things. It is quite remarkable that any one man can be so often wrong on such a wide variety of topics," Sophia said.

"You hate him," Aldreth said, studying her face.

"But of course, darling. However, that Caro is married to Westlin's heir is quite satifying."

"And you did not serve your daughter ill by seeing her mated with Ashdon?"

"They are well mated. She loves him. He loves her in equal measure."

Aldreth nodded again, almost serenely. "You are certain that Amelia will be well mated by the end of this?"

"Well mated, well loved, Aldreth," Sophia said. "Trust me to see it done."

"There are many who would call me a fool for trusting you, Sophia," he said, his blue eyes twinkling.

"And all go by the name of Lord Westlin," she said lightly. "What does Zoe think?"

"Zoe trusts you nearly as much as she trusts me."

"Oh, more, I should think," Sophia answered with a smile. "We have no contracts between us, legalizing neither trust nor payment."

Aldreth lost his pleasant look. "That is for Jamie. I would not leave either of them without . . . without . . ."

"Without," Sophia said, laying a hand upon his forearm briefly in pacification. "Which is precisely as it should be, for a man of honor, your grace."

"Your brother, he is a man of honor as well, I think. If

Mr. Grey had been with you twenty years ago when you first saw London, I think none would have touched you, Sophia. He is not a man to provoke, is he?"

"No, he is not," she said, using her fan to hide her mild agitation at the memories his question aroused in her. Memories she kept carefully bound. "If John had been with me . . . but he was not. He was in the forests of Canada and I was here. It took years for us to find each other, years and continents. The world is wide, Aldreth. The world is very wide."

"That it is," he said simply. "They look at us, Sophia, and they wonder what binds us."

"John can guess," she answered, "but the others, these young men of ours, they likely believe I am trying to seduce you."

Aldreth ducked his head and smiled. "Zoe would have my head on a platter."

"And I would hand her the carving knife," Sophia said with an answering smile.

&

"I wonder what they're discussing?" Dalby said, looking at his mother and Aldreth across the room from them.

"They have known each other for many years," John Grey answered quietly. "They share many memories."

"That sounds pleasant," Dalby said.

"Does it?" John asked.

"Shouldn't it?" Hawks said, looking at his father, noting how Aldreth looked very nearly relaxed. Odd. Aldreth never relaxed, and certainly not in his own home.

"What do you know about it, John?" Dalby asked his uncle.

John looked at Lord Dalby with all the emotion of a piece of flint. Matthew Grey, John's youngest son, chuckled. Dalby fidgeted with his cuff and dropped the subject.

"I didn't think Aldreth knew Lady Dalby," Hawksworth said. Having spent many confusing hours with Dalby's Indian relatives had taught him that most topics of conversation that would be considered innocuous by anyone were not considered proper by these particular Iroquois. As he did not know any other Iroquois to make a comparison, he was not willing to do so. After all, Sophia's relatives might be peculiar.

He was inclined to think so.

John Grey, Sophia's brother, looked precisely how one would expect an American Indian to look. He was hard-featured, dark-skinned, laconic of speech. He was, to be precise, a most dangerous-looking man. His behavior did not dispel the impression.

George Grey, John's eldest son, was on his way to becoming famous for his blatant pursuit of Hawksworth's cousin, Louisa. It was even being whispered by some that, if not for his blatant pursuit, Louisa might not have found herself wed so quickly. Hawks did not agree with that assessment in the slightest. Louisa had got herself well and truly ruined and George Grey had had nothing to do with it. George was, however, the most talkative of John's three sons. He thought British customs were unusual and sometimes comical, and he was not shy about saying so.

John, the middle son, was called Young, as he was the younger John. He rarely had anything to say, but was a very watchful sort. He resembled Dalby quite strongly, except that Dalby was far more conversationally inclined.

Matthew, the youngest, had startlingly blue eyes in a very dark-skinned face. That was the first impression. The second impression, albeit likely due to the fact that Matthew was barely out of boyhood, was that Matthew was very often bored—unless he was hunting. In the very brief time that Hawks had spent in the fields with the Greys, he had been astounded by their skill at the hunt.

It was very nearly chilling.

"There is much a son cannot know about his father," John Grey said in answer to his speculation.

"Or a son about a mother?" Dalby asked.

"In the making of a life, a history is made," John said. "Sophia and Aldreth have a history."

"I had no idea," Hawksworth said. "But then, I rarely see Aldreth."

John nodded, but it was clearly not in approval. "A man wants his sons about him."

Which was preposterous as Aldreth didn't want anyone about him, unless it was his French mistress. She'd been *about* him for as long as Hawks could remember.

"My mother has a history with quite a few men," Dalby said. His tone of voice was not what one would call cordial.

"You are very young, Mark," John said, using a very abbreviated version of Dalby's name. "You know very little."

It was not the most polite of remarks, but then Hawks had realized within minutes of meeting John that one should not spend time with him if one required civility.

"I know enough," Dalby said.

"Yet nothing of importance," John said. That remark, which could truly be termed a rebuke, ended all conversation for the moment. The sounds coming from the vestibule, male sounds, preempted whatever conversation might have been forthcoming.

"Here they come," George Grey said, his dark eyes shining in mirth.

Mirth? There was nothing remotely amusing about the situation. Why, Amelia was being made a laughingstock, at the very least.

Before Hawks could say anything, not that he was convinced he would actually have said anything, the door to the library opened and Amelia came in, looking a bit harried, truth be told, followed by a score or more of gentlemen. A score of gentlemen could harry the best of girls, which Amelia certainly was. Or had been.

It was a tangle, wasn't it?

Twenty

It was a complete tangle, and she had no idea how to go about untangling it. Cranleigh was at her side, scowling, as was his practice, and surrounding her were more dukes and earls and lords of this and that than she knew what to do with.

One husband. She only required *one* husband. What was she supposed to do with the rest of them? Throw them out upon the street? Having just got them off the street, and away from Gillray, who she was almost certain she saw at the edge of the Square, scribbling, she was not eager to toss them back out upon it. It was entirely possible that another satire might erupt from this . . . this tangle.

How looking for a husband among the cream of London's crop had turned into *this* she had no idea.

Amelia's gaze strayed to Sophia, who stood next to Aldreth, smiling. She had *some* idea, anyway. Sophia was flirting outrageously with Aldreth. It was nearly obscene. At least it was better than watching her ogle Cranleigh.

The men made their bows, the women their curtseys,

and Yates, followed by four footmen, brought in more glasses and more refreshments. It was a quite busy day for Aldreth At Home. He didn't look too terribly displeased, which was slightly inexplicable. The fact that Sophia stuck to his side like a, well, like a thorn, might have explained part of it. The rest of it? Could it possibly be that Aldreth was that eager to get her married off?

It didn't seem likely, unless that satire had changed everything, which of course, it had.

"If you'd just left the Prestwick ball from the conservatory, none of this would be happening now," Cranleigh said at her side.

"With my dress torn to pieces? How was I supposed to do that?" she snapped.

"I meant the first time in the conservatory," Cranleigh said. "When I pushed you."

"You didn't push me. I wasn't pushed! I would never allow you to *push* me, Lord Cranleigh!"

"Right," he said on a snort of air.

"Did I hear you correctly?" Lord Penrith asked politely, when it could hardly have been polite to blatantly overhear their private conversation. "You *weren't* pushed into the roses by Lord Cranleigh?"

"I most certainly wasn't," Amelia said. "I merely mis-stepped and found myself snagged."

"Quite a misstep," Lord Dutton said.

One would have thought that, having been thrashed, Dutton would have slunk home, or at least into a corner of White's. How he had the gall to come into Aldreth's very home with the dust of the street on his pantaloons perfectly displayed the arrogance of the man. She had never liked Dutton. Now she knew why.

"Lord Dutton," she said, feeling quite put-upon and entirely exhausted by it, "I do think that you should hie off and pull yourself together. You look entirely too . . . shopworn."

The Duke of Edenham chuckled.

"I should think, Lady Amelia, that you would be the last person," Dutton said, the bruise Cranleigh gave him coming up nicely purple, "to use that particular phrase."

The Duke of Calbourne coughed.

Amelia felt Cranleigh at her side, felt the solid mass of him, the waves of his anger rolling against her, and found herself caught up in it. Caught out of her shame and annoyance, lifted into something stronger and harder, something hot and urgent. Cranleigh always did that. Cranleigh always freed something within her, something she was certain was slightly sordid and not at all pleasant, but something most assuredly free, even fearless.

Before she could answer Dutton, and did she want to, Cranleigh said, "And I should think, Lord Dutton, that you would understand that you have no place here. I can demonstate that for you, again, if necessary. Will it be necessary?"

Dutton's gaze flickered, his blue eyes shadowed for a moment, and then he bowed to her and left without another word. Amelia let out a sigh of both relief and disappointment. She could have got off at least one insult if Cranleigh hadn't bullied Dutton out of the room.

"I can't think what's got into Dutton these past few days," Penrith said. "He used to have a reputation."

"He still does," Cranleigh said, "though perhaps not the one he wants."

Amelia very nearly sniggered.

"I, for one, don't care a fig about Dutton or his reputation," Calbourne said. "I do care about redeeming myself in regard to Lady Amelia's list."

"You're off, Cal," the Duke of Edenham said. "Learn to live with it. I, however, have yet to be interviewed. I am on your list, am I not, Lady Amelia? Please don't tell me that I have been discarded without being fully considered."

He *was* very handsome and his title was very, very old. But he did have that nasty habit of killing off his wives, who by all reports had been exceedingly agreeable and quite proper. And Cranleigh *still* hadn't properly asked for her hand. He'd done nearly everything but, and as Edenham was so very eager to be considered and it would enrage Cranleigh so . . .

"Why should you want to be considered?" Calbourne asked tartly, distracting her from her thoughts. "You have two children. Your line is secured."

"And you have your heir as well, Cal," Edenham answered. Turning his rich brown eyes upon Amelia, he said, "A man should have a wife for more than the heirs she provides him."

"Oh?" Cranleigh said. "And what is that?"

"The civility she brings to his home, for one, and for another, her sweet companionship," Edenham said.

"Which will lead most swiftly to more heirs," Calbourne said. "Toss him out, Lady Amelia. Turn your attention upon me."

"Her attention is now and forevermore turned upon me," Cranleigh said, sounding not at all pleasant. The sound of his voice, however, and the sentiment he expressed sent a shiver of awareness down her spine to settle in her hips, where no proper woman wanted to experience sensations of awareness.

"If Lady Amelia's attention is truly turned upon you, Cranleigh," Lord Raithby said, "then her list parameters have clearly widened. That being so, I should like to be interviewed. Would you be so kind as to consider adding me to your list, Lady Amelia? I am most respectable, have a quite lovely estate in Lincolnshire, and am in the pink of health."

"I've seen his estate," Penrith said. "It's a bit small for you, I should think, Lady Amelia. And does anyone truly want to live in Lincolnshire?"

"Why are you involved, Penrith?" Calbourne asked a bit rudely. As he was a duke, no one thought it particularly offensive. "Do you seek placement on this famous list of gentlemen?"

Famous list of gentlemen? Is that what it had become? Amelia cast a glance at Sophia, who was now in polite discussion with her brother, the Indian. They were not looking in her direction, which ought to have relieved her, but didn't.

"Not at all," Penrith replied. "My mother has declared that I am entirely too young to marry, and I quite agree with her. I am involved only as an interested third party, a moderator of sorts. I hope that does not offend you, Lady Amelia?" he asked, turning his remarkable green-eyed gaze upon her.

"No, I—" she began to say, not at all certain what she would say that would sound respectable, not at all certain there *was* anything that would sound respectable. Cranleigh, as was to be expected, cut her off completely.

"It offends *me*," Cranleigh said, his arm just barely touching her shoulder. She ought to move away. She didn't. "There is no list. There is no competition that involves her."

"Of course there is, Cranleigh," Iveston said, coming up from behind them both. Iveston had brushed off the worst of the dust and looked none the worse for his altercation with Cranleigh. As to that, Cranleigh no longer looked annoyed with Iveston. Did brothers often do that? Hit each other by way of sport? Most peculiar, though there were times when she wanted to hit Hawksworth. Being male might have slight advantages, but only of the violent sort. "Everyone knows there is a list. There's no denying it. There's also no denying that every man in Town wants his name upon it."

"That's absurd," Cranleigh barked.

Iveston shrugged. "It might be absurd if any other woman but Lady Amelia had compiled a list of potential husbands, as most women on the marriage mart are not nearly so discriminating. As she so clearly is, being on her list is something of a major coup. I, for one, am delighted to have been included."

And, lovely man, he bowed to her at the end of his very detailed explanation of things as they presently stood.

"There is no list!" Cranleigh said, a bit loudly as more

than a few people in the library turned from their conversations to look at them. One of them her father. "There is no honor in being upon it! If there even was one. Which there isn't."

Raithby turned to Calbourne and said, "I take it he's not on the list."

Cal shook his head and shrugged dismissively.

"Oh, is he not?" Iveston asked her politely. "I should hate to see my brother so maligned. Could you not see a way to put him on it, Lady Amelia?"

Cranleigh looked almost close to bursting a blood vessel. It was rather funny to see him so abused. Certainly, after the entire shawl experience, he deserved some slight abuse.

"I do not believe Lord Cranleigh wants to be on my list, Lord Iveston," she said with as much charm as she could manage. She could manage quite a bit for such a worthy cause.

"Whyever not?" Calbourne said.

"That can't be correct," Edenham said. "All men of quality and distinction want to be acknowledged, publicly if possible, for their quality and distinction."

"But not by a woman who has complied a list of men she might consider for marriage," Cranleigh said hotly.

"How else should I have proceeded, Lord Cranleigh?" she replied, just as hotly, not that she should have shown these lovely gentlemen that sordid side of her nature, but Cranleigh deserved a hot rebuke and she was going to give him one. "Should I have, oh, perhaps, succumbed to the first man who got me alone in a corner and kissed me?"

By the look on his face, perhaps her rebuke needn't have been quite so hot.

"Would it even require a corner, Lady Amelia?" he shot back.

Iveston cleared his throat into the stunned silence that followed that insult. Amelia, quite able to ignore Iveston and his throat, Calbourne, and Edenham to focus all her attention on Cranleigh, answered, "Better to ask if such a man would even require getting a woman of good family and careful upbringing alone, Lord Cranleigh. Such a man would grab his chance where he could, wouldn't he? Grab as grab can."

"Catch as catch can, Amelia," he snarled. "And what can be said for a woman, no matter what she says of her family and breeding, who allows herself to be caught? Does not the catching declare all?"

"Even the innocent may be caught, Cranleigh. In fact, it is the innocent who are most easily snared. As I am quite certain you know."

"When the lure is tempting enough, anyone may be snared," he answered, his eyes like chips of ice in blue glass. "Even a man of good family and careful upbringing."

"Hence the marriage dance, Cranleigh. A lure, a snare, and a marriage," she said sharply. "Not my invention, I assure you, but finding myself upon the hunter's field, what can I do?"

"What can you do?" he said, his voice dropping, though all in the room listened regardless. "Amy, you can retreat. You can go home."

"Cranleigh, I am home. Look about you. I am encompassed."

"And not at all unhappy about it," he said.

"No, not at all," she said softly, gazing up into his eyes, captured once again by the look in them. It was this approximate look that had snared her that first time. Every time. "Cranleigh, I *will* marry."

"Someone on your list," Iveston said quietly into the web of unspoken words that surrounded Amelia and Cranleigh. Amelia jerked slightly. Cranleigh did not, but he did allow his gaze to shift to his brother.

"But not you, Iveston," Cranleigh said. It sounded nearly like a threat.

"No, not I," Iveston said. This time Cranleigh started. "Lady Amelia, having conducted her interview, found that we would not suit."

"Would not? Why not?" Cranleigh asked, shifting his

gaze back to Amelia. She wished he would stop doing that; she found it very difficult to concentrate on being perfect and lovely when Cranleigh stared at her.

"Because, Lord Cranleigh," she answered, "*we did not suit*. Did you think I would simply go to the highest bidder?"

Cranleigh provoked her by merely raising an eyebrow in answer.

"We know that you will not go to the tallest," Calbourne said.

Edenham smirked. Amelia smiled in spite of herself.

"I do have my standards, after all," she said.

"Hence, the list," Iveston said, "which I have admired from the start and, even finding myself elimated from it, continue to admire. But, Lady Amelia, please do consider adding Cranleigh to your list. If only for familial pride, I must entreat you. How would it look to have him omitted from the most famous list in Town? Why, 'twould be in the vein of getting sacked from White's."

"Hell and blast, Iveston," Cranleigh muttered, shaking his head in disapproval. "Don't encourage her in this idiocy. She's in deep enough now."

"Lord Iveston," she said, ignoring Cranleigh completely, which he hated thoroughly, "you can see my problem. Your brother is . . . unacceptable, and worse, he is happy to be so. What is a woman to do with such a man?"

It was not, perhaps, the wisest way with a phrase, for Cranleigh, suddenly, and with just that barest of provocations, gave her such a look that her heart stopped beating for a full five seconds. Starting up again, it pounded against her breasts. Yes, her breasts, for that is where she felt the full effect of Cranleigh's attention. Without a by-your-leave, he took her by the arm and led her, not at all gently, from the room, bowing an excuse or an apology, impossible to tell as he said not a word, to her father, and nearly dragged her out of the room, into the drawing room at the rear of the house. It was a large room, as they all were, but it was not inhabited and that made it a very dangerous room indeed.

Lord Cranleigh had quite a history going of what he could accomplish in an empty room.

"Unacceptable, Amy?" he said, his voice a hoarse whisper in the vastness of the drawing room. "Is that what I am? Because I am no duke nor ever will be, unless both my father and my older brother die? Am I to wish for that so that I may have you? Is that what you would drive me to?"

"No!" she said, wrenching her arm free of his grasp. He allowed it. She knew enough of his strength to know that. "And do not pretend with me, Cranleigh. You had to know from the start what I wanted and you would not . . . and still you kept on and on, kissing me. What am I to do? I want to marry!"

"A duke," he said, the light from the north facing windows illuminating his face with a chill cast.

"Why should I not think of dukes, Cranleigh? Whom else should I think of?" she said, lifting her chin.

"Aldreth wants this for you, that I know," he said.

"I do not see Aldreth often enough to know what he wants for me, Cranleigh," she said, staring up at him. "I have made my own plans for my life. What else was I to do?"

"And what of what I must do, Amy? What of my plans?"

"What plans? To return to the sea?" she whispered. "I know nothing of your plans. Don't you see that I must plan for myself?"

"I see only you, Amy," he said, taking her face in his hands. "Only you. If I ever had a plan beyond that, it is lost to memory."

And then he kissed her. Gently, a soft nuzzle against her face, the corner of her mouth, the line of her jaw. She lifted her face to him, giving herself to him. She always did, from the very first kiss to this, possibly the very last one. It was what she told herself every time he kissed her, that this time could well be the last, that this time, this moment, this stolen and hushed moment might be the last time he touched her, breathed upon her, against her, in her.

Cranleigh slid his hands to her arms and took her shawl from its drape across her elbows, dragged it down, down, until it was snug against her hips. And then he pulled the ends of the shawl behind him, forcing her body against his, his mouth against her throat, kissing her skin, robbing her of thought.

"Want me, Amy," he breathed against the pulse point at the base of her throat. "Want me above every other want and every other man."

She shook her head, but that was all. She did not fight him. She did not end the moment, this last moment, for it had to be the last. She could not do this for one more day. Having him without having him was killing her.

"Kiss me," she said, wanting him to kill by kisses all the whispers in her head, all the longing and rejection that collided whenever she looked into his cold blue eyes.

He did. His mouth moved up her throat, caressing her as his hands never did. He never truly touched her, in all their kisses, he barely, rarely touched her. Even now, the shawl held her against him, not him, not his hands, not the firm grasp of his muscular hands.

She had studied those hands that would not touch her, studied them from the golden glimmer of the small hairs on the backs to the angle of the veins to the shape of his knuckles and the precise shade of pink of his fingertips. She was more than half mesmerized by his hands, by the hunger in her that grew month after month to have him touch her with them. But he only used his mouth, which was enough, but just.

With his mouth, he devoured her.

With his tongue, he invaded her.

With his teeth, he nipped her.

With his lips, he caressed her.

And with his hunger, he seduced her. But only her mouth. Could a woman be truly seduced with only a mouth upon hers? Two years ago, before that first kiss, she would have sworn it to be so. Now she knew better that a man's mouth, his kiss, could torment and tease, but not truly seduce. Not truly. For if truly, she would have been ruined and she was not.

Cranleigh had sworn to her after that first time, that first kiss in her father's house, that he would never ruin her. That he had more honor than that and that he honored her more than that. She'd believed him. She'd been right to believe him. He had not ruined her.

There were, perhaps, worse ways to be ruined. Or rather, other ways.

If he would not marry her, she'd marry elsewhere, a duke perhaps, why not? Did it matter? If she could not have Cranleigh, and he could not truly want her, could he? If not Cranleigh, another man. She would marry. She would not wait any longer for an offer that never came. She would marry and marry well, a duke, and Cranleigh would disappear over the sea. And she would somehow survive. She would be a duchess and that would have to sustain her because Cranleigh would not make her his countess.

Why? Because she had welcomed his kisses too soon and too well? Even thinking that, she could not stop. He was a hunger inside of her and she demanded to be fed.

When Amelia thought of marrying her duke, she never thought of kissing him. Kisses were Cranleigh's domain. She would leave kisses behind, leaving Cranleigh behind with them. She would be a duchess and she would give her duke heirs, and it was even possible that her duke might touch his lips to hers every now and again. But he would not kiss her. Not like this. There never would be anything like this again.

So, she kissed him. She kissed him whenever she could, whenever he reached for her, whenever his mouth moved down to claim hers, she lifted herself up to be claimed.

And when she dreamed of her duke, she did not dream of this.

"Touch me," she said against his mouth, pressing her breasts against him. "You never touch me."

"You are not mine to touch," he said, nuzzling her ear, kissing her throat.

"Yet you kiss me."

"I must eat. I must drink. This is that, to me," he said hoarsely. "Would you starve me, Amy?"

"No," she said, "but I should stop you. We must stop doing this."

He pulled the shawl taut, forcing her breasts to rub against his chest. Her nipples ached in delicious torment, her breasts heavy and full. She wanted his touch more than air.

"Stop me," he said. "Can you? If you cannot, then it will not be done for I cannot stop myself from tasting you. You must know that by now, Amy. Only you can stop me."

But she never did, and she never would.

The sound of footsteps against the polished wooden floors stopped them both. He released her shawl and it dropped to the floor, a blue stain upon the golden wood. He did not step away from her. She did not know if she could. Her knees were weak and her breathing ragged. She took a half step back, turned to the windows lining the north-facing wall, and tried to catch her breath. She had not quite caught it before Hawks opened the heavy door into the room.

"Aunt Mary is here with Eleanor, Amy," Hawks said. "You should greet them, shouldn't you?"

"Yes, I will," she said, turning to face Hawks. "I'm coming."

And with that, he was through the doorway and back into the library, and so was she, and so was Cranleigh. The library was even more crowded than when she'd left it.

Standing on the other side of the room were Aunt Mary and Eleanor. Aunt Mary looked outraged. Eleanor looked intrigued. It was never to be a peaceful, pleasant encounter when Eleanor had that particular look. They were speaking to Sophia, who looked entirely pleased to see them, and to the Duke of Edenham, who looked entirely disinterested to see them, which was rather nice of him.

But then Sophia called out, across the room, mind you, showing not a jot of discretion. "Oh, Lady Amelia. You've returned. How nice. But where is your lovely shawl? Not ripped, I hope. That would be a peculiar coincidence and it would put Lord Cranleigh in the most unflattering light."

And then, naturally, every one in the room, Aldreth included, stopped speaking to stare at her, and she didn't have her shawl as she'd left it on the floor of the drawing room because Cranleigh did have that effect on her, of making her forget precisely where certain items of her clothing were at any particular moment. And, because everyone was staring at her she couldn't think of a thing to say, but of course Cranleigh could because he was so very good at stepping in and cleaning things up, as it were.

"Lady Amelia and I enjoyed a cordial conversation just now and I convinced her to give up her rather nice shawl to Miss Prestwick. As a gift. By way of exchange. For the red shawl that became entangled on her rose shrubs. Lady Amelia thought it was a splendid notion and—"

"And I," she continued, "I told Yates to bundle it up and send someone right over to deliver it. Now. As doing it as soon as possible would be the nicest gesture."

At which point Yates left the library, where he had been standing near the door to the vestibule and clearly not in any position to have been spoken to even a second earlier, and, to make matters even worse, that young Indian, Matthew Grey, the one who had looked the most innocent of the lot of them, which wasn't saying much, came through the door from the drawing room with the shawl wrapped around his neck. He looked ridiculous and yet not one bit amusing, treacherous somehow, which had to be absurd as he was only a child of Eleanor's age, but what was worse and really the entire point was that he clearly proved by way of that shawl that everything she had just said was a complete lie. Naturally, lying was perfectly acceptable in certain extreme circumstances, but only if no one knew a lie to be a lie.

She had just been proven as a liar.

She truly was horrible at it. She should have left it to

Cranleigh. He lied with aplomb. Every kiss had been a lie, hadn't it?

"How very thoughtful of you, Lord Cranleigh," Sophia said, "to consider so thoroughly both Miss Prestwick's feelings about her ruined shawl and Lady Amelia's reputation in Society. Though, perhaps a bit late on both counts?"

"I beg your pardon?" Cranleigh said, nearly scowling at Sophia.

"Not at all necessary, Lord Cranleigh," Sophia replied. "Though perhaps you should beg pardon of Lady Amelia. If not for the extraordinary perfection of her reputation, she might find herself in a most peculiarly uncomfortable situation now, her standing in Society quite ruined. But as she is quite above suspicion as it has been her practice to be nearly unnoticed and certainly unremarked upon these past two Seasons out, no one can bring themselves to believe anything but the most innocent of explanations now, which is entirely to her credit, isn't it?"

Amelia felt her lungs shrink and her heart explode at the insult, for what else was it? No one thought her capable of attracting a man in any degree that would result in her being ruined? Why, she could have been ruined many times over by Cranleigh. Countless times, in fact, if not for the inconvenient truth that she had counted them. Forty-three encounters, with multiple kisses exchanged on thirty-one of them. She certainly did not think any other proper girl in either Town or Country had nearly that number. Why, Louisa had been ruined for a single misstep in a single evening. Sloppy bit of work, to be frank. That she had been flitting about kissing Cranleigh nearly at will and not a bit of suspicion cast in her direction was to her credit, not to her shame.

That she felt shame now was entirely due to Sophia's phrasing.

"As well as to mine, I should think," Aunt Mary added, which was entirely off point as Aunt Mary was perhaps the worst chaperone ever to be conceived.

That Amelia had not been ruined years before now, and indeed not mere moments ago, was due entirely to her careful protection of her public image and Lord Cranleigh's determination not to be the cause of her downfall, which was surely a lovely thing for a man to do. That was beyond obvious. Of course, Cranleigh's behavior of the past few days had been less than discreet . . .

"Oh, but darling," Sophia said to Aunt Mary, laying a kind hand upon Mary's arm, which Mary did not look kindly upon at all, "that is not quite accurate, is it? Lady Louisa, under your very amiable gaze, went quite astray, though very happily astray, as is usually the case. Certainly one must be forced to draw the conclusion that Lady Amelia, quite on her own, is above any sort of speculation, which is why her father has not come undone in the slightest degree upon seeing Gillray's satire. The fault must lie in exaggeration, which artists are so fond of doing. Why, certainly Romney's portraits of Lady Hamilton prove that point most well. Lady Hamilton, though lovely, is not quite *that* lovely, but one does not make a reputation for oneself by displaying less than intriguing, that is to say, captivating subjects in the realm of art. Hence, the satire can be discounted as it was clearly designed for monetary gain. And succeeded admirably at it, too, as I'm told it was sold out within the hour."

Somehow, within that convulted speech, Amelia heard two things most clearly. One, that she was not *that* lovely. The other, that Cranleigh couldn't possibly have succumbed to desire for her among the roses of the Prestwick conservatory, or anywhere else for that matter.

"Perfectly logical," Edenham said. "I agree profoundly, Lady Dalby. Lady Amelia is quite the innocent. Why, one has only to look at her to see how naïve and positively untouched she is by the tempest of that ridiculous satire. Or anything else."

Edenham was, to be fair, a profoundly handsome man. If he hadn't have been, one could hardly have expected him to attract any wife at all after the first. That he'd totaled up to three to date and was now, remarkably, looking at her as if she should make an agreeable number four was slightly alarming.

Cranleigh certainly didn't look pleased. Which was the slightest bit gratifying. Cranleigh looked positively enraged. His incredible blue eyes were shards of ice and his scowl was formidable. The moment was near perfection and quite irresistible.

"Duke, what a perfectly lovely thing to say," Amelia said, smiling up at Edenham. He *was* a very handsome man, quite like a Greek statue in many ways, certainly all the important ones. "If you would like to be interviewed, as everyone insists upon calling a simple conversation, then I should be delighted to accommodate you. Shall we retire to the drawing room?"

"Alone?" Calbourne said.

"She's in her own home!" Aunt Mary said, outraged at the question that every inch of Aldreth's home not be plainly recognized as perfectly respectable and acceptable.

"I didn't have the opportunity of talking with Lady Amelia alone," Calbourne said, not at all graciously. "I can't think how that's a fair comparison."

"But, darling," Sophia said, "you were discounted for your impressive height, and certainly a woman does not have be alone with you to determine that."

"She does if she believes it to be a . . . a hindrance," Calbourne said, quite more robustly than was in good taste. Why, Aldreth was looking at them entirely too closely. He might decide to end the entire adventure as it pertained to dukes.

"Why, Calbourne," Sophia trilled. "You astonish me! Certainly a girl of such refinement and obvious innocence wouldn't have the wherewithal to consider such . . . hindrances."

"No one is that innocent," Calbourne maintained, crossing his arms over his chest.

"She is," Cranleigh said. "And will remain so. No one else talked to her alone and I shouldn't think it necessary for Edenham to require solitude."

"You did," Sophia said brightly to Cranleigh. "Fair play should require you to allow Edenham the same privilege. And indeed, Calbourne as well. I won't say Lord Iveston because he did have his time alone with Lady Amelia in the Prestwick conservatory, didn't he? None would know that better than you, Lord Cranleigh, and none should know how completely innocent such brief though private conversations can be. Nothing did happen, did it? The satire is a complete exaggeration, is it not?"

Well, that did put a nail in it. What was Cranleigh to say to that?

Twenty-one

EDENHAM and Amelia walked into the drawing room alone. It was quite a pleasant room done up as it was in pink and white marble with a frescoe of prancing Greeks upon the high ceiling and dark red damask drapes at the windows. There were two elegantly proportioned settees covered in plum-colored silk damask and eight chairs sitting in a very polite line along the back wall, covered in the same dark red damask as the drapery. Certainly a girl's reputation could not be ruined in such a room. All that marble and a small settee? Impossible.

"How long do you intend his punishment to continue?" Edenham asked once they had sat on facing settees, his long legs stretched out in front of him.

"I beg your pardon?" she said with a start, wishing she had her shawl to wrap around her, anything to help her hide from Edenham's scrutiny. His lovely brown eyes were very observant. As to that, he had married three times; it was only to be expected that he might actually have learned something about women in all that time. "Whose punishment?"

"Lady Amelia, you are a very beautiful woman and beautiful women are very accustomed to getting exactly what they want, however long it may take, and upon whomever's shoulders they may be required to step on to get it."

Put that way, it sounded extremely unattractive.

"I have made no secret of the fact that I am ready to marry," she said, which was perfectly true.

"Yes, but to whom?"

"Why, to the man who is . . . that is . . . the man with whom I find the sweetest compatibility," she said.

It was a most difficult thing to phrase, this list of requirements. And wasn't Edenham interviewing *her*? Not at all the way this was supposed to progress. She hated to admit it, but Sophia did keep things so nicely on target, even with the most difficult of men. Edenham, it did appear, was going to be one of the difficult ones. Although, weren't they all in one fashion or another? Certainly Hawksworth was very nearly horrid most of the time, and he was only truly at his best whilst asleep.

"And you have yet to find that man?" he asked.

"Obviously. Do you hope to be that man?" she dared to ask.

"I must, or why else am I here?" he asked. "Unless it be to annoy another man into offering for you."

Oh, dear. He really was too very observant for a girl's enjoyment.

"If he must be annoyed to do it," she said, "I can't think that he'd be at all desirable as a husband."

"Can't you, Lady Amelia?" he said, smiling marginally. "But as to our interview, we have spoken before, though only briefly. Do you remember it? It was at the Earl of Quinton's, a dinner to celebrate his son Raithby's first win at Newmarket, or something of the sort. A year ago? Do you recall it?"

She most certainly did. Cranleigh had got her alone in the end stall of Quinton's mews and kissed her until she could barely see clearly. In fact, she'd stumbled for a full five minutes after leaving the mews. It was encounter number twenty-two and no one, as usual, had seen anything.

Except, apparently, the Duke of Edenham.

"Yes, Duke," she said. "A filly out of Ravenbolt, wasn't it? I fear I have forgotten the name of the winner."

"I believe, my dear, that Amelia Caversham was the winner that day," Edenham said. "But I don't mean to torment you." Pure rot. "I only wish you to know that I am an old hand at matrimonial dances and if I can aid you in any way, I am entirely at your disposal."

That sounded nearly too good to be true. But what to do with him, if true? How could Edenham, indeed any man, aid in bringing Cranleigh up to snuff?

"You believe to know my mind, my intentions? I did not realize we were that well acquainted," she said, shifting her weight on the settee and forcing herself to stare into his eyes. He had quite nice eyes, not the arresting blue of Cranleigh's but quite compelling in a different fashion.

"And I did not realize that you had any interest in being more well acquainted with me than you are, Lady Amelia, no matter the intrigue offered by your proposed interviews. Tell me, have you discovered anything but that you are more determined to have Cranleigh than ever before?"

Amelia chuckled before she had quite got hold of herself.

"I must apologize for being rather more forward than is considered in good form," she answered, "but you must know that it is and has been my intention since leaving the nursery to be a duchess one day. It has been brought to my attention that, far from being subtle, I have made no secret of my desire. That being true, whyever would I want Lord Cranleigh? He is no duke."

"Are we to pretend that a woman's desire is subject to plan?" he answered.

"Only if we pretend that a man's desire is likewise planned."

Edenham laughed softly and nodded in acquiescence.

"Lady Dalby suggested the list, the interviews?" he asked.

"Yes," she said, not entirely sure why she was confiding in Edenham, though the fact that he had known of her indiscretion with Cranleigh for a year and said nothing likely had much to do with it. "A scandalous proposition, but upon reflection, scandal seemed the only course left me. Being virtuous had achieved little."

"But not too virtuous," he said.

Amelia stiffened. "I would not have you believe so little of me or of Lord Cranleigh. A simple kiss is not a mark of indelicacy or indiscretion. If I believed it were, I would never have allowed the kiss and Lord Cranleigh, who is a man of considerable honor, would never have attempted it."

"Of course," Edenham said agreeably, and then ruined it by adding, " a simple, single kiss is no such thing as indelicate, indiscreet, or dishonorable. A man would be a fool to argue otherwise."

"Thank you for not acting a fool, Duke," she said, rising to her feet. Edenham rose at her cue. "And thank you for allowing this little interview; I believe I am not wrong in thinking we understand each other very well. It was very gracious of you and I do hope it does not tarnish your reputation in any way."

"I should hope it adds to my luster," he said. "But there is nothing I may do to aid you in your quest? No little nudge I may aim in Lord Cranleigh's approximate direction?"

"I can think of nothing, I am sorry to say. I should not have minded at all marrying a duke and being a duchess," she said. "I did want it very badly, and I was very firm in my plans. And then Cranleigh kissed me." Amelia very nearly shrugged, which would have been most improper. "I suppose I am not very sophisticated, to allow a kiss to accomplish so much, but it did and Lord Cranleigh has been most stubborn in not . . ."

How to say it? He had kissed her, confused her, she had righted herself, and then he had kissed her again. She had, to be perfectly fair with herself, kept her decision to marry a duke very firmly at the forefront of her thoughts despite a single kiss. Despite a single encounter of kisses. It was when the kisses had passed a score that she had become rather disinterested in dukes as a concept and wholly interested in Cranleigh.

What could be done about it? She had made plain her interest in Cranleigh, and Cranleigh, beyond kissing her, had not made plain an interest in her. She could have got herself publicly ruined and settled the matter, but Cranleigh had not publicly ruined her and the matter had not been settled.

Cranleigh should have understood that, by her continual availability to being kissed, she would not be disinclined to accept an offer of marriage from him.

Cranleigh had made no offer.

Not after the first kiss and not after the fifty-first kiss.

To say that it had broken her heart was not an understatement. To say that she had cobbled herself together and put a good face on it was also not an understatement. To say that she had come up with a plan to salvage her heart was obvious.

Whoever would have thought that getting married would be so complicated?

"Understanding your preference?" Edenham offered, finishing the thought for her.

"Yes. Precisely," she answered, for it was as good an explanation as any.

"Perhaps there is a way to encourage Cranleigh past his stubbornness," Edenham said as they walked to the doorway that led to the library, and quite a bit of commotion was coming to them from that direction, too. Why, it sounded nearly like a brawl.

It seemed to be a day for brawling, which might be precisely how marriages were arranged. She had seen nothing to hinder that conclusion and rather a lot to reinforce it. One only had to remember Louisa's night of ruination to hammer the point home.

It was as she was thinking of Louisa and how happily, one might even say passionately, she was married to the man who had seduced her by surprise, that Cranleigh burst into the drawing room looking like a tiger on the hunt.

Amelia started, jumped actually, Edenham took her hand and placed it on his arm, smiled at Cranleigh and said, "Ah, Cranleigh, you haven't seen Aldreth about, have you? I must speak to him immediately. Lady Amelia and I have reached a most cordial and most unexpected understanding."

"You can't have done!" Cranleigh nearly shouted. It was rather blatantly insulting, in certain lights.

"I beg your pardon?" Edenham said, lifting an eyebrow and looking very ducal all of a sudden.

"I said you can't have done," Cranleigh repeated, staring at Amelia. "Calbourne is even now insisting that he and Amelia have reached an understanding and this business of his being too tall was simply a jest they were playing upon the Town until Aldreth returned from the Continent and could be approached for her hand."

Really? Whyever would Calbourne say anything like that?

The name of Sophia Dalby sprang instantly to mind.

"Calbourne is known for his peculiar sense of humor," Edenham said dismissively. "Didn't he strike the Earl of Dutton in White's as some part of a wager or a jest or some ill-conceived entertainment?"

"That was the Earl of Ashdon," Cranleigh said, and then nodding as if remembering further details. "Followed by Henry." As Henry Blakesley was Cranleigh's younger brother it should not be considered that Cranleigh was in any confusion as to who struck whom.

"Upon a single day?" Edenham asked, losing the point completely.

Men did become so distracted by anything to do with fighting or horses or wagering. As the three so often went together, men were very nearly always distracted and therefore not at their best. It was a gracious assumption for it assumed that men did, at times, behave better than they ever did. Gracious and presumptive as she had never seen actual evidence of better behavior. Why, one only had to consider Hawksworth. And then there was Cranleigh.

"No, but within a single week," Cranleigh said tersely. "I do not believe Dutton found it entertaining."

"How unsociable of him," Edenham said blandly.

"As to being unsociable," Amelia cut in, "I should—"

"We must go see your father," Edenham said, cutting her off, and not at all apologetic about it. "I will have this intrigue with Calbourne settled and him promptly removed."

"Yes, do that," Cranleigh said. "I would speak with Lady Amelia while you do so."

Edenham raised one eyebrow arrogantly and said, "I am not at all certain I find that acceptable."

"Then become certain of it," Cranleigh barked.

"A most peculiar family," Edenham said as he walked into the library. "Must be the American strain introduced by the Duchess of Hyde."

"Damned arrogance," Cranleigh murmured, watching Edenham leave the room.

"As to arrogance," Amelia said. "I can't think why you thought it your place to intrude upon my interview with the duke. We were getting along famously."

"I can bloody well see that. You seem to be getting on famously with all the men."

"All the men on my list, yes. Did you presume otherwise?"

"No, of course not," he said, being as perfectly obstinate as he always was. "I know how well behaved you can be when the right eyes are watching you, Amy. 'Tis a fine performance you give, quite worthy of the boards."

"You make me sound quite common, Cranleigh, when the simple explanation is that I'm behaving as I was taught to behave."

"And when you're with me?" he asked, leaning close to her, his body tantalizing in its nearness.

"I behave as *you* taught me to behave," she breathed, taunting him boldly. Would he never declare himself? Would he never simply ask to have her? "Did you expect otherwise, Cranleigh? What did you think would happen after countless kisses in corners and stair halls? Did you think I would not—"

"Develop an aversion to corners and stair halls?" he said, missing the point entirely, as was his practice. One would think he did it on purpose, being as stupid as a stump, but she was very afraid he came by it naturally.

Perhaps, just perhaps, the spirit of blunt speaking upon her after talking to Edenham, she ought to simply explain what it was she wanted of Cranleigh. Things could hardly get worse; even honesty could do little harm now. It was a sign of the death of civilization as she knew it to even think such a thought. Where would Society be if such thinking took over?

"But not an aversion to you, Cranleigh," she said, taking the bull by the horns, very nearly literally. She pressed her head against his chest, feeling the heat of him rising up to caress her. She laid her hands upon his ribs and held her breath. In all their encounters, he had been the instigator, she the willing participant. Would he be willing now? Could she, by laying her head against his heart, force him to act?

Cranleigh lifted his head and sucked in a hard breath. One hand came round to hold her to him, his hand gentle on the small of her back, his other arm held away from both his body and hers, as if he were afraid of touching her with both hands, holding her to him, pressing her against him. She drank in the scent of him, feeling his cravat on her face, wanting what he would not give her. Himself. Fully and completely himself.

It was just ridiculous. Two years of this, and nothing. Oh, of course he kissed well enough and she'd decided she wanted him and only him one year, eleven months, and some odd days ago and in all that time and within all those kisses Cranleigh had decided nothing. He had not acted.

He had not pursued. He had not done anything. Except kiss her.

It was really too-too impossible of him. She just might marry a duke after all, just to annoy him. He deserved it.

"Yet it appears you have an aversion to me," she said, pulling out of his tepid embrace. "I'm so sorry to have intruded, Lord Cranleigh. You shan't be bothered by me again, I assure you."

She turned and stalked to the doorway to the library, half expecting and half hoping he would stop her, some violent rush of emotion, some blazing declaration, perhaps a tussle on the settee. But no. Nothing. She walked out of the drawing room without hindrance on his part or hesitation on hers.

Very well. If that's how he wanted to play it, then she would win it, by whatever means possible. And the means had names: Calbourne and Edenham. Either one, if properly motivated, would marry her. She even knew the name of the proper motivation: Sophia Dalby.

Twenty-two

"SHE looks determined," Aldreth said.

"And unhappy," Sophia said. "That's an interesting combination, isn't it? I should think things are going to get quite lively now."

"They've been quite lively for some time."

Sophia glanced sideways at Aldreth and smiled. "You need to get out more, Aldreth."

Aldreth made some noise, but said nothing. Well, but what could he say? His daughter had been not quite as discreet as she ought to have been in her amorous adventures and it had landed her in a very peculiar position. Cranleigh, of course, had mismanaged the thing entirely, but men did that so regularly that it really bore no comment. When the sun came up every day, was it necessary to remark upon it? So with men. They did try, by every appearance, but they succeeded so rarely that a woman was hard-pressed not to pity them their awkward incompetence, particularly in regards to women.

Why, just look at Amelia. She had, like any healthy girl of good family and pleasing looks, wanted to marry as well as she possibly could. Nothing wrong with that, nothing at all. Cranleigh, like most men, had stumbled into her orbit, been rendered nearly helpless by desire and appreciation of the most basic type, and proceeded to clumsily woo her. Clumsily, badly, and ineptly. Nevertheless, he had, quite obviously, ruined her for any other man.

They were at complete cross-purposes, which anyone could see, anyone who'd seen them kiss over the past two years, that is. In this room alone, she estimated that there were at least three who'd seen them kissing. Hardly discreet, but that was part of the charm of first love. Discretion required a certain level of sophistication and experience. It was almost sweet that Cranleigh, a man who had been out upon the world, had fumbled it so completely with Amelia.

How completely like a man lost in love.

That Amelia couldn't see how lost Cranleigh was only proved how lost in love *she* was.

As a couple, they could not have been more beautifully suited.

"I do think we'd suit," Calbourne said to Aldreth. "It's perfectly obvious by the look on her face now that she and Edenham did not get on well together at all."

"I beg your pardon," Edenham said to Calbourne. "She looked perfectly delightful when I left her. 'Tis Cranleigh who's responsible for her current ill temper. As to that, I was under the impression that Lady Amelia was quite docile and extremely pleasing in her character."

"Only if one finds docility pleasing," Sophia said. "Not every man does, you know."

Edenham looked at her conspiratorially, which was not at all discreet. Men. They did miss so many nuances of communication because of tromping about being indiscreet. Calbourne, not a fool by any measure, took good note of Edenham's look.

"You're not interested in her at all, are you?" Calbourne said. One could almost describe it as an accusation.

"Of course I am. I'm not opposed to marrying again. I quite enjoy being married," Edenham said. "But what of you? You surely never thought of marrying again until this list was thrust upon you."

"I certainly did," Calbourne said. It was perfectly obvious that he was lying. "It's just that I didn't think to find myself on some young woman's list."

"But were so flattered to find yourself upon it, once it was created?" Sophia said.

Calbourne didn't answer.

Sophia sighed inwardly and looked at Aldreth. Aldreth was looking across the room at Raithby. Raithby, standing with Penrith, was smiling at Amelia quite cordially. And Amelia, looking only slightly distracted, was smiling back.

Cranleigh came into the room then from the drawing room, scowled at Amelia, scowled at Raithby, Penrith, Calbourne, Edenham, Sophia, John and his boys, and, really, the list was too long. Better to say that he didn't scowl at Eleanor Kirkland or Lady Jordan or Hawksworth, though he might have frowned at Hawksworth. It was so difficult to tell from across the room. He positively ignored Markham, and what he had done?

Lady Jordan, Eleanor firmly tucked at her side, which by the expression on Eleanor's face was entirely Lady Jordan's idea, joined their conversation without any hesitation, or indeed, preliminary.

"Is this what you intended? To make mockery of my family and my ability to properly chaperone my nieces?" Mary, Lady Jordan, said, obviously directing her charge at Sophia. Aldreth raised a single dark eyebrow and waited for Sophia to respond.

"What I intended? I don't know what you mean, Lady Jordan. Certainly my wish is for Lady Amelia to enjoy her Season and to make a fine marriage. Isn't that what we all wish for her?"

"I do," Eleanor said swiftly, her charming little chin lifted in defiance of whatever Aldreth or Mary might say. "I wish the same for myself, Lady Dalby, and when I'm out, I shall very certainly seek your counsel."

"You most certainly shall not!" Mary said, her cheeks

quite flushed by the statement. By her tone, one would assume in horror and not delight. Ah, well. "I agreed to allow you to . . . to . . ."

"Yes?" Aldreth prompted. As Amelia was his daughter and Mary his sister by marriage and Amelia's chaperone, what Mary had allowed was entirely of interest to him. Mary seemed suddenly and uncomfortably to realize that. Also, belatedly. "You allowed what, Lady Jordan? Precisely what?"

"I, ah, I," Lady Jordan said, slightly flushed. Eleanor looked on in frank delight. What a charming girl. She would be a true delight once formally out. As this visit was to her uncle's home during an At Home, it was hardly to be construed as being truly out. "I agreed to allow—"

"*You* agreed," Aldreth interrupted. "Interesting. Please continue."

"I thought it was in Amelia's best interest to allow her some freedom, that is, to allow Lady Dalby to aid Amelia in seeking, that is, in finding—"

"A husband," Edenham said. "Yes, that bit has always been very clear."

"Yes," Mary said. "A particular type of husband. When the list was proposed, it seemed, I mean to say, it didn't seem, there didn't seem to be any—"

"Any reason not to attempt it," Sophia said. "And it did do so brilliantly precisely what it was intended to do. You were very wise and very brave to take your niece's future so firmly in hand, Lady Jordan. Aldreth could not have chosen a better chaperone."

A remark that resulted in Eleanor letting escape the smallest giggle.

"And the results," Sophia said, "the results speak for themselves. Lady Amelia will be married as soon as she wishes, I should think."

"You mean that," Calbourne said, his eyes starting to shine with mirth. "The list. The interviews. The men. All designed, all approved, and now Lady Amelia shall have her husband. Who, I should like to know? Edenham has clearly been your agent through all."

"Clearly? How flattering," Sophia said. "Edenham, I had no idea you were so devoted to me. We must do something about that, mustn't we? I do feel I've been shortchanged, not even a bracelet to mark your devotion. How niggardly of you."

"Calbourne, you mistake the situation entirely," Edenham said, staring at Sophia in frank appreciation. She did so enjoy it. "Once there was an affirmed list, all dukes or heir apparents, how could I not be found on it? I do not bear insults of that type or degree. I am a duke. I deserve to be on a list of dukes. 'Tis no more complicated than that. As to marrying, I do believe I shall marry. Perhaps not this Season, but some other one."

"You were delighted to be considered as a possible husband for Lady Amelia," Calbourne said. His tone was not flattering.

"Why not?" Edenham said.

"Yes," Aldreth said stiffly. "Why not?"

Calbourne had the grace to look slightly uncomfortable, which was only proper, then he smiled and regained his good humor, as was only proper, and said, "No reason at all, Aldreth. Your daughter is quite lovely in every regard. The man who wins her will be fortunate, indeed." Which was, again, only proper.

"I don't think Amelia cares about her list anymore," Eleanor remarked, sounding as casual as she possibly could, but not quite casual enough. They all turned to stare at Amelia, who was standing in quite animated conversation with Raithby and Penrith, both men looking completely charmed by her. Cranleigh, who was standing near John and his boys, did not look charmed in the least.

"I do agree, Lady Eleanor," Sophia said. "The list is crushed and beneath Raithby's boot, I should say. Or might it be Penrith's? So difficult to discern at this distance. Aldreth, I do wish you had smaller rooms in this house. Anything, anything at all, could happen at this distance."

She did hope so.

Twenty-three

CRANLEIGH was not so distant from Amelia that he couldn't see everything. He could hear nothing, but that hardly mattered. What he saw was more than enough. But what could he do? He'd done too much already.

He'd kissed Amy, and he'd kissed her again. Again upon again upon again. He'd lost count of it all. He'd lost his way. He'd come near to losing his honor. But he hadn't lost the most important bit: a duke for Amelia.

He would not steal that from her.

He was no duke. He was only a man who could not resist her.

He could not remember precisely when it had started, what had started it, why he had succumbed to the temptation of her mouth. Had he not always wanted her? Had he not been born with this fascination, this hunger for her? It seemed so.

It had started when he met her, a simple meeting, a shared look, nothing to cause remark. But he had felt the jolt, felt something break loose upon looking into her eyes.

He had ignored it.

It would not be ignored.

He had watched her that first day in her father's house. Watched her play the pianoforte. Watched her at cards. Watched her walk in the gardens. Watched her as she wandered into the gallery.

He had followed her. He had spoken to her, which had made it all worse, a thousand times worse. She was such an odd sort of a girl, so careful and proper, so cautious and deliberate. On the surface. Just beneath, she raged with passion and ideas. She sent off sparks of wit and wry humor. Did she know he had seen through her mask of demure propriety? Had she let him see past her defenses because he was a man she would never marry?

He hadn't thought so. Not at all. Not then.

He had approached her in the gallery, drawn to her nearly magnetically. Her hair had played with the light of the room, soft eastern light, yet she sparkled in it. Her eyes, her smile, her voice, had beckoned, called to him like nothing had ever called before and he, listening, had fallen.

Fallen and still falling.

Kissed and still kissing.

A hard fall, a forever fall.

What was to be done?

What a man did when he fell like that for a woman like that. Leaving her, he had sought out Aldreth and Hyde, eager to gain their permission to marry Amy, certain he would be granted it. Why not?

Why not?

He hadn't meant to eavesdrop, but voices carried so very well over marble and glass. Aldreth saying that he did expect Amelia to marry well, his voice low and deep as he murmured that he had hoped Iveston would have come, that the pairing of their two children would have been a tidy arrangement for both their houses. Hyde murmuring in response that if any girl was suited to being the next Duchess of Hyde, it was the delightful Amelia Caversham.

He was no fool. A casual conversation between two dukes, discussing their marriageable children, was not a thing to make a man change his life's course. But it was a thing to make him pause and consider.

He was a second son with brothers aplenty behind him. He was not needed to ensure the Hyde line, the proof being, if proof were required, that he had been sent off to sea with his American uncle without a single restraint put upon him. He was, not to put too fine a point on it, expendable, or at the very least, replaceable. Did a father who sought a duke for his daughter want such a man?

Yet he was an earl and that was no small thing.

It was when Aldreth then told Hyde that Amelia had cherished the thought of being a duchess from her youth and he would willingly see her attain her desire that Cranleigh felt his plans crash into dust. But not his heart. His heart stayed true, centered on Amy, but he could not act. Not beyond seeking her out, kissing her, tormenting her for rejecting him before he had even had the chance to win her.

She wanted to be a duchess. It was a fact well known, but he had not known because he had been at sea. Her father wanted her to be a duchess. His father thought that she would make a fine Duchess of Hyde.

That was where he had rebelled. A small rebellion, but important. She could not marry Iveston. Anyone but Iveston. He was aided in that Iveston rarely went out in Society. Hyde would never push for a loveless marriage and Aldreth was forced to let the matter drop. And Amelia, little Amy, was without her duke, Iveston or otherwise.

And as far as he could tolerate it, she was without him.

He only kissed her whenever he could not resist. His resistance was pathetically inadequate. But he had not touched her, not fully, not as a man, not the way he wanted. Some small honor remained, and he would not compromise her. He wanted her to have what she wanted for herself and what her father wanted for her.

He did not know how else to love her.

Let her have her duke, then. Let her find some duke. But not Iveston, not his brother. He would not, could not, imagine her in Iveston's bed, in Iveston's arms. His brother. Not that close, not in his own family.

She could have another. But not Calbourne. Calbourne was too coarse.

And not Edenham. Edenham was too experienced, too many wives had Edenham enjoyed. Where would Amy fit among that list? Just another wife. Another woman to bear another child.

That damned list.

Everything, while not fine, had been regular, had fit the pattern of his life. Amy wanted her duke, but no duke, indeed, no man noticed her. She was too quiet, too proper, too careful. It was not like her, not truly, but if she thought a man wanted that, wanted proper and careful, he said nothing to dissuade her. He had some honor left him, but he wasn't a fool.

Invisible to them, but not to him. He had hoped, in time, that she would want more than his kisses. He had hoped that, his kiss still hot on her mouth, she would abandon her dream of dukes and want him.

And then there came the list and everything had broken loose. He had sworn not to ruin her, not to dishonor her that way, and he had not. Barely, but he had not. But with the list, all rules were shattered. The list, the interviews, the scandal of it—her reputation was hanging by a thread. She was, by most measures, already ruined.

He could have her now. He could ruin her in fact, if she would only act like a ruined woman.

She wanted a duke, that was all. She wouldn't allow him to ruin her because she would have her duke at any price.

That blasted list, Sophia's list, he was certain. It was just like Sophia to think of a list, to make a list of men. And it was just like Amy to agree to it. She wanted her duke. She would risk anything to be a duchess.

But Lord Raithby was not a duke. Neither was Lord Penrith.

He was willing to give her up to some nameless duke,

not the dukes he knew of course, but some other one yet to be determined, but he was not willing to give her up to anyone or anything less. Raithby's father was an earl and Penrith was a marquis. Very well then, a marquis was ranked just lower than a duke, but he was an earl in his own right and that ought to count for something in her mercenary little heart.

"You look like you want to kill someone," the Earl of Dalby said. He was very young and Sophia's son, not at all experienced, hardly worldly, but at that, he was correct. He wanted to kill everyone, starting with Raithby and working his way up, or down, however it fell out.

"Ridiculous," Cranleigh said. "Maiming will do."

Dalby chuckled. Hawksworth, Amelia's inconvenient brother, did not.

"Lord Cranleigh," the Marquis of Hawksworth said, "I believe there is some history between you and my sister, some bad feeling perhaps, some misunderstanding."

"No, no misunderstanding, Lord Hawksworth. We understand each other entirely too well," Cranleigh said.

"If that is true," Hawksworth said slowly, watching him, "then you know she deserves the best in life. I would see her get it."

Cranleigh dragged his gaze away from Amelia to look at Hawksworth. He was young, inexperienced, and he was Aldreth's heir. Hawksworth would be a duke.

The best in life. A duke for a husband. Is that what Hawksworth meant?

Of course it was. Brother and sister, they would see the world through the same eyes, value life on the same scale.

"As would I," Cranleigh said softly.

"The best in life," George Grey said mockingly. "What is that? You English." And he shook his dark head in derision.

"And you're not English?" Cranleigh asked. "You are Sophia's nephew."

"Our family history is a tangled one," John Grey

answered softly. "Sophia is my sister, our mother English, our father Mohawk. That is a true and clean answer. The deeper truth is not so clean."

"Is any family history clean and simple?" Cranleigh said. "I know of none."

"Then take your woman," George said gruffly. "Make a tangled history with her."

"She is not my woman," Cranleigh said, the words tearing out of his heart.

"Then she will be Raithby's woman," George Grey said. "She will go, as women do, to the man who steps forward to fight for her."

Cranleigh stared at George, then at John, then at the two younger Iroquois sons. They stared into his eyes, measuring him.

John said, his dark eyes glistening. "Would you lose your woman by not fighting? It is a hard thing, to lose a woman."

"If I fight for her, I will win her. But in that, I may lose her completely," Cranleigh said, saying more to these savage men than he had to anyone in his life.

"You speak like an Englishman," George Grey scoffed.

Likely true. He was an Englishman. But he was also a man.

"Cranleigh," Dalby said quietly, "what have you to lose?

Amelia, once and for all. Amelia.

It was then that Raithby smiled and Amelia laughed and something burst free inside him. Let her hate him. Let her curse him for robbing her of her duke. Raithby was no duke. If she could consider Raithby, then she could and would consider him. And take him.

He meant to have her.

Twenty-four

Lord Raithby was very handsome and very amusing. Lord Penrith was very handsome and very compelling. Neither one, however, was Lord Cranleigh, who was handsome, compelling, and not one bit amusing. Lord Cranleigh was a stubborn sod who wouldn't know if a woman was throwing herself at him if she wrapped herself around his neck.

Which she might yet do if things grew truly desperate.

Things were not quite truly desperate as yet because Cranleigh was in the room, watching her, smoldering in anger, and that was as good a beginning to a proper courtship as she could imagine. Having never seen a proper courtship her standards were perhaps a bit low.

Of course, while flirting with Raithby and Penrith, who was more amused by her efforts than was flattering, she kept her eye upon Cranleigh. He did look furious. She was not encouraged. He often looked furious and did nothing about it. Nothing but kiss her, that is, when no one was looking.

"You must put me on your list, Lady Amelia," Penrith was saying. "I'm simply too young to endure being discarded so completely. My mother has no tolerance for such slights. She's Italian, you know, and they have such strong opinions about marriage and suitability. She would rail for a month if I failed to meet your standard of perfection. It's a heavy burden I bear, I assure you."

"You look to bear it very well, Lord Penrith. I shan't pity you in the slightest," she said, with a smile aimed precisely at annoying Cranleigh.

At that instant, Cranleigh walked across the room like a wild animal, graceful and purposeful, his light blue eyes hard with intent. One could only hope *amorous* intent.

"Lord Penrith, Lord Raithby," he said in greeting. It was not a very pleasant greeting as he looked like he wanted to knife someone. She did hope it wasn't her. "Lady Amelia," he said in an undertone. A shiver went up her spine and down again. "This business of your having a list, it's true that you have compiled one?"

He looked furious and . . . something else, some expression she had never seen before. She tried to ignore it. Cranleigh and his various disapproving expressions had never hindered her before and they would not now.

"Yes, it's true," she said, lifting her chin proudly. "I can't believe you doubt its existence. Certainly these gentlemen don't."

When Cranleigh stared at the gentlemen, his blue eyes gleaming with a dangerous light, they merely smiled weakly in response. She didn't fault them in the least; Cranleigh was behaving very aggressively, which did bode so well for her.

"Very well then," Cranleigh said, stepping nearer to her and very nearly looming over her, "as there is a list, I insist on being first upon it. That won't be a problem for you, will it, Amy?"

Amy? He called her that here, now, in sight of Penrith and Raithby and . . . her father? Aldreth. Her heart leapt up and plummeted down. What would her father think of her? She had lived her life as an exemplary example of womanhood, the perfect daughter for a powerful, distant duke. He hadn't seemed to notice. And so she had been more perfect. He hadn't seemed to notice that either. The conclusion she'd finally reached at the advanced age of nine was that dukes and duchesses were free of the requirement of perfection, yet able to require it of others. Once she was a duchess, she could leave off trying to be perfect. All she had to do was to marry a duke and then her life could begin in truth.

Yes, well, the initial problem with that plan was in finding a duke to marry her.

And the second problem, which had arisen approximately a week after meeting Cranleigh, was that Cranleigh had, by repeated effort and seductive force, caused her to forget about dukes entirely.

"I'm afraid you don't fit the requirements, Lord Cranleigh," she said politely. Then hissed under her breath, "And don't call me Amy in front of Aldreth . . . and everyone else!"

"I don't fit the requirements?" he asked, taking a step nearer to her, which forced her to take a step back, nearly bumping into Yates with a tray of refreshments. "I think we both know I fit them perfectly. Top of the list, Amy, and tear the rest of it up."

"I most certainly will not! And I decide who qualifies, Lord Cranleigh, not you. It is *my* list!"

"And you are quite done with it," he said, taking her arm.

She shook off his hand, which did not put her in the best light but she had such trouble remembering to be proper and perfect when Cranleigh was in the room. When he touched her, she couldn't remember it at all.

"I am quite done with *you*!" she snapped.

"No, Amy," he said, "you are not. You are not done with me and you never shall be. In fact, we have only just started."

Her mouth dropped open as she stared up into his eyes. Was he actually . . . was he actually ordering her about? In her father's own house? Was that look in his eyes that she couldn't identify lunacy? Had kissing her driven Cranleigh round the bend?

Penrith and Raithby, she could only just discern as Cranleigh filled nearly every thought, obliterating nearly every other physical reality, drifted quietly away. Cowards. Did gentlemen leave a lady to face a tiger? For that's what he was now, a tiger. Intent. Focused. Relentless. Dangerous.

She shivered, a long shiver down her spine that burrowed into her womb and nested there, throbbing with life.

Cranleigh, by a subtle shift of expression, seemed aware of her shiver and the throbbing.

Blasted inconvenient, being in the same room with a man who read desire in her so readily. Two years of kissing had apparently provided him with a map. Topographical.

Just thinking *that*, and staring into his eyes, and her nipples tightened painfully.

"Come, Amy," he said, taking her arm again.

She yanked her arm free again, looking now around the room. They were being stared at, which was entirely predictable. She looked at Hawksworth. Hawksworth stared.

She looked at Calbourne. Calbourne shook his head in mild disapproval.

She looked at Edenham. Edenham winked.

She looked at Aunt Mary. Aunt Mary was drinking Madeira, and rather sloppily, too.

She looked at Aldreth. Aldreth simply returned her look, shifting his gaze to Cranleigh and then back again to her. Was he going to do nothing?

Apparently so.

She looked, finally, at Sophia. Sophia was speaking softly to Aldreth, saying perfectly horrid things, Amelia was certain. She never should have trusted Sophia Dalby. The woman was unscrupulous, devious, and cunning. And that was her list of attributes.

The Indians, Sophia's odd family, the Earl of Dalby included, were staring at her with an odd look of expectancy. She couldn't fathom why. Was she supposed to do something? To allow Cranleigh to push her about and have his way with her?

Her stomach dropped into her ankles at the thought.

Ridiculous. Cranleigh having his way with her resulted in kisses that were as equally torrid as they were equally proper. He never actually *touched* her, did he? Entirely proper, if one only discounted his mouth, which was not terribly easy to do.

"I don't know what you think you're doing, but you're not going to do it to me," she said.

"Of course I am, Amy. To you and none other," he said, and then, without another word, he lifted her in his arms and carried her out of the library. Without her shawl. Without a squeak of protest from anyone, Aldreth included, though she did seem to hear a woman's muffled chuckle. Sophia, no doubt.

He was touching her. He was fully and completely and, by all appearance, enthusiastically touching her. His arms held her effortlessly to his chest, his breath smooth and even against her cheek. Yates watched Cranleigh lift her like a parcel, blinked a bit more forcefully than was usual, but said nothing. He even closed the door to the library behind them, leaving them in the relative privacy of the vestibule. But Cranleigh did not stop in the vestibule. He continued right on, carrying her as if she were some sort of war prize into the small anteroom connected to the dining room.

"You are not going to ruin me in a closet!" she said, twisting in his arms.

There had been quite enough ruining going on in closets the past week or two; she saw no reason to add to that number. Besides, it was such an undignified way to get a man to the altar. She did think to have done better. As to that, didn't Cranleigh have higher standards? As annoying as he was, she had thought better of him than that. To simply ruin her, and in a closet. Why, it was becoming very nearly a cliché.

"Quite right," he said. "The dining room table would be more comfortable."

"Cranleigh! I shall not allow you to ruin me!" she snapped, delighting in the way the light turned his eyes to icy blue.

"Not in the closet or not in the dining room?" he said, setting her on her feet in the anteroom, pulling the neckline of her dress down before she could whisper a word of protest, and kissing her delicately on the back of her shoulder. His arm was wrapped around her waist, pulling her against his very obvious enthusiasm, while his mouth worked its way up to her ear, which he bit.

"Not at all!" she said. "What were you thinking, to grab me up and carry me from the room that way. It was not at all proper."

"I was thinking that I was going to ravage you in the first empty room I could find. And how much I was going to enjoy it."

She pulled away from him.

He pulled her back against him, grinding his enthusiasm against her hip.

"Why, Cranleigh? Why?"

"Because I want you, Amy, and when a man wants a woman, he takes her."

It was shameful; it was delicious; it had the most startling effect on her. She could scarcely breathe, was the truth of it. Worse, she didn't actually want to breathe. She wanted only to melt into Cranleigh's arms and never come up for air again.

"But to be ruined, Cranleigh," she protested, softly, but she did protest. It was an important detail and one she intended to insist Cranleigh remember. "I don't want to be ruined."

"Don't worry, Amy," he said, lifting her hair to kiss the nape of her neck, "I can make you want it."

That didn't sound at all respectable. She very nearly giggled.

"Giggling?" he said. "Not at all what I want from you, Amy. You shall have to do better. Proper girls don't giggle when they're being ruined."

"I'm not being ruined, Cranleigh," she said, holding very still so that he could kiss her neck a bit longer. "You've kissed me before. I was not ruined."

"More than kissing this time, Amy," he said, lifting at her skirts with his hand, pulling her hard against him, nearly lifting her off her feet.

More than kissing. How often she'd wanted more than kissing. She'd wanted touching and caressing, skin and heat. Man and woman. She'd wanted things from Cranleigh that she couldn't even name, except to know that she wanted them from him.

She pushed at his hand, pushing her skirts down. "I'm not going to be ruined! *Everyone* is getting ruined this Season."

"Quite right," he said, holding her away from him, studying her as if she were an exhibit at the museum. "We must do it better, mustn't we? Something to make them sit up and bark, shall we?"

"What? That's not at all what I meant, Cranleigh."

"I'm sure it must be precisely what you meant, Amy. I shall prove it to you, shall I?"

And before she could draw breath to argue, which she surely would have done, he put her over his shoulder so that her hair quite tumbled down out of its pins and her derriere was quite alarmingly in his face, and carted her into the dining room, where he laid her on its gleaming wood surface and properly ravaged her.

No, no, that couldn't be right. A girl couldn't possibly be *properly* ravaged.

But it did feel lovely.

He put his hands all over her and, having waited for the weight and heat and texture of his touch for a full two years, it was quite as remarkable an experience as she had hoped, indeed dreamed. Why, for the past year her dreams had been quite uncomfortable on the subject of Cranleigh and his hands, causing her to awake in the dead of night with the most violent *throbbing*. It was such a convenience that she slept alone.

What would it be like to awaken at night, throbbing, with Cranleigh in the vicinity to tend to things?

She trembled just thinking of it.

"Enjoying this, are you? I thought as much," he said, one hand in her hair and the other, the other, oh dear, the other quite where it had no business being. She could not possibly have been more delighted. It was quite obvious that Cranleigh could be pushed only so far and then pushed not a fraction more. "And what of this?" So saying, the cad, he trailed his fingers up her stocking until his hand met the bare skin of her thigh. "Your skin is like velvet, Amy. I could touch you for hours."

She certainly hoped he meant that.

"Cranleigh, I do think you should stop," she said, for she was certain it was expected of her to say something along those lines.

"If you think that, I'm doing something wrong," he said, and then he kissed her.

That effectively killed all arguments she could have devised.

She was tossed into a vortex of sensation centered and controlled by his hands and his mouth, his weight and his heat. He was a hot, hard man, who touched her with soft seduction and relentlessly pleasured her.

Her skirts hiked up.

Her resistance was trammeled.

His kiss was gentle, thorough, leisurely. His hand the same. She was a meal, laid out for him and he ate of her softly, without haste and with great relish.

She moaned into his mouth, a sound of submission and of joy.

"Are you mine, Amy?" he breathed against her mouth. "Have I made it impossible for you to want any other man?"

"Stop talking. Kiss me," she commanded under her breath, pulling his head down to hers and biting his lower lip.

He kissed her. He always did. Cranleigh, so reliable. So very reasonable of him.

He nibbled her lips and his tongue danced against hers, his fingers played with the top of her stocking, touching skin briefly, skipping down to play with her garter, skimming up again to brush a fingertip against her trembling flesh.

Her groin ached. Her hips thrust upward toward his hand as she moaned into his mouth.

"Why did you wait so long for this?" she asked, panting out the words, clutching his hair, feeling the shape of his skull and the slick texture of his hair. "Why did you resist?"

"Resist?" he said, sucking at her throat, his hand clasping her knee and forcing her leg outward until it pressed against the confines of her narrow skirt. Blasted skirt. "I could not resist you for an instant, Amy. The whole trouble, that."

Trouble?

Was that a jest? Idiotic moment to be making jests.

"Cranleigh, you know perfectly well that you have been completely obstinate about the whole thing," she said, nudging his hand upward, past the insurmountable barrier that was apparently her garter.

"The whole thing? The whole duke thing?" he said, removing his hand altogether, completely proving her point that he was obstinate.

The whole duke thing? Didn't he understand anything?

Blast. It was beginning to look as if he might have lost the thread and wasn't going to properly debauch her after all. And after two years of waiting, too! He really was nearly hopeless. Did she have to arrange *everything*?

"Cranleigh, you are going to plead for my hand, are you not?" she said, trying not to sound petulant, but not entirely succeeding.

"Before or after I ruin you, Amy?" he said, his hand moving up her thigh again.

What a perfectly hideous thing to say, and while lying on top of her, too. Being brutish was one thing, she quite often enjoyed that, but there was no excuse for being common.

Amelia jerked her head back on the table, her hands fisted in Cranleigh's blond hair, her skirts jumbled past her knees, and said sharply, "Before, I should think. In fact, I'm entirely certain that I don't wish to be ruined, Cranleigh. Kindly desist."

"No," Cranleigh said, looking not even remotely put off. He barely lifted his chest from hers, and not before kissing her lightly on the cheek. "You have been ruined now, fully. The thing is done. You are mine."

"You appear to have expected me to fall into your lap, Cranleigh, with almost no effort at all on your part." And she had been so busy on his behalf, too. It was positively monstrous. "It isn't going to happen quite that way."

Cranleigh rose up from his prone position on the dining room table, and as it was a finely made table it didn't even squeak in protest, though she was tempted to. *Blasted sailor.* Cranleigh offered her his hand, which she took, and slid off the table, her skirts hiking up even more, which she did think might be to her advantage in a thorny negotiation of this sort.

Ruined? Of course she wasn't ruined. Not fully, anyway. She had an entire room full of people who, because of their desire to be on her list, would never breathe a word that would get them thrown off of it. Why, being on her list had become the most important measure of . . . something . . . of the entire Season. One only had to look into Aldreth's crowded library to see the truth of that.

"You may believe that a man may cart off a woman and that instantly makes her his, but I don't believe that for a moment. A man must do far more to win the woman he wants; simply escorting her from the room is hardly sufficient."

"You were more than simply escorted, Amy," Cranleigh said.

Escorted? She'd been carried. If she'd had her wits

about her, it would have been kicking and screaming, but she hadn't had her wits about her, and still didn't, quite. Things were getting terribly complicated very quickly. She didn't know what to think anymore, beyond the fact that she had felt wonderful thinking that things between she and Cranleigh were resolved, once and for all.

But they were not resolved, at least not to her satisfaction.

"I do think you could show a bit more fervor, Cranleigh," she said, arranging her hair. It was a complete disaster.

"Any more fervor and I shan't be able to walk," he said stiffly. "You are ruined, you know. There's no way out now."

Yes, well, the line of his pantaloons was a bit strained, as well it should be.

"How charmingly put," she snapped, turning to face him. He looked quite annoyed. Quite handsome, as usual, but quite annoyed. Entirely usual for him, actually. "You know, Cranleigh, you've had more than two years in which to ruin me, and yet you did not. You were so very careful that no one should ever know that we had stumbled into a few scattered improprieties. And yet now you are not careful at all. You want to ruin me now? Why?"

"You may have stumbled, Amy, but I fell," Cranleigh said, his voice low and hoarse, his eyes shining so blue that they seemed to pierce her heart. "I was trying to protect you from scandal. Was I wrong to do so?"

"No," she said softly, resisting the urge to walk into his arms, resisting the lure of his kiss and his touch and his very scent. Two years. Two years of stealing kisses, haunting her dreams, and tormenting her days, and he had not once asked for her hand in marriage. There was no avoiding the sting of it. "Shall I tell you that I wanted to be ruined? I very nearly prayed for it. If only someone had seen us, all would have been taken out of our hands and we would have found ourselves married. Such a simple way to get a man, don't you think? Look how Henry achieved Louisa. In a single night, he managed what you could not do in two years. Why? Why did you not want me in marriage?"

She was close to tears and it shamed her. She did not want to cry her way into his heart. She wanted to soar there on a strong and sturdy love that welcomed her in.

"I wanted you," he said in a throaty murmur.

"Not enough," she said, her voice tight.

Cranleigh grabbed her arms and shook her lightly, his blue eyes cold bolts of anger and longing, his lips compressed in a hard line of determination. "I will ask him for your hand, Amy. This time you will accept me."

"But you never asked me, Cranleigh, did you? You never once asked me. You've said many things, but not that."

"I did it for you, can't you see that?" he said, holding her in his arms, pressing her against his chest.

"No, I can't," she said, pushing away from him when every bone in her body wanted to collapse against him. She had done too much of that. And what had it got her? A man who could not do the most simple of things: ask for her hand. "What was it, Lord Cranleigh? You couldn't be seen to be a fool for love? Your brother Henry was developing a bit of that, wasn't he, before he married Louisa. I don't wonder that, watching him, it put you off romantic declarations. One fool for love in the family was quite enough, I suppose."

Why else hadn't he ever made known whatever feelings of regard he had for her, and he must have more than a few feelings to have been so singular in his attempts at kissing her for more than two years, and his care in protecting her reputation. Or had he merely been protecting himself?

"You wanted a duke and I am not one!" he said gruffly.

He sounded nearly ashamed. He should be. It was a ridiculous excuse. Did he love her or did he not? Did he only want her because it was convenient? Did he only want her because of that blasted list? Did he want her at all?

"No, you are not," Amelia said. "That has not changed. Nothing has changed, has it? Now, if you will excuse me, Lord Cranleigh, my reputation grows more fragile by the half hour."

Cranleigh stood rooted to the spot, staring at her, his tongue trapped behind his teeth. Fat lot of good it did there.

"You won't marry me?" he asked in a whisper. She could hear the pain in his voice, bleeding through his heart and into hers. She did not care. She would not care, that was all.

"No, Lord Cranleigh, as you have not asked for my hand, as you have not declared yourself lost in love for me, as you have not abased yourself to Aldreth in your determination to have me in marriage, I will not, as it seems perfectly logical to me, marry you."

❧

LADY Dalby was waiting for her in the vestibule. Amelia was not in any frame of mind to face her; she was afraid that showed on her face most completely. Lady Dalby did not seem to care, which was entirely typical.

"It seems I am ruined, Lady Dalby," Amelia said wearily. "Cranleigh assures me of it."

"Only as ruined as you'd like to be, Lady Amelia," Sophia said placidly. "And is that why you sought me out? So that you could be ruined by Cranleigh and lay the responsibility upon me?" Sophia asked.

Amelia felt the weight of guilt of her intentions sweep up and bury her.

"I can't think what you mean," she said on a thin breath of air.

"Can't you? Why else agree to a most obviously ruinous plan to interview dukes? How else could it end but in ruin, for in ruin it began? Darling, did you think I would not notice that you were determined to ruin yourself? I can assure you that I know very well what is acceptable behavior and what is not. And I am equally assured that you know it as well as I."

Blast!

If there was one thing that was reliably aggravating

about Sophia Dalby, and there were many more traits than one, it was that she had the most appalling way of stating what should never be put into words.

"If what you say is true," Amelia said stiffly, "then I certainly can't see how Aldreth has allowed things to progress to this state. I rather suspect that you have talked to my father about our little arrangement and that you persuaded him to allow you a free hand. How I can't possibly imagine. Aldreth may be a cold-hearted beast, but even he would not hie off to Paris, turning a blind eye to his daughter's ruination."

"But of course he wouldn't," Sophia said, drawing close to her and laying a hand upon her arm. Amelia found it strangely comforting, nearly maternal, and she felt the urge to weep again. She ignored it most thoroughly. "What was arranged was for me to make certain you did not end up truly ruined, a course which you were following at a gallop. Without aid, you would certainly have been ruined in a month, wed to Cranleigh by force of public opinion and to save your family name, and what then, darling? Would you have been delighted, do you think? Cranleigh forced to wed you. You, forced to give up your dreams of being a duchess, which is certainly a worthy dream and I, for one, never thought otherwise. How else is a woman to get on in the world without her goals and plans to see her through?"

"You saw us," Amelia said in shock. "When did you see us?"

"At Sandworth, darling, and a more well-suited couple it would be difficult to imagine."

"I don't understand any of this," Amelia said on a moan. Surely an understatement. She sat down upon a small chair and put a hand to her temple. It was pounding.

"That's quite obvious," Sophia said, sitting in a chair next to her and leaning back, looking very nearly relaxed. The noise in the adjoining rooms was growing louder, both from the library and the drawing room. Aldreth's At Home was turning into quite a brawl, from the sound of it. "You will not marry Cranleigh because he ruined you. You will marry Cranleigh because you want him, and he will marry you because he insists upon it."

"He *has* insisted upon it! Nearly."

"Nearly, and only because you were ruined, first by the list and then by the conservatory and then by the satire," Sophia said. "Amelia, darling, Lord Dalby pursued me to the altar, quite desperate for me to agree to marry him, as I nearly blush to admit, with far more vigor and determination that Cranleigh has yet to show you. You are the daughter of a duke. I was, as you certainly know, a courtesan. If a courtesan can be pursued, darling, certainly you can be. In fact, I am quite determined that you insist upon it. And so is Aldreth. And so, as long as I'm explaining how the world spins, does Zoe Auvray, whom I am certain you are aware of. Do you think she doesn't require Aldreth to pursue her every day, in one fashion or another? Men simply live for this sort of thing. What to do but provide them with their chief form of amusement?"

"I don't find it amusing," Amelia said, tucking her forehead against her palms and trying to breathe slowly and evenly. "I don't know what to do or even what to want anymore. It was all very clear to me once. I can't think how it got so confused."

"Can't you?" Sophia said with a rueful smile. "I think Lord Cranleigh must take the credit for that."

"All he did was kiss me."

"If all he did was kiss you once or twice, and all you did was allow his kiss, and if nothing of it made anything more than a slight impression upon you, then he did nothing worth comment," Sophia said. "But he did far more than that, did he not? And I don't mean merely kissing you. I trust you will believe me when I say that one man's kiss is not very much like another's."

Iveston. Her thoughts flew to that recent memory. Iveston's kiss had been nothing like Cranleigh's, even though the action had been the same.

"But if Cranleigh asks Aldreth for my hand," Amelia said, half hoping that he would, despite her angry and entirely justified words, "Aldreth will give it. I am ruined, Lady Dalby. That is the end of it."

"Aldreth will *not* give his consent, not until Cranleigh makes the proper effort to attain you," Sophia replied. "The thing that must be done is to arrange things so that Cranleigh makes the proper effort."

"I have tried, you know," Amelia said a bit sharply.

Sophia smiled, patted her knee, and said, "But I have so much more experience at it, darling. Rely upon me. You shall get your man, in exactly the fashion you want him."

Twenty-five

ALDRETH'S At Home had turned into the crush of the Season. During an At Home, people came, were admitted, made their greetings, took a turn about the room, and departed; it was as predictable and as innocuous as the ebbing tide. Until today.

No one was leaving. They came, and they stayed. Why, people came who had not spoken to Aldreth in ten years for one reason or another.

Westlin, for instance, had arrived and everyone knew that Aldreth and Westlin had had a falling out approximately twenty years previous, about the time that Sophia Dalby had thrown Westlin, her first and most infamous protector, out of her bed and onto his lily-white arse. The details of that break were murky and lurid, on those two points everyone agreed. How Aldreth fitted into it was complete speculation, which only made his involvement more interesting, obviously.

Then there was the Duke and Duchess of Hyde. That was a bit awkward. It wasn't that Hyde and Aldreth had any bad dealings between them, but there had just been that sordid satire done up featuring their second son and Aldreth's only daughter. Satires were just a bit of fun, everyone knew that, but they were also quite a good bit of scandal and, while one might laugh outright in the privacy of one's home, it was not considered in good form to admit to knowledge of one in public. How they would get on face-to-face, their children having been made mock of only that morning, was arousing considerable curiosity. And interest. Another reason why no one was anxious to leave Aldreth House.

And then there was Lord Cranleigh, who, after having carted Lady Amelia out of the room bodily, came back in alone looking entirely disgruntled and dissatisfied. Which pointed clearly to the conclusion that he had not got any satisfaction off of Lady Amelia, as was only proper, but which put a damper on the salacious qualities of his lugging her off. When Aldreth made it a point to thank and commend Cranleigh for his quick thinking and prompt action in removing Amelia, who'd been on the verge of either a faint or a cramp, no one could agree on which, that ruined any possibility of scandal about the event.

It was most disappointing. Strangely enough, Cranleigh looked equally disappointed, which invited more speculation. In short, no one was leaving Aldreth House any time soon, even if the servants had run out of food a quarter hour ago.

Of course, unspoken and unacknowledged was the determination to await the return of Lady Amelia to the gathering. That Lady Dalby was with her was assumed, though certainly Cranleigh had indicated nothing of the sort. As Lady Dalby was momentarily absent, her relatives drew the majority of gazes in that assembly; that Cranleigh was in their midst was a convenient miracle of proximity.

"I thought you meant to have her," Mr. George Grey said.

"Leave it alone, George," the Earl of Dalby said softly. "Just carrying a woman off does not equal a proposal of marriage."

Cranleigh looked at Dalby askance, hardly a friendly gesture, but said nothing.

"You could always just ask her," Matthew Grey said, the youngest of Sophia's nephews.

"Ask who what?" Lady Eleanor Kirkland said. Eleanor, now that her sister Louisa was married to Henry, was family. Cranleigh, for that reason alone, indulged her.

"Ask Lady Amelia to marry me," Cranleigh said.

"Oh, but why would you do that?" Eleanor said. "Amelia is only interested in dukes. I thought everybody knew that."

"People can change," Mary, Lady Jordan, said primly. Lady Jordan looked surprisingly sober. Aldreth must have run out of Madeira. "Time, and distance, can change much."

As Lady Jordan was looking at Mr. John Grey while she spoke, Cranleigh was fairly certain she was not speaking to his situation but rather to hers. But in regards to John Grey? That made little sense.

"Oh, but not Amelia," Eleanor insisted, "and never about that. She's quite firm about it."

"Of course, there is the satire," Lady Jordan said. "A thing like that can change the most firm of intentions."

As Lady Jordan was still staring at John Grey, Cranleigh became even more determined to disregard her opinions. And though she appeared nearly sober, there was no guaranteeing that she was. In the two years that Cranleigh had pursued Amelia, her chaperone had never proved a hindrance. Though pursued might not have been the precise word for it.

"I've yet to see it," Eleanor said to Matthew Grey. "Have you?"

"I have," Matthew answered.

"And?" Eleanor prompted, standing closer to Matthew. Matthew Grey was not precisely smiling, but he was not exactly frowning either. As Eleanor was now family by marriage, Cranleigh didn't think it quite proper to allow her to form any but the most tenuous of attachments to an

Iroquois, even if he were a relative of Sophia Dalby's. In fact, more so.

As was to be expected, Lady Jordan was ignoring the entire episode.

"And it is not proper for a young girl's gaze," Cranleigh said.

"He's in it," Matthew said, almost smiling.

"Doing what?" Eleanor said, her impish face aglow with curiosity.

Cranleigh sighed. Eleanor, like Louisa, was fair-skinned and ginger-haired. Still, they looked almost nothing alike. Eleanor's skin was heavily dotted with freckles, her red hair quite dark and nearly straight. Louisa's skin was flawlessly white, her hair brilliantly red and excessively curly. The only feature the two girls shared was a certain boldness of character and freedom in their speech, but that was likely due to the fact that the Marquis of Melverley was their father. A girl might well need to develop some special skills if forced to deal with Melverley on a regular basis.

"It's a satire," Cranleigh said. "It's not a portrait."

"Lord Cranleigh," Eleanor said with the most devilishly amused look on her pretty little face, "I do understand the difference. I have seen my share of satires. My father has quite a folio of them, and as he keeps the folio in the library and as he is never in the library, I have seen quite as many satires as I like. I should have seen Amelia's satire as well, but the shop was sold out. I shall be first in line when they run off a second printing, I promise you."

He was amused in spite of himself. She was clearly a spirited girl, and it was quite possible that this little sprite was the reason Lady Jordan drank. He found himself in some sympathy with Lady Jordan for the first time.

"Nevertheless, you will not see it here, and not now," Cranleigh said.

"I'll describe it to you," Matthew said.

"No, you shall not," Cranleigh said. "We do not subject our young and innocent girls to adventures of that sort."

"No, you subject them to different sorts of adventures,"

George Grey said with a cheeky grin. "Ones that involve torn clothing."

Her dark eyes wide with curiosity, Eleanor asked, "Did you truly and completely ruin Amelia? Does she hate you for it?"

"Eleanor!" Lady Jordan snapped. "That will be quite enough."

Eleanor closed her mouth and lowered her head, but she looked at Cranleigh with a frankly assessing gaze that he found discomfiting.

"It is perfectly plain that Lord Cranleigh has no interest in marrying Lady Amelia, nor she in him," Lady Jordan continued. "What's more, it is more than obvious that this satire is a complete bungle on Gillray's part. Everyone knows how these artists starve for nine months out of every twelve. A simple ripped shawl, an excess of imagination, and now he can eat for a month. Anyone who could believe that Lord Cranleigh has any interest at all in Amelia is a fool."

They were staring at him: John Grey and his three sons, Lord Dalby, Eleanor, even Iveston.

Who was the fool? That was the question.

It wasn't much of a question, was it?

"I want her," he said, more to himself than to anyone. "I am going to have her, no matter what it takes. I've wanted her from the moment I first saw her. Two years and more ago."

The women stared at him in shock. The men in approval, even Hawksworth, which astounded him somewhat. Not that he cared what anyone thought anymore. If that made him a fool, a fool for love, so much the better.

"That cannot be true!" Lady Jordan said, taking a step nearer to Cranleigh.

"Lady Jordan," he said quietly, looking down at her, "it is more true and more certain than the turning of the Earth."

"That explains the satire," George Grey said with a smirk.

Lady Jordan gave every appearance of being struck dumb.

"You don't mean there's any truth to it," Hawksworth said. Yes, well, as Amelia's brother he would be concerned about that.

"I simply must be told about it!" Eleanor demanded.

"It's not a bit true," Cranleigh said sternly, eyeing George Grey judiciously. George only grinned more fully in response.

"I did see one that I didn't think could possibly be a true rendition of anything," Eleanor continued, "but as Melverley was in it, and Lord Westlin, judging by the flaming hair, I studied it quite regularly as a child."

As she was little more than a child now at just sixteen, it was nearly an absurd remark. Lady Jordan, however, did not react as such.

"I'm quite certain you must be wrong," Lady Jordan said swiftly. "I have never seen any satire that had anything to do with your father."

"Haven't you?" John Grey said, not particularly kindly.

Lady Jordan blanched. Eleanor looked on avidly. Cranleigh was momentarily intrigued. What was the connection between John Grey and Lady Jordan? Clearly there was one, though how could it have been formed, and when?

"Describe it," Matthew prompted. "Then I'll describe the Cranleigh satire."

"I believe that matter has been settled," Cranleigh said.

"It's a fair trade, sir," Matthew said. "You are not her father, nor the man to protect her."

"No, Cranleigh is not a man to protect her, not Eleanor and not Amy," Hawksworth said, sounding more energetic than Cranleigh had ever heard.

His head jerked upward and he glared at Hawksworth. Hawksworth was a pup, young and untried, but he held his gaze. Cranleigh was reluctantly impressed.

"I don't need protection," Eleanor said on a disgruntled huff of air. "I have seen satires. I do not fear them."

"You are not a girl who fears much of anything," Matthew said, his eyes shining in approval.

"Indeed, I am not," she said, shining back at him.

Melverley would not be pleased to see his young daughter forming an attachment to a young Iroquois. Cranleigh had seen Indians in their natural habitat while with Uncle Timothy in America; he was not fooled by an Indian in a well-tailored coat. Little Eleanor could hardly understand the difference. Indeed, most of London's elite could not. It was why he distrusted Sophia so thoroughly. She was an Iroquois; he could see it clearly, no matter her muslin gowns and well-set jewels. There was a ruthlessness, a deviousness about her that chilled his blood. How no one else could sense it in her he couldn't understand. Even his own brothers, Iveston and Blakes most specifically, liked her. As to that, his own mother considered Sophia a friend.

"I do not see any woman here who requires protection," Cranleigh said, looking down at Eleanor. She looked pleased by the comment. She might well be pleased but he was not leaving her alone with the Iroquois in the room.

"How convenient for you," Hawksworth said chillingly.

"Tell me about your satire, Lady Eleanor," Matthew said, turning the subject.

"It was an old one, by Gillray, which is a coincidence, isn't it?" Eleanor said.

"Is it?" John Grey asked softly, his dark eyes glittering.

"Isn't it?" Eleanor asked, looking mostly at Matthew Grey, the most amiable of the three sons, and certainly more approachable than his father.

"Tell me," Matthew prompted, crossing his arms over his chest.

"Very well," Eleanor said. "It was—"

"I don't see any reason—" Lady Jordan interrupted.

"Let her speak," John Grey said, and Lady Jordan grew quiet.

Even Eleanor now became more watchful and hesitant, even more focused on Matthew.

"Go on," Matthew Grey commanded.

"It was Melverley, certainly, and the old Duke of Cumberland and perhaps Aldreth? I couldn't quite tell. But the Marquis of Dutton, the old one, not this one, he was very clear," Eleanor said, her voice having gone very quiet. "They were pictured in a wood and . . . there was a woman. Dressed, or nearly so, in leaves and things, woodland things. The men looked like satyrs, the woman like a nymph, the satyrs hunting the nymph, or so it looked to me."

"A happy woodland nymph?" Matthew asked quietly.

Eleanor frowned and shook her head, "No, it all looked rather frightening, if you must know, as satires sometimes do. But like something out of a myth, not real, but not unreal either. It's not one of my favorites, but as Melverley was in it . . ." She shrugged, her recitation at an end.

The Earl of Dalby excused himself and walked away, across the room toward Penrith and the Prestwicks, who had just arrived.

"That explains much, does it not?" a voice said from the edge of their number.

Cranleigh turned. It was the Marquis of Ruan, looking particularly somber, as indeed they all did.

Yes, it did explain much, though Eleanor understood little of what she had seen. She was too young to understand, thank God.

Now Sophia's motives were clear. She had aided Amelia in her list game, damaging her reputation and ruining her chances of marrying a duke, for revenge against a twenty-year-old injury done to her by Aldreth, among others. Aldreth, who had been of that scandalous party in that scandalous wood, the nymph none other than Sophia herself before Dalby had made her his countess.

"Explains what, Lord Ruan?" Eleanor said.

"Be still, Eleanor," Lady Jordan said.

And for once, she was.

"How old is that satire?" Ruan asked Lady Jordan.

"Twenty years now," Lady Jordan said, looking at John Grey as she said it.

"And now there's a satire of Aldreth's daughter," Cranleigh said, also looking at John Grey. "Hardly coincidence."

"Who can say?" John said.

"*I* can say, that's bloody well who!" Cranleigh said, taking a step nearer to John, his fists clenched at his sides.

"But the point," Hawksworth said, "is not who drew the satire, but who provided the fodder for one, isn't it? Is that a coincidence, Lord Cranleigh, or did you hope to force my sister into an alliance with you?"

"Lord Hawksworth, your sister is not a woman to be forced into anything. She is a force unto herself and quite the most determined female of my experience," Cranleigh said, staring into Hawksworth's eyes.

Unfortunately, it was a remark that could be taken in more than one way, not all of them flattering to Lord Cranleigh.

It was at that moment, when things were taking a definite downturn, that Amelia reentered the room, Sophia Dalby at her side. They looked both composed and resolved, which did not precisely suit his purpose. Cranleigh wanted Amelia to look disheveled, marked somehow by his hands upon her, his mouth devouring hers. And resolved? Resolved to do what?

As to Sophia, he wanted her as far away from Amelia as possible. Canada would serve nicely. Sophia, with a whispered word to Amelia, walked directly toward him.

Cranleigh felt every nerve vibrate with expectancy.

"I don't suppose anyone has ever told you," Sophia said without the least bit of preamble, "how it was that my mother came to be married to a Mohawk warrior, Lord Cranleigh?"

It was the last thing he expected her to say, the absolute last. He couldn't think why it should matter to him, particularly now. He stared into her dark eyes and waited, certain she would continue. She did.

"She was a captive, you realize, and not at all happy about it, as who would be? But she was not content to remain a captive and thought it much preferred to be a wife. My father's wife, in particular. And so she married him."

"Fascinating," he said in a tone that said nothing like.

"You miss the point, darling," Sophia said with a brief smile. "What could possibly induce a warrior of my father's stature to marry a captive woman? Indeed, he not only decided to marry her, he was determined to do so. So much so that he fought for her. He bled for her, Lord Cranleigh. Which is precisely how it should be, don't you agree?"

Cranleigh stared into Sophia's eyes, her black, glittering Indian eyes, heard the challenge in her words, the mockery, and the wisdom. She was trying to help him, he realized with a shock, and she was trying to help Amelia, which was all he needed to know.

No wonder his mother considered Sophia a friend. She made a good one.

"If Amy wants my blood, she'll have it," he said. "Who do I have to fight to make her mine?"

"There's the spirit, Lord Cranleigh," Sophia said with a smile. "You'll need to fight Aldreth for her, I fear, and perhaps Lord Hawksworth. They are not pleased at the way Lady Amelia has been treated, which I'm sure you can understand."

Cranleigh bowed to her and said, "I can. I will do all to make everything right. Immediately. Lord Hawksworth, would you have a piece of me?"

Hawksworth, which was entirely to his credit, said, "I would."

Cranleigh nodded crisply and the two men walked across the room toward the Duke of Aldreth . . . who was gone. In his former place stood Amelia. She stood alone, her back to a window, her eyes hot, sultry blue in the western light.

"If you'll excuse me for a moment, Hawksworth," Cranleigh said. "You may have whatever scraps of my hide Amelia leaves for you."

He stood before her, her brother at his side, his competitors for her at his back. But Amy was before him, the sight of her filling his eyes and his heart. Nothing else mattered, nothing but having her and holding her, keeping her forever. He'd always known it, known it for what seemed a lifetime. Let his father and hers find other dreams. He had found Amy and he wasn't letting her go.

"Amy, I—" he began.

"A man must grab hold of what he wants, Cranleigh, that's what you told me," she said, cutting him off. "But I want more. I want words, Cranleigh. I want bold action. I want—"

"Me to be a fool for love," he finished softly. "Amy, I will do anything you ask, be whatever you want, but there is no being a fool for love. There is only being in love." And standing there, in the crowd of Aldreth's At Home, he dropped to both knees and said for all to hear, "I love you. I want you. I ask that you pity me and marry me, Amy. I am a fool without you, as must be perfectly plain to you and to this entire company. I love you." Taking her hands in his and turning the palms upward, he kissed the inside of her wrists, one after the other. "I love you," he whispered against her skin.

With tears in her brilliant blue eyes and laying her hands against his cheeks, she said, "About time, too."

Twenty-six

AFTER that, no one seemed to want his blood, not even Aldreth. Hawksworth followed Cranleigh into his reception by the Duke of Aldreth, and a cold welcome it was, too.

"Do you know why I allowed you to behave in that fashion in my house with my daughter?" Aldreth asked from the relative quiet of the dining room.

"No," Cranleigh answered, the blows starting to be felt now. A bruised eye, certainly, the left one, a cracked lip, and a bit of blood on the right brow. And that was just what could be readily seen. He was aware that, at the moment, he did not appear the most reputable of husbands for Amy, but surely the duke had been in a brawl or two in his time?

"Because, Cranleigh, I want better for my daughter than what her mother got."

That took a bit of deciphering as he was still cataloguing his injuries. His right hand ached, as was to be expected.

"I understand," he said, not understanding at all but wanting to move this along.

"Cranleigh, I am a duke," Aldreth said. "I presume you understand what that means?"

"I do," he said. His father was a duke, after all. He did have the gist of it.

"It means," Aldreth said, answering his own question, Cranleigh's reply extraneous, "that I can do what I want, have what I want, and not do what I don't want. Do you know what results from that particular condition?"

"No, I don't," Cranleigh said, fairly certain by now that no matter what he said, Aldreth would keep talking. Best to keep the man happy; he did want his daughter, after all.

"Nothing," Aldreth said, leaning back in his chair, his legs extended, considering Cranleigh in an almost friendly manner. Cranleigh was not fooled. This man was not his friend. "A profound habit of doing nothing, of feeling nothing." And here Aldreth gave Hawksworth a very hard look. Hawksworth cleared his throat.

"I see," Cranleigh said to fill the pause in the conversation. He didn't see. Hyde was not busy about his life doing nothing. He had been a general in the American conflict and he was busy in politics now.

"Oh, I don't mean to imply that the protocols are ignored. Hardly. I was instructed from an early age to marry well, to make influential friends, and inconsequential enemies, if I must have enemies at all, which I was very strongly encouraged not to do. My father, the first duke, was a very careful man."

"I've heard only good things about him," Cranleigh said. He'd actually heard that the first Duke Aldreth had possessed skinny legs and an ability to belch on command, but that didn't seem to the point. The man had been dead for more than twenty-five years. One's legacy lived only so long, even if he were very careful.

"The thing is, Cranleigh, that I've come to want differently for my children, for Amelia." Cranleigh's attention refocused on Aldreth more acutely. "And so, I agreed to this adventure in impropriety."

That sounded dismal. Cranleigh was nearly certain that Aldreth's next observation was going to cast him in a horrid light, not that he didn't deserve it, but one did hope to retain some dignity when asking for a woman's hand in marriage.

"Sir?" Cranleigh prompted.

Aldreth cast him an impatient look and sat up more erectly in his chair. The light was quite soft now, the afternoon quite done, the servants not got to lighting the candles yet, small wonder as to why. Aldreth and Cranleigh sat in growing shadow, the light going gray and dim, the edges of the room blurred.

"I wanted her to find bliss, which sounds perfectly ridiculous when said aloud, but there you are. A duke for a husband was what I thought she'd set her heart on. But she met you and that appeared to be that. Only it wasn't, was it?"

Cranleigh was slightly astounded. He didn't know what to say that wouldn't make him out either a scoundrel or a fool. Perhaps he was both. He thought it likely.

"Sir," he said, rising to his feet to stand nearly at attention.

Aldreth looked at him curiously. "It turned into quite a puzzle, you see. You seemed to want her, but did nothing. She seemed to want you, but . . ." He shrugged. "You do want her?"

"Completely."

"Yet you made no effort before now."

"I wanted her to have what she wanted."

"And she didn't want you."

"I didn't believe so, no."

"Yet, she kissed you," Aldreth said, steepling his fingers. "Are you implying that my daughter is a jade?"

"Not at all!"

"Then what did you think she was doing, kissing you all over Town?"

"It was hardly that," Cranleigh argued, and then seeing the frosty look in Aldreth's light blue eyes, added, "We didn't think anyone knew about that."

"You knew about it. Did you think she did that with everyone?"

"No."

"Only you, then?"

"Yes," Cranleigh said, though of course he hadn't given it any thought at all, not precisely.

"Yet you concluded it meant nothing to her, that you meant nothing to her," Aldreth said.

"I concluded nothing."

"Yes, that's quite obvious, isn't it?" Aldreth said, standing abruptly. "It's in your favor that I am as dull about these things as you appear to be. It all had to be explained to me, by a woman, in fact. Women are given to scrupulous dissection on matters of the heart, which can be a bit of a bother, but one must forgive them as their observations are occasionally quite astute. As in this case."

"Yes," Cranleigh said, not sure he was following exactly, but aware that Aldreth seemed to have warmed toward him in the last few minutes. "Then you'll give your consent?"

"Naturally. You've proven yourself nicely, if a bit irregularly. I had thought the wedding to have been months ago now, got all prepared for it. Even talked to Hyde about it, got the papers in order and signed, the financial details worked out to everyone's satisfaction; naturally you'll want to look it over, but I suspect all will meet with your approval. Your father didn't tell you, I see."

Cranleigh was certain that he was as white as a sheet. He felt nearly light-headed.

"Tell me?" he repeated stupidly. "You talked to Hyde? About *me*? Not Iveston?"

"Iveston? What does he have to do with my daughter? I don't suppose she's kissed him as well?"

"No, naturally not," Cranleigh said. The less said the better. Sound policy. He saw no reason to change it now.

"I must confess, this was all far more complicated than I anticipated, likely due to the obvious fact that you're both stubborn as stumps, but you clearly want to marry each other and that's the most important thing, isn't it?"

"The most important thing, yes," Cranleigh said. "The most important thing. We do get on, don't we?"

"Don't you know?" Aldreth said.

"Yes, I do. I do know," Cranleigh said, grinning like a fool. He didn't care. Dignity be damned. What did he need with dignity if he had Amelia? "I should like to marry her at the earliest opportunity."

"Tomorrow?" Aldreth said. "I arranged for a special license immediately after Amelia sought out Lady Dalby's help. Things do seem to explode after Sophia gets her hand in, or that has been my experience. Would you agree?"

"Yes, sir," Cranleigh said, very nearly laughing. "Yes to all."

He hardly noticed that his blood was dripping on the carpet. Aldreth noticed, of course, and determined that the man had suffered just enough for the privilege of gaining possession of his daughter. Hawksworth, however, surprised himself by being undecided as to the matter.

❦

"WHAT if he doesn't say yes," Amelia said, standing with Sophia. They were hardly alone, the crowd at Aldreth House having spilled into every part of the house save the dining room.

Sophia was facing the windows that lined the back of the room, overlooking the mews. She turned to look at Amelia, her expression serene. "Aldreth? He has little cause to deny Cranleigh's suit, does he? That's been most efficiently arranged. I do hope you want him, because he is most decidedly yours now."

"Of course I want him!" Really, how ridiculous. Was there any reason to think otherwise?

"Then there is nothing wrong with letting him know it," Sophia said. "Indeed, if more women let their wishes be known, there would be far less confusion on the part of poor, hapless men."

"Certainly he must already know it," Amelia said. "I've been, that is, I was quite intrigued by him from the start." She was starting to flush just thinking of it.

"And when was that, darling? From first look or from first kiss?" Sophia asked.

"From first . . ."

She paused, thinking back to that day, that first meeting in that crowded saloon at Sandworth. She'd been nervous, eager for her come out, eager to impress Aldreth with her perfect manners and her perfect wardrobe and her perfect conversation. Aldreth had behaved typically, no matter her perfection; he had busied himself with his male guests, looked at his children in mild recognition when he happened to find himself in the same room with them, and neither confirmed nor denied the stellar quality of her perfect imitation of a perfect woman.

There had been no unmarried dukes about, no Lord Iveston, no one to pretend an interest upon. No one to be perfect for.

And then she had seen Cranleigh. He had walked into the saloon like a sailor walking a ship's deck. He had walked through the room with barely a nod to the other guests, to the back wall of windows, and stood looking out at the gardens, his rough hands clasped behind his back. The room faced west, his golden hair had gleamed in the sunlight, his blue eyes had looked like shards of crystal, and he had captured her.

No, it hadn't been that simple. It couldn't possibly have been that simple.

But he had captured her attention, and held it.

When he kissed her in the picture gallery, he had held her heart, capturing her completely.

The problem was that he hadn't acted upon it. What was she to have done? What was any woman to do? Pine, as Louisa had done over Dutton? Throw herself in Cranleigh's path and hope for the best?

No.

She was Aldreth's daughter and she wasn't going to make a fool of herself over any man, especially a man who didn't seem at all eager to marry her.

"From the first . . ." she said again.

"Be honest," Sophia prompted.

"Look," Amelia said with a rueful smile. Did it matter now? She and Cranleigh were to marry. It was a fact, nearly. Aldreth had approved, certainly. "I'm so relieved that he's finally proposed."

"And after just the right amount of applied force, too," Sophia said brightly. "It's very difficult to get a man to propose in the best of circumstances, and certainly with Cranleigh it has never been the best of circumstances. Why, he was planning to run to China to avoid you, darling. Very difficult indeed to get a man to do the proper thing when he's half a world away, but of course you knew that, which was the entire point of the list, and of your decision to pursue that path. How else to drive a man to desperation but to be so obviously and relentlessly pursuing another man? As to that, an entire list of them."

Amelia looked in horror at Sophia. Had she understood *everything*? Every nuance of Amelia's urgent plan to force Cranleigh to do the right thing, namely, claim her for his own?

"Why deny it, darling? It was a perfectly devious plan and quite cunning of you, and of me, of course. And didn't it all end beautifully?" Sophia said with a deliciously amused smile.

Amelia smiled. And then she laughed. And it wasn't at all proper, naturally not, but still laughing most indecorously, she gave Sophia a hug of pure feminine delight.

"There you are, Amy," Cranleigh said, coming up behind her and laying his hand on her waist, scowling at Sophia. Poor Cranleigh. He would never understand; as he was a man, she did not expect him to. "Aldreth has agreed that we may marry. If that suits you."

She was relieved, of course. Obviously. Naturally. But there was something in his tone, in the look in his amazing eyes that gnawed at her. *If that suits you?* Was that any way to phrase a proposal? Couldn't he be slightly more relentless? After two years of being assaulted by Cranleigh, deliciously assaulted, this was how matters were to be resolved?

She wanted her tiger back, not this cool man with his cool blue eyes standing sedately at her side.

Amelia cast a glance at Sophia.

Sophia cast a very supportive glance back at her.

Relentless, that's what she wanted and that's what she would get. Perhaps even dangerous. Dangerous would be lovely.

"Don't you want to carry me off, Cranleigh?" she whispered, tugging on his arm. "Carry me off and ravage me, fight Chinese pirates for me, but carry me off and make me yours."

Cranleigh looked at her askance. She looked normal, no fever, no glassy-eyed stare, no hysteria. Of course, her request indicated a complete collapse, which he did hope wasn't permanent, mother of his children and all that, but he continued to study her, looking for signs of . . . something.

Carry her off? Ravage her? When he'd just now won her, finally and permanently from her father? Everything all legal and complete . . . which she didn't yet know because he hadn't told her that bit. The only thing left for them to do was to say their vows, a pretty formality, a social necessity.

She wanted to be carried off?

Very well. As to that, he'd imagined it himself more than once. The ravaging bit, too. Very much more than once.

"Where would you like to be carried, Amy?" he said, leaning down to her, speaking into her ear.

"Someplace *dangerous*."

"Someplace close?" he suggested with a grin. He couldn't remember the last time he'd felt like laughing, couldn't remember ever feeling such nameless joy.

No, not nameless. *Amy*.

"If we keep talking about it, it's not going to work," she said.

"What, exactly?"

"Being ravaged," she whispered against his coat. "Being

taken by surprise. As you always do. Only *more* this time. Much more."

"How much more?"

"As much as there is, Cranleigh," she said, lifting her face to look up into his eyes, teasing him, provoking him, challenging him.

The look in her eyes, seductive and hesitant, married within him to drive him to distraction.

"Go to the vestibule," he said in a low voice. "I'll find you there, and take you."

"You won't carry me off from here?" she said, sounding almost disappointed.

"I would, but I don't think Miss Prestwick would survive it. She's seems a very conventional girl, very observant of every rule of decorum."

"Of course she is, Cranleigh. How else is she to win herself a duke?" Amelia said, her eyes twinkling mischievously. "In the stair hall, then. Hurry, will you?"

"Not to worry," he said, bowing as he left her in the drawing room. He had to find Aldreth first and make certain that all the legal documents were signed before he touched her. Amy might be feeling reckless now, but this was just the sort of thing that a woman used against a man in the future. He had that on good authority, and he didn't doubt it for a minute.

❧

"I'M relieved that's done," Molly, Duchess of Hyde, said under her breath, watching as Amelia wandered past from the drawing room into the stair hall. Cranleigh, nearly on her heels, wandered with rather too much precision for actual wandering into the library. "You don't think it's possible for them to mangle it now, do you?"

"I can't think how," Hyde said. "The contracts have been agreed to and signed. Aldreth has nothing to kick about. Cranleigh should be delighted."

"I suppose you're right," Molly said, sounding not entirely optimistic. "It has been a coil. I can't think how we should have managed it without Sophia guiding things. That was a rare bit of luck, Amelia Caversham seeking her out, though it did raise quite a scandal. Still, once the first child comes, no one will remember a thing."

"Oh, some people remember, Molly," Hyde said with a rare smile.

Hyde was not given to outward displays, or indeed many inward ones. He was a restful man, something of a safe haven, which she did so like about him. In fact, that quality drew her to him immediately and resolutely.

"Hyde, you know perfectly well that Sophia would never breathe a word. She's far too discreet."

"I would have said she's far too devious," Hyde said mildly.

Molly laughed. "A woman may be both, dearest Hyde."

"But not you, dearest Molly," he said, taking a sip of tea to cover his nearly appalling sentimentality.

"Hyde, do I still turn your head?" she said, smiling up at him. Hyde was very tall and she was very petite; it was an arrangement she enjoyed for a multitude of reasons.

"Would I have ruined you if you did not?" he answered. "How else to make sure your father would agree to the match? I did what was necessary."

"Being a duke and a general in His Majesty's army wasn't enough, you didn't suppose?"

"I wasn't going to take the chance, colonials being what they are."

"And what they are is?"

"Unpredictable," he answered stoutly.

"Hyde, what a lovely compliment."

He grunted, grinning.

"After all these years, I can still surprise you?"

He grunted again and sipped his tea.

"Oh, there's Cranleigh again. Whatever is he doing?" she said, laying her hand on Hyde's arm and encouraging him to lead her to the doorway to the stair hall. Amelia was there, tucked into a shadow, looking quite animated.

Cranleigh came into the stair hall, saw Amelia, saw his

parents, bowed to his father, shrugged, picked Amelia up and threw her over his shoulder, and then proceeded to carry her down the stairs. Her muffled giggles rose up from the shadows.

Hyde and Molly stood silently for a moment, staring down the stairs. Molly then said, "He is *so* like you, Hyde. It does take me back to that autumn day in Concord."

"Tenth October, 1772," Hyde said gruffly.

"Hyde! You romantic!" Molly said brightly.

The Duke of Hyde blushed pink.

Twenty-seven

CRANLEIGH carried her down the stairs to the ground floor, past the servants, past the grooms, and into the mews. Three stableboys stopped raking out the stalls to stare. Cranleigh barked an order and the stableboys, whom she could only identify by their dirty shoes, upside down as she was, were gone. Far gone, she hoped.

Cranleigh slapped her lightly on the arse, hoisted her over his shoulder as she was still squealing in outrage, and dumped her into a pile of fresh hay.

"You wanted danger? How'm I doing?" he said, staring down at her, his hands on his hips. He looked, dare she admit it, like a sailor.

"You didn't have to strike me!" she said, pulling a piece of hay from her bodice, where it itched.

"Didn't I? Sorry," he said, sounding not the least bit sorry. "I was going for danger. I shall just have to keep trying, shan't I?"

And with that, he knelt in the hay at her feet, lifted her skirts with both hands to her knees before she had a chance to artlessly kick him in the chest. Which she did. Which he ignored.

"Cranleigh! What are you doing?"

"Ravaging you, what did you suppose?" he said. "It goes rather quickly, this ravaging damsels bit. I thought you knew that."

"Cranleigh, stop! Just . . . stop!" She was holding her hand out, as if to push him away, when of course he couldn't be pushed, not if he didn't want to be, and he clearly didn't.

"No, Amy, I don't think I will. This idea of yours to ravage you in dangerous fashion has definite appeal. Try to relax and enjoy it. There's a good girl."

And before she could say another word of protest, which she was completely certain she would have done, he lay on top of her and kissed her. Of course, none knew better than she that Cranleigh definitely knew how to kiss. He kissed her quite thoroughly, his tongue quite fully engaged in ravaging her mouth, his hands doing things they had never done before.

He seemed to have more hands than two.

He was tugging at her bodice, which collapsed.

He was lifting her skirts, which ripped.

He was holding her face and popping her breasts free and sliding down her garters.

All at once. All, impossibly, at once.

Why, she was helpless to stop him. She could not resist him. He was relentless. Ruthless. Dangerous. And very, very thorough.

This is what all those endless months of kissing had been leading toward, this destination, this explosion of sensation and want and throbbing necessity.

Why was she wearing so many clothes? Why was he? Mountains and mountains of clothing piled up between them.

Her skin tingled and she shivered beneath his touch. Her nipples ached and she arched her back to thrust them into his hands. He caught them, clever boy, and seemed to know exactly what to do with them.

"You seem very experienced at this, Cranleigh," she said, gasping against his mouth.

"Do I?" he said, grinding his hips into hers, pressing her down into the hay, the scent of it rising in the air around them, golden sparkles in the last light of the day.

"Ravaged many women, have you?" she said.

"You're my first wife," he said, tracing a finger against her sex. She moaned and bucked against his hand.

"That sounds rather debauched."

"Perfect then," he said under his breath, his mouth at her breast, his hands . . . everywhere.

"Cranleigh," she gasped, "wait . . . wait."

"I'm done with waiting, Amy. You're mine, and you'll stay mine."

It was a remark tinged with dangerous overtones. She nearly trembled with delight. In fact, she did tremble.

Cranleigh shifted his knee between her legs, moving upward, forcing her legs apart. His hands were at her breasts, at her belly, at the folds of her sex, at her lips, at her hips, at her . . . at her . . . and at her.

Remarkable bit of work.

She couldn't think how he did it.

She couldn't think at all.

"Ravaging," he whispered, his lips at her breast, his tongue licking a path to whatever destination he chose. "What do you think of it?"

"I think," she panted, clasping her hands around his shoulders, his muscles bunching beneath her hands, "I think it's perfectly obvious why it's such a popular pastime."

"Thinking of taking it up, are you?" he said, a smile in his voice.

"I may. With you," she said, reaching down to clasp him on the arse. "Hurry up and ravage me completely, Cranleigh, for then, knowing how, I shall ravage you."

And with that, he lifted her knees high and wide and plunged into her without another word. Good thing, too, as she had nothing more to say.

Except scream, that is.

❧

THE crowd at the drawing room windows overlooking the Aldreth mews heard a scream, a most feminine scream of a most specific type.

The Duke of Edenham sighed and said, "I didn't think he had it in him. Twenty pounds, then. Monday next? I'll send my man around with it."

Sophia Dalby smiled and said, "I'm to wait more than a week? And then take your money off some grubby messenger? You bring it round yourself, Edenham, and tomorrow, if you please."

Edenham laughed lightly. "And if I don't please?"

"Then you shall learn why I can hardly scare up any wager at all anymore. I nearly always win, and I'm quite ruthless about getting paid."

"Nearly always?"

Sophia shrugged. "I was being polite. I *do* always win. I can't seem to help it, not that I'd want to. I'll expect you tomorrow, then? Around six?"

"As long as I'm not to be interviewed, then I shall be there."

"Oh, that's long over. Who else would possibly want a duke for a husband?"

Edenham laughed, as did Sophia, as it was a very ridiculous comment to make. At least Penelope Prestwick thought so.

❧

"BLAST, I've just lost thirty pounds to Sophia Dalby," Lord Iveston said quietly.

"You didn't think they'd marry or that he'd ruin her or that he'd ruin her in a stable?" Lord Ruan asked.

They were both standing staring down at the mews with most of the guests at Aldreth House. It was a complete crush, actually, which was hardly surprising.

"Oh," Iveston said, ducking his head down and shaking it slightly, "only that I didn't think Cranleigh would make his move today. He's been . . ." Iveston let his voice trail off, clearly feeling he was about to betray a confidence.

"Interested?" Ruan supplied diplomatically.

Iveston didn't so much as nod, but his agreement with the word was implied.

"I thought it would take a bit more prompting, that's all. I can't think how it happened so quickly, after such a prolonged period of interest."

Well, that was diplomatic. Ruan couldn't confess that he'd been aware of any special interest between Lady Amelia and Lord Cranleigh until the business in the conservatory, but once aware of that, it was more than obvious that something had been going on between the two of them for some time. Things just did not progress that quickly from a dead start. Especially with a virgin. Why, just look at how slowly he was making his way with Sophia, and she was anything but a virgin. He did think he should have got further along at this point, but she was playing it very coy, a response he couldn't fathom. He was not completely unattractive. He was experienced. He was young enough to do her some good service.

She was toying with him and he couldn't think why.

Most peculiar.

He had thought to taunt her with some other woman at his side, but upon further study, he was more than convinced that such a ploy would merely amuse her. Something else must be done. The more she resisted, the more intrigued and determined he became.

Yes, he was very well aware that that was nearly certainly the very reason for her coyness, but he was still intrigued, even against his better judgement, of which he had little at the moment.

Sophia was driving him mad.

He found he didn't care. He was having too much fun being driven round the bend.

Remarkable woman. He simply had to have her. And he would. He was a patient, thorough man. And even more to the point, he was experienced at more than seduction, which he knew would tantalize her. In fact, he did think in his more cheerful moments that she was nearly tantalized already.

Ruan smiled and kept his gaze out the window and down to the mews. But he was thinking of Sophia, not innocent Amelia, though by that scream she wasn't innocent anymore.

∽

"THERE goes her innocence," Mary, Lady Jordan, said on a sigh. "And not to a duke, either. I can't think how she wandered so far from the path she had determined for herself."

"Can't you?" John Grey asked.

They were standing nowhere near the drawing room windows, but at the single library window that overlooked the mews. They were nearly alone in the room. Eleanor was sitting on one of the sofas in the room, talking to John's sons, or rather trying to get them to talk to her. The Duke and Duchess of Hyde were engaged in a seemingly pleasant conversation with the Duke of Aldreth, all clearly delighted to have their houses joined in marriage. Lord Dalby stood listening politely, his attention drifting.

Mary looked up at John. He still looked so much like the man she had met at Spa more than fifteen years ago. He'd been looking for Sophia. They'd lost each other somehow as children; Mary never had got the details. She'd been too busy trying to seduce him. And she'd succeeded, too. Her marriage had been . . . unpleasant. Her husband nearly dead, hence the trip to Spa, an effort to restore his health that hadn't worked and that had depleted all their resources.

It had ended in death and debt, but there had been John.

She had used him miserably, and he had forgiven her for it. She sometimes nearly hated him for that. Nearly.

He'd been roaming the continent, searching for Sophia. He'd asked her, and she'd lied. She knew Sophia, and hated her. Hated her for being beautiful and scandalous and successful. A common courtesan, she'd snared not only the

Earl of Dalby for herself, but the Duke of Aldreth for her friend Zoe Auvray. As Aldreth was married to Mary's sister, that was quite unforgiveable, wasn't it? She'd been justified in claiming no knowledge of Sophia Grey. She'd been justified in using John for her own pleasure, sensual, forbidden pleasure, because wasn't she entitled to that? Sophia had everything, without justification, without reason or honor or family connection. Certainly, certainly she was allowed to use Sophia's brother to satisfy her own ends?

Her own ends. What had those been? She couldn't think what. And so one bottle became two, became three, and life grew more bitter and cold with each passing year.

John, not finding Sophia, and finding her not enough, had kept on searching, leaving Spa and disappearing from Mary's life. What she could not hold, Sophia could not lose.

"I meant to ask you, John, but you'd left for Marshfield Park," she said. "Do you know who is Eleanor's true father?"

"Melverley is her father," John said, turning back to the window, crossing his arms over his chest.

"But, do you think he can be? Truly?"

"Truly? I don't know what that means, Mary. Melverley is father to Eleanor. There can be no one else."

He was lying. She knew it. But as she had lied to him, she had no weapon now to force him to anything.

She turned to the window again and stared out of it, seeing nothing but the past.

Epilogue

As everyone knew perfectly well who had been responsible for the Earl of Cranleigh finally marrying Lady Amelia Caversham, Lady Dalby was very nearly the guest of honor at their marriage the day following what was quickly being rumored as the most appallingly organized At Home of this Season or any other.

The Duke of Aldreth didn't seem to mind the scandal, however, as his daughter was now firmly connected to the Duke of Hyde, and everyone knew that Hyde was not only excessively rich from his own connections but from having married a very wealthy woman in the person of Molly Hyde. As Amelia had been out for two full years, some unkind remarks had been whispered about her finding herself on the shelf. Amelia, now the Countess of Cranleigh, was having the last laugh, which was the very best sort of laugh to have.

Sophia sat in the white salon of Dalby House, quite despairing of ever getting it redone. She simply couldn't seem to find the time, what with one woman and another seeking her help in acquiring a man. When had it ever been so much bother to acquire a man? They were everywhere. One simply couldn't avoid them, even if one wanted to, which she certainly did not.

Lord Ruan was most definitely making a delicious nuisance of himself, which was perfectly adorable of him. He simply turned up everywhere. What *was* she to do with him?

She was quite certain she would think of something.

Freddy came in, looking a bit harried, which was quite unlike him.

"Mr. Gillray is here, and Markham is wandering through the house looking like a bat in a graveyard," Freddy said.

"That sounds unpleasant," Sophia said, rising to her feet. "Mr. Gillray is in the yellow salon? I'll be in directly. And if Markham wanders this way, ask him to wait for me in here, will you?"

Freddy nodded and left the white salon, Sophia ran a hand over her hair, and then walked into the yellow salon to greet a very anxious-looking Mr. Gillray.

"Countess Dalby," he said, bowing.

"Mr. Gillray, how good to see you. As ever, your work is not only timely, but lovingly executed. I simply could not have asked for more. You received payment from the man I sent round? There's no problem, I hope."

"No, not at all. I only wanted to make certain that you were satisfied. I do feel a certain confusion as to your purpose, Lady Dalby, but that is not a new experience for me."

"Mr. Gillray, you are hardly alone in that, but as long as my money does not confuse you, we may continue to work well together. I may well require the position of muse to the great artist again. You will be available?"

"Certainly, Lady Dalby, and thank you. I'm glad you found the print acceptable."

"Mr. Gillray, please don't be so modest. Your prints are not merely acceptable, they are beautifully useful. Until next time, then."

It was as Mr. Gillray was leaving that Markham happened to nearly stumble upon him. Most unfortunate, but then sons did so often get under foot. A condition of too much energy and too little occupation. Markham was going to benefit greatly from his trip to America with John and the boys.

"Mother, that was Gillray, wasn't it?" Markham said, following her into the white salon.

"Yes, darling, certainly. I've known him for years. Such a talented man."

Sophia sat on one of the white sofas and leaned back. This was not going to be pleasant so she should at least be comfortable.

"He did the satire of Lady Amelia, didn't he?"

"You know perfectly well he did, Markham."

"You commissioned it, didn't you?"

"I most certainly did, which speaks so well of the man's talent as he got it out so quickly. I paid extra for that speed, but it was worth it, don't you agree?"

Poor Markham. He looked quite appalled. He truly did need to get out of London and away from Society so that he could learn something useful, such as how to manage people and events to suit his needs.

"What of Lady Amelia?"

"What of her? Do you think she was ill served by that satire? When she has the man she wanted mere hours after the publication of the print? I'm quite certain she's delighted. I would be."

"Not everyone is you, Mother."

"How very true," she said, leaning back against the cushions and stretching her legs out in front of her.

Freddy came in then with a tray of tea and biscuits, which was most welcome. Freddy stayed, which was not at all unusual. Freddy was not entirely typical as butlers went, the result being that he was invaluable.

"About that other print," Markham said, looking completely miserable, poor darling, "the old one, the one Lady Eleanor described."

"Darling," she said, before he forced himself to say more. She reached out and took his hand in hers. "That was long ago, long before you, long before Dalby. Best just to forget it, as I have."

"Did Father know?" he asked softly, his dark brown eyes staring at their entwined hands.

"Of course he knew," she said, squeezing his hand. "He knew everything. Do you think I would have married him otherwise? Darling, some may think me devious, but no one can claim I am deceitful. No one."

He sighed and took a deep breath, raising his gaze to look her full in the face. He had such a beautiful face, this son of hers. He looked quite like Dalby, and quite like her, too. The best of them both, she liked to think.

"There's much I don't understand, isn't there?" he asked.

"Who told you that?"

"John."

"Yes, well, no one is required to understand everything, so you are quite in the clear, darling. Now, when do you leave for New York? Have John and the boys not had their fill of England yet?"

"Not quite yet. I believe they want to stay for a bit more of the Season."

"Not hunting at Marshfield Park? I'm astounded."

Markham grinned, his normally cheerful aspect returning, "I believe it was George who said that there was more exciting hunting in Town."

"My, my, George may well turn into a Town buck. Whatever will John do if that happens?"

"Shoot him?"

"And he'd deserve it, too," Sophia said.

Freddy eased out of the room and came back in directly. "Miss Penelope Prestwick to see you, Lady Dalby."

"Now why would Miss Prestwick be calling upon you, Mother?"

"Darling," she said, rising to her feet and checking the condition of her dress, "how am I to know that? She is calling upon me. Am I to refuse her? Do you have some objection, some secret knowledge of Miss Prestwick of which I am unaware?"

"No, no," he said, holding up his beautiful hands in surrender. "Just, please, no more scandals. My reputation, I fear, is suffering a mortal blow."

"Darling, you are so young. Reputations cannot suffer mortal blows, they can only die of neglect."

Markham smiled, shook his head at her, the way boys will do with their mothers, which was so very amusing to their mothers, and left the white salon by the doorway to the dining room.

Before Freddy admitted Miss Prestwick, he said, "He doesn't know about that first satire? The one with Melverley and Westlin and all the rest?"

Sophia shook her head. "He's had one revelation and I fear more of a like nature would crush him. That he knows of the satire is quite enough for him. If he knew that I'd commissioned it . . ." Sophia shrugged and smiled. "Please show Miss Prestwick in, will you, Freddy? I am aquiver with curiosity. This is a busy Season, isn't it? I do enjoy a busy Season."

Miss Prestwick entered the white salon with all the determination of a general attacking a wildnerness fort. It was completely charming. She was dressed beautifully, her black hair and eyes set off to perfection by the whiteness of her muslin and the crimson red of her shawl. She wore no jewels at her ears or throat, but only a lovely golden bracelet of filigreed design.

She made quite a pretty curtsey and then they were seated and staring at each other with almost no subtlety at all. How remarkable.

"Lady Dalby, thank you for receiving me," she said. She had a very lovely speaking voice, quite melodic. One could not but wonder if she could sing. Such an advantage, to have a talent of that sort.

"How lovely of you to call, Miss Prestwick. You are

quite recovered from hosting your wonderful ball? Truly, it may be remembered as the event of the Season."

"Yes, that would be lovely," she said, clearly thinking of how to broach the reason for her visit.

It had not escaped Sophia's notice that it was half five and Miss Prestwick was not unaware that the Duke of Edenham was due at six. If all went well, Miss Prestwick might still be at tea in the white salon when Edenham arrived.

Sophia had not yet decided if all would go well.

"And how are your marvelous roses doing?" Sophia asked. "Not damaged in any way when poor Lady Amelia became entangled in them? Roses are fragile, are they not? Even with their thorns? Of course, the very reason roses have thorns is because they are so fragile, or so I have surmised. Would you agree?"

"I would, Lady Dalby," Miss Prestwick answered, licking her lower lip somewhat distractedly.

"Then your roses have quite recovered?" Sophia asked, nearly certain that Miss Prestwick didn't know a thing about roses beyond the fact that they were flowers.

"They give every appearance of being so," Miss Prestwick said, a bit tartly.

How delicious. A woman with a temper, and not terribly shy about showing it.

"How do you take your tea, Miss Prestwick?"

"Lady Dalby," Miss Prestwick said, ignoring the offer of tea entirely. What a delightful, entertaining girl. "I am quite aware, indeed, all of Society is quite aware, that you have a particular talent, one could even say, a passion for matchmaking. You have done so, quite obviously, with three women of gentle birth in the past month, one of them your own daughter."

"But of course with my own daughter, Miss Prestwick, how else was she to marry without my guidance and permission?"

Miss Prestwick shook her head briefly, as if she had lost her train of thought and was regaining it.

"Clearly true, Lady Dalby, I was only recounting my observations. If I may continue?"

"Please do."

"If one includes Mrs. Warren, which I feel I must as she is a close family friend, then the number jumps to four. Four women within a month. Four women who have made stellar, if not to say, unexpected matches with respectable and honorable men. Is that an accurate recounting of events, Lady Dalby?"

"I am completely charmed that you've taken such trouble, Miss Prestwick. I do think, however, that if your accounting is to be precise, the true number is four women in not quite three weeks. You seem to me to be a woman who values precision."

"I do, Lady Dalby. I also value results, which I suspect you do as well."

To which Sophia nodded, completely enchanted by this woman, and indeed, who wouldn't be?

"Then, Lady Dalby, I have come to ask if you well help me as you've helped the others. Will you make it five, Lady Dalby? I should like a husband. I have only one requirement and, having met that, he can be whomever you think best. I am quite convinced that you know what you're about. The women who have sought your aid seem to me to be entirely delighted by, if not the chain of events, by their conclusion. Will you help me, Lady Dalby?"

Was ever a more delightful woman created? She was a wonder. How on earth did her father manage her? Although it was perfectly plain that her father did not manage her in the least particular.

Sophia leaned forward and stared deeply into Miss Penelope Prestwick's dark eyes. "And what is your one requirement, Miss Prestwick? I confess to being curious."

Miss Prestwick also leaned forward and met Sophia's gaze without hesitation. "I want a duke, Lady Dalby."

"Many girls want dukes, Miss Prestwick. Indeed, I should say all girls would like one. Why should you get your duke?"

Penelope Prestwick smiled, and with a tilt of her dark head said, "Because, Lady Dalby, I can afford one."

Sophia nearly laughed out loud. She didn't, but it was a near thing.

"Darling, we are going to get along famously."

Turn the page for a preview of
the next historical romance from Claudia Dain

How to Dazzle a Duke

Now available from Berkley Sensation!

London 1802

Miss Penelope Prestwick stood in the middle of the conservatory of her father's Upper Brook Street home and stared at the roses. The roses were a disaster.

The roses, purchased to make a pleasing and, one hoped, impressive display of her horticultural talents to the marriageable men of the ton, none of whom had any need to know she did not possess horticultural talents until one of their number was securely married to her, had not done the job at all. All her roses had done was to somehow become involved in getting Lady Amelia Caversham married to the Earl of Cranleigh.

Which, actually, was perfectly lovely as Lady Amelia had been rather obviously on the market for a duke. As Penelope was also on the market for a duke, it would certainly have become awkward very quickly. Her roses, ruined now, had done a good bit of work, now that she considered it.

Penelope Prestwick was a girl who considered everything, a trait she found quite admirable and certainly useful. Her future husband had no need to know that either.

Men were so much more pleasant, which is to say, manageable, when they did not understand too much.

"What will you do to them now?" her brother, George, asked her, rather ironically, given the direction of her thoughts. "Throw them down some distant well?"

"Don't be absurd, George," Penelope said stiffly. "How can I get rid of the evidence of my spectacular talent with roses? I must save them, somehow. I can't simply get rid of them, can I?"

"They did serve their purpose. What point in keeping them, Pen?"

"George," she said with strained patience, "everyone at our ball, indeed, everyone in Town, knows that I keep roses and that they dwell in my conservatory. Having played a part in Lady Amelia's marriage, how can I ever be rid of them now? Besides, everyone thinks I'm rose mad. I shall have to continue on with it, shan't I?"

"I don't suppose you could simply inform people that they'd died of some malady. That would be too simple by half."

"Who would ever believe a word of that? These roses are famous. I can't be rid of them now. No, the thing to do, obviously, is to use them somehow. I wish I could think how."

"As to using things, there's that shawl."

Yes, there was *that* shawl. Of course, it was quite well-known that Lady Amelia, a duke's daughter, had behaved in quite questionable fashion and that a scandalous satire had been done of her, and of Penelope's roses. As a result of all of it, or a part of it, no one was quite certain, Lady Amelia had been promptly married to Cranleigh.

It was, to put it mildly, a scandal.

Penelope had the shawl, ripped, and the roses, ruined, and knew she had to do something with both, but was not at all sure what.

Lady Dalby would know.

Yes, that was undeniable. Something had to be done. And when something had to be done, particularly concerning men, Sophia Dalby was the precise person one should see. Of that, Penelope had no doubt whatsoever.

"George, we're going to see Lady Dalby," Penelope said firmly. "You, of course, will wait for me outside. I do not think this will be an appropriate conversation for a gentleman to hear."

"Going to talk marriage, are you?" George said wryly.

"Precisely," Penelope said as she walked away.

She was going to change her dress. She was not going to face Sophia looking even slightly less than perfect. That it was coming on five and the Duke of Edenham had an appointment with Lady Dalby for six o'clock was not a coincidence to be ignored. Indeed, Penelope did not believe in coincidence. All could and should be arranged to suit oneself beautifully. Relying on coincidence was for spoilt girls, and she was no such thing. She was a determined, logical, precise sort of girl, and she had determined to marry a duke, or an heir apparent at the very least. Logically, she had made it a point to overhear Edenham make his six o'clock appointment with Sophia. She planned to arrive at Dalby House at precisely half five. There was no need to look *too* precise about running into the duke, was there?

Of course not.

❧

Dalby House was quite lovely, though the Dalby House butler was not. He was a rugged-looking man, not at all what one sought in a butler as to physical appearance, and he was of somewhat irregular demeanor and perhaps just slightly indiscreet in his responses, which was also not at all desirable in a butler. Why, he very nearly grinned when he accepted her card. And then he was bold enough to stick his head out the door and twist his neck around until it was perfectly obvious he'd spotted George loitering across the street, fussing with his waistcoat, most like.

What a perfectly horrid beginning to what was certain to be an awkward exchange once she put her request to Lady Dalby in the flesh.

In the flesh was not the sort of expression common to Penelope, but when one was dealing with Sophia Dalby, it was the expression that sprang most vigorously to mind. Sophia Dalby was, without question, the most famously seductive woman that anyone in two generations had occasion to know. Even Penelope's father, Viscount Prestwick, who did not know Sophia personally, knew nearly everything about her and found her fascinating. It was one of the main reasons that Lady Dalby had been included on the guest list for the ball. One of *his* main reasons. Penelope's sole purpose in wanting Sophia to attend was that if a woman was as famously seductive as Sophia was reputed to be, and indeed she was, then all the most interesting men in Town were certain to follow her about like cats after cream.

And so it was.

Very nearly everyone who had been invited, and her guest list had been aggressive and high reaching, had attended. Hence the horrid crush of people. Hence the attendance of two dukes and one heir apparent. She hadn't dared to even hope for that, but come they had, trailing in Sophia's wake. Penelope was far from being outraged or insulted or alarmed by Sophia's blatant allure, for what good would that do? Besides, Sophia had married well and had provided the proper heir to the Dalby earldom, what need had she for a husband now? No, Penelope was nothing so foolish as to be jealous of Sophia. What she intended was to make use of such a valuable lure. How could she not? With so many perfectly eligible men of the proper rank buzzing around Sophia like so many bees, it would make catching her own man so much easier, wouldn't it? It was a perfectly logical and, dare she admit it, nearly effortless way to get a man.

But naturally, she did not want just any man. She wanted a duke. And for that, she rather suspected she would require expert assistance. If any woman was an expert in getting a man, that woman was Sophia Dalby.

Penelope was no fool. She wanted the best, both in

husbands and in aid. Sophia was the best. Penelope had absolutely no qualms at all about seeking the proper help.

Although, perhaps, just perhaps, she did have the slightest qualm about actually putting into words what she wanted when faced, well and truly, by Sophia's perceptive gaze.

Which was precisely the situation she found herself in when the Dalby House butler, with quite a bit of cheek, announced her to Lady Dalby and she entered the famous white salon.

It was a beautiful room, famously done up in white damasks and white velvets, pale blue braid here and there. An exquisite and clearly priceless Chinese porcelain vase in celadon green was the strongest spark of color in the pale room. Penelope, as diligent as anyone in listening to pertinent gossip, and surely it was *all* pertinent, had known of the famous porcelain in the famous white salon, though she had supposed the porcelain to be white, which only proved that gossip was not as reliable as it ought to be. Still, it was Chinese porcelain and it clearly was the centerpiece of the room, so she was not too disappointed in the reliability of casual gossip. According to the most popular report, the vase was a gift from Pitt the Younger for some aid she had done him in the Commons two decades past, but another version had it that it was a gift from the Prince of Wales for one night in her bed.

Penelope did not have an opinion on the matter one way or the other. Of course, there were many more speculations on the origin of the vase, which in some reports was a bowl or even a cup, but there was the porcelain and Sophia had done *something* to earn it, and that was quite enough information for Penelope.

She made her curtsey to Lady Dalby with the grace she had been tutored to display, sat prettily on the edge of her white upholstered seat, arranged her crimson shawl attractively over her arms, and proceeded to the task at hand.

"Lady Dalby, thank you for receiving me," she said, mentally commanding herself to hold Sophia's dark gaze.

It was most peculiar, but she had the most uncomfortable sensation that Sophia not only knew why she had come, but found it utterly amusing.

"How lovely of you to call, Miss Prestwick," Sophia said. "You are quite recovered from hosting your wonderful ball? Truly, it may be remembered as the event of the Season."

As the Duke of Aldreth's daughter, the inconvenient Amelia, had been nearly ruined at the Prestwick ball, Penelope should not be a bit surprised. Of course, it would be remembered as the most *disastrous* event of the Season, but Sophia was too experienced at conversation to make such a bald statement.

"Yes, that would be lovely," Penelope said absently.

There was simply no point in discussing the ball. It had not yielded the desired fruit: no duke or heir apparent had considered her as a prospective wife. She knew enough of men to know that, at least. Men got a certain look when they were considering a woman, for anything. No man had looked at her in any fashion beyond the bare necessity of civil conversation. It was very nearly insulting.

Oh, very well, it had been completely insulting, and she was such a handsome-looking girl, too.

"And how are your marvelous roses doing?" Sophia asked. "Not damaged in any way when poor Lady Amelia became entangled in them? Roses are fragile, are they not?"

Oh, bother; this is just the sort of nuisance that the roses were clearly going to become in Society. Everyone now would expect her to practically give horticultural lectures on the peculiarities of roses. And what was she to say? That she was fairly certain they required watering on some sort of regular basis? That she thought the blooms quite pretty, when they could be bothered to appear? All the roses were to have been was a point of interest laid at her very petite feet; she was not supposed to be required to actually discuss them upon command. This was all Lady Amelia's doing, without question.

"Even with their thorns?" Lady Dalby continued, a certain malicious light in her dark eyes. "Of course, the very reason roses have thorns is because they are so fragile, or so I have surmised. Would you agree?"

"I would, Lady Dalby," Penelope answered. Anything to end the flow of words, and pointed questions, about roses. She very nearly regretted buying the stupid things in the first place.

"Then your roses have quite recovered?" Sophia asked, displaying a rather bold streak of cruelty, as it was perfectly plain that Penelope had no wish to speak of her annoying roses.

"They give every appearance of being so," Penelope said tartly, quite unable to stop herself and nearly unapologetic about it.

Sophia gave her a considering look, her eyes twinkling, and then asked, "How do you take your tea, Miss Prestwick?"

Bother. Now, if the pattern held, Sophia would engage her in a perfectly pointless discussion about various teas for the next quarter hour. The Duke of Edenham was due to arrive at Dalby House in less than thirty minutes, but if Penelope did not have Sophia firmly in her corner by then, Edenham would prove useless. She knew that as well as she knew her own name. Unless aided by Sophia, there was not a duke in Town who would fall into her very deserving lap. They hadn't yet done, had they? Without the proper aid, they clearly never would. Sophia, as annoying as she could clearly be, was the proper aid, indeed the *only* aid. That was more than clear.

"Lady Dalby," Penelope said, ignoring the subject of tea entirely. "I am quite aware, indeed, all of Society is quite aware, that you have a particular talent, one could even say a passion, for matchmaking." Penelope paused briefly to study the look on Sophia's face. She looked not one whit alarmed, or even surprised. She did look entertained. Penelope was perfectly willing to be the source of humor for Sophia, as long as she got her duke in the end. "You have done so, quite obviously, with three women of gentle birth in the past month, one of them your own daughter."

"But of course with my own daughter, Miss Prestwick," Sophia interrupted, needlessly. "How else was she to marry without my guidance and permission?"

Penelope shook her head in annoyance and continued. "Clearly true, Lady Dalby, I was only recounting my observations. If I may continue?" She was not asking permission, which was perfectly obvious to both of them.

"Please do," Sophia said with a smile, leaning back against the cushions.

"If one includes Mrs. Warren, which I feel I must as she is a close family friend, then the number jumps to four. Four women within a month. Four women who have made stellar, if not to say unexpected, matches with respectable and honorable men. Is that an accurate recounting of events, Lady Dalby?"

There. She had got it all out without further interruption. Penelope was aware that she was holding her breath, her spine very straight as she held Sophia's gaze. It was, surprisingly, not a particularly awkward moment. Sophia made it so, of that she was certain. No huffs of outrage or looks of offended dignity; no, she was completely at ease, calm as a shallow pond. Strangely, Penelope realized she had expected nothing less.

"I am completely charmed," Sophia said softly, "that you've taken such trouble, Miss Prestwick. I do think, however, that if your accounting is to be precise, the true number is four women in not quite three weeks. You seem to be a woman who values precision."

And indeed she was. How unusual and how pleasant for someone to have noticed that about her. But then, she was under the rather firm impression that Sophia noticed everything about nearly everyone.

"I do, Lady Dalby," Penelope said. "I also value results, which I suspect you do as well."

To which Sophia Dalby nodded and smiled in clear delight. Perfect. Things were going so well and so very quickly, which is just as things ought to go. Penelope plunged in to the full; whatever hesitation, and indeed she had nearly none to start with, cast away in the pure pleasure of such plain speaking.

"Then, Lady Dalby," she continued, "I have come to ask if you will help me as you've helped the others. Will you make it five, Lady Dalby? I should like a husband. I have only one requirement, and having met that, he can be whomever you think best." A gamble, certainly, but the events of the past three weeks had proven sufficiently to Penelope that Sophia was a woman to gamble upon. "I am quite convinced that you know what you're about. The women who have sought your aid seem to me to be entirely delighted by, if not the chain of events, their conclusion. Will you help me, Lady Dalby?"

There was no taking the words back now. No, nor the wish. She wanted a duke. She didn't see any reason at all why she shouldn't have one. Having come to Sophia for aid, it would have been a ridiculous bit of foolishness to not be forthcoming about what she wanted, wouldn't it? Penelope had decided her course and she would hold to it, with Sophia's help or not. But she did so want Sophia's help as her own efforts had produced not a solitary duke or heir apparent. Surely, she could do no worse with Sophia on her side.

Sophia, far from looking shocked, such a relief, leaned forward and stared in some fascination at Penelope.

"And what is your one requirement, Miss Prestwick? I confess to being curious."

Penelope suspected rather strongly that there was no mystery as to her one requirement, but she played along, not a bit put off by plain speaking, as should be perfectly obvious to the most obtuse of persons, which Sophia Dalby clearly was not.

Penelope leaned forward upon her seat, matching Sophia's pose nearly completely. "I want a duke, Lady Dalby," she said calmly and clearly.

Sophia did not so much as blink. "Many girls want

dukes, Miss Prestwick. Indeed, I should say all girls would like one. Why should you get your duke?"

Penelope smiled and tilting her head playfully, said with the utmost earnestness, "Because I can afford one, Lady Dalby."

Sophia blinked. "Darling," she said with a smile, "we are going to get along famously."

Oh, she did hope so. She did so very much want her duke, or heir apparent; she was not unreasonable, after all.

Claudia Dain is an award-winning author and two-time RITA finalist. She lives in the Southeast and is at work on Sophia's next attempt at matchmaking.

Enter the rich world of historical romance with Berkley Books.

Lynn Kurland

Patricia Potter

Betina Krahn

Jodi Thomas

Anne Gracie

Love is timeless.
penguin.com